STORM FROM
THE NORTH

T.J. COULTON

CONTENTS

1

It was a long way down.

The man reached out to press his fingertips against the floor-to-ceiling window pane. Then he leaned forwards, resting his forehead against the chilled glass.

He squinted down at the Beijing city street 22 floors below him. He could just make out the traffic crawling through the smog. Neighbouring skyscrapers loomed around him like ancient spirits.

His spacious office was on the north side of the building. As custom dictated for a man in his exalted position. Nearer to heaven.

On the street, he would have passed unnoticed. He was of average height with a slim build. His hair was receding and his cheeks were mottled from a childhood skin complaint.

His dark suit was a cut above but only a tailor would have appreciated the needlework. His tie was standard blue.

On closer inspection, a passer-by might have noted the intelligence lurking behind the thick-framed glasses. Eyes constantly on the move, registering and appraising.

His alertness had served him well over the years. He had risen through the ranks, skirting the pitfalls his rivals had blundered into.

His prodigious capacity for work coupled with unerring political judgement had finally prised open the door to the top-floor office. He had been in post for three years.

But staring into the deepening gloom of that winter evening, he felt unsettled. Change was in the air.

He did not need to consult one of Beijing's fortune consultants. He was well able to gauge the way the wind was blowing.

Before long, a new man would take control at the very top. His arrival would herald a clamp-down. Officials raking in the spoils during the fat years would flee for cover.

He would not be among them.

He had accrued billions through graft. He was intent on safeguarding his fortune.

He had contacted specialists in Hong Kong. Experts at spiriting funds into havens beyond the reach of the authorities. The process was already underway.

When he judged the time was right, he would follow. Turning his back on the country of his birth.

Before the hammer fell.

2

At six o'clock in the morning, Hong Kong's Victoria Park was already filling up.

Clustered under the trees, elderly Chinese were performing their daily tai-chi. Some brandished swords, others wafted fans or handkerchiefs.

The unhurried movements were deceptively simple. The leaders of each group demanded exact adherence to the example they set.

The small man sitting on the park bench kept his distance. He was content just to observe.

Not that he had much to learn. He himself was a practised exponent of the ancient art. At daybreak he would exercise on his roof-top in Yokohama, filling his lungs with the scents of the harbour as the sun rose over the bay.

A stranger would struggle to guess his age. Possibly early fifties.

His face was round and his unblemished features almost childlike. His head was shaved. He had a slight potbelly.

Oddly, he wore a pair of white silk gloves.

He had been summoned two days earlier.

He had booked into one of the high-rise hotels overlooking the park. He had only brought with him one small overnight bag and a large briefcase.

People in his position rarely travelled alone. But that was always his preference. He felt less encumbered.

The meeting the previous day had been on the Kowloon side. A limousine had picked him up from the hotel soon after his arrival.

He did not recognise the men in the car. In his line of business, staff turnover was a constant.

The Mercedes plunged into the Cross-Harbour Tunnel and then headed for Whampoa. No one spoke. The man readied himself.

They pulled up outside a large conference centre. The man was escorted to a spacious, well-appointed room on the fifth floor.

It could have been a business meeting like any other. He made his presentation to the attendees. Those designated took detailed notes.

There was a lot to go through. Every aspect of the project was put under the microscope. Finance, management, timescales.

When the questions came, there were no niceties. They landed like punches. He needed all his wits to defend his position.

By the end of the meeting the man was exhausted. He was dropped off back at his hotel. The following day, they said, he would have the decision.

That night he slept uneasily. At one point he thought he heard someone outside his door. He opened it, only to peer out on an empty corridor.

Lying in bed, he kept going over everything in his mind. His instructions had been clear. He hoped his solution would pass muster.

Japan was, after all, his area of expertise.

He had deep roots there. When the Chinese immigrants first arrived, the Japanese penned them in the Yokohama settlement, fearing unwanted foreign influence on the local population.

When restrictions were eventually lifted, the family decided to stay. Yokohama became their home.

There were perilous times. The Great Earthquake in 1923, the war with China. Invariably the blame was laid at their door.

His grandfather recounted how the Japanese would maraud through the streets, venting their anger on the hapless Chinese residents. But, despite all the ordeals, the family hung on.

It paid dividends. As a gateway to the rest of the world, Yokohama offered rich pickings.

Foreign crews came ashore seeking exotic entertainment. His family were adept at catering for all tastes. As the port grew, so did their fortunes.

The international settlement lived according to its own rules. The Japanese largely left the enclave to its own devices.

Over time the criminal landscape evolved. New opportunities emerged.

To exploit them, the family decided to form an alliance. Hooking up with a major Hong Kong criminal organisation catapulted them into the big league.

It came at a price. They had new masters to answer to. If the call came, they were expected to respond without hesitation.

Sitting in Victoria Park, the man glanced at his watch. He needed to head back to the hotel.

At the prescribed time, his phone rang.

"You can proceed."

There was no elaboration. The man's bag was already packed. He checked out of the hotel and took a taxi to Chep Lap Kok Airport.

As the plane took off for Tokyo, the man in the white gloves was already considering his next moves.

3

Ms Sekikawa turned and stared at Yamaguchi sitting in his glass-panelled office. She could not help likening him to some caged animal.

He was bent over a thick document. Beside him lay an A4 pad. His pencil poised.

His notetaking, she noticed, had improved. Gone was the cursive cat's cradle of old. Now, as chief of the International Liaison Department, he churned out screeds of neatly-formed characters.

His promotion had followed a high-profile case. Against the odds, the pair of them had managed to thwart a potentially devastating terrorist plot.

It had been touch-and-go. In the process, they had disregarded orders from their superior and standard police procedure.

Despite the top brass commending them for their initiative, other voices had disapproved of their gung-ho approach. Opinion was divided.

Yamaguchi's superiors at Tokyo's Metropolitan Police Headquarters came up with a neat solution. They tucked the maverick officer away in a glass box and buried him in paperwork.

It went against the grain. Yamaguchi was a field detective to his fingertips.

But once the decision was made, he buckled down to his new role. He spent long days ploughing through the mountain of files in his in-tray.

Ms Sekikawa knew him too well. She was not fooled by the statistical charts taped to the glass panels or the bureaucratic terminology he had taken to spouting.

On the infrequent occasions they met for a drink, she queried him about his new role. He remained tight-lipped, refusing to comment. He was never one to complain.

If she pushed him too far, she would be met by one of his blank looks, his jaw slightly protruding. She knew when to take a hint.

They had established a close rapport since transferring to Tokyo from Osaka some years before. Facing Yamaguchi across the desk every day, Ms Sekikawa reckoned she knew what made him tick, despite the difference in their age and rank.

But that was in the past. Yamaguchi had the whole department to consider now. Ms Sekikawa understood she no longer had any special claim over her boss.

As she mulled over these thoughts, Yamaguchi glanced up and met her look. He nodded briefly before returning to his reading.

A few seconds later Ms Sekikawa's phone rang.

"Can you come in, please?"

Typical, she thought. She crossed the office and entered the glass cube.

"Close the door, please."

Without waiting to be invited, she plonked herself down

on the chair opposite him. After everything they had been through together, she felt entitled.

As he shuffled the papers on the desk in front of him, she took a moment to study Yamaguchi.

He was largely unchanged from when they had met eight years previously. Physically, he was in excellent shape from his intensive martial arts training. A few wrinkles had started to appear and his close-cropped hair was thinning slightly on the crown.

She wondered how he saw her. Like him, she kept fit from her regular sessions at the swimming pool. Her split times had hardly changed in the intervening years. The youngsters in the club still struggled to keep up.

She never took much notice of her appearance. She kept her hair short, wore a modicum of make-up and felt most comfortable in her work clothes.

Yamaguchi laid his palms flat on the desk. The signal he was ready to start.

"Sekikawa-san. We have a new officer joining us next week. He'll report to you."

"To me?"

"Yes. I'd like you to take him under your wing. He's transferring from Yokohama."

"I see."

"I realise this is a new role for you but I have no doubt you will manage perfectly well."

"Thank you for your confidence. Do we know much about his background?"

In response Yamaguchi slid a sheet of paper across the desk.

Ms Sekikawa glanced through the officer's details.

"A Chinese speaker?"

"Yes. I felt we could use one in the department."

In recent years Japan had become a magnet for tourists from mainland China. They came with money in their pockets. For many of them, it was their first trip abroad.

When they found themselves in difficulties, the International Liaison Department was often asked to step in and assist. Having a Chinese speaker on the team would be a big help, especially when dealing with the Chinese authorities.

Ms Sekikawa skimmed through the résumé. Top marks in Chinese studies at Tokyo University of Foreign Studies. She nodded her approval. Only the most able students were accepted at this prestigious public university.

After entering the police force, he had completed the six-month graduate conversion course at the Metropolitan Police Academy. He then joined the Chinese specialist section in Yokohama.

"He seems to fit the profile."

"Yes. He'll be starting next Monday. He'll take the desk opposite you."

Ms Sekikawa raised her eyebrows. It had been unoccupied since Yamaguchi had vacated it for the glass box.

It would be good to have some company at last.

4

The following Monday morning, a young officer stood rigidly to attention in front of Yamaguchi.

He was taller than the average Japanese. He had a firm chin and prominent nose. He shared Yamaguchi's minimalist cropped hairstyle.

From her desk, Ms Sekikawa watched the interview unfold. The young man did not appear to falter. As Yamaguchi rattled off questions, the new recruit responded without hesitation.

Eventually the process drew to a close. Yamaguchi shut the file in front of him and led the way out of his office into the heart of the department.

"If I could have your attention, please?"

Heads popped up from behind computer screens. Officers stopped in their tracks.

"This is Detective Hayashi. He's joining us from Yokohama to assist with our Chinese liaison work. I have no doubt he'll prove a very useful asset to the team. Please make him welcome."

Hayashi bowed.

"*Yoroshiku onegai shimasu.*"

The team responded in kind.

The group introduction over, Yamaguchi marched over to Ms

Sekikawa's desk with Hayashi in tow.

"This is Detective Sekikawa. You will report to her."

With that, Yamaguchi turned on his heel and retreated to his office. He was soon fully immersed in his reading once again.

Ms Sekikawa smiled at Hayashi.

"Welcome. Here's your seat. Please get settled in and then I'll brief you on your duties."

"Thank you."

Hayashi sat down opposite her. He glanced around the room as if fixing his coordinates before unpacking his briefcase and storing the contents in his desk drawer.

Then, reaching forwards, he switched on his computer. Soon his fingers were rattling over the keyboard.

Ms Sekikawa had decided to throw him in at the deep end. In front of her was a weighty United Nations report on human trafficking. Its focus was the Philippines.

Yamaguchi had summoned her to his cube the previous week.

"Can you have a look at this, please?"

"Of course." She glanced at the cover. "Human trafficking?"

"Yes, it seems the United Nations and the Philippine government feel the Japanese authorities are sitting on their hands. You'll see the figures inside. Only four trafficking convictions in 2010. Forty-three victims identified."

"That's barely scratching the surface."

They were both well aware of the spread of this lucrative trade throughout East Asia and beyond. They also knew it was extremely hard to prosecute. The victims were in fear of their own lives and those of their loved ones back home.

"Exactly. Anyway, we've been asked to investigate."

"Just from the Philippines angle?"

"To start with. Statistically they make up the largest group trafficked into Japan."

"Any suggestions on our approach?"

"Well, first find out as much about the trade as you can. How it operates, the main perpetrators. Try to track down any victims and take witness statements. Then we'll need to compile a report with a recommended action plan."

Inwardly, Ms Sekikawa groaned. Reports had a habit of sitting in someone's drawer until the question was raised again.

Still, it was a subject close to her heart. In 2004 she and Yamaguchi had investigated the abduction of a Swedish child from Thailand in the aftermath of the Asian tsunami. In the process they had waded into the unsavoury mire of human exploitation.

After giving Hayashi some time to get settled, Ms Sekikawa walked round to his side of the desk. She shoved the report in front of him.

"Right. Here's something to get your teeth into."

He listened carefully as Ms Sekikawa explained what was required. He asked a series of pertinent questions and then immediately set to work.

Ms Sekikawa left him to it, intrigued as to how he would approach the task. At intervals throughout the morning, she stole quick glances across the desk.

His concentration never seemed to waver. He flicked through

the pages without ever taking notes.

Ms Sekikawa had the distinct impression he did not need to. That he had committed all the information to memory.

She decided to test her theory. Referring to her own notes, she asked Hayashi a random question related to one section of the report. His reply was word perfect.

"You can remember that?"

Hayashi looked up as if surprised by the question.

"Yes. It's something I've always been able to do."

Ms Sekikawa raised her eyebrows and returned to her own work. She doubted Hayashi was going to be much fun to work with.

Exactly the type she approved of.

5

The woodpecker fell silent.

The man had his binoculars trained on the bird, studying its distinctive red and green plumage. After a short break, it resumed its attack on the bark of the Japanese cedar.

He recalled when first he had heard a woodpecker in the forest. It was years before as he had been climbing the steep winding path from the valley floor.

Somewhere in the dark woodland recesses, the bird had introduced itself. Its faint Morse code signalling its presence.

Weeks later, he had spotted colourful flashes between the trees. Finally, he was granted a private audience: the woodpecker in full view hammering out its meal of grubs.

Subsequent generations had become bolder, more assured. They had started to feel at home.

The binoculars were heavy and cumbersome, but he would not consider parting with them. They had been a gift from a close Japanese friend. His name was embossed in gold lettering.

He panned the treetops, tracking the contours of the mountainside up to the peak. In early spring, a thick band of ice and snow still lay against the sky.

Then he turned his attention to the village below. The traditional dark-tiled houses squatted precariously on soil all too prone to slip.

Raising his sights, he studied the city in the distance. He could just make out its streets lined with high-rise office blocks. Only the multi-storied castle at its heart stood as a reminder of its place in history.

He avoided Yamashiro. On the rare occasions they needed to go to the supermarket on the outskirts, Hiroko went alone. For her, it was a treat.

Adjusting the focus again, he swept the horizon, settling on a distant sliver of water between two mountains. Every spring he and Hiroko made a pilgrimage to this vast lake to welcome home the migrating Siberian swans.

The mobile phone vibrated in his pocket.

He was expecting the call. Through his binoculars, he had spotted the large black saloon threading its way up the narrow track towards the house. He had half-hoped he would be left in peace.

He did not answer. It was a signal he and Hiroko used. Two rings to tell him to head home. It saved the cost of a call.

He swung the binoculars behind his back and set off. The path down was steep, strewn with loose rocks. He picked his way between them with surprising agility for a large man.

The saloon was parked in the shadow of the barn. The driver, in a dark suit and sunglasses, sat behind the wheel flicking through a newspaper.

He lifted his head when the man emerged from the forest. He watched him shimmy along the stone wall separating the paddy fields.

Normally people did not interest him much. When his eyes were not on the road, they were on the racing pages.

The man approaching him was tall and well set. He could

have been a wrestler.

He wore a pair of ballooning blue *mompe* trousers typical of women during the war years. They were held up with a homemade belt of braided straw. Under a frayed judo top was a tee-shirt emblazoned with a picture of Mickey Mouse.

His long hair was tied back in a ponytail. His face was heavily whiskered.

The driver did not come across many non-Japanese. Certainly, none looking like this. He stared until the foreigner met his gaze.

The old farmhouse stood on its own. The nearest neighbour was at the bottom of the track leading down to the village.

Its steep roof and solid timbers were built to resist the severest winters. The mountain winds barrelling down the valley worried away at any weak point.

When tiles became dislodged, Sean Peters clambered up to replace them. When gaps appeared in the walls, he covered them with odd lengths of timber.

Any expense was spared. It made the building an untidy patchwork. But it was watertight and resilient.

As he approached the front door, a Japanese woman in a simple skirt and quilted top appeared.

"Hurry up, Sean! He's arrived."

6

They sat in the lounge. It was cramped and cluttered.

Despite being midday, there was little natural light. Tears in the paper *shoji* screens had been repaired with sticky tape. The loose ends curled back on themselves like scorpion tails.

Large wardrobes crowded the walls. Any free space between them was crammed with cardboard boxes.

In the centre of the room was a *kotatsu* table. Its feeble electric element on the underside was rarely switched on, even during the winter. The house's main heat source was a wood-burning stove in the kitchen.

The Yamashiro city mayor was perched on a cushion. He wore an expensive suit and looked ill at ease.

Sean Peters knelt opposite. He was still perspiring from the walk down the mountain. Reaching across, he picked up a small cotton towel to wipe his brow.

The silence was broken when Hiroko arrived with the tea. She served the mayor and Peters before herself.

"Thank you."

The mayor sipped his tea. It was insipid.

"So, you've come to see us…?"

"Yes."

The mayor put his cup down.

"It's a difficult situation."

The mayor addressed his comments to the woman. He avoided eye contact with Peters.

"As you know this is a poor community and opportunities like this don't come along often. We need to seize them when they do. But we all need to act together."

He reached for his teacup. He liked to punctuate significant utterances with sips of tea.

Hiroko looked at Peters. She wondered whether he was even listening.

He was. Years in Japan had taught him speech was an overrated faculty. Listening was much more useful.

Sometimes locals interpreted his silence as lack of understanding. They wondered if he still struggled with the language.

Hiroko invariably acted as their spokesperson. They would address her and she would answer on his behalf.

She mostly represented his views accurately. There was little about which they did not see eye-to-eye.

Hiroko turned to the mayor.

"I'm sorry. This is our home. We would never consider moving."

The mayor stared at her. Anyone could see they were living on a shoestring. Alone, he was sure the woman would jump at the chance. She was one of them, after all.

But Peters was different.

The mayor had run across people like him in the past. People who stuck their toes in. But when the price was right, they always signed. It was just a question of time.

After all, what were they fighting for? Their mountainous property was unproductive, just full of lumber too expensive to extract.

But today the land could sell at a premium. A once-in-a-lifetime opportunity.

The mayor decided to push.

"Of course, you love your home. Many of the families have lived in the village for generations. You aren't the only ones with strong links. But we can't halt progress. A development like this will bring prosperity to the whole area. Provide vital employment, a better infrastructure, a brighter future for our children."

He glanced at the couple to see if his words were having any impact. He pushed ahead.

"Without this project, we'll continue as a backwater. We are responsible for the whole community. You're the only ones who haven't agreed to sell. Please reconsider."

"We're not moving. That's final."

Peters' Japanese was unadorned, not open to misinterpretation. The mayor stared at the perspiring foreigner across the table.

He sighed, realising he had overstayed his welcome. As soon as convention permitted, the official made his excuses and stood to leave.

Hiroko saw him out, watching until the black saloon disappeared from view at the end of the track. When she came back to the room, she leaned against the doorframe, her arms folded.

Peters stood up and drew her to him. She hugged him,

breathing in his familiar earthy scent.

"Don't worry Hiroko. It'll be all right. They can't make us move."

He smiled at her and kissed both her eyes. She pinched the fold of skin at his waist, before pushing him away.

"OK?"

She nodded. He padded over to the entrance and started to put on his working boots.

"Well, the onions need weeding."

He swung a hoe over his shoulder and threaded his way towards the vegetable patch.

Hiroko came to the door, biting the side of her thumb. She watched him for a few seconds before closing the door.

7

The room was packed.

The men and women were smartly dressed. The *lingua franca* was English. The topic was the financial markets.

The group met socially once a quarter for a wine tasting or art exhibition. But the aim was to leave with a snippet more information than when they had arrived.

Often, it was no more than a passing comment, a whispered aside as the vintage wines loosened tongues. But it was attributed a value and filed away for future reference.

The prime mover of the event was in his early forties. Charles Fancourt worked the room with handshakes and a ready smile. He knew how to turn on the charm when he had to.

Sometimes, he singled someone out. Then he would bend to whisper in their ear. To make them feel special.

He was always in the know. A step ahead. An invaluable source of information. But when he did someone a favour, he expected one in return.

For three years, he had presided over these get-togethers. He chose a suitable venue, decided on the theme and sent out invitations.

A paltry effort considering the return.

"Charles!"

Fancourt turned to face an elegant Japanese woman.

"Hello Yuki. Glad you could make it."

"Oh, I wouldn't miss this for anything. You know that."

He did. The previous year he had made an unguarded comment. It had cost him.

Charles Fancourt never forgot. And he never forgave.

"You're looking stunning."

"Thank you!"

From her piled coiffure to the tips of her Jimmy Choo shoes, Yuki Morigami exuded opulence. She was tall and toned. Every lunchtime she worked out at her exclusive fitness studio under the watchful eye of her personal trainer.

With Charles Fancourt, the cracks were appearing. His time in East Asia had taken its toll.

His jawline was blurred and his waistline expanding. Only his eyes retained their acuity.

His days were long, the pressure unrelenting. He rarely left his desk from dawn to dusk. When he did, his attention was constantly on his smartphone.

But however hard he pushed himself, others were pushing him harder. People entrusting him with their money.

"How's business?"

Yuki Morigami flashed him a smile.

"Fine, fine. Keeping one step ahead."

The product of an American education, Yuki Morigami's English was impeccable. She was smart and ruthless.

Fancourt studied her. Even if she had just lost her shirt on the Tokyo Stock Exchange, you would never know.

He was the same. They all were. They could not afford to show the least sign of frailty.

"Splendid. You're moving, I hear?"

"You're well informed as always, Charles. Yes, we need room to expand."

Charles Fancourt understood they were cutting back, ditching their prestigious city centre office.

Yuki Morigami took a long sip.

"Excellent wine! Where did you find it?"

"A specialist outfit in Ginza. A friend at the club gave me the tip."

There was only one club. The Tokyo American Club. For the foreign investment community in Tokyo, joining was de rigueur.

"You must mail me the address. We're having a do shortly and this would be perfect."

Yuki Morigami took another sip, her hair falling back to reveal a set of diamond earrings.

Fancourt allowed himself a second to study her graceful neck as she drank. As she intended.

He was forgetting himself. Picking up a knife from the table, he chinked his glass. The fragile sound reverberated through the room. Everyone stopped talking and turned towards him.

"Good evening, everyone. Welcome to another of our soirées. It's good to see so many of you here, especially with the markets so jumpy. I can only assume it was the lure of these rather fine Bordeaux."

"Hear, Hear."

"Two pieces of news, I wanted to say bon voyage to Juan Garcia who returns to Spain at the end of the month and a warm welcome to Kurt Hirsch of Green Stream Management who joins us."

Fancourt pointed out the two men. They raised their glasses in salute.

"Finally, just to say our next meeting will be in June. If you have any suggestions for a theme, do let me know, otherwise I shall exercise my usual prerogative as your secretary."

That concluded the evening. The guests did not dally.

Fancourt waited for the room to clear before heading for the lift. Outside in the spring evening he hailed a cab and slid in.

"Shinjuku."

The driver nodded and swung out into the Roppongi traffic. Fancourt sat back, his fingers drumming a tattoo on his knee.

His earlier bonhomie had vanished, his face expressionless. His guests would hardly have recognised him.

8

Peters worked his hoe briskly between the rows of onions. There would be a good crop that year. As long as he could keep the pests off.

"Sell? Not a chance."

He spent a lot of time on his own. He often found himself talking to himself as he worked.

There was no likelihood of anyone overhearing. No one ever came near the property. The couple kept themselves to themselves.

Hiroko was occasionally expected to pitch in with community activities, but Sean rarely showed his face. The villagers interpreted their reticence as lack of community spirit.

People had grumbled about the newcomers at first. But over time they had been ignored and then largely forgotten.

But now Sean and Hiroko were the centre of attention.

When the developers had first publicised the meeting, the villagers were agog with interest. No one spoke of anything else.

No one knew exactly what it was all about, but speculation was rife. One woman's daughter worked in a hair salon. She had heard an international consortium was involved and the project was large-scale.

Everyone had dismissed the rumour. But it turned out the daughter was right on the money.

The day arrived and the community centre was decked out with colourful bunting. The villagers assembled in good time. When the doors opened, they pushed forwards to secure the best seats.

A hush fell as the city mayor strode onto the stage. He had a reputation for being a pompous windbag. The villagers steeled themselves for one of his typically rambling speeches.

They were surprised when he simply introduced the presentation team and sat down.

A man in a subdued dark suit stood up. He was well-built, late thirties, with tightly-cropped hair. He exuded confidence.

After introducing himself, he started his pitch. He was articulate and persuasive.

He said he understood the difficulties facing the community. Lack of facilities. Poor roads. Unemployment. They were there to help.

He asked his assistant at the back of the hall to dim the lights. A short film would follow.

As they watched, the villagers were left open-mouthed.

The mountains behind their village were to be sculpted into a Swiss style resort. There would be a championship golf course and an extensive winter ski area, on a par with venues in Europe and America.

Improved transport links would follow. A new industrial park. The latest health care facilities. The whole area would prosper.

The film ended on a rousing patriotic note. The locals could play their part in helping their region back on its feet.

The man returned to the stage and invited questions. It took a while for the villagers to raise their hands, but then there was a steady stream.

The presenter had the answers off pat. His team had mostly anticipated the issues.

But then a hand went up at the back of the room. When Sean Peters stood up, the villagers nudged each other.

His question was in fluent but unadorned Japanese. He came straight to the point.

"What will the environmental impact of this development be?"

The presenter did a momentary double-take as he sized up the unconventionally-dressed foreigner. Then he started to list environmental prizes the development group had won.

Sean Peters interrupted.

"No. I want to know the effect on the area's wildlife."

One of the local wits could not restrain himself.

"What's he talking about? Wild boars?"

There was an undercurrent of laughter. The man on the stage ignored it.

"The wildlife will be unaffected. It will roam freely throughout the mountains as before."

The meeting closed to enthusiastic applause.

The man came down from the stage to mingle with the villagers. He tried to locate the foreigner who had asked the question. It appeared the couple had already left.

Subsequently all the neighbouring landowners had jumped at the chance to sell. Despite being in their families for generations, the land was effectively worthless. The current offer was way above the going rate.

But for the project to proceed, the developers needed to secure the key tranche of land linking all the others. Without Hiroko and Sean's property, the project was not viable.

Over the weeks the pressure mounted. People made their views known.

But Sean Peters was not one to succumb to pressure easily.

9

Akira Kato's personal assistant tapped on the glass office door. She was always fearful of disturbing her boss.

She waited until he signalled her to enter before tiptoeing across the room with some papers clutched to her chest.

"Excuse me Kato-san, these documents require your signature."

As he read each page carefully, she stood at his side, her hands clasped behind her back. She could not help glancing at him.

He was unconventional. As the owner of the company, he could afford to be.

His copious hair fell to his shoulders. While he worked, he kept it pinned back out of his eyes with a lacquer headband.

He wore a blue velvet three-piece suit with gold watch and chain. On his feet, a pair of pointed tan leather shoes.

His personal dress style echoed his earlier artistic ambitions. As a child, he spent every spare moment doodling, scenes and characters leaping from the page with just a few deft pencil strokes.

His gift was plain for anyone to see. As a teenager he won prizes and dreamed of a future in his own atelier, poised in front of an easel.

But there was more to becoming an artist than being a

talented draftsman. Eventually he had bowed to pressure.

His parents had guided him towards a more established profession. After graduating with a top degree in architecture, Kato had joined a prestigious firm of architects to learn his trade.

He spent his formative years slaving over drawings, churning out one corporate facsimile after another. Finally, he decided it was time to make his move.

He established a small boutique to realise his own personal vision. He wanted to put his particular stamp on the city around him.

It was an immediate success. Clients sought him out. The freshness of his designs set him apart from the competition. In the trade, he was soon recognised as a coming man.

He simultaneously discovered a surprising knack for business. He quickly learned how to woo investors, how to work the system to achieve his goals.

In time, his small-scale start-up morphed into a fully-fledged property development company. The staff expanded. The firm moved into sought-after city centre premises.

Kato was too filled with ambition to contemplate a reverse in his fortunes. He took on ever more complex projects, ignoring the financial risks involved.

When the 2008 crash came, Japan's property developers were caught napping. The wind suddenly dropped from Kato's commercial sails.

The banks called in their loans. His situation became increasingly desperate.

Then, just as he was staring bankruptcy in the face, he was thrown an unexpected life-line. A new client approached him with a project for a major leisure development in the north.

He had jumped at the chance. Anything to stave off his creditors.

The project was bigger than anything he had attempted before. It would stretch his resources to the limit.

He did not hesitate. It was all or nothing. His future was on the line.

His phone rang.

Before answering, he waved his personal assistant out of the room. She gathered up the papers and hurried out.

He waited until she had closed the door behind her, before answering.

"So, what's the latest?"

He had been expecting the phone call from the local mayor of Yamashiro. The hold-up to their development in the village to the north of that city was becoming critical. Everything depended on resolving the impasse.

"I went to see the couple as we discussed. They won't budge."

Kato stabbed the desk with his pencil in frustration.

"So, what's going to change their minds?"

The mayor went silent for a second before answering.

"Difficult to say. At a pinch, I think we could persuade the woman. But the foreigner is another matter."

Kato recalled the initial report from his team at the village meeting. The environmental questions the wild-looking *gaijin* at the back had raised. His people had immediately sensed potential trouble.

"Is there any pressure we can bring to bear?"

The mayor frowned. He was standing outside his office in the parking lot. He glanced around.

"There's a limit to how much we can do. We can't force them to sell."

"You'll need to think of something. Your role was to handle the local community. At the moment everything is on hold. A lot of money has been invested. People are becoming impatient."

The mayor bristled. He had been a fool to become involved. He thought it would be easy, business as usual.

Handle the planning department. Pour oil over any objections. Nudge people to sell.

But he was stuck. He had taken the developer's coin. He was obliged to deliver.

"I'll get back to you. I'll try to think of something."

Kato rang off and threw his phone on the table. He removed his hairband and reset it on his head.

Glaring at his phone as if it was the enemy, he swept it up again and punched in a number. One he knew by heart, not contained in his regular contacts.

This was not a phone call he was looking forward to.

10

Hiroko sat on the tatami floor folding the washing. She never saw the point of ironing.

She always attended to Sean's clothes first, smoothing out the creases with the flat of her hand. As if they carried traces of him in their weave.

As she worked her hair dropped forwards over her face. She paused to sweep her tresses back and knot them behind her head. Then she took a sip of tea and bent to her work again, her brow puckered in concentration.

People always took her for a much younger woman. She had a practical fringe above her soft eyes and petite nose. When she smiled, her face lit up.

Under her unflattering dress, her figure was unchanged from when she was a teenager. Her long, straight legs were the envy of her friends. She had always been considered a beauty.

As she worked, her mind strayed to Sean. He was never far from her thoughts.

They had met in London. She was working in a noodle bar near Piccadilly. It was a part-time job to save up for a trip around Europe.

They always said it was love at first sight. As if in a flash, their lives changed for ever.

It took him time to pluck up courage to ask her out. Several trips to the restaurant, always sitting in the same seat, always ordering the same dish.

She was constantly on the look-out for him, hoping. When eventually he appeared in the doorway, her heart leaped.

He would make a beeline for the rear of the restaurant. He never seemed to notice her. Her eyes never left him.

His order was always the same despite spending minutes puzzling over the menu. When he looked up, she was waiting patiently.

"Hello, what can I get you?"

"I'll have the *miso ramen*, please."

She would write it down on her pad, taking her time.

"Something to drink?"

"Just water, please."

Her smile held a string of urgent messages. About seizing the moment. Taking a chance.

Then one day, instead of heading for the back of the room, he approached the counter.

"Can I speak with you, please? Alone?"

She felt the eyes of the other restaurant staff on her. But she did not care.

Her thoughts were only for the man in front of her. She felt light-headed.

He turned on his heel and walked out of the restaurant. She did not hesitate. She took off her apron and followed him.

She was only twenty-one at the time. It was her first spell living abroad.

Back in Japan her future was mapped out for her. A well-paid job until she married. Then children. Family responsibilities.

A comfortable, predictable life. Just as her father expected.

When Hiroko rang from London to tell him she was living with an Englishman, the lines burned hot. Words were said that could never be unsaid.

Hiroko made her choice there and then. To stay with Sean. Whatever the cost.

She was proud. She would never back down.

Her father was an exceptionally clever but small-minded man. He had won a place at Tokyo's most prestigious public university through ability and hard graft. It was a great honour for the small village where he had grown up.

Once in the capital, he did not look back. After graduation, he was snapped up by one of Japan's top trading companies.

He was a catch for any girl. In no time, he married into an affluent Tokyo family.

But when Hiroko was five, her mother died. Her father compensated for the loss by lavishing attention on Hiroko and her younger sister Akemi.

They wanted for nothing. He never re-married.

Hiroko was always his favourite. She had a sweet nature and good looks.

Akemi, three years her junior, was the polar opposite. Plain and plump, she was increasingly jealous of the exclusive relationship enjoyed between her father and her elder sister.

After Hiroko decided to turn her back on the family, her father broke off all contact. He vowed to have nothing more to do with her.

Akemi stepped in. She stoked the fires, burning Hiroko's

bridges for good.

Only when their father was dying of cancer did Akemi decide to contact Hiroko. It was already too late. By the time Hiroko arrived in Tokyo, her father had slipped into a coma.

They never spoke. Never had the chance to reconcile their differences.

When the two sisters faced each other across the dying man's bed, the battle lines were drawn. After the funeral, Hiroko hastened back to England to be with Sean.

Some weeks later, her father's lawyers contacted her. She learned her sister Akemi had inherited the vast majority of her father's sizable estate.

Hiroko had only been left the former family home in the north, together with the mountainous tract of land it sat on. It had been in the family for generations. A gift for war-time services rendered to a local *daimyo,* centuries before.

The deserted farmhouse was in poor repair. Apart from some logging, the land was of no practical value. A costly encumbrance.

Hiroko had been scathing about her inheritance. Describing the property to Sean, she had painted an unflattering picture. A worthless piece of scrub land in the middle of nowhere.

As she complained, Sean Peters was gazing out of the window of their North London flat. His eye travelled across the rain-smudged grey rooftops of the city.

He had turned to her.

"It sounds perfect. Let's go."

She had stared at him in disbelief. But he was adamant. In no time they had thrown in their jobs and were heading for a new life in rural Japan.

When they arrived at the property, they realised the enormity of the task facing them. The dilapidated walls, the caved-in roof, the rampant weeds.

But Peters was undaunted. He patched up the farmhouse and laboured from dawn to dusk to restore the garden. They had finally found somewhere to call home.

Over time, they managed to eke out a meagre existence on the unforgiving terrain. They kept themselves to themselves, living within their means.

Sixteen years had passed. They could not have been happier.

Hiroko smoothed the last piece of laundry. Folding it, she laid it on the pile.

11

Ms Sekikawa and Hayashi waited silently until the waitress had served them their lunch. Pork fillet tonkatsu on a bed of sliced cabbage, miso soup and rice.

The set meal was always dependable in the family-run restaurant in Akasaka-Mitsuke. Ms Sekikawa rarely bothered to go anywhere else.

The new member of the department had completed his first week and Ms Sekikawa decided it was time to take stock. She was keen to find out what made him tick.

Hayashi had spent most of the week glued to his computer screen. He only spoke when spoken to. He rarely took breaks. He seldom interacted with the other officers in the department.

Ms Sekikawa took her new responsibility seriously. She was anxious to make a success of it.

She found herself becoming quite maternal towards Hayashi. Only the family cat had ever inspired similar emotions.

"*Itadakimasu.*"

Snapping his chopsticks apart, Hayashi ate with concentration. When he finally came up for air, Ms Sekikawa took her chance.

"So, how are you settling in?"

"Fine, thank you."

"Can you manage the work?"

"Yes, thank you."

"No concerns?"

"No. Everything's fine."

"Good."

Ms Sekikawa retreated to her own meal. She had interviewed criminals who were more forthcoming.

After glancing at the top of Hayashi's bristled head for a couple more minutes, she made a fresh sally.

"So how are you finding the commute from Yokohama?"

Hayashi looked up as if surprised at the question.

"Nothing to complain about. An hour or so."

"Do you live far from the station?"

"About twenty minutes."

"Not too bad then."

"No. It's fine."

With this conversation in danger of hitting the buffers too, Ms Sekikawa tried another tack.

"So, what made you study Chinese at university?"

Hayashi paused. Ms Sekikawa anticipated another dead end.

"My mother is Chinese."

Ms Sekikawa's chopsticks hovered in mid-air.

"Really? So, you spoke Chinese as a child with your mother?"

"Yes. But later we only used Japanese at home. My parents thought it was for the best. Less confusing for me at school."

Hayashi seemed anxious to return to the remnants of his meal.

"Well, your Chinese skills will be very useful for us in the department."

"Yes. I hope I can make a contribution."

"I'm sure you will."

It was slow going again until coffee.

"So, what made you choose the police force."

Hayashi frowned as if searching for an acceptable answer.

"When I was young, I was given a toy police car with flashing lights. I think it all started then."

Ms Sekikawa spluttered into her coffee.

"Sorry?"

Across the table Hayashi smiled. He suddenly seemed a different person.

"I've still got the toy car."

"You don't bring it to work, do you?"

"No, it's quicker by train."

Ms Sekikawa chortled, keen to encourage his humorous vein.

"So, that was that. A toy car and suddenly your career was mapped out."

Hayashi's smile faded.

"The truth is I witnessed a lot of crime growing up in

Yokohama Chinatown. It left its mark on me."

Ms Sekikawa nodded.

"I can imagine."

She glanced at her watch.

"Well, we'd better be getting back."

She headed over to the counter to pay while Hayashi waited outside the restaurant.

"Thank you."

"You're welcome."

They walked back to the office without talking. On arriving back at their desks, Hayashi immediately immersed himself in his work.

Looking across, Ms Sekikawa wondered if she was any the wiser about her new understudy.

12

When Akira Kato entered the hotel restaurant opposite the bullet-train station, the man he was due to meet was already shovelling down a substantial breakfast.

The man jumped to his feet, bowed and introduced himself as Ito. No name cards were exchanged.

The man signalled to the waitress. Kato ordered a coffee and then sat back and studied the man opposite.

Even in an Armani suit, he would have looked scruffy. Evidence of recent meals daubed the front of his tie. His hair stood on end as if he was in a permanent state of shock.

"You came highly recommended."

Ito nodded.

"It's gratifying to hear that."

"My contacts say you are very thorough. That you get results."

"I've had my share of successes. So, how can I help you?"

As Kato gave Ito the background, the man took laborious notes. Kato became increasingly irritated.

He could have briefed Ito over the phone. He wondered if he had been dragged north just so the private investigator could sponge a meal off him.

Kato had made an early start, taking the Tohoku Shinkansen

from Tokyo Station. During the journey he had time to reflect.

He had contacted the local mayor for an update. The official confirmed he had been unable to make any further progress.

He said he had spoken with the woman again on the phone. Despite using all his powers of persuasion, she had been insistent.

They were not going to sell under any circumstances. She asked to be left in peace.

Kato had sat for the next half an hour staring at the project plans spread out on his desk. The detailed scale drawings amounted to nothing without the missing tranche of land.

He realised he had no choice but to take control of the situation himself. The unappetising private investigator sitting across the table was his next line of offence.

"So, do you have everything you need?"

Ito stared at his notebook, mentally ticking off the points.

"Yes, I believe so. If there's anything else, I'll call you."

"Contact me on this number."

"OK. I'll give you the first progress report at the end of the week."

"I'll be waiting."

"Right. Thank you for breakfast. I'll be in touch."

The man closed his briefcase and left the restaurant. Kato lingered. The return train was not for a couple of hours so he had time to kill.

He looked out of the window at the featureless city. It stretched away towards the encircling ring of mountains to the west.

He should never have got into this.

He had first met the client at a discreet café in Tokyo's Higashi-Ginza. Kato had been sceptical until the small man opposite had mentioned the sums of money involved.

The man had explained he represented a very wealthy consortium. One that was keen to take advantage of Japan's historically-low rural land prices.

Kato had his doubts. The man did not come across as a well-heeled property investor with his ill-fitting clothes and incongruous white silk gloves. For Kato, dress sense mattered.

He arranged for some initial background checks. To his surprise, he found the funding held in the Cayman Islands was exactly as the client had outlined.

Kato chose not to probe any further. No need to look a gift horse in the mouth.

He had set up a working group. A few weeks later, the team had reported back.

They had pinpointed a remote corner up north. The land prices were favourable and there were enticing tax breaks. The local authorities were only too delighted to facilitate the venture.

Given the project's importance, Kato had headed up-country to evaluate the site first-hand. As he drove through fields of plum trees framed by the mountain backdrop, he found himself nodding his approval.

The area's potential was obvious. Kato had no difficulty visualising this rural backwater transformed into a popular visitor destination.

He had personally presented the plans to the client at the same café where they first met.

The client had set the ground rules early. He only dealt with Kato. And never at Kato's office.

Kato was no innocent. As time went on, he had few illusions about who he was dealing with. But by then, he was in too deep to back-pedal.

When Kato received the green light for the development, he moved fast. He lined up the local politicians and initiated the land purchases.

At the outset, the client had been quite explicit. Kato should not hesitate to let him know if there were any major road-blocks. He had, he explained, resources at his disposal.

During one of their most recent discussions, Kato had mentioned the couple who were reluctant to sell.

The client had interlaced his gloved fingers and leaned forwards across the table. His voice emerged as a growl.

"Don't bother me with such trifles."

13

Charles Fancourt always arrived at the office early. It was just a short stroll from his luxury apartment in the monied heart of Tokyo.

He cut through side streets, avoiding the early morning traffic. His building was visible up ahead, the 54-story Roppongi Hills Mori Tower.

Entering the air-conditioned lobby, he glanced up at the information board listing the tower's corporate tenants. It gave him a kick to see his company rubbing shoulders with household financial names.

Despite the early hour, the elevator was packed.

"*Nijukkai de gozaimasu.*"

The elevator's metallic voice bleated out the floor numbers. Fancourt had absorbed enough Japanese to know when they had arrived at the twentieth.

He wrestled his way through the other occupants of the elevator car with no word of apology. Brushing himself down, he strode along the glazed walkway to his office.

Work was already in full swing.

"*Ohayoo gozaimasu!*"

Fancourt's personal assistant was waiting with her notebook at the ready. Whatever he needed, from executing complex financial transactions to flight reservations, she handled everything.

She was mid-forties, turned out as always in a charcoal-grey pin-striped suit, her hair raked back in a bun. Business-like, efficient, completely discreet, she kept a cool head even under the most testing circumstances.

There were many such occasions. Fancourt played a high-stakes game.

Clients contributing to his hedge fund expected above-average returns. When the market turned against them, they clamoured to know why.

At those times Fancourt needed to draw on all of his assurance. But he knew how to talk the talk, smooth ruffled feathers.

He always stressed he was in the same boat as them. The financial rules demanded he take a sizable personal stake in his own fund. If they went down, he went down with them.

"In here. Now."

The personal assistant followed Fancourt into his office. She was impervious to his curt manner.

Throwing his bag into the corner, he perched on his chair. Simultaneously he reached across to flick on his computer.

His multiple screens lit up, crammed with up-to-the-second global financial information. Alongside the data sat his portfolios. Like a surgeon he drilled down to the source of his discomfort, figures throbbing red.

He had been wide awake in the dead hours of the morning, mentally sifting through his trading positions. On his way to the office, he had crystalised his strategy.

His P.A. stood ready to take instructions. Nothing needed repeating. She was familiar with all the components of his trades and his complex dealings.

Once she had been briefed, she raced out of the office. Every second counted.

In the cramped back office, she barked out orders to the skeleton staff. Even before she finished, they were pounding at their computer keys and ringing brokers.

When Fancourt met his clients, they were entertained in the smart meeting room along the corridor. They never set foot inside the office itself.

He screened them from an unsettling reality. Only he and five others managed their multi-million-dollar investments.

They were blinded by the returns. They salivated over the percentage figures Fancourt achieved, even in times of economic downturn. He had the Midas touch.

While his P.A. oversaw the back-office executions, Fancourt was planning bold new moves. At lunchtime, he leaned back in his chair and stretched.

Once he had shored up his trading position, he turned his attention to other matters. Ones he alone was privy to.

His speciality was manipulating a complex web of shell companies stretching around the globe. From one secretive tax haven to another, money flowed through a labyrinth of offshore accounts.

The paper trail would throw the most persistent investigator off the scent. It was virtually impossible to identify the source of the funds.

Fancourt sat at his desk issuing instructions to his confidants in exotic locations. Opening and closing accounts, making a chain of transfers and withdrawals.

Every detail was in his head. Nothing committed to paper.

Account numbers, the composition of fictitious board members, the corporate minutiae. He could recall them all at will.

It was a unique talent. A great deal rested on his shoulders. He was highly-prized and jealously guarded.

Charles Fancourt was worth a fortune.

14

Hiroko looked forward to her fortnightly trips to the city.

That morning she checked her shelves to see what they needed. Never more than the bare essentials.

Once she had compiled her list, she totted up what it would all cost and checked her wallet. She saw she was running short of cash. She avoided using credit cards.

She spent almost nothing on herself. No new clothes. No visits to the hairdresser. No beauty treatments.

Sometimes, she wondered what it would be like to have a regular income. To be able to afford treats.

It would have been different if they had had children. That would have changed everything.

But she could not conceive. A doctor had earlier confirmed she had complications.

The day she learned the news she had wept in the car. She wanted nothing more than to have children with Sean.

Returning home, she could not bring herself to tell him. She felt she had failed.

Sean could see something important was troubling Hiroko. But he did not press her.

It took her two days to open up. He was sitting beside her on the bed that morning with a cup of tea.

She turned to face the window, pulling the bedclothes up to her chin. The words tumbled out. She told him about the visit to the doctor and the diagnosis.

"I'm sorry, Sean. I'm sorry."

There was a moment's silence before he reached over to squeeze her shoulder.

"Hiroko, all I want is you. Just you and me together. That's it."

She felt the warmth of his hand. She turned to look at him.

Sean Peters sipped his tea. Then, as if reaching a decision, he started to speak.

"In the past, when you asked me about my family, my childhood, I always skirted the subject. Fobbed you off."

It was true. Despite all the years they had been together, she knew little of his early life. After being cut off by her own father, it had become an unspoken pact between them: the past was another country.

He stared straight ahead and then cleared his throat.

"I grew up in Plymouth. It was a shithole and I lived in the shittiest part. Devonport, right by the dockyards. I never knew my father. He was a Dutch merchant seaman. He and my mother were together for just a few months. Then he left. After that, she got into drugs in a big way. She was always out in the evenings, down Union Street. On the game."

He stopped for a second, staring at the teacup resting on his thigh. Even after all these years together, Hiroko struggled to understand Sean's English when he lapsed into his native dialect. But she always managed to get the gist.

"She'd come back pissed, always with some new bloke. I used to lie awake at night hearing them going at it. The houses were rubbish, put up after the war after the Germans had flattened the city. We lived in a block of flats just behind the Dockyard walls. Nobody gave a shit. People would just chuck stuff out they didn't need. Old mattresses, whatever, and leave it to rot in the street."

"That's terrible!"

"I got beaten up a lot. There were some really mean bastards in the area. I didn't get much of an education. Mum was useless. She slept it off during the day. When I came back, she was already getting set for another night on the town. She would shoot up before she went out. I suppose it helped her get through it all. But eventually it fucked her up completely. She'd come home with really rough blokes off the ships. They'd be pissed and shouting in foreign languages. Sometimes she got messed up by them. I was too young. There was nothing I could do."

"And you were in the next room?"

"Yes. I had to listen to it all."

"What happened?"

"When I was sixteen, I came back to the house one evening and found her lying there. She had her gear beside her. She was dead. I called one of the neighbours and he phoned the police."

"Oh Sean. How terrible!"

"I suppose it was a blessing really. She had a shit life and it was only going to get worse."

Hiroko turned and held him tightly, burying herself into his chest. She felt his hand rest on the top of her head.

She understood. From then on, it would be just the two of them. All the family they needed.

She recalled the scene as she steered their little car down the steep track to the village.

It had worked out fine. In the end, it had bound them even closer together. They had never brought the subject up again.

This was the life she had, the one she had chosen. As long as she had Sean, nothing else mattered.

She was not a very confident driver. Sean would always grimace at her slow reactions and erratic decision-making.

She concentrated on the road ahead. Passing though the village, she had to slow down for some traffic lights.

A mother with two children was walking along the pavement next to her. Hiroko knew the woman quite well. She ran the local convenience store.

The woman glanced at the car waiting at the lights. Catching her eye, Hiroko smiled and mouthed a greeting.

The woman blanked her, bending down to say something to the children. The lights changed and Hiroko set off again.

As she drove, she felt angry and upset. This was not the first time she had been given the cold shoulder by the villagers.

When she reached the supermarket on the edge of the city, she did not dawdle along the aisles, as she liked to do. Instead, she quickly gathered the items on her list and hurried back to the car.

She could not wait to be back home.

15

Akira Kato's mobile rang. He was in a taxi heading across the city to a meeting.

"Yes?"

"Kato-san? Ito here. Can we speak?"

"Go ahead. What have you got for me?"

The ill-kempt private investigator he had met in the station hotel came straight to the point.

"I've carried out the preliminary checks as you requested."

"And...?

"The couple have a single bank account in the woman's name. From what I've discovered they live an extremely frugal existence. No debts. They keep themselves to themselves."

"Family?"

"No children. The woman's parents are dead. She has one sister in Tokyo."

"What about the man?"

"Not much to go on. A bit of an odd-ball. Seems he's a keen environmentalist."

Kato frowned.

"American?"

"No, English."

"Find out more about him."

"OK. I'll get onto it."

"What about the land ownership?"

"All in order. The woman inherited the land from her father. It's been in the family for generations."

Inheritance and property rights sometimes gave Kato room for manoeuvre.

"Any health issues?"

"No. Country life agrees with them."

"What do the locals say about them?"

"I chatted with a few of their neighbours. According to them, resentment is building in the village. They don't like the way the couple are blocking the development. People there have a lot to lose."

"Enough resentment to make life uncomfortable? To force them out?"

"I doubt it. The man is known to be a pretty tough character. The villagers I spoke with seemed rather wary of him."

Kato sat thinking as the taxi dawdled at the interminable traffic lights. He needed more. There was always some point of leverage, something to pressurise a reluctant landowner into selling.

It was not uncommon for developments to be held up due to someone sticking their toes in. It could lead to sizable losses for the developer.

Kato glanced over in the direction of Roppongi Hills. The mega-complex was a case in point.

Some of the original landowners had held out until the developer was forced to re-house them in the new site itself. It had cost the project millions.

But though the Japanese could be hard-nosed, they were also pragmatic. Eventually they would agree when the terms were right.

Foreigners played by different rules. This particular Englishman, Kato speculated, could become a painful thorn in his side.

"So, what's next?"

"I'll keep digging. Something usually turns up."

"Time is against us. Don't waste any. I need an answer right away."

In his mind's eye, Kato pictured the private detective tucking into a steaming bowl of noodles before buckling down to the task at hand.

To dispel the distasteful image, he turned his attention to the buildings along the way. Several were recent additions, new since he had last passed that way.

Tokyo constantly renewed itself. Today's new builds would be in the skip in a few years.

As they turned into the tree-lined Omotesando avenue, they passed one of his own early projects. It had helped to launch his career with its daring modernistic design.

It still had the power to impress. With its sleek lines and imaginative fusion of glass and metal, it more than held its own against subsequent offerings up and down the fashionable boulevard.

He remembered the opening. The pride he had felt at being in the forefront of Tokyo's up-and-coming architects.

It seemed like a lifetime ago. Now, when one of his developments opened its doors, he barely gave it a second thought. He had no time to dwell on his successes.

Beneath his lush velvet suits, the idealism of his early years was threadbare. His priorities had changed.

Everything now depended on the development in the north. He had to make it work. Whatever the cost.

In the back of the car, he squeezed his knee until it hurt. Behind his tinted glasses his eyes watered.

16

The man was flicking through a tabloid newspaper. He let his mobile phone ring twice before answering it.

"Health Entertainment Agency."

There was a brief silence at the other end. The caller was caught off-guard. He expected to be speaking to the girl portrayed in the advertisement.

"I need a Health Delivery."

"Certainly, sir. How long for?"

"An hour."

"What did you have in mind?"

The man listened as the voice at the other end of the phone detailed what he wanted.

"40,000 yen."

The arrangement was confirmed. The caller provided the address. The agency representative said they would be there within the hour.

The man struggled into his jacket, thrusting his newspaper into the pocket. He crossed the office to the room at the back.

It was cramped. Three women sat side by side on a small sofa.

Two of them were watching a television in the corner. The other was browsing a fashion magazine. It could have been a dentist's waiting room.

They all glanced up before quickly looking away. They tried their best not to catch his eye.

The man stared at each of them in turn. He liked to spin it out. Then he nodded at the girl reading the magazine.

"You."

The other girls muttered with relief.

The girl who had been selected chucked her magazine on the pile and stood up. She brushed her short skirt to remove the creases before taking her coat from the peg.

"See you later."

Her accent was pronounced. The women all spoke Japanese during business hours. The clients expected it.

Ligaya Santos still struggled with the language. Unlike the Chinese women lounging around downstairs, she spent her days trapped in a small room on the first floor.

There, speed was of the essence. The economy special offer was restricted to a mere 10 minutes. But in those straitened times, there was no shortage of takers.

It was not the life Ligaya Santos had looked forward to when she arrived in Japan. She had been told she would be an entertainer.

A Filipino broker had spotted her in a local talent contest in Batangas, her home city south of Manila. She had a pleasing voice and looks to match. The Filipino broker had taken her aside to explain what the future held for her.

Ligaya Santos had swallowed the bait. Her home situation was desperate. Her husband had long since taken off for the capital. She had no means of supporting her child.

She thought it over for a couple of days. She decided she had no alternative. The offer was too good to ignore.

She had left her six-year-old son Cesar in the care of his grandparents. After all, it was only a year. Time to put her life back on track and save some money.

She arrived in Japan on a circuitous route via Singapore and Hong Kong. When she finally landed, she was met by the Filipino broker's Chinese associates. There and then, she was presented with a bill for expenses totalling six million yen.

The next day she was ordered to start paying it off. The real nature of her employment became apparent. She was not expected to sing.

Ligaya Santos refused point blank. It took a full three weeks to break her.

Repeated brutality and destabilising drugs left her powerless to resist. At the end of the onslaught, she was unrecognisable as the bright-eyed woman boarding the plane in Manila with such high hopes.

Her shift was 12 hours a day, seven days a week. By the time she had paid her rent and keep, she had nothing to send home. A year later, she still owed almost all of her original debt.

Escape was not an option. Her passport was locked in the office safe. Her meagre savings were retained by her employers.

They made it clear her family would suffer if she ever attempted to contact them or go to the authorities. Over time, the exhausting, demeaning schedule eroded her powers of resistance. She no longer contemplated making a run for it.

She sat on the narrow bed. A lightbulb hung in the corner emitting a feeble glow. Just enough to see what she was doing.

Her hands rested on her bare thighs with her shoulders slumped forward. Her feet hardly reached the floor.

She had taken off her precarious high-heeled shoes. They were ready to slip back on when required.

She found herself staring at her feet. She used to make her friends laugh on the beach at home, how she could spread her toes like a hand.

"Go on Ligaya! Do that thing with your toes!"

She would refuse, pretending to be angry. Then she would give in. They would all scream with laughter, rolling on the sand until the tears streamed down their cheeks.

She tried hard to remember the faces of her friends. But she could only visualise other faces. Faces drenched with sweat, contorted with effort.

Along the corridor, she heard footsteps approaching. She slipped her shoes back on.

She shuddered as she waited for the doorhandle to turn.

17

In Kato's experience, families could often exert a beneficial influence.

It did not take Ito, the private investigator, long to track down Hiroko's sister, Akemi Watanabe. Kato rang her and asked if he could drop by to discuss some property matters.

After being initially reluctant, Akemi Watanabe had given way. She was clearly intrigued by the mention of Yamashiro. She agreed to meet the developer at her company headquarters.

As he headed west across Tokyo to the appointment, Kato skimmed through the profile Ito had prepared on Akemi Watanabe.

She was, it seemed, a successful businesswoman. She ran a chain of deluxe pet hotels.

The animals received five-star treatment – the best food, luxurious sleeping arrangements, daily walks and constant attention. At the end of the stay, they returned to their owners in peak condition, even more pampered than when they had left home.

The owners paid a hefty fee for the service. But peace of mind was all that mattered when it came to their adored pets.

Kato pulled up outside the two-storey building in Kami-kitazawa. In the background he could hear some of the company's customers baying for attention.

He was welcomed at reception and shown into a plush consultation room. Pictures of dogs with glossy coats pranced across the walls.

A few minutes later, Akemi Watanabe joined him. After the introductions, Kato politely enquired after her business. She quickly warmed to her theme.

"The idea came to me when we were about to go on an extended family holiday to Europe. We couldn't find anywhere suitable to leave our miniature poodle."

Kato smiled sympathetically. Akemi Watanabe trundled on.

"Such a sensitive little thing. I couldn't bear the thought of leaving her in one of those disgusting kennels."

Kato sipped his tea, waiting for a chance to change the subject. Eventually Akemi Watanabe registered his waning interest.

"So anyway, Kato-san, how can I help you? You mentioned on the phone something concerning my sister, something involving Yamashiro?"

"Yes. Well, as I explained briefly, we are engaged in a large-scale development project there. Very exciting. It will transform the area and bring the community significant benefits."

Akemi Watanabe could not care less about the area or its inhabitants.

"I see. And my sister?"

"Your sister's property straddles the intended development. Our project's success hinges on purchasing that parcel of land."

Akemi Watanabe immediately saw where this was leading.

"I assume they are refusing to sell?"

"Unfortunately, that is so."

The portly businesswoman expected nothing less. Some years earlier she had run into her sister and been introduced to the Englishman for the first time.

It was at the funeral of a close relative in Yamashiro. Protocol demanded both daughters should attend.

Akemi Watanabe had heard rumours. Her sister, she understood, had returned to Japan with her Englishman and taken up residence in the old property. The funeral gave her the excuse to dig a little deeper.

At the funeral parlour, she ran her eye over the faces of the mourners. It took her a moment before she singled out Hiroko.

Her older sister had changed. The striking looks had faded prematurely. She was thinner and bore a harried expression.

Akemi Watanabe was not displeased to see the effect the years had wrought. She was conscious how well turned out she herself was in comparison.

Relatives at the funeral gathered round Akemi Watanabe, expressing their admiration for her successful business venture. Cut from the same cloth as her father, they all said.

Conversely, they gave Hiroko and the tall Englishman a wide berth. The couple were left standing on their own at the side of the room.

Akemi Watanabe had no intention of going back to Tokyo without finding out as much as she could. She crossed the room and addressed Hiroko, ignoring the Englishman completely.

"You're back, I see."

"Yes. It's already been a while now."

"Goodness. How's life out there in the sticks?"

"Wonderful. Sean and I love the nature. All the animals and birds."

At the mention of the Englishman, Akemi Watanabe glanced at him. Sean Peters bowed awkwardly and mumbled a formulaic greeting in Japanese.

Akemi Watanabe turned back to her sister.

"So, what exactly are you doing up there?"

"Looking after the property."

"Farming?"

"On a small scale, yes."

Akemi Watanabe's lips pursed, ready to laugh.

Hiroko ploughed on.

"It's a good life. Growing our own produce. Living off the land."

"What does he do?"

"I've just told you."

"No. I mean, does he have a proper job? One that earns money?"

"We get by."

"Really? That explains the way you look."

"What do you mean by that?"

"You should be ashamed coming to a family funeral in such a

state. He should be looking after you properly. It's a disgrace."

Sean Peters had sufficient Japanese at that stage to follow what Hiroko's sister had said. He decided it was time to come to Hiroko's defence.

It was a valiant effort. Akemi Watanabe laughed, answering him in English.

"You've been here all this time? And that's all the Japanese you can manage. It's embarrassing."

With that she had turned on her heel and walked away. She now knew everything she needed to know.

Sitting with Kato in reception, she smiled to herself as she recalled the encounter, the last time she had met her sister.

"Well, I'm very sorry, Kato-san. If it was my property, I would sell it to you without a moment's hesitation. But my sister has different, quite misguided ideas."

"Perhaps you would consider pressing our case? It would surely be to her benefit. It's a very generous offer."

"I'm sure it is. Sadly, my sister and I have been estranged for many years. She would never listen to anything I had to say, far less act on it."

As Kato sat in the taxi on the way back to his office, he rued his luck. He could see he was dealing with the wrong sister.

18

Charles Fancourt was in one of his regular haunts in Roppongi. A lively English pub, popular with expatriates.

He was sitting by himself at the bar with a gin and tonic. He was manoeuvring a piece of lemon around the glass with a plastic straw.

He did not notice the Japanese man sidle up to him.

"Excuse me, are you from England?"

Fancourt looked up and scowled.

"Sorry?"

"Are you from England? Would you mind if I practise my English?"

Fancourt stared at the man. He was early twenties wearing a light-blue sweater. He held an orange juice in his hand.

"Fuck off."

"Excuse me?"

"Fuck off."

The man was taken aback. He knew the word. He had rarely heard it used. He turned and slipped away into the crowd.

Charles Fancourt returned to prodding the piece of lemon.

"Hi Charles."

He looked up again, anticipating another unwelcome

interruption.

"Oh, it's you Frank."

Frank Deluca slipped onto the stool beside Fancourt and pointed to the Englishman's drink.

"Freshener?"

"No. I'm on my way soon."

If Fancourt had to talk to Deluca, he preferred to keep it brief.

"I'm glad I caught you, Charles. Great event the other week."

Deluca was one of the regular attendees at Charles Fancourt's quarterly social events. Like Fancourt, he was a hedge fund manager. Unlike Fancourt, he was in trouble financially.

He was small and compact. He had wrestled his way out of New York's Lower Manhattan and had acquired a veneer of sophistication along the way. But you did not have to scratch far below the surface to find the street fighter.

Fancourt nodded.

"Yes, not a bad turnout."

Deluca sipped his beer and stole a look at Fancourt. He found everything about the Englishman distasteful but the man had his uses.

Deluca had the gift of the gab. When it came to schmoozing clients, no one was better. But he lacked Fancourt's analytical brain.

Recently he had made some unwise investment decisions. His clients were asking questions. He needed a cash injection and fast.

"So, Charles, anything in the pipeline?"

Fancourt skewered the piece of lemon to the bottom of the

glass.

"What?"

Deluca looked over his shoulder to make sure they were not being overheard. He lowered his voice.

"You know. It's been a while."

"Shut your trap."

"Come on Charles. No one's listening. You can level with me."

"You know the rules. I'll tell you when I'm ready. Not before."

"OK, Charles. Take it easy. I get it."

Deluca took a long slug of his beer.

Fancourt regretted including the pint-sized American in his exclusive investment club. He had come highly recommended. All the right attributes. A player with significant funds at his disposal.

He should have trusted his instincts. When they first met, Fancourt had had his reservations. Beneath the gloss, the man did not add up.

Deluca was not going to be put off so easily.

"What are you doing later, Charles? Drink up and let's head over to Shinjuku."

"No thanks. I'm having a quiet night."

"Hey, come on Charles, loosen up."

"Goodbye Frank."

Fancourt stared at his drink. Deluca finally got the message. Slowly he unpeeled himself from his stool and joined a group of ex-pats on the other side of the room.

Fancourt drank up quickly and left the bar.

19

"Mama?"

"Ligaya? Daughter? Is that you?"

Ligaya Santos was crouching in a small cupboard, trying to muffle her voice. Her eyes were fixed on the door, fearing it would burst open at any second.

The connection to the Philippines was scratchy. But clear enough to recognise her mother's voice.

"Mama! Mama!"

"Ligaya! Where are you?"

"In Tokyo."

"What's going on? Why didn't you call?"

"I can't explain."

Ligaya wiped the tears away with the back of her hand.

"We tried to contact you, Ligaya. To find out where you were. The woman who arranged for your trip to Japan never returned my calls. I even went to the police but they were no help."

"Mama, I haven't got long."

"What do you mean?"

Ligaya lowered her voice. Her hand cupped the receiver.

"I can't speak for long."

"What's that? I can't hear what you are saying. Is something wrong?"

"I don't have time. Quickly Mama. How is Cesar?"

"That's why we tried to contact you. Cesar is in hospital."

"What do you mean?"

"He had an accident. He was on his bicycle and a car hit him. He has some bad injuries. The doctors are worried. There are complications. They are keeping him there."

Ligaya steadied herself by pressing her hand against the wall. The cupboard seemed to be shrinking.

She tried to focus. Every second was precious. She would not have another chance to phone.

The women were kept in the rooms on the top floor. They had no privacy. When their shift was over, they lay down on any spare futon available.

Sleep was never a problem. They were too tired even to cry.

Once a fortnight they were taken out in pairs to shop for personal necessities. They were always accompanied by two of the minders. They were hustled into a car parked outside the front door and driven to a supermarket some distance away.

It was not much but the trips out were enough to keep her sane. To see other people going about their daily business. To remember what life used to be like.

It always made her pine for home.

On one occasion as she left the brothel, she managed to peek into the office on the ground floor. She spotted a phone lying in its cradle on the desk closest to the door.

Back in her room, as the men came and went, it was all she thought about it. A link to home. Just an international dialling code away.

Eventually, she knew she had to try. Whatever the repercussions.

That morning before dawn, she had stepped over the other sleeping women and crept downstairs. If she was caught, she would have no excuse.

The house was silent. She tried the office door. It was open. She reached in and grabbed the phone from its cradle.

She had noticed a small cupboard across the corridor. She squeezed inside and shut the door.

She knew her mother's number by heart. She listened as the line connected. Then the familiar ringtone at their family home in Batangas. Then her mother's voice.

She had wanted to blurt out what was happening to her. To ask her mother for help.

But now it was no longer about her own predicament. Her concern was only for Cesar.

"What do the doctors say?"

"They've set his broken leg and arm. But they are worried. He has other problems. Infections."

"Is he in pain?"

"They give him drugs but he is very poorly. He needs you Ligaya, my angel. You must come home and look after him."

"I have to go now Mama."

"Ligaya? What's wrong?"

"Goodbye, Mama. Kiss Cesar for me."

Her finger hovered over the button to cut the call. Reluctant to sever the link.

She listened. No one was stirring. Emerging from the cupboard on her hands and knees she straightened up and tiptoed across to the office. She replaced the phone in its cradle, making sure it was as she had found it.

Mounting the stairs, she scurried into the toilet. To have an excuse in case someone saw her.

When she crept into the bedroom, the other women were fast asleep. She lay down, being careful not to disturb the people next to her.

As she pulled the thin duvet over her head, she pictured Cesar in the hospital. His tiny face on the pillow, his eyes wincing in pain.

She only had a couple of precious hours sleep before she would have to get up. She needed all the sleep she could get.

But instead, she lay awake thinking. Planning.

20

Masanori Inoue threaded his way through the old town's narrow streets. The ancient castle towered above the houses.

He had lived in the city all his life. He had no reason to leave. He was settled.

He had married a local girl. Her family were rice growers and supplied the local saké producers.

His parents considered themselves a cut above farming stock but grudgingly had given their consent. Their son was not the brightest. They had to be realistic about his chances.

They ran a small kimono shop with a loyal clientele. His mother was a skilled seamstress. They were not prosperous, but comfortably off.

The young couple's married life ran along predictable lines. In no time, they were blessed with two unexceptional children, a boy and a girl.

As the years passed, their offspring eventually left home. Inoue was close to his daughter. When she moved out, a wave of loneliness engulfed him.

He looked at his wife and contemplated a dreary future. His wife had separately reached the same conclusion.

Though nothing was ever articulated, it was mutually understood henceforth they would pursue their own interests.

His wife took the moral high ground. Every weekend, she was away with her trekking club scrambling up mountain peaks in the surrounding area.

Inoue's new interest was more down-to-earth. It centred on a small bar near the station.

She was the same age as his daughter. The antithesis of his wife.

She had no interest in the outdoor life. She rarely strayed from her small flat. She had her meals delivered. She spent all day glued to the television.

Work was her priority.

Several men shared her favours. Each one knew his relative position in the pecking order.

Gifts were the key to advancement. The more splendid the presents, the higher the donor's ranking.

Inoue was constrained by his limited income. He languished on the bottom rung of the ladder.

He worked in the local City Council offices. The salary was less than generous.

The work was ideally suited to someone with Inoue's limited abilities. So much so that, over time, he even succeeded in rising to the coveted position of section leader.

His advancement happened by default rather than talent. As others died or retired, Inoue found himself stepping into the resulting vacancies.

His forte was following orders. He and his colleagues in the City Council might not be lavishly rewarded but their careers shunted along well-defined tracks.

His salary was managed by his wife. She supervised every

penny spent.

Inoue's meagre monthly entertainment allowance did not come close to the expectations of his new girlfriend. He sought another source of income.

He turned to his doting mother. She was too soft to argue. She handed over what he asked for without question.

After all, she reasoned, she and her husband had enough. He was their only child and would inherit everything eventually.

But recently she had had to tighten her sash. The kimono business was not what it once was.

Inoue felt the pinch. And so did his girlfriend.

That was when he bumped into the stranger. The chance encounter took place in the bar where his girlfriend happened to work.

The girl was busy with another customer, pouring drinks and making flirtatious small talk. Inoue was nursing his drink at the counter and watching her out of the corner of his eye.

When he turned to his right, he was surprised to find the stranger perched on the bar stool beside him. Inoue had not seen him come in.

They had started to chat. The stranger was excellent company. Inoue soon fell under his spell.

Inoue's neighbour was large and wore a creased suit. Above his jolly red cheeks was a mop of erratic hair.

He reminded Inoue of a popular comedian. Inoue remarked on the similarity and the two men chortled together.

After an hour or so of pouring each other drinks, the man

leaned over and whispered in Inoue's ear.

"Inoue-san, you work at the City Council, don't you?"

Inoue looked at him in amazement.

"Yes, I do. How do you know that?"

"It's common knowledge. It's pretty important work, after all."

Inoue sat and thought about it. He had never considered his work as much to brag about. But perhaps he was selling himself short. Local government after all had a lot of clout.

"Well, I suppose it is."

"You see, the thing is…" the big man glanced around, "there's something I need. As you work at the City Council, you might be just the person to help me."

"What do you mean?"

"Well, I'd like some background details on one of your citizens. I need to have a peep at some family records."

Inoue turned in his seat and looked squarely at the man.

"Who?"

"Well, that doesn't matter at the moment. Of course, I could make an official request. I just wanted to avoid all that unnecessary red tape."

Inoue nodded. He knew all about red tape.

"As you work there, a senior administrator, I wondered if you could dig out what I need."

"You really ought to go through the proper channels."

The big man nodded in the direction of Inoue's girlfriend. Looking across and catching his eye, she giggled.

"Of course, I wouldn't expect you to go to all that trouble for nothing. Naturally. Perhaps your girlfriend might like something special? Some new clothes? Or jewellery? A swanky holiday?"

Inoue looked at the man and then across at his girlfriend. The man seemed remarkably well informed.

"Well, I don't know. I'll have to think about that."

The big man smiled and poured Inoue another drink. He signalled to the barman, waving the empty bottle.

"Of course. I quite understand."

21

Ms Sekikawa sat facing Hayashi in a cramped, windowless meeting room. Slapping her hands on the table, she jumped up.

"Let's go out for a coffee."

She had been concerned about Hayashi's progress. Every day he beavered away from dawn to dusk but she had yet to see any tangible results.

When Yamaguchi bumped into her in the department, he had asked her how the new man was settling in.

"He's getting on fine. Very dedicated and industrious. No complaints at all."

Yamaguchi cut to the chase.

"So, what's he actually produced?"

"He's finalising the trafficking report you requested."

"Yes, well. Tell him to hurry up. I'm getting pressure from above."

In fact, Hayashi had already completed the document. He was only waiting for an opportunity to present his findings to Ms Sekikawa.

Ms Sekikawa led the way out of the building, Hayashi following in her wake. They threaded their way through the maze of government buildings to Detective Yamaguchi's café of choice in Akasaka-mitsuke.

Ms Sekikawa took her boss' seat while Hayashi slotted into her usual place. She took a few moments to appraise the world from Yamaguchi's perspective.

Despite only being 10.30 in the morning, Ms Sekikawa could not resist a pastry. She ordered a large chocolate croissant. Hayashi chose a custard cream to keep her company.

Ms Sekikawa took a large bite and waved the stub of the croissant at Hayashi.

"Right, off you go."

Hayashi leaned forwards over the table and spoke in a low, conspiratorial voice. Quite unnecessary, given they were the only customers in the café.

"I started by going back over relevant crime reports. Surprisingly few. Victims seem reluctant to come forward. Partly fear of the criminals running them and partly doubts about the protection the authorities can offer."

"Did you identify the main trafficking hubs?"

"Mainly large cities, but not exclusively. Sometimes the girls are dispatched to rural backwaters. The victims are often shuffled from place to place. It's a deliberate ploy."

"How so?"

"It's harder for the authorities to track them and the victims don't have time to establish ties with people who might help them."

"I see. Who are the main perpetrators?"

"The crime syndicates principally. Chinese groups have taken a much bigger stake in the trade in recent years. They have a reputation for being extremely ruthless."

Ms Sekikawa licked her fingers and then stabbed them at the

remaining crumbs on the plate.

"Do you have any specific examples?"

Hayashi gathered his thoughts. The custard cream lay untouched in front of him.

"One case concerned a Chinese woman trafficked into Japan. She came from an impoverished part of China. She arrived in Tokyo expecting to work as a waitress in a Chinese restaurant, only to discover it was a fabrication. The traffickers presented her with a sizable bill and told her she had to work as a prostitute to repay the debt she owed."

Ms Sekikawa grunted. Standard operating procedure for traffickers. Hayashi sneaked a bite of his pastry before resuming.

"The woman was a virtual slave for over a year. She was watched day and night. Never allowed out by herself. If she made a mistake or a customer complained, she was physically punished, though not so as to impact her work. She was mostly engaged in Health Delivery."

Ms Sekikawa nodded again. She knew what that entailed.

"She was always accompanied by a minder. He would take her to the address, wait outside, collect the money and then drive her back. It was a Chinese operation top to bottom."

"What happened?"

"Eventually she managed to get away. One of her regular clients helped her. They headed for Kochi City on Shikoku to lie low."

Not a bad choice, thought Ms Sekikawa. Kochi was on the southern tip of the least populated of Japan's main islands. The coast was cut off by deep forests and mountains. Traditional bandit country.

Hayashi gulped down the remains of his custard cream before carrying on.

"Eventually the relationship ran its course and the former client deserted her. Left by herself, she only really had one alternative. She had no means of support. She gave herself up to the local police."

"Was she able to point the finger at the Chinese gang in Tokyo?"

"She refused to give the police any details."

"Where is she now?"

"Deported back to China. The case has been closed."

Ms Sekikawa was already eyeing up the pastry selection again.

"It would be good to speak with a trafficking victim directly. Can you look into it?"

"Yes, of course."

Later, back at her desk, Ms Sekikawa asked for a copy of Hayashi's file. It was extremely thorough.

He had assembled a great deal of information. It was well organised, making it easy to extract all the salient points.

She was sure Yamaguchi would be impressed.

22

The police officer stared across the desk at the woman.

Long dark hair, almond skin, revealing outfit.

He knew the type. Shaking his head, he returned to his paperwork.

She had literally fallen into his police box. She did not make much sense, could hardly speak any Japanese and was highly distressed.

He sat her on a chair opposite him and told her not to move. Ringing through to the main station, he requested specialist help. They said they would send someone over without delay.

The woman's eyes were fixed on a spot on the floor. Her fingers constantly picked at the hem of her skirt.

The policeman tried to ignore her, bent over the latest Japanese police box procedural update.

Ligaya Santos had never been so scared. She still could not believe the risk she had taken.

She had crossed the line. She knew she had put herself in grave danger. Possibly her family too. But her only priority was Cesar.

Images of her son flooded back to her. How she had nursed him as a baby through one crisis after another.

She remembered how, when he was a toddler, she would sit

for hours on the beach watching him play at the water's edge. Always poised to sprint and rescue him from the waves.

He was an impulsive child. Always getting into scrapes.

She remembered how pleased he had been with his new bike. Then how she had fretted as he raced pell-mell along the dusty lanes.

She should have stayed with him in Batangas. What was she thinking of, coming to Japan, leaving him?

She knew her chances of escaping from the brothel were slim. The odds were stacked heavily against her.

She had no money, no documents and did not speak Japanese. How would the Japanese authorities react, even if she was able to reach them and claim sanctuary?

But she had no choice. She had to return to the Philippines. That outweighed any other consideration.

After the phone call home, she lay in bed thinking. Forcing herself to figure out a way.

She had to come up with a solid excuse to leave the brothel. Something plausible. Once outside, she would need to find a way to make a break for it.

It took a couple of hours, but, by first light, she had sketched out a rough plan of action.

She decided to act the very next day before she talked herself out of it. Before the obscene, degrading routine eroded her resolve any further.

"I need to go to the doctor."

The minder sitting at the end of the first-floor corridor eyed Ligaya Santos with distaste. He was there to manage the queue. To keep the punters in line. To make sure the girls did not kick up a fuss.

"What's wrong?"

"I've got a problem here."

She pointed. The man nodded.

"Show me."

"Only the doctor."

The man sniggered and opened his newspaper.

"OK."

"You'd better be quick. I don't want to infect any of the customers."

The thought had already crossed the man's mind. A sore throat, or a headache, who cares? But ailments of this nature needed swift attention.

"Go back to your room."

He leaned forwards and fished his mobile out of his back pocket.

"One of the whores needs to go to the clinic."

He rang off and carried on reading the paper.

A few minutes later another man came up from the office below. He was slim, in a close-fitting suit, his hair gelled tight against his skull.

"Where is she?"

Ligaya Santos was marched out of the building into the street. The Toyota RAV 4 with darkened privacy windows was waiting outside, the engine ticking over.

She was shoved into the back seat. The driver activated the

central locking.

The SUV looked out of place in the narrow street. It struggled to negotiate the advertising boards, parked bicycles, pedestrians. When it reached the main road, the driver swore under his breath and put his foot down.

Ligaya did not bother to look out of the window. All the streets seemed the same. She stared down at her hands, concentrating.

She needed to plan ahead. She could not allow the doctor to examine her and find nothing the matter. She had to make her move first.

It was hard to think clearly. The regime of drugs fuddled her brain. She forced herself to focus.

The clinic was in a semi-residential area. There was an unobtrusive sign in Japanese in the window. Passers-by would not give the place a second glance.

The thug pushed Ligaya through the door into the ground-floor waiting room. Several of the women were dressed similarly to her in miniskirts and tight tee-shirts.

Ligaya squeezed onto a spare seat near the door. Her neighbour grumbled before budging up to make room.

The clinic specialised in gynaecological examinations. The doctor was discreet and professional.

If he found a skiver, he made sure the people who paid him were made aware. He was well rewarded.

As her turn approached, Ligaya became increasingly desperate. Something needed to happen before it was too late.

Suddenly, her minder got up. He strolled over to the receptionist and muttered a few words to her. She pointed down the corridor.

He was going to the toilet. Ligaya had a precious window of opportunity, a minute or two at most.

This was the chance she had been waiting for. But she had to move fast.

Ligaya launched herself at the door. Then she was out in the street, sprinting for all she was worth.

She was hampered by her high heels. Shocked passers-by flattened themselves against the wall as she clattered along the pavement.

Back at the waiting room, pandemonium had broken out. The minder, returning from the toilet, found the receptionist shouting and gesticulating towards the door.

He looked at the empty seat. Yelling in fury, he raced out onto the pavement.

"Which way?"

The receptionist waved her hand to the right.

He sprinted up the street. As he passed pedestrians, they indicated the direction the woman had gone.

They voiced their disapproval. Someone needed to put an end to all this racing around in broad daylight.

Ligaya had a head start but knew the man would be right on her tail. As she rounded a corner, she almost ran into a young couple with a baby buggy.

She had no idea where she was going. She just knew she needed to run and run.

If she was captured, she would never have another chance to escape. It was now or never.

She turned her head only to spot the man racing after her. He was not far behind.

She was too slow in her cumbersome high heels. She kicked them off, continuing barefoot.

The people on the pavement parted to let her through. She could hear the man closing fast.

He started yelling as he ran. She was worried a Japanese pedestrian might try to interfere.

She found herself screaming in panic. The pounding feet were, by then, right behind her.

There was no escape. Her fate was sealed.

Then, as she rounded a corner, she spotted a police car parked beside a small square building. She made a final effort, straining every sinew.

The policeman inside the *kooban* leaped out his chair as the girl lunged through the doorway. She collapsed spreadeagled on the floor.

Behind, her pursuer hove into view. He stood in the entrance of the police box, panting and glaring down at the woman.

In a trice, the policeman rounded the desk, his hand reaching for his police baton.

The man snarled and shouted something. Then he took off, back the way he had come.

23

Ligaya's minder rushed into the office.

"She's escaped! Gone!"

His boss was sitting at the large desk dominating the cramped room. He stopped fiddling with his smart phone. It took him a moment to react.

Then, throwing back his chair, he strode across the room. His hand shot out and grabbed the gang member, still out of breath, by the lapel.

The man cowered. He knew what Wang was capable of. He had witnessed his violent rages before.

"What?"

"She ran out of the clinic while I was in the toilet. The police have got her."

Wang whirled round and shouted at the girls in the adjoining room.

"Upstairs. Now!"

They scuttled past him, anxious to make themselves scarce.

The man did not see the blow coming. It caught him squarely on the side of the head. He dropped like a stone.

Wang took an unused mobile phone out of his desk drawer and stabbed in a number. The phone was kept in reserve for emergencies. As the call connected, Wang slammed his palm repeatedly against the desk in frustration.

"Yes?"

The voice at the other end of the line had its own distinct cadence. Other-worldly, full of menace.

Wang spat out what had happened. He was allowed to finish without interruption.

Then he stood to attention awaiting instructions. A vein on the side of his neck started to pulse.

Wang already knew what was coming. It was always the same whenever there was potential police involvement.

Close everything down. Clear out without delay.

Wang shouted up the stairs to summon his subordinates. As he waited, he drove his foot into the man lying on the floor for good measure.

The woman was a liability. She could scupper the whole operation.

He should have realised she was a potential flight risk. He should have got rid of her earlier.

He had good reason to be concerned. Ligaya Santos was already sitting opposite a young officer in West Shinjuku police station.

A squad car had been dispatched to pick her up. The officer at the police box had escorted her to the vehicle, checking up and down the street for any signs of trouble.

As the squad car pulled away, he saluted and returned to his desk. He had sighed as he poured himself a cup of tea.

Enough excitement for one day. Soon he was flicking through the procedure manual again.

Once inside the police car, Ligaya Santos had started to feel safe. Now, sitting on the eighth floor of the police station, she felt a good deal safer still.

"Can you speak English?"

Ligaya Santos nodded. English was the second language at home.

"Where are you from?"

"Bantangas, the Philippines."

The officer started to make notes.

"Please tell me what happened."

"I was imprisoned by Chinese criminals. They made me work for them. I managed to escape."

"What type of work?"

"As a prostitute."

Ligaya Santos looked down at her feet. She struggled to articulate the word.

The policeman continued scribbling. He kept his tone even.

"Did you come to Japan for the purposes of prostitution?"

"No, I was told I would be an entertainer. I'm a singer back in the Philippines."

"Did you get paid as a prostitute?"

"No, never. They told me I was re-paying my debt."

"Do you have your passport with you?"

"No, it was taken from me when I arrived in Japan."

"Were you free to leave the building where you lived?"

"No, someone always went with me."

"So, how did you manage to escape?"

"I told them I needed to go to the doctor. Then I ran for it. I was just lucky the police box happened to be nearby. Otherwise..."

Ligaya Santos shivered and then leaned forwards.

"Please sir, it's my son Cesar. He's in hospital. I have to get back home to the Philippines to look after him."

The police officer stopped writing and looked up. He could plainly read the desperation in the woman's expression.

Detective Nakagawa was a specialist at working with victims of trafficking. He knew the rule book better than most.

The method of questioning followed a prescribed pattern. The priority was to establish if the interviewee was an innocent victim or simply a working girl, a common criminal.

Detective Nakagawa had interviewed enough women to reckon Ligaya Santos fell into the first category. Having her passport confiscated, having to repay debts, being violently coerced into prostitution, were all tell-tale signs.

The detective shook his head. It was a miracle the Filipina had managed to escape.

He knew only too well what would have happened if she had failed. He had witnessed enough corpses in the morgue in his time on the force.

He closed the file in front of him and stood up.

"Please come with me. You are under our protection now. No one can hurt you here."

24

The man in the white gloves was relaxing in his small, untidy office. He was staring through a smudged pane of glass at the bustling streets of Yokohama's Chinatown.

He always left his window slightly ajar. To allow the tempting aromas from the surrounding restaurants to find their way into his room.

He had grown up on these streets and knew every nook and cranny. He belonged here.

In the world beyond this Chinese enclave, he still felt like a foreigner. Even after all these years.

Not that any Japanese he met ever suspected he was not one of them. He went by an adopted Japanese name. He shared their looks. He spoke their tongue.

But when the penny dropped, he would note the hesitation, the rapid re-assessment. The exclusion as doors slammed shut in his face.

But he was fine with that. As far as he was concerned, the Japanese were cash cows, pure and simple.

He did not like Thursdays. They tended to be trouble. Events invariably seemed to conspire against him on that particular day of the week.

So, when his phone rang, he steeled himself. The ensuing call fully lived up to his worst expectations.

He listened as his trusted lieutenant Wang explained one of the whores had managed to escape. That she was at that moment at a police station, spilling her guts.

It happened from time to time. However attentive his men were, the women's motivation to escape was strong.

There was a simple protocol to follow in such circumstances: close up shop and leave no trace.

Wang knew the drill. Wang was dependable, smart and loyal.

And Wang understood the importance of his boss remaining invisible at all times. No one should ever be able to detect his superior's hand on the organisational tiller.

Chen, his boss' Chinese name, was a secret to all but a trusted inner circle. And even they were ignorant of his alternative Japanese name.

Wang was one of the privileged few with direct access to Chen. An unavoidable risk. A significant slice of the business was channelled through him.

But Chen was not concerned about Wang. He would never talk. It was more than his life was worth.

If Chen was careful about keeping his business at arm's length, he was even more scrupulous about distancing himself from people in general.

It stemmed from his youth. The doctors discovered early on he had a very rare condition: he was allergic to human touch.

Chen remembered the weeks he had spent in hospital one long humid summer. The skin all over his body was ablaze with livid rashes. Try as he might, he could not resist the urge to scratch and scratch.

Eventually they resorted to embalming his body with thick

ointment before covering him head to toe in plastic. He had been left for days and nights, unable to move, his body swimming in grease.

Since then, he had learned to live with the affliction. But it meant foregoing any physical contact with another person.

Hence the white silk gloves. Just in case he happened to brush against a stranger.

Chen was still digesting the conversation with Wang, when the phone rang again. This time it was Kato. As if one problem was not enough, suddenly another landed in his lap.

"We've tried everything to make them sell. It's no good."

The underworld capo peered through the window again. A man was dashing past with five ducks hanging from a pole slung over his shoulder. Their heads lolled from side to side.

"What exactly have you tried?"

"The woman has a sister. I spoke with her. She's very switched on. A businesswoman. I thought she could bring some pressure to bear on the woman."

"And?"

"No use, I'm afraid. They loathe each other, it seems. Some long-standing family feud."

A street vendor wheeled a mobile noodle stand directly in front of the window. It blocked the light.

"You're not trying hard enough."

"There's a limit to what we can do. We can't force them to sell."

"Under the right conditions, people will always do what you want them to do."

Kato remained silent. Waiting for his client. Eventually the thin voice responded.

"Well, perhaps you'd better leave it with me. Was there anything else?"

"No. The rest of the project is moving forwards well. We have completed the other land purchases. There are a lot of details still to tie up but we're making good progress."

"About time."

"So, shall I wait to hear from you?"

By way of answer, the line went dead.

Since Chen had presented the plans in Hong Kong, too much time had elapsed. His masters were becoming impatient.

They expected rapid results. The word "obstacle" did not feature in their vocabulary.

They demanded frequent status reports. On each occasion, he found himself on the defensive. The criticisms were harsh and unsparing.

He understood the game. Where money was involved, there were no niceties. No excuses were tolerated.

At the most recent project update, he had referenced the couple's reluctance to sell. He had tried to brush over the matter.

They had jumped on it. How could two nobodies be holding up one of their projects? What did he think he was playing at?

He soaked up the invective, each insult landing from across the sea like a slap in the face.

Afterwards he wondered why his family had decided to sell

out to mainland Chinese scum like this. One day he would get even. No one got away with speaking to him like that.

In the short term, he realised he needed to take control of the situation. To nip the problem in the bud.

It was time to raise the stakes. The couple would find him a man not to be trifled with.

25

Masanori Inoue was sitting on a bench in the castle precinct. He had chosen a secluded corner beside the tea ceremony building.

He was wearing a cap pulled down low over his eyes. He was anxious lest a colleague might happen by and recognise him.

He was surrounded by a screen of cherry trees. Beyond them stood a row of ancient pines, the weight of their outstretched branches supported by bamboo splints.

He opened his lunchbox and started to eat. He was nibbling the last of his pickles when the ruddy-cheeked man he had met in the bar hove into view. Inoue half-raised a hand in recognition.

Spotting Inoue, the man walked across to the bench and sat down. Inoue mumbled a greeting.

When they last met, the man had spelled out the specific information he was looking for. Inoue did not anticipate any difficulties. It seemed a straightforward-enough request.

All hard copies were held in the City Council records section. Inoue knew to steer clear of any digital files, anxious not to leave a data trail.

That morning he had paid the records section a visit. Having located the document in question, he pottered over to a nearby photocopier. He felt exposed and hoped no one would sneak a look at what he was up to.

As Inoue waited for the copier to warm up, he glanced through the document. He wondered what could be so important about it.

Just an ordinary family register. The usual list of names and dates.

Nothing special. The stocky comedian's generosity seemed out of all proportion to the task. It struck him as odd, but it was not his concern.

When he had finished, he gathered together the printouts and replaced the originals in their files. Then he marched out of the records department trying to look as if he was on official business. No one paid any attention.

Back at his desk he placed the documents face down in his in-tray. Later in the day, he squeezed them into a city council envelope which he slipped into his black briefcase.

That was all there was to it. He sat back for a second, relieved.

For the rest of the day, he pondered how best to spend his reward. The priority was not to attract any unwelcome attention.

Tempting as it might be, an overseas jaunt was out of the question. It would be impossible to justify.

He finally settled on a long weekend in Tokyo as the optimal solution. Only two days' absence from the office. Easy enough to explain away.

He needed two excuses: one for his wife, the other for his colleagues. As he kept home and office strictly separate, no one was likely to stumble on the inconsistency.

He decided to inform his wife he had to attend an important conference in Sendai. Not that she ever showed any interest in his comings and goings.

Meanwhile his colleagues would learn of the sudden death of one of Inoue's uncles. The funeral would necessitate an unavoidable trek up to the capital.

He had decided to book himself and his girlfriend into a five-star hotel at Tokyo Disneyland. She rarely had the chance to go to Tokyo, and never first class.

He imagined them nestled together on the Disneyland rides. They would visit DisneySea, with its romantic water-world settings. According to the website, it was a firm favourite with dating couples.

His girlfriend would adore it. She would shower him with affection. His rating would soar.

"So, Inoue-san. Have you got what I asked for?"

His large companion spoke without turning his head. Inoue continued to stare into his empty lunchbox.

"Yes, it's in my bag."

The man leaned over and prised open Inoue's bag. Locating the envelope, he pulled out the pages and cast his eye over the contents. Satisfied, he pushed the documents back in the envelope which he stuffed into his coat pocket.

"That seems to be all in order. Did you have any trouble?"

"No."

The man nodded.

"Excellent."

Inoue stared at him, waiting.

Smiling, the man reached into his inside pocket and produced a stuffed envelope. With a flourish he dropped it into Inoue's bag.

"As agreed."

Inoue snapped the bag shut, glancing around the park.

"So, are you going anywhere nice?"

Inoue did not feel like sharing his plans. He did not want to sully them.

"I haven't decided yet."

The man nodded, amused at Inoue's reticence.

"Well, anyway, please enjoy yourself. Thank you for your assistance."

He started to get up from the seat. Inoue reached over and laid an arm on his sleeve.

"Just before you go, can you tell me why you need the information?"

The man sat back down. His cheerful bonhomie had deserted him. He stared at Inoue.

"Sorry?"

"I just wondered why you needed this information so badly."

The large man removed Inoue's hand from his coat sleeve, twisting the wrist slightly. Suddenly Inoue experienced a sharp pain as the nerves reacted all the way up his arm.

"Let's get one thing straight. You'll mention this to no one. No one. Remember I know where to find you."

Inoue's lunchbox clattered to the ground.

"I understand."

The large man loosened his grip and stood up. Straightening his jacket, he strode away along the path, disappearing out of sight behind the castle.

Inoue sat trembling. He was not used to being treated like that.

After a couple of minutes, he opened his briefcase. He peeked inside the envelope and thumbed the wad of cash.

It was all there. The man was right, the rest was not his business.

Standing up, he hurried out of the park by a different exit.

26

"Do you have a moment Yamaguchi-san?"

Yamaguchi looked up from a document he was reading. Seeing it was Ms Sekikawa, he beckoned her into the office.

She marched in and sat down opposite him. Hayashi's report was under her arm.

Yamaguchi leaned back and perched his glasses on his forehead. It was a recent habit of his. Ms Sekikawa was not a fan.

"Yes?"

Ms Sekikawa could see he did not welcome the interruption.

"I've been going over your comments on Hayashi's report on human trafficking."

"Yes?"

"Well, I'd like to discuss them with you."

Yamaguchi had reviewed the detective's report the previous day. He had scribbled notes throughout and left it on Ms Sekikawa's desk early that morning.

"Of course. Though now isn't really the best time."

Ms Sekikawa's eyes drifted to the title of the document in front of Yamaguchi. "Racial stereotyping in the United States penal system."

He followed her eyes and placed his hand over the cover.

"I'll be brief. Excuse me for saying so, but I thought your comments were rather ... picky."

"Picky?"

"Yes, well, missing the point, actually."

"I see."

Yamaguchi looked at Ms Sekikawa. Waiting for her to continue. She stared at him.

"Missing the point, you say?"

"Yes. After all, I threw Hayashi in at the deep end, asking him to produce a report on a complex issue with little background knowledge of the subject."

"Very commendable."

"And then you send it back covered with all these comments."

Ms Sekikawa leafed through the report, waving her hand at the offending items.

Yamaguchi raised his eyebrows. She ignored him, pressing ahead. She had a lot she needed to get off her chest.

"Well, I thought Hayashi made an excellent effort. He has made some pertinent observations. It seems to me you neglected to comment on those."

Yamaguchi retrieved his glasses from his forehead and lay them carefully on the desk in front of him.

"So, you don't agree with my comments?"

"I'm sure they're all perfectly valid, but they just seem a bit...."

"Picky?"

"Exactly."

"And you felt you needed to come and tell me that?"

"Yes. I did."

When she had skimmed through Yamaguchi's comments that morning, Ms Sekikawa had bristled. She felt defensive on Hayashi's behalf.

She wanted to set the record straight. To stick up for Hayashi.

Now, however, face to face with Yamaguchi, she feared she might have been precipitous in tackling her boss. She should have cooled down first.

"Detective Sekikawa. As Hayashi's supervisor, you are responsible for making sure any report he writes is of the required standard. Hayashi's draft needs considerable polish before it can be circulated to a wider audience of senior officers. I have indicated the areas requiring further attention."

Ms Sekikawa stared at her boss.

She was trying to visualise the Yamaguchi of old. The one with a protective arm around her on the US aircraft carrier's deck after her perilous sea rescue. The one powering a police car through the streets of Tokyo. The one posing on Mount Fuji's summit with an idiotic smile on his face.

She was having trouble joining up the dots.

In swimming competitions, she was always too tense on the blocks, anticipating the gun. Her coaches tried to help her to relax but she found it impossible. She always found herself having to make up ground in the water.

She was feeling like that now. Her jaw was set tight. Her voice emerged as a throttled mumble.

"Yes, well, thank you for that, sir. I'll make sure Hayashi is fully briefed and the next version of the report will adhere more closely to the guidelines. I apologise for the poor initial presentation. I'll make sure it does not happen again."

With that, she retreated from the office.

Yamaguchi followed her progress back to her seat. Sighing, he put his glasses back on and resumed his reading.

It took a minute or two to focus on the text.

Ms Sekikawa also struggled to regain her composure. She found herself staring at her computer screensaver. A golden beach somewhere in Hawaii.

Across the desk, Hayashi stole a quick glance at his boss. He was weighing up whether this was a good time to interrupt.

"Excuse me, Detective Sekikawa?"

Ms Sekikawa unclenched her jaw and tried to breathe normally.

"Yes?"

"I've just received word from a police station in Shinjuku. Apparently, they have a Filipina in detention. It seems she was trafficked a year ago and managed to escape only yesterday."

"Go on."

"I wondered if we should go over to Shinjuku to interview her before she is transferred to a different facility."

Ms Sekikawa jumped to her feet and grabbed her bag.

"Excellent Hayashi! Time for some real police work!"

She spoke rather louder than she had intended. Her colleagues nearby raised their eyebrows in surprise.

As she strode towards the lift, Hayashi once again found himself struggling to keep up.

27

Ligaya Santos was curled up on the bed in the police cell. She felt safe behind bars.

Detective Nakagawa had arranged for her to be kept in protective custody, separated from the other detainees. Later she would be transferred to secure accommodation.

A female doctor had examined her. She confirmed Ligaya Santos was unhurt apart from the trauma. She gave her some tablets to help her sleep.

The Filipina lay facing the wall, re-living her escape. She could still hear her minder pounding along the pavement behind her. She visualised the alarm on the bystanders' faces as she hurtled past.

She still could not believe she had managed to get away. She shuddered at what might have happened otherwise.

She was only too aware of the Chinese boss' explosive temper. Calm one minute, savage the next. Even his underlings were petrified of him.

She shivered under the blanket. She closed her eyes and sucked her thumb. Her mother had tried to break her of the habit as a child. But, at times like these, it was a comfort.

When the light through the small barred window started to fade, she took two of the tablets the doctor had left for her. Soon she was asleep.

During the night, a female police officer looked in on

her through the observation slit. Detective Nakagawa had ordered a regular watch.

The next day, the detective came to her cell. He explained two police colleagues would like to talk with her.

She had agreed. She tidied herself up as best she could and was then escorted to an interview room on the floor below.

Ms Sekikawa and Hayashi were waiting. Ligaya Santos sat down and Ms Sekikawa drew up a chair beside her.

"Ms Santos, thank you for agreeing to speak with us. It would be very helpful if you could explain exactly what happened to you. In as much detail as you feel able."

Ligaya Santos started uncertainly, stumbling over her words.

"It's all right. Take your time. You're in no danger now."

Ligaya Santos took a deep breath. She turned to address her comments directly to Ms Sekikawa in a whisper.

"I had to escape. My son's in hospital."

"Your son? I'm very sorry to hear that. You must be extremely worried. How did you hear about his condition?"

"From my mother."

"You spoke with your mother?"

"Yes."

"You were allowed to make phone calls?"

Ligaya Santos explained about her perilous excursion in the middle of the night. As Ms Sekikawa listened, Hayashi took notes.

"When did you last see your family?"

"Over a year ago."

"During your time here, have you always been held in the same place?"

"No, at the beginning I was somewhere else. Another part of Tokyo, I think. Then they moved me. About nine months ago."

"How many other women were with you?"

"About ten. Sometimes more. Mostly from the Philippines, like me. Some from Thailand. A few Chinese. They were treated better."

"Better?"

"They went out on appointments. They were allowed to sit around in the office. They slept in a separate room."

"What kind of appointments?"

"They were taken to hotels or private houses. The rest of us waited for customers to come to us."

"Can you describe the location of the building where you were kept?"

"I don't know. I'm sorry."

"Would you recognise it if you saw it again?"

Ligaya Santos thought. All the streets seemed the same to her. Just a baffling series of shop fronts and bars.

"The few times we were allowed out to shop, we were always taken by car."

"Could you identify the people in charge?"

"Yes. I'll never forget them."

"Do you remember any of their names?"

"No, they always spoke Chinese."

"How many were there?"

"About six men altogether, I think. One man was the boss."

"Was he Chinese?"

"Yes."

"Can you describe him?"

"Very violent. Horrible. Everyone was afraid of him."

Ligaya Santos looked down. Ms Sekikawa had to lean forwards to hear what she was whispering.

"He was the one who punished us."

Ms Sekikawa read the distress in Ligaya's face. Nevertheless, she continued asking questions until it was obvious the recollections were causing Ligaya Santos too much discomfort.

With a nod to Hayashi, she called a halt to the interview.

"We understand you've been through a terrible time. Perhaps we should leave it there for today?"

"Thank you."

"But we'd like to talk to you again. Would that be all right?"

Ligaya Santos looked at Ms Sekikawa. It was such a long time since anyone had treated her with respect.

"Yes. Of course."

As Ms Sekikawa started to get up, Ligaya Santos reached across and took her wrist.

"When can I go home and see my son?"

Ms Sekikawa sat down again. She was not in a position to make any promises.

"First, you'll be taken to a safe place. I'm sure it won't be long before you see your son again."

"But I need to see him urgently…"

Ms Sekikawa's heart went out to the woman but her hands were tied. If she had her way, she would put Ligaya Santos on the next plane home.

"I'm sorry, but in cases like yours there are procedures to follow. We'll do everything we can to speed them up. Please be patient."

Ligaya Santos gradually released her grip. She had growing confidence in this approachable policewoman.

As she was escorted out of the room, she turned at the doorway to give Ms Sekikawa one final look. The message was unmistakeable.

28

Akira Kato sat in the same seat at the station hotel restaurant waiting for Ito.

The private investigator had rung the previous Friday to request a follow-up face-to-face meeting. Kato had been reluctant to make the trek north again.

"Why?"

"Some new information has come to light. I'd rather not discuss it over the phone."

"New information?"

"Yes."

"And you think it's absolutely necessary to meet again in person?"

"Yes, I do."

Despite his misgivings, Kato booked himself once again onto the nine o'clock bullet train heading north. Something in the private detective's tone suggested it would not be a wasted journey.

Kato was dredging his miso soup for chunks of tofu when the private investigator bustled into the restaurant.

"Good morning."

Without replying, Kato pointed at the buffet with his chopsticks. Ito nodded and set about charging a tray with food. Kato wondered if he had eaten since they had last met.

It was obvious nothing was going to be discussed until Ito had taken the edge off his hunger. Eventually the pace slowed.

"Delicious breakfast. Thank you."

Kato sat drumming his fingers on the table. Taking the hint, Ito pushed his tray to the side and leaned across.

"I've got something to show you."

Ito pulled an envelope out his bag and handed it to Kato.

Kato opened it and laid the contents on the table. He immediately identified the pages as copies of a *koseki,* an official family register. He glanced up at Ito, eyebrows raised in enquiry.

"What's this about?"

"The woman Hiroko Iwasaki's *koseki.* Please read it."

Kato scanned down the pages. Nothing out of the ordinary. He looked back at the private investigator.

"So what?"

Ito reached across and swivelled the photocopies so they could both see.

"Look. Here's the woman's father, and beside his name is that of his wife."

"OK...."

"Here are the two daughters."

"I fail to see what you are driving at."

"Now look at the entry for Hiroko Iwasaki."

Kato stared. He was starting to lose patience. A trip north on a Monday morning, cancelling all his appointments to squint at the small print of some family register.

"What about it?"

"There's nothing there!"

Ito sat back and rewarded himself with a slurp of coffee. Kato continued to look confused. Ito expected people to be quicker on the uptake.

"Don't you see? There's no mention of the Englishman."

Suddenly the red-cheeked man with the erratic hair had Kato's full attention. He was starting to understand.

"I checked with a lawyer friend of mine. As everyone knows, when you get married, your wife is added to your *koseki*. Standard practice.

"OK."

"But in this case, the husband is a foreigner. He has no *koseki* of his own. So, under Japanese law, he is added to his wife's *koseki*. He effectively joins her family."

"Right..."

"But the lawyer said foreigners are treated differently. They are not shown as married in the normal way but added as a remark on the *koseki*. A footnote."

Ito pointed at the space on the *koseki* reserved for footnotes.

"But, as you can see, he's not there. There's no reference anywhere on the *koseki* to the Englishman."

Kato finally caught on.

"So, if the Englishman isn't shown on the *koseki*, you're saying they aren't actually married?"

"Exactly. That's what the lawyer confirmed."

"What about in England?"

"I had my contact over there look into it. No marriage registered there either."

"So, if they aren't married, he has no rights. He's not recognised under Japanese law."

Ito nodded.

"The property is hers and hers alone."

Kato sat back and looked at Ito. He was impressed.

"What made you think of checking?"

"Just a hunch. Apparently, the Iwasaki woman never uses the man's surname. Not that unusual in marriages with foreigners, but I thought it was worth following up."

"So how did you get hold of this?"

Kato waved one of the photocopies.

"I had to grease a palm in the local council office. You'll find it on my next invoice under miscellaneous expenses."

Kato nodded. Ito drained his coffee and prepared to leave.

"Well, if you don't mind, I'd better get on. Hopefully something can come of this. You never know."

After he had taken his leave, Kato stayed at the table. He continued to stare at the *koseki* as he waited for his train back to Tokyo.

It was not much. But sometimes small details could make all the difference.

29

Sean Peters walked onto the mat in the dojo at exactly six o'clock.

All the students had already taken their positions. They knelt in rows, senior students at the front.

He faced them. Then he bowed. As one, they responded.

Assisted by the most senior student, Peters demonstrated the move they would be practising. As the student attacked, Peters moved aside and applied the hold. The next moment the student was on his back, immobilised.

It was deceptively simple. It required relaxation, timing and years of practice.

Peters had dedicated the last 20 years to this martial art. When he had first set foot in the dojo in North London, something had clicked.

He practised every moment he could. He had aptitude and made rapid progress through the grades.

But the move to Japan set him on a steeper trajectory. The Yamashiro region boasted a long martial arts tradition and some of Japan's top practitioners.

He trained under the best. As his understanding of the art deepened, he embarked on a profound personal journey.

In time, he was accorded the status of teacher. A distinction rarely conferred.

He moved around the dojo, helping each student. He demonstrated the form over and over again, explaining the subtleties.

Normally, he left any worries at the dojo door. It was one of his rules.

But today was different. He lacked his usual composure.

The previous day, Hiroko had noticed a car parked on the track below their house. She had not given it much thought.

She was on her way to feed the chickens. She always looked forward to that.

Peters used to laugh at her, the trouble she took with them. She had given them all names. She would stroke them, muttering words of encouragement.

On cold nights she would even tuck them up with extra blankets. They rewarded her by laying daily, eggs with rich yolks.

As she walked back to the house, the car was still there. She shielded her eyes from the sun. She could just make out a driver and one passenger.

She mentioned it to Peters over lunch. He said it did not concern them.

Later, while washing up, she peered through the small window above the sink. The front of the car was still visible. It had not moved. What on earth were they doing?

At three o'clock, Hiroko brought a thermos of tea up to the garden where Peters was working. He had cleared a section with a hoe. Steam rose from the freshly-moved earth in the afternoon heat.

They sat together, enjoying the peace, watching the

dragonflies buzz to and fro. Suddenly a car horn sounded near the house.

"I wonder who that is."

Peters got up. Walking to the edge of the garden, he looked down at the house. He could not see anyone.

"I'd better go and check."

He trotted down the path. No sign of any visitors. The car Hiroko had described had disappeared.

He shrugged and walked to the front door. Sliding it open, he stood quite still.

Lying on the wooden floor of the hall were two of Hiroko's chickens. Their heads had been cut off.

The people Hiroko had seen in the car had left their calling card. Crude and cruel.

Peters picked up the birds and took them outside. He placed them in a bucket. Then he went inside to fetch a mop to clear up the blood.

When he was sure the floor was quite clean, he retraced his steps to the garden.

"Who was it?"

Peters looked at Hiroko. He never kept anything from her. They faced life's hardships together.

"The people you saw in the car."

"What did they want?"

"They wanted to leave us a message."

"Message?"

"Yes, to tell us to sell the land."

Hiroko looked thoughtful.

"Did you speak with them?"

"No."

Hiroko frowned, trying to put it together. Peters walked towards her and held her tightly.

"They killed two of your chickens."

"My chickens?"

Hiroko freed herself and whirled round to pick up her basket. Peters held her wrist.

"Hiroko, listen. They want to frighten us. We need to be careful."

He followed her down to the house. She had already found the bucket with the dead birds.

Hiroko picked one of them up, her favourite and smoothed its feathers, whispering to it. Then she dropped the bucket and rushed down the track, screaming at the top of her voice.

"You're inhuman! Inhuman."

Peters waited in silence. He felt something stir inside him, something ugly and unexpected.

Eventually Hiroko returned. She wiped her hand across her face and went back into the house without a word.

That evening they sat opposite each other at the table as they always did. Hiroko had her mending box out and was repairing some clothes in silence. Peters was whittling away at a piece of wood.

Eventually Hiroko looked up.

"Sean, perhaps we ought to sell the land."

In the dojo, the students suffered the repercussions. The falls were that much harder. The exercises more prolonged. The next day several found themselves nursing strained wrists.

30

She and Sean rarely disagreed. When they did, Hiroko took it to heart.

After the death of her chickens, her resolve started to weaken. Everyone was against them. It was time to throw in the towel.

She had grown up in Tokyo, a long way from Yamashiro. Despite her deep family roots in the region, she felt no particular affinity for the rambling mountainous property.

But she knew the land meant a lot to Sean. And what made him happy, made her happy.

It was what made her struggle out of bed at first light to complete her long list of daily chores. To survive without the luxuries she had always been used to.

Once Sean laid bare his troubled upbringing, she understood why he was so tied to this particular place. It was the home he never had.

But they could buy a similar plot of land anywhere. Easier to work. More productive.

When she broached the subject, he had listened. She tried her best to persuade him.

With the money on offer, they could find somewhere else, miles away from all this unpleasantness. As long as they had each other, what did it matter?

He fell silent. He had a way of jutting out his jaw when he was being stubborn.

He mumbled something about checking the car's oil. He shut the front door behind him. She waited for his return.

Eventually his footsteps approached the house over the loose gravel. He kicked his boots off in the *genkan* entrance as he always did and padded into the front room. He sat down opposite her.

"Hiroko, I've been thinking it over."

She studied his face. To see if he had had a change of heart. She could tell immediately he had not.

"You can't allow people to walk all over you. Sometimes you have to take a stand."

Hiroko shook her head, railing at him.

"But Sean, this won't stop, don't you see? Eventually we'll have to give in. Better now than before anything else happens."

"Nothing else will happen. I promise. This is our home. I'll look after you."

Hiroko knew he would not budge. Sean was not one to turn his back on a fight.

The following day she suffered one of her sporadic migraines. When they came, she was knocked for six. All she could do was spend the day in bed with the curtains drawn.

The following morning, Peters had made her a cup of tea.

"Drink this. It may help."

She struggled onto her side and, her hand shielding her eyes from the daylight. Peters knelt on the floor beside her.

As she sipped her tea, he reached across and stroked her hair.

The roots were quite grey. Dyeing her hair was her only vanity.

Every few weeks, she would hide herself away in the small bathroom and daub the roots with an old toothbrush. She would later appear, wondering if Sean would notice any improvement.

She clasped his hand against her cheek and felt the warmth. Absorbing his energy. Then she lay back and looked at him.

"Everything will turn out all right, Hiroko. You'll see."

Slowly her eyes closed, wincing at the throbbing pain. She sought the refuge of sleep.

Sean Peters did not move. He continued to stare at her.

Before Hiroko, life had had little meaning. She could never know how much he owed her. He could not bear to see her suffer.

Doubts started to surface. Was his refusal to sell just pig-headedness? An unwillingness to face facts?

Slowly, he stood up and left the room. He slid the door behind him so as not to disturb her.

Downstairs he busied himself with the washing-up. Just a few dishes and a single pan for simmering vegetables.

Then the phone rang.

He generally avoided answering the phone. Hiroko usually dealt with the few calls they received.

"Yes?"

There was no response.

Peters held the receiver to his ear and listened. In the background he could hear light breathing. The person wanted him to know someone was on the line.

Peters knew better than to show his anger. Little was achieved by anger. It was a waste of energy.

Eventually he heard a man's chuckle. Then the person hung up. Peters walked back to the sink and carried on with the washing-up.

A few minutes later the phone rang again. Again, the sound of breathing. Peters rang off and reached down to disconnect the phone at the plug.

He felt a surge of indignation at this cowardly intimidation. His fists clenched. For a second, he pictured what he would do if he met the man in person.

His hand strayed for the eight-inch kitchen knife. It was razor-sharp. Its edge never seemed to dull.

Sean Peters understood knives.

31

He remembered the cold most of all. The sub-zero temperatures as they inched through the minefield.

The route had been recced before. But that did not make it any the less nerve-wracking.

He focussed on the man in front. He tracked his movements over the uneven ground.

They crept forwards, each man lost in his thoughts. Wondering how they would measure up in the battle to come.

Ahead of the company lay the mountain, their objective. As they moved closer, steeling themselves for the assault, the naval bombardment started.

The air screeched with missiles, the ground bucking with each impact. Hard to imagine anyone surviving up there on the granite face under such an onslaught.

But they had. They were dug in and waiting. Suddenly the mountain came alive with sputtering flashes from the heavy machine-guns. He watched as the ground in front of them spat and hissed.

His training kicked in. All the endless exercises at the Royal Marine Commando Training Centre on Devon's Exe estuary. All the gruelling night marches on the wild reaches of Dartmoor. Damp, cold, hungry, exhausted.

This was all he had to rely on. That and his bloody-mindedness.

Far to the west the diversionary tactics began. The rattle of gunfire. Flares lighting up the night sky.

He remembered the briefing. Now it was their turn to advance.

They started to climb, scrambling for safe positions. The guns held them. There was no way through.

Behind the gunsights he imagined the Argentine conscripts. The enemy.

He had been told never to put himself in their shoes. Never to give the enemy a face.

But it was hard not to. They were young men like himself, given a weapon and told to fight.

At least he had made a choice. Not much of a choice admittedly.

After his mother's death, he had few options. But one employer was always ready to recruit tough young men.

The introductory training course quickly weeded out anybody not up to it. Not Sean Peters. He was more than equal to the task.

He ran, he swam, he scaled whatever they put in front of him. He passed with flying colours. His reward was the coveted green beret.

His plan had been to leave Plymouth far behind. But after passing out from the training centre at Lympstone, he joined 42 Commando Royal Marines. They were based just a few miles away from the city of his birth on the southern fringes of Dartmoor.

But it might have been another world. His days were spent

exercising on the unforgiving upland terrain. He grew to love its unpredictable bleakness. How it could turn in an instant when the barometer dropped.

It was the perfect preparation for the Falklands.

The men started to fan out. The air was strident with gunfire. In the midst of the bedlam their discipline held. Orders were given.

One soldier rushed a machine-gun post and silenced it with a grenade. He fell as he did so. Others followed his lead.

The advance was halted by spirited resistance. The word was these soldiers would buckle, that they were full of bluster with no stomach for a fight.

It was not that way. He knew it would not be. These men had passion and courage.

As they pushed on up the hill, mortar fire steadily wiped out the enemy, position by position.

One Argentine conscript alone at the summit covered his comrades' retreat. He kept up a steady stream of fire with his heavy machine-gun.

He could have been strolling along a boulevard in Buenos Aires, dropping into his favourite café, chatting with his friends. Instead, he chose to die on a freezing rock in the Atlantic at the dead of night.

Eventually the mountain was theirs. Sean Peters had just been old enough to take part but his age was irrelevant.

He had played his part. He had been in at the kill, blooded in action.

He rarely thought about those days as he trekked through the mountains in Japan. They were a lifetime away. A past he had all but forgotten.

Meeting Hiroko had been a new start for him. With her, his defences crumbled. For the first time he understood tenderness.

Moving to Japan was the final step in his rehabilitation. Suddenly he was airlifted into a different world. A chance to re-invent himself. He had seized it with both hands.

His martial arts teacher had shown him a new way. To side-step aggression. Not to meet force with force.

But now the old spectres started to return. They peopled his dreams.

The violence in his soul, so long suppressed, was surfacing. Once again, he started to hear the drum beat. The call to arms.

These days he was constantly on alert. He watched the road, keeping close to the house. He threw a protective net over everything he loved.

Hiroko noticed the change in his behaviour. She understood he was standing guard.

"Do you think we are in danger?"

He looked up from their simple meal of boiled rice, pickles and omelette. He read the concern in her eyes.

"No. But it's better to be safe than sorry."

Hiroko nodded, snaking her hand across the table to grasp his. They stayed like that for a few moments until they resumed their meal.

In Tokyo, Akira Kato opened an envelope. It was marked for his personal attention.

It was from the private investigator Ito. The promised report on the Englishman.

The detective's contact in England had been thorough. A particular section was highlighted. The Englishman's years as a Royal Marine commando.

Kato puzzled over some expressions. "Mentioned in dispatches." "Commendation for bravery under enemy fire."

But he understood the overall gist. He swivelled his chair to stare out of his office window.

This man was going to be a serious problem.

32

The unmarked police car weaved its way through the narrow streets.

Ligaya Santos peered at the buildings they passed. She sat in the back seat next to Ms Sekikawa. Detectives Hayashi and Nakagawa were upfront.

"Do you recognise anything?"

Yet again, the Filipina shook her head.

Initially, Ligaya Santos had been afraid to help in the search. To leave the safety of the police station. She only relented after Ms Sekikawa promised she would come to no harm.

The clinic was their starting-point. The doctor and the receptionist had been taken in for questioning while officers carried out a systematic search of the premises.

The records yielded little of interest. Unlike the clinic's bona fide clients, the criminal fraternity submitted fictitious registration information and paid exclusively in cash.

According to Ligaya Santos, the car journey to the clinic took about half an hour. The police team focused their search on well-known red-light areas within that radius.

They had been trawling the streets for three days without success. They were increasingly resigned to coming away empty handed.

Ms Sekikawa and Hayashi had been seconded to the

investigation full time. They were both glad to be out of the office.

Ms Sekikawa had chosen her moment carefully. Yamaguchi had just finished his daily routine of press-ups inside the glass cube.

No one in the department batted an eyelid at their department chief's somewhat eccentric behaviour any more. They understood he was cut from a different cloth.

"Do you have a minute, please?"

"Of course."

They had not spoken much since Ms Sekikawa had taken umbrage. Yamaguchi had decided to let the dust settle.

Ms Sekikawa was still feeling rather abashed. She should not have let her emotions get the better of her. It now seemed all very petty in hindsight.

"Hayashi and I have been making good progress with our investigations into people trafficking."

"Good. Excellent."

Yamaguchi sat down at his desk, wiping a towel across his bristled head.

"We've had the chance to interview an actual victim. To get some first-hand input."

"Did it prove useful?"

"Yes. The victim we spoke with is a Filipina. She recently escaped from a brothel run by members of a Chinese crime organisation."

"Where is she being held?"

"At Shinjuku police station. She's in protective custody."

Yamaguchi sensed this was leading up to something. He sat back and waited.

"Anyway, Hayashi and I have managed to gain the woman's trust. She speaks hardly any Japanese."

"I see."

"I thought it might help if we were temporarily assigned to the case."

Yamaguchi nodded. As he suspected.

"What about your other work?"

"Not much on our plates at the moment. Apart from finalising the trafficking report, of course."

Yamaguchi contemplated his colleague across the desk. He could read the signs.

"You're not getting too involved, are you?"

Ms Sekikawa tried to look nonchalant.

"No, not at all. I just think we can make a useful contribution."

"Let me think about it."

A day later Yamaguchi gave his permission to proceed. He had spoken with Detective Nakagawa. The Shinjuku detective had welcomed the assistance of Yamaguchi's two officers.

But after a third day's fruitless trawling through the streets, the detectives had to admit defeat. They called off the search.

They had been unlucky. At one point they had only been one street away from where Ligaya Santos had been held.

Not that the Filipina would have been likely to recognise the building. It was already under new management.

The frontage was covered in scaffolding and the interior gutted. The partitions separating the cramped rooms for entertaining clients had been demolished. The building was due to re-open shortly as a macrobiotic health food store.

Back at the station, Ms Sekikawa reviewed all the information they had gathered from Ligaya Santos. After consulting with Detective Nakagawa, Ms Sekikawa put in a call to a colleague at headquarters.

"Hello? Yes?"

Noriko Muratani knew her telephone manner needed work. She felt far more at home with computers.

She and Ms Sekikawa were close friends. When it came to anything technical, Ms Sekikawa always turned to her geeky colleague for help.

Ms Sekikawa needed to put together a photofit. Ligaya Santos had agreed to work with the police to provide a physical description of the man in charge of running the brothel.

Creating a police photofit had come on in leaps and bounds in recent years. Gone were the days of a police artist sketching with a box of crayons. The latest facial imaging software achieved a superior likeness in a fraction of the time.

But the best results required a combination of skilled software manipulation and accurate eyewitness recall.

Later that day, Noriko Muratani, Ms Sekikawa and Ligaya Santos huddled together in a spare interview room in Shinjuku police station.

They emerged an hour later with a close likeness of the man. Looking at his photofit, Ligaya Santos could not help shuddering as she recalled the brutal treatment meted out by him.

33

The mayor was waiting for his lunch guest.

The restaurant interior harked back to an earlier age. The low ceiling was criss-crossed with wooden beams over the tatami-matted dining area. Waitresses in kimonos had to stoop to deliver their trays of food.

A family party was at the next table. The children were fractious and demanding. The mayor clicked his tongue in irritation.

Finally, the restaurant door slid back. A tall man with a skeletal frame ducked into the room, escorted by one of the waitresses.

"Sorry to keep you waiting."

The mayor waved away the apology. His guest squeezed into his seat opposite. Laying his glasses on the table, he buried his face in the piping-hot *oshibori* towel the waitress had handed him.

The mayor studied the man as he then craned over the menu. Competent, hard-working, smart. Unlike many of his colleagues, the man had risen through the ranks entirely on merit.

As city land registrar, every property transaction went through his office. Every document received his personal scrutiny. His attention to detail was legendary

The two men chatted about local issues until they had

finished eating. As the registrar started mining his mouth with a wooden toothpick, the mayor finally broached the subject.

"I'm interested in some background on a particular property."

The registrar paused in his explorations.

"Which property?"

"The Iwasaki family's place."

Kato had phoned the previous day. The mayor had not appreciated Kato's tone. The developer had not minced his words.

"I've just learned the Iwasaki woman and the foreigner aren't actually married."

"Really? That's news to me."

"My point exactly. Anyway, I'd like that fact corroborated. And any other useful background details you can find out. Assuming you have the time, of course."

The mayor's first port of call was the man currently sitting opposite him in the restaurant. If he did not know, nobody did.

The city registrar screwed up his eyes in thought and then nodded.

"Yes, I remember. The father lived in Tokyo. Died in 1995. The older daughter, Hiroko Iwasaki, inherited the property."

The mayor stared at the registrar in astonishment. The registrar smiled modestly back.

"You see, I dealt with the land transfer myself. That's how I remember it so well. The father used to consult with me on land issues over the years. Rather a difficult type, in point of fact."

The mayor nodded.

"So, the land transfer was straightforward?"

"Yes, absolutely. All the ownership documents were in place. The property has been in the family for well over a century."

"The older daughter owns everything outright?"

"Yes, she does."

The mayor lit up a cigarette.

"Did you know Hiroko Iwasaki is living up at the property with an Englishman?"

"Yes, she told me as much after her father's death."

"She met with you?"

"Yes. Hiroko Iwasaki wanted some advice on inheritance matters."

"Inheritance?"

The registrar bent forwards and took a sip of tea. He was in his element. He relished the opportunity to show off his unrivalled grasp of his specialist field.

"When the daughter registered the land transfer after her father's death, she needed some advice about writing a will."

"A will?"

"Exactly. She wanted the *gaijin* to inherit the property in the event she pre-decease him."

The mayor tried to conceal his growing interest. He puffed on his cigarette and blew smoke in the direction of the next table. The children fanned their noses in disgust.

"And this will. I assume it's lodged with the notary?"

The registrar shook his head.

"In fact, it isn't. Iwasaki-san wanted to avoid the unnecessary expense of having a legal document drawn up. She just drafted a simple document, clearly stating her wishes, which she has in safe-keeping at home."

"And that has legal force?"

"Oh yes. Absolutely. I remember specifying all the elements to include in the document. Standard clauses describing her wishes, the need for her official stamp and so on."

"And this will would make the Englishman the sole beneficiary?"

"Yes, exactly. Of course, if they were married, he would inherit the land automatically."

"So, you mean they aren't actually married?"

"No, according to Hiroko Iwasaki, the couple decided not to marry. Surprising I know, but each to their own."

The mayor stubbed out his cigarette.

"Well, that's foreigners for you. Unpredictable."

"Quite so. We Japanese like to do things by the book."

34

"Kampai!"

They clinked glasses and took a long draught of chilled beer. It was a while since Sean Peters and Hiroko had ventured out in public. That day they made a special effort.

The nuisance phone calls had ceased and everything seemed to have returned to normal. Hiroko was back to her usual self and Peters had relaxed his close watch over the house.

The couple never missed the annual cherry blossom celebrations. The trees bloomed later in the northern highlands than further south, holding back their fragile flowers until the winter chill had abated.

As always, Peters and Hiroko arrived in good time to reserve a secluded spot in the corner of the village park. They liked to keep themselves to themselves.

The park was already busy. Groups of junior employees from local companies were staking out the most desirable pitches under the trees with plastic sheeting.

Peters and Hiroko listened to their excited conversations. Where was the best place for the barbecue? Where to store the cold boxes full of food and drink? Who should sit where?

Everyone looked forward to *hanami*. For once, the locals could let their hair down and have some fun. Karaoke machines added to the general hubbub.

"It's lovely, isn't it Sean?"

Peters nodded and smiled at Hiroko. He knew how much it meant to her. Another small mystery of Japanese life.

The blossoms were now at their best. The park was a riot of colour, each tree vying for attention.

It would not last long. That was part of the appeal. It would only take a strong gust of mountain wind for the petals be strewn on the grass.

"Yes, perfect."

He moved to sit closer to her so their shoulders touched. He was never very demonstrative about his feelings.

She understood. It did not matter.

As dusk fell, the park started to fill up. More revellers arrived to enthusiastic shouts of welcome. The newcomers bowed, bobbing up and down, before slipping off their shoes and joining their group on the plastic sheeting.

The smell from barbecues drifted across the grass. Plastic cups of drink were filled and refilled.

Gradually everyone relaxed. The usual strict formality underpinning their lives was temporarily set aside. *Hanami* was no time to stand on ceremony.

Sean Peters and Hiroko unpacked their own hamper. It was modest in comparison.

Peters set to work on the mini barbecue. Hiroko held her hands to the coals as they caught.

She always felt the cold and the spring evening was chilly. She tugged a cardigan around her shoulders.

She could not help looking enviously across the park at the festivities. As a youngster she would have been in the thick of it. Laughing and joking with the rest of them.

Now she could not help feeling excluded, left on the side lines. With the land issue hanging over them, she felt further ostracised.

Peters knew. He understood the sacrifice she had made to be with him. And he was well aware of her current sense of uneasiness.

The nearest group to them was sitting under a tree some 20 metres away. A family from their village together with relatives from further afield.

All ages were represented. The elderly, their backs bent from a lifetime labouring in the fields. Their children keeping an eye on the next generation as they rushed about making a nuisance of themselves.

Hiroko smiled as she watched the youngsters playing. One of them, a girl of about five, her hair bunched on top of her head with an elastic band, caught her eye.

Hiroko waved and the child, after hesitating for a second, waved back.

Her mother broke off from attending to the barbecue. She looked across, screwing up her eyes to see who was sitting under the trees opposite.

When she saw Hiroko, all the pleasure drained from her face. She quickly turned and muttered something. Now the whole family group stopped what they were doing and stared in their direction.

Hiroko looked away, edging closer to Peters. Not here, not now.

All at once, the oldest member of the family struggled to his feet and slipped on his shoes. He tottered across the grass towards Hiroko and Peters.

He stood looking at them for a few seconds. His wrinkled face alive with *saké*. He was known as a man who never minced his words.

"You stupid bastards. Ruining it for everyone. You should be ashamed."

With that, he spat on the ground. Another member of the family rushed over and shepherded him back to the mat.

The family group clustered together, muttering. The fun seemed to have gone out of their party. Even the children, sensing a problem, huddled close to their parents.

"Let's go home, Sean."

Even though they had hardly touched their food, Peters started to pack up their things.

They slipped out of the park and started the long climb back to their house. Behind them the festivities continued long into the night.

35

Chen sat at the folding table. He was wearing a thin jacket with the collar turned up despite the spring warmth.

As always, he was composed, his gloved hands resting on his thighs. He looked straight ahead, deep in thought.

Opposite him, a man in a dark suit and thick glasses bent over a chart spread across the table. It was covered with Chinese characters and symbols.

No words were exchanged. The man broke off only to jot something down on the pad beside him. Then he would exhale loudly before immersing himself again in his calculations.

It was an arcane, complex procedure. Reaching the correct conclusion required discipline and considerable knowledge. It took time and great patience.

The two men's serenity was in stark contrast to the bustling street scene surrounding them.

Pedestrians jostled with one another on the cramped pavements. Customers formed long queues outside popular restaurants offering cut-price lunches. Cars revved to no avail in the choking gridlock.

No one was going anywhere fast.

At the far end of the street stood the massive ornate gate. The entrance to Yokohama's Chinatown.

Chen's undivided attention was on the man opposite. He waited patiently as the soothsayer teased out his future.

He had been coming to this table for years. It was a family tradition.

The man was not like other fortune tellers on the street. Charlatans reading tourists' palms, shaking Kau Cim incense sticks for a pittance.

He was privy to an ancient world of divination passed down through the generations. His services were the reserve of a clique of extremely well-heeled Chinese.

The man could have afforded luxurious premises. Pleasantly-appointed rooms with sweeping views of the bay. An attractive receptionist to attend to his clients' needs.

Instead, he chose to remain on the streets of Yokohama. Where his own family had its roots.

He sat in exactly the same spot as his forebears. At the same antique table inlaid with deep red lacquer.

He preferred to keep things constant. Change, to his mind, often heralded unintended consequences.

Chen shared his distrust. Two days earlier Kato had sought a meeting with him.

The venue was the same as always. A discreet French-styled café opposite the Kabuki Theatre in Tokyo's Higashi-Ginza.

When Kato arrived at the café, his client was in his usual spot at the rear of the shop. He had his hands folded in front of him on the table like a cat, gazing into space.

Kato sat down opposite and ordered. He looked across at the man who had yet to acknowledge his presence.

As the developer waited, his eyes were drawn to the white

silk gloves. Intrigued, he had always wondered why the man was never seen without them.

But he had the good sense never to ask. He steered clear of anything remotely personal.

There were only two other customers in the café. Two large men adjacent to the entrance with untouched iced coffees in front of them.

Once the waitress in her lacy French outfit had served Kato his coffee, Chen finally engaged.

"What's so important?"

Kato recalled their first meeting in this same café at the start of the project. When the two men had laid down the ground rules for the multi-million-dollar development.

Kato remembered his initial impression of the diminutive businessman. He took him for a pushover, a lightweight. Not in his league.

But, by the time Kato had left the café, he had revised his opinion. He had hurried to flag down a cab, anxious to distance himself. By then, he had a clear idea who he was dealing with.

Subsequently their business was managed remotely. An arrangement Kato favoured. But sometimes there was no alternative to a face-to-face meeting.

Kato cleared his throat. He needed to broach this subject with care.

Chen listened to Kato's preamble. His small hands sought out the delicate French porcelain cup and raised it to his lips. Only when it was safely restored to its saucer did he interrupt.

"So, in summary, the couple still refuse to sell?"

"Yes."

Chen patted his mouth with his paper napkin. He glanced at the dark stain from the coffee before folding it and placing it beside him.

"Extremely displeasing."

It seemed his people's initial low-key attempts to pressurise the couple had proved ineffective. It was time to raise the stakes.

The crime boss stared across the table. Kato avoided his gaze by busying himself with his mobile phone.

But Chen was a past master at reading human behaviour. His livelihood depended on it.

The people he dealt with day-to-day were devious and mendacious. He had learned early on how to peel back the mask, to understand what was really on their minds.

Kato presented a straightforward challenge. Chen could read him like a book.

"Kato-san, there's something else you would like to tell me. Spit it out and stop wasting my time."

Kato looked up from his phone. The keen brown eyes fixed on him like a pit-viper.

The developer thrust his phone into his pocket. As he started to speak, he felt disembodied, as if he was observing himself from across the room.

"Well, as it happens, some new information has come to light. I've discovered the couple are not, in fact, actually married."

"Not married?"

"No. Not in Japan or England. I checked thoroughly."

"I see."

Chen waited. He knew when to take his time. The French porcelain cup travelled to his mouth again. His mouth pursed around the rim as he sipped.

Kato felt obliged to fill the vacuum.

"Of course, just because they aren't married doesn't alter the situation greatly. The Englishman can still persuade his partner not to sell."

"Exactly. So why are you bothering to tell me this?"

Kato looked away as he spoke. As if that made it easier.

"It's just that it would make a difference if anything were to happen to the woman. The Englishman would have no rights to inherit the property. Under normal circumstances."

"Because they aren't married?"

"Exactly. The land would go to the closest relatives. In this case, her only surviving sister in Tokyo."

"To her only sister?"

"Yes."

The white gloves swivelled the cup in its saucer as if trying to establish a specific compass point.

"Under normal circumstances?"

Kato glanced away across the room. As if hoping the waitress polishing cutlery in the corner could come to his aid.

"Yes. I understand the woman has written a will bequeathing the property to the Englishman."

"A will, you say?"

"Yes. Not a will lodged with a notary in the normal way. A do-it-yourself will she drew up herself and keeps at home. Legally binding by all accounts."

"A legally binding will which she keeps at their house?"

"Yes. In the event of her death, the man would simply present the will to the authorities for him to be confirmed as her beneficiary."

"A sort of bearer bond?"

"Yes. Exactly."

"Interesting. Tell me more about this will ...."

On leaving the café, Kato had glanced back through the window. He suddenly wished he could go back in and retract everything he had said.

The two men by the door watched the developer as he hurried off down the street. They smirked at each other.

Now, two days later in the street in Yokohama Chinatown, the fortune teller sat back and rubbed his eyes. He had concluded his calculations.

He did not need to articulate his findings. He simply nodded.

Chen thanked him. They then sat drinking tea and observed the melee around them.

So many lives. So many potential unforeseen outcomes.

36

Hiroko was not herself.

After the unpleasantness at the cherry blossom celebration, she had gone into her shell again. Peters was increasingly concerned.

He knew she was prone to mood swings. Sometimes elated, other times wrestling with depression.

The rift with her father had been hard. She had a special bond with him. Being forced to choose between her family and Sean had taken its toll.

Sometimes, when she thought she was alone, Peters would hear her muttering to herself. Justifying her decision.

In true Japanese style, she never brought it up with Peters. It was her burden to bear.

But often he found himself contemplating her slender shoulders as she sat darning. Trying to imagine the recriminations churning inside her.

Their meals together were generally happy times. They would discuss the chores they needed to tackle. How they were going to make their finances stretch. All their immediate pressing concerns.

They rarely discussed the world beyond. It had little relevance to them, tucked away in their remote mountain home.

Sometimes after supper, they would sit together and browse wildlife books. Over the years, Sean Peters had become an ardent naturalist. He spent much of his time studying the local flora and fauna.

Often, he disappeared overnight with a rucksack and a tent into the high forest. Hiroko rarely accompanied him, secretly preferring her creature comforts.

Peters' pride and joy was a top-of-the-range camera. When he returned from one of his expeditions, the couple would spend enjoyable evenings identifying the different species he had come across.

That day Peters had trekked into the high peaks. He had the good luck to spot a northern goshawk in flight.

He managed to track it to the branches of a fir tree perched at an angle on a rocky outcrop. Lying flat on his stomach in the undergrowth, he had reeled off a series of pictures of the bird at rest.

Suddenly it had sensed his presence. With a huff, the hawk launched itself into the clear mountain air and soared away on the up-currents.

The next day, as he made his way back home, he hoped his photos might help to raise Hiroko's spirits.

He found her in her usual place sitting at the *kotatsu*. Unusually, the television was on. She was watching a quiz show.

They very rarely watched television. And never during the day.

On the screen two comedians, dressed in bizarre outfits, were regaling a group of celebrities. Peters did not recognise any of the participants.

Hiroko glanced up at Peters as he came in. She gave him a quick nod and then her eyes returned to the screen.

Peters had trouble concealing his disappointment. He had longed to show her the pictures of the goshawk, but could see now was not the time.

"Are you enjoying the programme?"

"It's all right. Something to pass the time."

Peters sat down opposite and freshened the tea pot from the large thermos on the table. He glanced across at her.

She kept staring at the television as if anxious not to miss anything. Eventually Peters' patience wore thin.

"What's up, Hiroko?"

"Nothing. I'm just watching a television programme. That's all."

"In the middle of the day?"

"Well, there's not much else to do."

"Sorry?"

She looked him full in the face. Her eyes burned.

"Out here. Stuck in the middle of nowhere. With no friends. Where everyone hates us. Living in this dump."

The words flew out like arrows. They found their mark. Peters recoiled.

"You don't mean that, do you?"

"What do you think, Sean? You saw them at the *hanami*. How they behaved. How can we put up with this?"

"We'll get through it."

"You may, but not me. You don't know what it's doing to me. I can't bear it."

Peters crawled around the table and stretched out his arms. She fended them off, flailing her hands at him.

Then the floodgates opened. All the years of repressed guilt and tension gushed out in a torrent of raw emotion.

Peters gripped her. It was like clinging onto a mast in a violent storm.

He waited for her outpourings to subside. Slowly he felt her breathing return to normal, the words coming in snatches.

In the background, the two comedians continued their antics. He desperately wanted to reach over and switch the television off.

Then Hiroko looked up at him, her eyes red, her nose running.

"Don't you understand Sean? I want to sell up. Get out of here and leave all this shit behind."

37

The teacher observed Sean Peters as they sat drinking tea.

The elderly Japanese could tell something was wrong. Not from anything Peters said. They rarely indulged in much conversation.

The training session had been gruelling. There was much to reflect on.

Whenever Peters came to the rambling old house in the mountains, he needed to be on his mettle. To expect the unexpected.

Prior to the session, he sat in meditation on the dojo mat. As always, he started to become aware of all the insignificant sounds he had overlooked.

Tiny wings beating in the garden outside. A leaf twitching in the breeze. A ripple across the pond.

The time spent meditating sharpened his senses.

He never knew what was in store for him. That was up to his teacher.

Peters was big-framed. A physique inherited from his Dutch forebears. And in his late forties, given his constant manual work, he was supple and strong.

He needed to be.

The teacher knelt at the front of the dojo. Peters and the teacher's son knelt side-by-side facing him. It was a private session for only the most advanced exponents.

Peters had studied under the teacher since arriving in Japan. He remembered how clumsy he had been at the outset.

He had soon learned the black belt gained in London cut little ice. The teacher, with his compact, birdlike frame, could best him with ease. Strength was an irrelevance.

For Peters to progress, he was forced to return to first principles. As they revisited the basic moves, Peters was introduced to subtleties never part of the syllabus at the London martial arts school.

The teacher started the session, issuing a brief instruction.

Peters turned to face the son. They bowed.

"Onegai-shimasu."

The moves were choreographed. The two men threw and were thrown, their bodies spinning through the air. They hardly seemed to contact the mat as they landed, back on their feet in an instant.

If the teacher's son found an opening, he exploited it. Peters would find himself pinned, tapping for quarter.

That day he was found wanting more often than usual. His concentration wandered.

He could not help thinking of Hiroko. How upset she had been. Imploring him to capitulate and sell.

Typically, he had stuck his toes in. He had said they were not quitters. He was damned if anyone was going to force them out of their own home.

Hiroko begged him to change his mind. Saying it was not worth all the unpleasantness.

Land was cheap, she said. With what they were being offered, they could live in peace. They would never need to worry about money again.

He could see she was near the end of her tether. He could sense her desperation. In the end, he had asked for time to mull it over.

Sensing his distraction, the teacher could have gone easy on his student. Instead, he piled on the pressure.

The son was dispatched to bring real weapons to replace the wooden facsimiles. A sword and a knife. Both razor-sharp. One mistake could result in a severe injury.

The sparring continued with a new edge. Peters needed to be totally engaged.

At the teacher's insistence the attacks were delivered with real intent. There was no room for error.

As the blades descended, the defender side-stepped and engaged the appropriate counter grips. It required perfect timing and years of practice.

At the end of the session, the son bowed and withdrew. He had a busy day ahead of him. Rotavating the fields to prepare for the following month's rice planting.

As they sat together, sipping tea, the teacher studied his student.

He had heard about Peters' troubles. Word travelled quickly through the grapevine of small communities.

The development project was common knowledge. The couple's unwillingness to sell was a frequent topic.

"Steel sharpens the mind."

Peters looked at the teacher. The old man had a penchant for enigmatic statements.

At the end of the training session, Peters drove slowly home. He was in no hurry. He threaded his way along the narrow tracks bordering the paddy fields.

The journey gave him a chance to think. At one point, he parked, got out and leaned against the car.

His eye roved over the landscape. In every direction, fertile tracts of land stretched far into the distance.

Many fields lay fallow, elderly villagers no longer able to cope with the backbreaking work. They needed someone younger with energy to pick up the baton.

By the time he reached their village, he finally had things straight in his mind. He knew what he wanted to say.

A crocodile of children in yellow caps were filing through the village. Two teachers kept them in order. The children were excited but did what they were told without question.

Peters thought about himself at that age. Bloodied, beaten, bullied and learning nothing. A different world.

When he turned into the track leading up to the farmhouse, he noticed a small car parked at the bottom. It was outside their nearest neighbour's property.

Local plates. Nothing to be concerned about, he thought. Just someone paying a visit.

38

The woman had observed the Englishman leave the village. As always, he was bang on schedule.

She had been sitting waiting on a bench outside the primary school. Once he had disappeared, she gave it five minutes before walking across to her car.

She drove to the bottom of the track and parked. From there, she could just make out the front door of the farmhouse.

She knew the couple's routine inside out. According to her information, the Englishman's partner would also be leaving the house, but her timetable was less set in stone.

The minutes ticked by. Suddenly it was already an hour since the Englishman's departure.

The woman drummed her manicured fingernails on the steering wheel. She was concerned she would not have enough time to complete her mission.

She sat behind the wheel of her rented Suzuki Kei car. The box-shaped run-about was perfect cover but, with its 600cc engine, not made for a quick getaway.

She was wearing a broad-brimmed straw hat over her head towel. Her clothes were also village standards: an apron, baggy *mompe* working trousers and rubber boots.

No one passing would take a second glance. Just a villager readying herself for a day's work in the fields.

Her rural get-up bore no resemblance to her usual wardrobe. Chic outfits from Shinjuku's designer boutiques.

Her milieu was the Tokyo smart set. She attended parties, receptions, art events. Anywhere the rich and famous rubbed shoulders.

While others longed to be noticed, her intention was the exact opposite. To slip beneath the radar, to melt into the crowd. To remain inconspicuous.

Her conversation was unmemorable. Her appearance unremarkable. She left no lasting impression.

Her metier was stealing secrets, gathering information, identifying people's weak spots for others to exploit. She was highly trained, technically savvy and had nerves of steel.

She muttered under her breath as she glanced at her Cartier watch. As the minutes passed, there was still no sign of the woman.

She started to worry. She was cutting it fine.

She knew she needed to be patient. It would be better to return the following Thursday than risk exposure.

Suddenly the front door slid opened. Hiroko emerged in a faded skirt and a cardigan.

She turned at the entrance to lock the front door. She rattled it once to make sure it was secure.

Then she disappeared into one of the outhouses and emerged with her bicycle. Mounting it, she cycled down the track.

Seeing her coming, the woman took out her phone and simulated a conversation, her head bowed forwards.

When Hiroko reached the car, she glanced across. Not recognising the driver, she gave her a nod before freewheeling down to join the road.

The woman in the car checked her rear-view mirror. When Hiroko rounded the corner, she waited for a few minutes to be sure the coast was clear.

Then she got out of the car and walked briskly up the track towards the house.

This was her chance. She needed to make every second count.

The front door posed no problem. She locked it behind her, just in case. Standing in the hallway, she rapidly prioritised her search.

Pulling on a pair of latex gloves, she first slipped into the living room. She frowned at its untidiness, but she knew she had to be wary.

The couple stared at the same disorder every day. They would be likely to notice any change.

She started with the small writing desk. It was strewn with papers. A cardboard box stuffed with correspondence stood to one side.

She tried the drawers. They were unlocked. She found passports, certificates, bills and bank statements.

Everything except the document she was looking for.

She looked at her watch. Time was marching on.

She ignored the kitchen and headed down the corridor. She glanced into the bedroom.

The futons and bedlinen had been cleared away into the large cupboards to the side. The room was empty apart from suspended bamboo poles acting as clothes hangers.

The woman crossed the corridor to the tatami room

opposite. It was empty apart from the family *butsudan* shrine and two swords lying on a rack fashioned from deer antlers.

The squat, hardwood *butsudan* displayed the usual items of veneration: a painting of the Buddha, scrolls, an incense burner, a small bell and an offering of fruit.

The woman turned her attention to the small drawer at the base of the *butsudan.* In a trice, she had it open. The document she sought was in plain view.

She unfolded it and skimmed through the contents. The text was simple and unequivocal. Hiroko's signature and seal were displayed at the bottom.

She stuffed the document into her pocket. Looking at her watch again, she realised her time was up.

Rushing back along the corridor, she glanced into each room, checking to make sure she had left no trace. She knew she had not.

She was just pulling her rubber boots on in the *genkan* entrance, when she froze. Through the frosted glass, she saw the Englishman's car draw up.

There was no escape that way. Undeterred, she grabbed her boots and scuttled back into the interior.

It always paid to do her homework. When she had first checked over the house, she had noted an unlocked rear window in the lounge. Her back-up escape route.

Sliding it open, she climbed out with impressive agility. Reaching back, she closed the window behind her as she heard the Englishman unlock the front door.

She gave him time to go into the house. Then she picked her way back to her car, avoiding being seen.

39

Thursdays meant a lot to Hiroko. While Sean had his regular training session at the teacher's dojo, she cycled to a tiny hamlet further up the valley.

It was easy going along the well-surfaced road. The gradual incline took her past farmhouses, rice paddies and fields of fruit trees.

She enjoyed the peace and quiet. And the chance to be on her own for a while.

She loved being with Sean but sometimes she needed a break. That particular day, she had a lot on her mind.

She rarely bumped into anyone else on the road. An occasional car would trundle past, the occupants nodding a friendly greeting. Solitary figures working in the fields would straighten to see who it was before bending to their tasks again.

After half an hour, she reached the small house tucked away behind two large cedars. She leaned her bicycle against the dilapidated fence and slid open the front door.

"Sorry to intrude!"

There was an answering call from somewhere inside. Seconds later, an elderly lady appeared.

She hobbled towards the front door, doubled over, her arthritic hands brushing down the front of her white apron. But there was nothing slow about the two bright eyes and ready smile.

"Come in Hiroko-chan. Thank you for making the journey over. You must be ready for a cup of tea."

It was always the same when Hiroko came to visit Auntie Mieko. She was her father's first cousin, the last member of the family still living in the area. She was her father's favourite relative, and Hiroko's too.

Since Hiroko and Sean had moved to the area, Auntie Mieko had done everything she could to make them feel welcome. She would turn up unannounced with bundles of plants, pickles she had made, odd assortments of household goods she thought might come in handy.

She never stopped for long. Her next-door neighbour always gave her a lift. As soon as they arrived, he would be turning the car in the drive ready to head back home. If she dallied too long at the front door, the car's horn would sound.

But Thursdays were different. Auntie Mieko looked forward to spending a leisurely time with Hiroko, sipping tea and nibbling snacks together.

They were never short of topics to discuss. Auntie Mieko rarely strayed far beyond the locality where she had been born. She had never been abroad in her life. But it did not stop her taking a lively interest in the world at large.

Her husband had died several years previously. Apart from the tabby cat stretched full length on the mat beside the window, the television was her closest companion.

Auntie Mieko soaked up everything she watched. Global politics, current affairs, all the burning issues of the day. She held firm opinions based on well-grounded common sense. Thursdays were her chance to air them with Hiroko.

For her part, Hiroko greatly looked forward to the weekly

sessions with her aunt. She was always amazed by her elderly relative's grasp of world events. Tea with Auntie Mieko opened her eyes to life beyond her village.

Hiroko could recognise her father in Auntie Mieko. The family resemblance was striking. Not only their physical similarity, but their quick, enquiring minds.

When Auntie Mieko finally exhausted her discussion topics for the week, she sat back and took a long hard look at Hiroko.

"So, tell me, what's happening with you? What about that development?"

Auntie Mieko kept abreast of the latest gossip around the village. She was fully aware the couple were under pressure. Whenever any of the locals brought the subject up, she staunchly defended Sean and Hiroko's stance.

Hiroko stared down at her hands. She did not know how Auntie Mieko would respond to the news.

"Since I last saw you, we've come to a decision. We're going to sell the property after all."

The previous week when Hiroko had arrived home from visiting Auntie Mieko, Sean had been waiting for her in the house. She had been surprised.

Normally she would have expected him to be working outside. It was a busy time of year and Sean was never one for sitting around.

He clearly had something on his mind. He had waited until she had caught her breath after her bike ride. Then he poured her a cup of tea and invited her to sit beside him at the table.

Sean never beat about the bush.

"I've been thinking it over. You're right, Hiroko. If we sell up, we can use the money to buy somewhere else. A long way away."

She had started to argue but he was insistent. She was afraid she had pressurised him into giving in. That it was not what he really wanted.

Eventually, after several more cups of tea, they had agreed. But they decided they would wait a while before contacting the developers, just to be sure they did not have any second thoughts.

As Auntie Mieko listened, she attacked a dirty smudge on the table top with a damp cloth.

"Is that right? Sean-san has changed his mind, then? He was dead set against selling up before, wasn't he?"

"Yes. At first, I was worried he was just doing it to make me happy. I made such a fuss earlier. But he was very definite. He said it was what he wanted too."

Auntie Mieko put down the damp cloth and turned to look at Hiroko.

"But what about you? Are you sure it's what you want?"

Hiroko shrugged.

"I'm just fed up. Everyone wants us to sell. I've had enough. At the end of the day, it's just a bit of land."

Hiroko had never told Auntie Mieko about the threats they had received, or any of the other unpleasantness. She had not wanted to upset her elderly relative.

Auntie Mieko had never been one for giving in. Quite the opposite. She was well known in the community for expressing strong opinions and sticking to them. She invariably turned out to be in the right.

"Hiroko-chan, nobody should be able to push you around.

You must do what you think is best for you two."

"I know. Sometimes I wish Dad hadn't left me the property. Maybe we should never have come back."

Auntie Mieko looked puzzled.

"But he specifically wanted you to have it."

"Really? I could never figure it out. Sometimes I wondered if it was his way of forcing me to come home."

Auntie Mieko frowned.

"Hiroko-chan. I think you've misunderstood his motives."

"What do you mean?"

"The land meant such a lot to your father. He always talked about it. Its historical significance. Its importance to the family. Whenever he came to visit from Tokyo, we always popped over together to have a look at the old place. Don't you remember?"

"I remember."

Hiroko pictured her father and Auntie Mieko wandering around the property. She and her sister, still children then, tagged along behind.

Then they would all sit together in front of the house, chatting and laughing. The adults delighted in recounting stories of times past. Hiroko always thought her father was at his happiest at those moments.

Auntie Mieko folded the cloth and placed it on the edge of the table. She reached across and patted Hiroko's hand.

"Not long before your father fell ill, he came to see me. He sat just where you are now. He wanted to discuss his plans for the old place. He must have known he was dying."

"You talked about the property?"

"Yes. He told me he had decided to bequeath you the land outright. He thought you would look after it properly. He wasn't sure your sister Akemi had the same respect for our family traditions and history."

"I never knew that."

Auntie Mieko leaned over and refilled Hiroko's cup.

"Think carefully my child. Don't let anyone push you about. It's your land. Your heritage."

40

Peters was late arriving back from teaching his evening class. He was glad to be home. He was looking forward to a bite to eat and an early night.

Hiroko was kneeling at the table in the living room. In front of her was the large wooden box where they kept their vegetable seeds. She was going through the packets, making notes on a pad of paper next to her.

Peters sat down opposite without interrupting. He watched her as she scribbled in her neat handwriting, forming the intricate characters with a flurry of tiny strokes.

Normally it was a task they did together. Working out what seeds they needed to buy for the growing season. As they made their list, he always found himself picturing the seedlings germinate and grow into strong, healthy plants.

After their decision to sell the property, the seed box had stayed on the shelf. Suddenly, it was no longer relevant.

Like almost everything else. Peters found it hard to come to terms with what was happening.

He was a creature of habit. Up early at first light, a cold shower to sluice away the humidity of the night, then out to do an hour's work before breakfast.

After they had reached the decision to sell, he had stuck to his routine. It was all he knew.

Then, one morning, as he sank his hoe into the rich soil, he had suddenly stopped. Wiping the tool clean, he had turned back to the house.

He had put the hoe back in its place on the tool rack and sat on an upturned crate, staring out of the window.

He felt like he was in limbo. It was as if the stitching of his life was slowly unravelling.

But a decision was a decision. Peters would not go back on it.

Since then, he had tried to adjust, to look ahead at the next phase of their life together.

Seeing Hiroko working her way through the seed box made no sense.

"What are you doing?"

She looked up and smiled.

"Seeing what we need for the planting season."

Peters frowned. Trying to fathom what she meant.

"The planting season? Sorry, I don't get you."

Hiroko picked up a packet of *gobo* seeds. Holding it to her ear, she gave the contents a shake.

"The planting season, Sean. You see, I've come to a decision. We're not selling up after all."

Peters sat back.

"But I thought we agreed to move on."

"I know we did."

"So, what's changed all of a sudden?"

"It's simple really. I now realise this is where I belong."

Peters shook his head. Hiroko always had the ability to

surprise him.

Hiroko put the packet of seeds down and smiled at Sean. Then she explained what Auntie Mieko had told her.

About the importance her father attached to the land. About how he had entrusted it to her safekeeping.

She had thought long and hard about it over the previous days. Finally, she had reached her decision.

"Don't you see, Sean? We can't just let it go now. Dad gave it to me to look after. I am responsible."

"Are you certain? Quite certain?"

Hiroko smiled at Peters. In answer she picked up another packet of seeds and gave it a shake.

"What about the neighbours? All the unpleasantness?"

"You'll keep us safe, Sean. With you here, what could I possibly fear?"

Peters nodded slowly.

"OK."

With that he got up and went to the front door. Pulling on his boots, he picked up his hoe and headed for the vegetable garden.

Hiroko stood and watched him from the window. In no time, he was hard at work, the hoe rising and falling with its usual steady rhythm.

After a while, she heard him start to whistle. She recognised it immediately. A sea shanty from back home.

She shut the window, a contented smile playing across her fine features.

She always knew when he was happy.

41

"Do you mind driving, Hayashi?"

Ms Sekikawa had requested a small unmarked police car. She did not want to draw attention.

They were in the car pool below police headquarters. The duty officer in the booth handed over the keys.

Hayashi grunted as he wedged himself into the confined driver's seat.

"Comfortable?"

"So so."

They set off up the ramp, out of the dark basement into the dazzling morning sunshine.

They were waved out into the traffic by the guard in front of the building who saluted as they passed. Hayashi skirted the Imperial Palace and then swung south towards Nihonbashi.

Ms Sekikawa sat back. She was looking forward to another chance to chat with Hayashi.

He was a model police officer. Quick on the uptake, incisive, industrious. Everything she could hope for.

But even after these weeks working together, she still had no idea what made him tick. Never shy, she jumped straight in.

"So, tell me Hayashi-san, any brothers or sisters?"

Hayashi was concentrating on the traffic. Queues of taxis

congregated outside Nihonbashi's office blocks waiting for fares. There was not much room to manoeuvre.

Nobody gave way for an unmarked police car with its plain-clothes occupants. Eventually the lights changed up ahead and the road cleared.

"Nope, it's just me."

"And you still live at home?"

"Yes. That's right."

"With your mother?"

"Yes. Just the two of us."

"She must appreciate your being there to look after her."

"Yes, I guess so. It works both ways, of course. She makes a fuss of me."

Ms Sekikawa glanced down at the slow-moving Sumida River as they crossed Eitai Bridge. Ahead lay the reclaimed expanse of Shitamachi.

She thought about her own upbringing in the United States, and then later in Osaka.

"I'm an only child myself. Never easy. Too much focus on you. Too many expectations."

Hayashi nodded, muttering as the car in front swerved erratically.

Ms Sekikawa could see Hayashi was uncomfortable discussing his home life. Fair enough, she thought. She had no business poking her nose in. She decided to switch to work-related topics.

They were headed for Kiba, once a thriving centre of the timber trade. Most of the old lumber firms had made way for housing developments, but a few hung on. Hardwood logs still bobbed about in the network of narrow waterways.

After weaving through the streets, Hayashi pulled up at their destination. An ordinary-looking building in an unremarkable housing estate. No signs on the exterior indicated its function.

The Tokyo Women's Consulting Centre was a shelter for victims of domestic violence and trafficking. It kept a low profile. Its location was never publicised.

The centre's female head met them and showed them into her spartan office.

"I understand you'd like to see Ligaya Santos?"

"Yes, please."

"Santos-san has been settling in well after a period of adjustment."

"That's excellent. Do you know how long she will be here?"

The centre's head straightened some papers on her desk.

"That depends on the authorities reviewing her case. It may be some weeks, even months. It's never a speedy process."

"Her child is in hospital back in the Philippines."

"Yes, so I understand."

"Isn't it possible to expedite matters, given the circumstances?"

"I'm afraid that's beyond my jurisdiction. It's up to others to decide."

Ms Sekikawa saw there was little point in pursuing the matter.

"I see. Well, if we can see Santos-san ..."

"Of course. Please follow me."

The centre's head led the way along the corridor. She knocked on one of the doors.

"Come in."

Ligaya Santos was standing next to her bed. She was wearing a tartan skirt and a white blouse. Her hair was trimmed. Quite a change from the traumatised woman they had met at Shinjuku police station.

The head arranged for two extra chairs to be brought to the room and then left them to it.

"How are you, Ligaya? Are you being treated well?"

"Oh, yes. The people here are very kind."

Ms Sekikawa looked around the room. Beside the small bed was a simple table with a light on it. Beside the light, a photograph in a frame.

Throughout her ordeal, Ligaya had managed to safeguard a precious family snapshot. It was creased and faded from constant handling.

It showed a family group sitting together on a beach. Ligaya Santos was in the centre. The adults were all laughing at a child in the foreground pulling faces at the camera.

Ligaya Santos sat on the bed. Then she leaned across and whispered to Ms Sekikawa.

"When can I go home? I need to see my son. You said you would help me."

42

Hiroko enjoyed her trips to the supermarket. Every other Friday, she drove to the store on the outskirts of the city to stock up on essentials.

She never bought much but she enjoyed her time browsing and simply being around other people. She even found herself humming along to the repetitive loudspeaker jingles.

Since taking the decision not to sell, all her anxiety had disappeared at a stroke. The smile had returned to her face.

Peters, while still vigilant, found himself relaxing his guard. There were no further unpleasant incidences. No communication from the developers. The neighbours kept their distance.

Everything, it seemed, was back to normal. The couple set to their regular tasks with enthusiasm, their eyes fixed on the future.

To celebrate, Hiroko and Sean had spent a day trekking. On the way up the steep mountain path, they had paused to take a break at a small clearing between the trees. They always thought of the concealed glade as their own special place.

The weather was perfect. The surrounding peaks looked close enough to reach out and touch, every detail visible to the naked eye.

The couple sat side-by-side on two smooth boulders. The rocks seemed deliberately aligned as if by some unseen hand.

They breathed deeply, soaking up the atmosphere. All around them small birds darted in and out of the canopy, their strident calls piercing the thin air. High above them, buzzards circled on the up-draughts.

"This place means so much to me, Hiroko. I can't explain the feeling. It's like I belong here. As if it's always been a part of me."

Hiroko had turned to look at Sean. In all the years they had been together, she had rarely seen him so emotional. Embarrassed, he had laughed, wiping his sleeve across his eyes.

"Sorry about that. I don't know what came over me. Getting a bit weepy in my old age."

She knew. She understood. She felt it too.

It was their land. They were the custodians. When they grew too old to cope, she felt sure someone else would step in to take their place.

She had reached over and laid her hand on Sean's arm. He had covered it with his. They had sat still without speaking before resuming their climb.

"Yes, everything's back the way it was," thought Hiroko. "Thank goodness. It's time to put all that unpleasantness behind us."

As she pushed her trolley along the supermarket aisle, she ran her eye along the shelves. Occasionally she would pick out an item and squint at the label. Invariably she would return it before continuing on her way.

Stretching along one wing of the supermarket was the seafood counter. The fish looked so fresh they could have been caught just moments before.

Dominating the display were the packs of raw tuna. Each contained bright red slices of fish topped with colourful garnish.

Sean loved *sashimi*. It was always a special treat when they could afford it.

She reached over and chose one of the smaller packets. Perfect for the two of them. She imagined the look on Sean's face when she showed him the shopping.

She understood how the unpleasant episode had taken its toll on Sean too. He was usually so calm, balanced. He rarely showed his feelings.

But she recognised the signs when all was not well.

She remembered how, when they first met, he would cry out in his sleep. He would only settle again as she cradled him in her arms.

They never discussed the past, except that one occasion when he opened up about his childhood. She understood Sean had put all that behind him. He was only interested in their future together.

He said he loved her. Would always love her.

Marriage was never considered. She accepted the situation.

It was enough to be with him. More than enough.

It had been a testing period but they had managed to pull through unscathed. Thank goodness for Auntie Mieko. Hiroko pictured her elderly relative with her sleeves pulled up, furiously wiping the table.

Hiroko could not help laughing out loud. Some of the shoppers nearby gave her a surprised look.

She dawdled around the shop, pausing to try some free

samples on offer. The salesladies looked at her askance, knowing a cheapskate when they saw one.

She did not care. She never expected to see anyone she knew at the huge supermarket. It was a forty-minute drive from home.

She enjoyed the feeling of anonymity. Of being alone in a crowd. It gave her a sense of freedom.

She chose the shortest queue at the cashiers. When it was her turn, her eyes never left the till display, checking the totals, making sure she had all the discounts she was due.

Before she bagged up her purchases, she ran her eye over the receipt. Any error would find her rushing over to the customer service counter to demand a refund.

Today everything tallied correctly. She packed the *sashimi* into the plastic carrier bag last to make sure it was not squashed on the journey home.

Then she pushed her trolley towards the exit. A man reading a newspaper was leaning against the wall. He glanced up as she passed.

She did not much like the look of him. Wispy beard, hard eyes.

He was probably waiting for his wife to finish her shopping. Hiroko did not give him a second thought as she pushed her trolley out into the fresh air.

The car park was quite large. It took Hiroko a second or two to remember where she had parked the car. Finally, she spotted it and threaded her way between the lines of vehicles.

Inside the supermarket the man folded his newspaper and put it under his arm. He made his way towards the exit.

He was not waiting for his wife after all.

Hiroko loaded her shopping and climbed aboard. For a second, she sat and gathered herself before starting the engine.

Gazing through the windscreen, she could make out the faint trace of the mountain peaks in the distance. Their home.

She had been away too long. As always, she looked forward to getting back.

43

The traffic lights turned green.

Hiroko pressed the accelerator and the small car spluttered before responding. It needed a long-overdue service.

She glanced in the mirror at the line of cars behind her. Back at the village, no one was in a hurry. Locals even pulled up for a chat, blocking the road, when they met acquaintances coming from the other direction.

Townspeople were so much more impatient. After all, what did a few minutes matter either way?

She was not a particular confident driver. She craned over the steering wheel, giving the road her full attention.

When she joined the main highway, the cars behind seized the opportunity to overtake. As they rushed past, Hiroko avoided making eye-contact.

She felt at her most nervous trapped in the fast-moving traffic. She kept an anxious lookout for the junction where she would turn off.

She breathed a sigh of relief when it came into view. Indicating early, she took the slip road and started the long climb up into the hills.

She only passed one car coming in the opposite direction, an elderly couple. They were going even more slowly than she was.

The old gentleman peered at the road, his hands clutching the steering wheel. Beside him, an old lady was peeling a *mikan* orange.

Hiroko passed through a succession of remote villages. Old people were hard at work in the fields. The women bent low with hand hoes while the men operated the rotavators. Everyone wore identical outfits, bought from the same farm shop.

Hiroko saw few young people. In common with the rest of Japan, the younger generation gravitated to the cities, leaving the old ones to muddle along.

Hiroko had been the same. In search of adventure. It had taken her all the way to England.

Strange how life had its twists. Now she was following in the footsteps of her forebears, working the same soil, eking out a living.

At the appointed days of the year, she tended the graves of her ancestors in the village cemetery. For all her independence of spirit, she was a stickler for Japanese traditions. She considered it important to pay her respects.

She doubted anyone would do the same for her. There would be no one to clean her tomb, light incense sticks and leave cut flowers in a vase. She would soon be forgotten.

Well, she thought, living is what matters. Make the most of it while we are here.

The mountainous road ahead climbed through long tunnels and precipitous bridges spanning rivers hundreds of feet below. At one time, it had been the main link between Yamashiro and its sister city to the north.

That was before the construction of the four-lane by-pass on the flatlands below. Now the route through the mountains was largely redundant. Only local traffic ever used it.

Hiroko steeled herself as she negotiated the tunnels and bridges. It would not do to make a mistake on these remote stretches. If anything went wrong, it would take a long time for help to arrive.

Eventually she reached the highest bridge on her route home. As she approached it, she glanced up at the towers bearing the high-tension cables to support the span. They seemed to rise up to heaven.

Below the bridge was a deep gorge. Sometimes when she crossed in the early morning mist, she had the sensation she was flying.

She was halfway over the bridge when she spotted a small blue car parked on the far side. It was tucked into a narrow space bordering some woods.

Hiroko thought it was an odd place to park up, in the middle of nowhere. Then, before she knew it, a young woman dashed out into the middle of the road.

She stood right in front of Hiroko's car. Hiroko had no option but slam on the brakes. The young woman was shouting, clearly in a state of panic.

She had something in her arms. A bundle. A child, by the way she was cradling it.

Hiroko first instinct was not to get involved. She needed to get home. This was no business of hers.

But she immediately banished the unworthy thought. Naturally she should stop and see what the matter was.

There was nowhere to pull in except a tight space directly behind the small car in the layby. As she manoeuvred the car, she considered what the problem might be.

Perhaps the woman had run out of petrol? It had happened to her once.

Or was it something more serious? A medical emergency? Perhaps the child was ill?

Hiroko let down the window. The woman approached, holding the baby close to her chest. It was wrapped in a white blanket, obscuring its face.

"Please can you help me?"

Hiroko could sense the woman's desperation.

"What's the matter?"

"It's my baby. He's terribly ill. He needs to go to hospital. My mobile phone battery has run out. Can you help me and ring for an ambulance?"

"Of course. Just a second."

Hiroko reached for her bag. She always carried their mobile phone with her when she took the car.

Sean insisted. After all, anything could happen on those remote roads with hardly any traffic.

Locating her phone, she opened the car door and started to get out. Suddenly, she was face-to-face with the man she had seen loitering at the supermarket.

Her defence mechanism kicked in. She tried to get back into the car but he was too quick for her, wrenching the door wide open. Then a second man appeared.

In seconds, she was overpowered. The two men were strong and knew their business. She tried to kick out but was lifted clean off the ground.

Between them, they carried her back onto the bridge.

"Help! Help me!"

Hiroko threw her head back, twisting her face towards the woman with the child. As she did so, she saw the woman chucked the bundle in the white blanket onto the back seat of her car.

Hiroko re-doubled her efforts to escape. She tried to scream but panic constricted her voice. Her cries emerged as only strangled yelps.

In no time, the men reached the centre of the bridge.

Suddenly Hiroko understood what was going to happen. Her body froze in their arms.

The men did not hesitate for a second. No time for last words.

In unison, they heaved her up and over the railing. She tried to grab on, but her strength failed her.

For a moment she seemed to float. Then gravity took over and she plummeted towards the riverbed far below.

As she fell, Hiroko saw the bridge disappearing above her. She was sufficiently aware to brace herself for the impact.

Her mind resolved into a single image – Sean. She reached out to him with her mind.

The impact came with shattering force. The riverbed was strewn with massive boulders interspersed with rusting debris - discarded refrigerators, wrecked cars, smashed TV sets.

Hiroko crashed amongst the detritus. Her life leaked out in the fast-flowing current.

The men waited only long enough to see her land. Her death

was a certainty.

They sprinted back across the bridge. The blue car's engine was already running with the woman waiting behind the wheel.

Back at the house, Peters had just finished preparing lunch. He had been expecting Hiroko back at any moment and had rushed to have everything ready in time.

He smiled as he thought of her at the supermarket, wheeling her trolley up and down the aisles. He knew how much she looked forward to it.

The trip to the shops will do her good, he thought.

44

Peters sat waiting in the front room.

The rice was keeping warm. The spinach was cut and scattered with bonito flakes. The pickles were laid out on the table in their jars.

It had all been ready for well over an hour.

Hiroko never specified the time she would be home. They preferred it that way. They did not tie themselves down to schedules.

But Peters was uneasy. As the minutes ticked by on the cracked alarm clock on top of the fridge, the feeling intensified.

It was already three o'clock. Even allowing for some last-minute change of plan, he would have expected her home by now.

Perhaps there was a traffic hold-up? Landslides in the mountains were common enough. Especially during the rainy season. If the road was blocked, it would entail a sizable detour for Hiroko to find her way home.

Peters was always worried about Hiroko's driving. She seemed slow to react, unaware of what was happening up ahead. Sitting in the passenger seat, he often found himself holding his breath.

He prayed she had not had an accident.

No, there was bound to be a good explanation. He just needed to sit tight and wait.

He picked up his favourite magazine from the shelf. It dealt with a range of topical environmental issues, everything from anti-whaling exposés to advice on how to build an organic compost heap.

Peters read it from cover to cover. It spoke of subjects close to his heart.

This month's issue had only just dropped through the letterbox. He and Hiroko always pored over it together, savouring one article at a time.

Try as he might, he could not concentrate. The Japanese characters swam in front of his eyes.

After half an hour, he gave up. He returned the magazine to the shelf.

He could not wait any longer.

He picked up the phone to check the connection yet again. As before, the dialling tone was as normal.

He had repeatedly tried to ring their mobile. On each occasion, a woman's recorded voice told him the phone was switched off and to try again later.

He re-dialled again, just in case. The same result.

He stood in the centre of the kitchen, arms folded, thinking. Once he had reached a decision about what to do, he acted swiftly.

He covered the food and put it away in the fridge. He did not know how long he would be.

Finding a pencil, he scribbled a brief note. He left it on the table where Hiroko would be bound to see it. Then he walked out of the house, closing the front door behind him.

He went over to the barn and dug out his old bicycle. He rarely used it. He pumped up the tyres and sat astride. It groaned under his weight.

He cut a comical figure as he pedalled through the village. His judo top flapping open in the wind, his ponytail streaming behind him.

But there was nothing comical about his expression. The bike responded to the relentless tempo of his legs. In no time he had left the village far behind him.

His pace did not slacken. This was the same road Hiroko would have taken to drive to the city. The only route through the mountains.

He steeled himself for the long ride ahead of him. Yamashiro was 45 minutes away by car, two and a half hours by bike.

He was spared most of the journey.

After a couple of miles, he reached the stretch of road where the tunnels and bridges began. He pedalled hard through the first tunnel and across the bridge beyond. He kept his eyes firmly on the road in front of him.

After the third tunnel he jammed on the brakes. Their car was parked in the layby beside the bridge. With a sigh of relief, he freewheeled towards it.

It must have broken down. He kicked himself. He should have had it serviced sooner.

Hiroko must have been very upset. Stranded alone in the middle of nowhere.

When he reached the car, he tried the door. To his surprise he found it was open.

He leaned his bike against a tree and climbed into the driver's seat. The key was still in the ignition.

On the passenger seat was her bag. He opened it. Everything was there as he would expect: her purse, her diary, their mobile phone.

He took out the phone and tested it. It was switched off.

He stared at all the items, trying to make sense of them. Then he slowly leaned forwards and turned the ignition key.

The engine fired first time. His eyes strayed to the instrument panel. Plenty of petrol. No warning lights.

He switched off the engine and got out. He checked the tyres. All fine.

Then he opened the boot. Inside was a carrier bag of shopping. On the top lay the small packet of *sashimi*. He closed the boot.

He stood up and looked around. The brush on both sides of the road was thick and impassable.

If she had been walking home along the road, he would have met her on the way. She would have no reason to walk in the other direction.

But why would she abandon the car unlocked, her bag on the seat and the key in the ignition? Why had she not rung him?

None of it made sense. Where on earth could she be?

Slowly he turned and stared at the bridge.

Thoughts started to invade in his mind. Thoughts he tried hard to banish.

He put his hand on the roof of the car to steady himself. Then he found himself striding onto the bridge.

He stopped near the centre of the span and peered down into the void.

Far below, wedged between the rocks on the river bed, he could just make out a crumpled figure.

Hiroko.

45

"You say she's dead?"

"Yes. Her husband is here with us."

The ambulance service had been first to arrive responding to Peters' emergency call. They had contacted the police station from the scene.

"Understood. A forensic team is on its way."

For a city the size of Yamashiro, violent deaths were a rarity. Occasional traffic accidents, the odd suicide, some climbing fatalities in the mountains. All well below the national average.

The ambulance team had scrambled down the steep incline to the river bank. They carried with them a stretcher and boxes of first-aid equipment.

The foreigner was kneeling at the woman's side. He had stripped off his judo top and covered her body with it. He sat motionless among the grey boulders, his head bent forwards.

The ambulance man in charge ushered Peters to the side. The others set about their preliminary assessment. They spoke in hushed undertones.

The victim's status was in no doubt once they drew back the *judogi*. The eyes were dull. The body crushed.

Peters already knew. He was no stranger to death.

He had searched for the pulse. He had run his fingers over

Hiroko, locating the break in her neck and the fractured limbs.

Finally, he had smoothed the hair away from her face. Mercifully, it had been spared the worst of the impact.

Then he had held her close to his chest. He never stopped whispering to her.

When he heard the ambulance's siren, he had laid Hiroko down. His first instinct was to cover her, protect her dignity.

"Please wait in the ambulance."

Peters turned to the ambulance man and sized him up. He was young but well trained. He was just doing his job. Peters did not resist.

One of the team draped a blanket around his shoulders and shepherded him up the slope. The other two team members waited with the dead woman.

More sirens were converging. Peters watched from the back of the ambulance as two police cars came to a halt on the bridge.

Uniformed officers jumped out and clambered down to join the emergency crew, while a plain-clothes officer approached the ambulance. There was a brief discussion between the officer and the paramedic out of Peters' earshot.

The plain-clothes officer approached Peters. There were no introductions. No words of condolence.

The officer pointed to the second police car.

"Please go with them to the hospital. We shall join you there."

"What about our car?"

"We'll bring it later. Do you have the key, please?"

"It's in the ignition."

Peters stood up and walked towards the waiting police car. Before getting in, he looked back down into the ravine. He wanted to fix the scene in his mind.

The police car turned and set off towards the city. Peters was sandwiched between two officers. No one spoke.

At the hospital, Peters was escorted into A&E. A middle-aged doctor and a nurse attended to him. He was taken to a private room and invited to rest.

The nurse offered him some water and a sedative. He drank the water but refused the medication.

The doctor insisted.

"Please. It will help you sleep. It is important after what has happened."

Peters finally complied.

When the medical staff left the room, he drew the blanket up to his chin. Through the open window, he could overhear people talking.

Everyday conversation. People unaware of what had happened to Hiroko.

His mind started to race. He was searching for answers, reasons.

But the medication clouded his mind. He dropped like a stone into sleep. He did not wake until the following morning.

A lot happened in the interval.

The forensic team at the scene had followed the rule book. Everything was scrupulously recorded. A full and thorough examination took place of the body and the surrounding riverbed. Hiroko was then bagged and transferred to the city morgue for a post-mortem examination.

The car received the same treatment. Afterwards, it was put on a low-loader and taken to the police workshop for analysis.

Two police officers were stationed outside Peters' room. Only the nurse was allowed in at regular intervals to check up on the patient.

At 7:00 the next morning, he started to stir.

The police officer outside the room heard the movements and summoned the doctor.

Peters sat himself upright on the edge of the bed. The sedative had left him confused.

He turned as the doctor came in. After a cursory examination, the doctor stood up and pointed to some clothes on the chair.

"Please put these on. I hope they fit. Your clothes are being cleaned and will be returned to you shortly."

"Thank you."

"If you feel up to it, the police would like to speak with you about yesterday. Only if you feel ready…"

"Of course."

"Well, we'll let you get washed and dressed and the nurse will bring you some breakfast."

With that, the doctor left the room.

46

"You didn't go shopping with her?"

"No. As I said, I was at home. She went alone. As she always did."

The grizzle-haired captain jotted everything in his notebook. He had been in the police force all his working life. He had a reputation among his junior officers as a hard taskmaster.

He preferred it that way. He expected work to be done properly. He made sure his officers knew it.

The interview had already lasted over an hour.

The police incident report identified the fall from the bridge as the probable cause of death. The ambulance crew's findings supported this view. There were no obvious signs of foul play.

The captain had read the report sitting in his office at the police station. He did not take long to reach his own conclusions.

The woman's death had all the hallmarks of a suicide. An open and shut case.

But what would make the woman jump? What was the motive? Was she under some kind of duress?

His train of thought had led inexorably to the foreigner. In his experience, foreigners were trouble. They had no business in Japan, let alone up there in the countryside.

The moment the captain walked into the room Peters was on his guard. As the interview progressed, he became even more wary.

Peters knew the type. Unbending, dominating, bigoted. He had spent his life trying to avoid them.

"Name, please."

The interview started predictably. Details about Hiroko. Details about their life.

The captain asked Peters to describe the events leading up to Hiroko's death. Then he asked him to run through it all again.

"What made you suspect something was wrong?"

"She was very late. I was worried."

"You didn't think she might have gone somewhere else? A spur-of-the-moment decision?"

"Not without phoning to let me know. We always have lunch together at home when she gets back."

"So, you decided to go and search for her. How did you know where to look?"

"I didn't know. I just took the route she always takes into the city. Then I came across the car."

"And what made you look under the bridge?"

"I can't explain. I just had a bad feeling."

"A bad feeling?"

"Yes."

"Could you see the body clearly from the bridge?"

"Yes."

The police captain had already checked with the officers on the scene this was possible.

"And when you went down, she was already dead."

"Yes."

"What did you do?"

"I rang the emergency services."

Throughout the interview, the police officer made notes. Peters watched as the tiny characters filled the page.

Cold facts.

The official did not describe how Peters had held Hiroko in his arms like a broken bird. How cold her cheek felt when he pressed her to him. These details had no place in the captain's notebook.

The captain sat back and studied Peters. He was used to grilling his own countrymen. They were not likely to forget the experience in a hurry.

But this foreigner was different. More resilient. A harder nut to crack.

"Please describe your relationship with Hiroko Iwasaki."

Peters was on his guard. The policeman's tone had changed. Suddenly he sensed he was being treated as a suspect.

"That's none of your business."

The captain leaned forwards. This was more like it. Finally, he was getting under the foreigner's skin.

"It is my business. We're trying to establish why Iwasaki-san jumped from that bridge. Why she parks her car, walks back to the centre of the bridge and throws herself off. What would make her do that?"

Peters knew the police officer was trying to rattle him. He tried to keep his composure.

"I don't know."

"Did you argue?"

"No."

"Did you beat her?"

Peters stared at the captain. He understood the provocation.

"Please can we end this interview now?"

The captain sat back and closed his notebook, snapping the elastic band around it.

"Of course. We'll continue at the station when you've recovered sufficiently."

The captain was satisfied with his progress so far. He would let the man stew.

Then they would have a proper chat.

47

Peters unpacked the shopping bag on the kitchen table.

He had been discharged from the hospital that morning. His car was still impounded so a young police officer had given him a lift home. His bicycle had been loaded into the boot.

He ran his hands over each item. To feel what she had felt.

She should have been there with him. As she always was. Not stretched out on a slab in some police morgue.

He cast his mind back to the interview with the police captain. He had felt the thrust of his questions.

Had Hiroko taken her own life? Was he, Peters, in some way responsible?

He knew he could be stubborn. Very difficult at times. Hiroko had had a lot to put up with, especially recently.

She had borne the brunt of the villagers' opprobrium, not him. She had acted as his shield.

But staying at the farm, refusing to sell, had been her decision. He had been ready to make a clean break. To put it all behind them. But she had insisted.

Afterwards, she had seemed like the old Hiroko again. Ready to tough it out. To face the future with him.

But how could he be so sure? Perhaps he had misread her?

Hiroko could be a conundrum at the best of times. Even after all these years living together, he was still apt to misinterpret what was going on inside her head. He often found himself wide of the mark.

Perhaps another Japanese might have spotted all was not well. That something was simmering beneath the surface.

But not him. His regimented mind could not appreciate these subtle shades. He was not privy to all the nuances of her heart.

Perhaps, deep down, she had been searching in vain to find a way to reconcile these conflicting demands. Had she finally succumbed to the pressure?

Was it some sudden impulse? Crossing the bridge in the car, she glances down. The chasm below draws her. She feels compelled.

He found himself gripping the packet of *sashimi*. The bright red flesh of the tuna had dulled, dried out, become inedible.

He pictured Hiroko buying it. How she would have stood at the fish counter, enjoying the prospect of the treat they would share together.

No, it did not make sense. Suicide? No, he simply did not believe it.

That last morning together, everything had been as usual. Her laughter ringing out in the kitchen at one of his dumb jokes. No sign of anything untoward.

Peters dropped the packet of fish in the waste bin. He set some water to boil on the stove. He knew he should eat but ended up simply making a pot of tea. He had no appetite.

He took his drink through to the other room. He sat cross-legged on the floor, cradling the cup in his hands.

Looking around the room, everything reminded him of her.

Photographs, bits of half-finished knitting, scribbled memos pinned to the cork board.

He reached over and picked up her pullover. Clutching it to his face, he breathed in her scent before it faded for ever.

Turning, he took down a photograph album from the shelf behind. Memories from a trip they had made soon after arriving in Japan. A long weekend at a hot-spring resort.

She was wearing a smart blue jacket. She still kept it in the wardrobe for special occasions. He was in a pair of jeans. They looked so young, smiling at the camera.

He closed the album and laid it on the table.

Earlier that day, he had ridden his bike back to the bridge. He had forced himself to walk to the centre and look down at the riverbed.

He pictured her plummeting onto the rocks below. He imagined the agony of the impact.

He had promised to protect her. He should have been there to stop her, to hold her close.

As he peered down through the guardrail, he thought of her kneeling at their *butsudan* at home with its incense and ringing dish. Her eyelids pressed tight in silent prayer.

He had no religion but he found himself muttering half-remembered phrases. Anything to ease her passing.

Then he had scrambled down the path beside the bridge until he reached the spot where she fell. He could still see the tell-tale signs. Less distinct now, fading as each day passed.

He picked a handful of wild flowers and placed them on the boulders where she had lain. He stayed for an hour before heading home.

The evening stretched ahead of him. He imagined her there with him.

Always busy. Pickling plums, making preserves. He could tell when she was concentrating. She would pucker her lips and start to whistle.

At first, he thought it was a discordant Japanese melody. Later he realised she was simply out of tune.

He pulled her leg but it never stopped her. Only death achieved that.

His mind was dragged back to the time he himself was in free fall. After the Falklands.

He had been deployed to South Armagh, Northern Ireland. He remembered the patrols through the danger zones. Constantly fearing the sniper's bullet.

The cold nights out on the moorland running down to the border with the Irish Republic. Lying in ditches, setting up road blocks, checking traffic movements.

Always exposed. Always assuming you were trapped in a rifle's crosshairs.

It gnawed away at you. The civilians' unconcealed hatred. The children hurling stones at the armoured vehicles.

Like drops of water, it eroded your resolve. Despite all his training, he knew he was burning out.

Only his comrades stood between him and the abyss. Men who always had his back.

Peters got up and reached for the battered address book by the phone. The entries were mostly in Hiroko's neat hand. There were a few he had pencilled in himself.

One was a Tokyo number. Picking up the receiver, he rang

and waited.

48

Yamaguchi glanced at his watch.

"Could be worse," he thought.

He was still almost as nifty over the five kilometres as in the old days. He towelled his head as he rummaged for his door keys.

His Sunday morning run was part and parcel of his weekend routine. Out at seven o'clock on the dot and then back for a light breakfast.

His route never changed. Along the river embankment to the next bridge upstream and then back on the other side. The shouts ringing out from the baseball teams practising on the pitches along the river bank spurred him on.

It was an excellent way to unwind after a week's work.

Inside the house, he kicked off his shoes and went to the fridge to pour himself a glass of orange juice. He took it through to his seat on the balcony.

Over the years, his shelves of bonsai had multiplied. His hobby had grown into an obsession.

He could hardly keep up with all the trimming and snipping. Then there was the re-potting, fertilising and watering.

They were demanding plants. On the balcony there was only just room for his small plastic chair. But he would never consider parting with any of his charges.

What with tending his bonsai, maintaining his two Japanese swords in pristine condition, cleaning the house and doing his laundry, his weekends were pretty much accounted for.

Normally he was able to switch off while performing these domestic chores. A welcome break from poring over stodgy reports.

But that weekend was different. Ms Sekikawa was on his mind.

After her visit to the Women's Consulting Centre, she had pinned him down in his office. As usual, there was no preamble. She had come straight to the point.

"Ligaya Santos has to go home. Without delay."

He liked to think the two of them always got on well. They had worked together in some very dicey situations where he had depended on her sound judgement and remarkable pluck.

They could be frank with each other. An unusual situation at police headquarters where tight-lipped formality was the norm.

But open discussion could have its downside.

He had sat back in his desk.

"Sorry?"

Ms Sekikawa expected people to be quicker on the uptake. Especially when time was of the issue.

"Ligaya Santos. The Filipina. The case Hayashi and I have been assisting with."

She raised her eyebrows at Yamaguchi. He still looked blank.

"The trafficked woman. The one who suddenly appeared at

the Shinjuku police box?"

Yamaguchi held up his hands in surrender.

"Ah yes."

"Anyway, we need to get her home."

"To the Philippines?"

Ms Sekikawa stared at Yamaguchi in exasperation.

"Yes. The Philippines."

"Why the urgency?"

"Her son is gravely ill. That's why she escaped from the brothel. She's desperate to get home and look after him."

Yamaguchi frowned.

"It's not that easy. There are legal procedures to go through first."

"Procedures?"

Ms Sekikawa glared at Yamaguchi as if he suddenly embodied those procedures.

"Legal processes as part of her repatriation."

"Can't we speed them up? After all the woman's a victim, not a criminal."

"I understand, but the police authorities have to do everything by the book."

"Well, can't we at least push things along?"

"I'll see what I can do."

"Thank you."

After Ms Sekikawa left the office, Yamaguchi had difficulty

concentrating on his reading. Ms Sekikawa had a habit of getting under his skin.

Eventually he picked up the phone. Every call he made was met with the same response.

It was just as he predicted. Procedures had to be followed. No special treatment for individual cases.

No amount of pleading for Ligaya Santos made a scrap of difference. Yamaguchi pushed it as far as he could before his colleagues started questioning his particular interest.

At that point, he had to admit defeat. He had done everything he could.

Ms Sekikawa did not see it that way when he updated her later. When she suggested other possible avenues to pursue, Yamaguchi had been unusually abrupt.

"I'm sorry but that's that. I have done as much as I can. Ms Santos will need to wait until all the necessary steps have been completed. Thank you."

Summarily dismissed, Ms Sekikawa had stomped out of his office.

The situation continued to play on Yamaguchi's mind. He was annoyed with himself. Once again, he had allowed his personal feelings to get the better of him, interfering with the smooth running of the department.

His tiny pruning scissors lopped off a side-shoot from one of his favourite bonsai. He looked at the plant in dismay as he realised his error.

Apologising to the plant, he put the scissors back in their box and retreated inside the flat.

49

The car drew up outside the house.

The engine revved twice before the ignition was cut. The car door opened and then slammed shut.

"Noisy bastard," Peters thought as he got to his feet.

He picked his way through the boots lying at the entrance to slide open the front door. His visitor was already standing outside, a hold-all slung across his shoulder.

"George."

"Sean."

George Trevillion clasped Peters' outstretched hand. After an awkward second, the two former Royal Marines hugged each other.

"Come on in."

Once inside the house, George Trevillion started to take his bearings. He glanced around the main room, noticing the dirty crockery on the table and the unmade futon in the corner.

"Tea?"

"Sure. Thanks."

Peters went out to the small kitchen to put the kettle on. Trevillion found a place to sit down on the tatami floor.

A photo album was on the table. It was open at some snaps of the couple's leaving drinks in London before they moved to Japan.

Trevillion remembered. It was a simple affair. Just beer and sandwiches in a pub in Holborn. A small group of well-wishers in attendance.

Trevillion had made a stumbling toast. Speeches were not his forte. At the end, he had raised his glass to Peters.

"Here's to the best bloke I know."

It was a while since they had seen each other. At one time, they were inseparable.

Peters returned with the Japanese tea on a wooden tray. He knelt down and poured, taking care not to spill any.

Trevillion took a long sip. It was bitter but at least it was hot. He would have preferred an English cuppa.

The long drive up from Tokyo had been a slog. First the packed expressway, then the twisting mountain roads.

It was the first time he had visited Peters' house. It was the first time he had been invited.

Trevillion had moved to Tokyo some years earlier. After the army, he had landed a well-paid job with an international communications company.

He always had a technical bent and was a quick learner. He had progressed quickly and when the chance had come to transfer to the Tokyo branch, he had jumped at it. After all, his best mate Sean Peters was in Japan.

Trevillion was put in charge of one of the specialised technical teams. He lived in a spacious expatriate flat in Azabu in the centre of the city. It could have comfortably housed three Japanese families.

Not long after arriving, Trevillion got in touch with Peters and invited him up to Tokyo. Initially Peters had made excuses but eventually Trevillion had managed to persuade him.

The visit had not been easy. Trevillion could see his friend was ill at ease.

Peters viewed Tokyo life with mistrust. The city's noise and bustle were a world away from his serene mountain retreat.

Trevillion had taken Peters to some bars to introduce him to his new circle of expatriate friends. He was proud of his former comrade. He had told them all about him.

But faced with high-flying bankers and self-satisfied company executives, Peters clammed up. Trevillion's new friends found him hard going.

Trevillion tried to bridge the gap, reminiscing about the old days. Initially the company showed polite interest in their military exploits before moving onto other topics.

Peters found himself staring at his drink. He was thinking about home, wondering what Hiroko was doing.

The two men were both secretly relieved when Peters boarded the Tohoku Shinkansen on the Monday morning.

It signalled a break with the past. They realised they lived in different worlds. Over the intervening years, they had gradually lost touch.

But when trouble came knocking, your old comrades-in-arms were the first people you turned to.

Trevillion waited. Peters would tell him in his own time, when he was ready.

All Trevillion knew was that Hiroko was dead. Peters had

only given him the barest details over the phone.

But that was enough. Trevillion had immediately cancelled his weekend plans and jumped into his car.

After tea, Peters leaned back against a cupboard and exhaled. He was ready now.

Trevillion was a good listener. He did not interrupt.

"It doesn't make sense, George. I know we disagreed over the land sale initially. But that was in the past. Hiroko had made up her mind to stay. Everything was back to normal. For God's sake, the day she died, she was even bringing home *sashimi* for us, a treat. I just can't understand it."

Trevillion agreed. He remembered Hiroko clearly. She was no quitter.

When they were in London, Peters had told him about Hiroko's decision to go against the wishes of her father. Trevillion understood what that entailed, the break with the family, the sacrifices she had made.

He had seen the two of them together. The chemistry was obvious. A solid bond not easy to break.

Trevillion shifted his weight on the tatami. He still found sitting on the floor a trial.

"And there's no other explanation?"

Peters frowned.

"What do you mean?"

"Well, I wondered if the police had offered any alternatives to suicide."

Peters looked straight at his friend.

"I don't get you."

"Well, I don't know, perhaps it was some kind of accident?"

"Accident? She fell from the centre of the bridge. The protective railing was almost two metres high. How could it be an accident?"

"OK. Not an accident then."

Peters continued staring at his friend.

Trevillion busied himself opening his hold-all. After rummaging through his overnight things, he pulled out a bottle of Scotch whisky.

"For old time's sake."

50

Charles Fancourt leaned against the wall, dripping sweat.

He was an average squash player, making up for his lack of talent with a refusal to succumb. In recent years, carrying more weight, he was slower around the court, tiring more quickly.

His opponent, an Australian, was in a different league. Slim, athletic, a shot maker.

They rarely played together. It was not really worth his opponent's while.

"Had enough?"

Fancourt did not answer. He brushed past the Australian and left the court, not bothering to shake hands.

Outside two players were warming up. They raised their eyebrows at the obvious mismatch.

"Good game?"

Fancourt ignored them.

They did not need to ask who had won. Fancourt collapsed on a chair outside the court, while the Australian looked as if he had hardly broken sweat.

Winning was the name of the game for members of Tokyo's exclusive American Club. Its roster boasted the cream of the expatriate community. A short jog up the hill from Tokyo Tower, it provided the elite with a sanctuary from the city's relentless hubbub.

The two men headed for the locker room. They showered and changed without exchanging a word.

The conversation only started later in the club's first-floor Café Med. Fancourt commandeered some seats in a quiet corner of the room, out of earshot of the other customers.

Here, the tables were turned. Fancourt was now the one calling the shots.

The Australian was one of Fancourt's cabal of investors. When the time came, he executed Fancourt's orders to the letter, without question.

Not that he would consider raising any objections. Fancourt, to his knowledge, had never put a foot wrong.

He had not met the other members of the group and had no wish to. The less he knew, the better.

He sat memorising Fancourt's instructions as he sipped his orange juice. At Fancourt's insistence, he then repeated back the details. Nothing was ever committed to paper.

At the end, he stood to leave. Fancourt dismissed him with a brusque handshake.

Losing at squash still rankled. He was a sour loser.

There was a lot at stake. As Fancourt stirred his coffee, he glanced out of the first-floor window.

He did not like what he saw. He did not like anything about Japan. The people, their secrecy, their irritating customs.

He longed to be back in Hong Kong.

He had made a killing there. Where regulations were more blurred, he had been able to sail close to the wind. Over time, he had established a reputation as a smart operator.

But it was not just the money. In Hong Kong, everything was possible. There were no holds barred.

He could dive into its human mire and then resurface spotless. And no one was any the wiser.

Until it all changed.

He remembered the evening meeting at the Happy Valley racetrack. A Chinese broker had arranged it. He was told it would be to his advantage.

Fancourt had found his way to the private box high up in the stands. He was shown in by two guards. An elderly Chinese and a plump younger woman were waiting for him.

The Chinese couple did not follow the races. They sat with their backs to the track.

They took it in turns to question Fancourt. The woman demonstrated considerable knowledge of the financial markets.

Fancourt started to feel uncomfortable.

"Excuse me, but what exactly is going on here? What are you after?"

The elderly Chinese exchanged a look with his younger companion.

"Mr Fancourt. We represent certain interests in Hong Kong and abroad. We have many resources at our disposal. We are looking for someone of the right calibre, a broad-minded person to help us manage these resources. We think it may be of interest to you."

Fancourt smelled a rat. He had been in Hong Kong too long not to understand who he was dealing with. He knew he had to proceed with extreme caution.

"I'm not sure I have the skills for what you have in mind."

"On the contrary, Mr Fancourt. You have exactly the right knowledge and experience."

The plump woman smiled at him in encouragement.

"Yes, we are extremely impressed."

Fancourt found himself sweating despite the air conditioning.

"No, really. I think I must be going. I'm not your man. There must be some mistake."

"No, no mistake at all, Mr Fancourt."

The plump woman reached in her bag and produced an envelope of photographs. She laid them out on the table as if she was about to play a game of Pelmanism. She smiled at Fancourt.

"You see, Mr Fancourt? No mistake at all."

Fancourt let out a gasp. He then sat with his head in his hands.

Displayed on the table in front of him was his deepest secret. The one that should never see the light of day.

At the end of the race meeting, losing race slips rained down like moths in the night sky from the tiers above.

After that he was their man. They ran him.

Success was a sure thing. Their inside knowledge and his financial know-how formed an unbeatable combination.

In the tight-knit Hong Kong community, his stock soared. He was fêted. Other investors wanted to cash in on the Fancourt phenomenon.

But his real value to his masters lay elsewhere, far from the public gaze. In the global money labyrinth he created and managed.

He was cocooned like a silkworm. His minders saw to everything. The peccadilloes of his past were airbrushed away.

Now, whenever he was seized by the uncontrollable craving, they made the necessary arrangements. Everything was organised with the appropriate safeguards in place.

Then, suddenly, without warning, they told him he was moving to Japan. They judged Hong Kong was no longer safe for him.

By then, he knew better than to argue. Reluctantly, he started packing his bags.

He would, they explained, be looked after by a business associate in Yokohama. A man who had been fully briefed.

A very savvy operator.

51

"The coroner's office has concluded Iwasaki-san committed suicide."

The police captain observed Peters closely as he delivered the news. He wanted to see how the Englishman would react.

He had personally overseen the police investigation. It had been rapid and thorough. All the evidence pointed to the woman taking her own life.

The local villagers were questioned. They were quick to level blame at the Englishman. They said he kept his wife isolated from the community. That he was the one blocking the land sale.

The police then contacted Hiroko's next-of-kin in Tokyo. Akemi Watanabe was horrified to learn of her sister's death. It was the first she had heard of it. She too railed against Peters.

The resulting report depicted a wife in thrall to a dominating foreign husband. An unhappy woman at the end of her tether with nowhere to turn.

"It's not true."

The captain was not used to being contradicted.

"Not true?"

"No, Hiroko would never commit suicide."

"Everyone is capable of taking their own life. You may not

know but we Japanese have a special affinity for suicide."

"I know."

"Ah, yes. You've lived here for many years. You understand our culture."

"I didn't say that. I simply meant I'm aware of the Japanese attitude to *seppuku*."

"Well then, you'll know when shame makes life unbearable, suicide can provide an honourable exit."

"Shame?"

"Yes. I understand you isolated Iwasaki-san from the rest of the community?"

"That's not true. Hiroko preferred to keep herself to herself."

"For your sake. A foreigner who did not fit in."

"No, it was her decision. We were happy together. Just the two of us."

"Really? We Japanese prefer the company of others, you know. It's not natural to be kept apart from friends and family."

"What do you mean?"

"I understand you didn't even allow her to see her own father."

"That's not true either. He couldn't accept our being together. Hiroko decided it was best to keep her distance."

"But her own sister told us quite the opposite. She said you discouraged Iwasaki-san from contacting her family."

"You've spoken to her sister?"

"Of course. As part of our investigation. Incidentally, she

knew nothing about her sister's death until we contacted her. Apparently, you had omitted to tell her."

Peters winced at his oversight. In his grief, he had forgotten to ring Akemi Watanabe. Naturally, she had a right to know.

The police captain hammered the point home.

"Why didn't you tell her?"

"I was confused. Upset. It slipped my mind."

"Then your neighbours complained at your stubborn refusal to sell your land like everyone else. You drove a wedge between yourselves and the community. Iwasaki-san must have found this situation intolerable."

Peters looked down. He could not deny it.

"It's true. She was upset. But in the end, she realised her home meant more to her than money."

"You persuaded her."

"No. She came to the decision herself."

"But, in the end, the pressure became too much to bear. There was only one possible solution. The terrible strain pushed her over the edge."

Peters glared at the police officer. He felt his self-control slipping.

"I'm sorry but I still don't believe it.

"Is there an alternative explanation?"

Peters could not stop himself.

"What if someone else was involved?"

The bottle of scotch, drunk over several hours, had raised this spectre. Sean Peters and George Trevillion had not shied away from facing up to the possibility.

On patrol along Northern Ireland's borders, death was an ever-present reality. What might be unthinkable to others came second nature to them.

"Someone else?"

"Have you considered she may have been murdered."

The captain put down his pencil and sat back in his chair. For the first time, his smug expression vanished.

Murder had never crossed his mind or his desk. And he was determined to keep it that way.

"This is just conjecture on your part. All the facts indicate otherwise."

"Your facts."

The police captain's jaw clenched.

"I suggest you go home now and accept the verdict of the professionals. Your car is ready for you to collect. The body has been released. You need to make arrangements for the funeral. I advise you to concentrate on the pressing issues at hand."

The police captain picked up the report and stowed it in his filing tray. The interview was over.

52

Peters' hand trembled.

With the metal chopsticks, he picked up one of Hiroko's bones from the tray of ashes. The larger ones lay on the top.

He was worried about dropping it. It was a relief when the teacher's son took the bone from him with his own chopsticks and placed it in the funeral urn.

With great care, they repeated the process. Eventually the transfer was complete and the urn filled.

Peters remembered how, when they first met, Hiroko told him off for taking food directly from her chopsticks with his own. That only happened at cremations, she said.

He had needed help with the funeral arrangements. His teacher, realising Peters was out of his depth, had sent his son to assist him.

The son had arrived first thing the next morning. He had started by visiting the neighbours to ask for their support.

Initially, Peters had been reluctant to involve the local community. After all, they had ostracised Hiroko when she was alive. To his mind, it was too late to make amends.

But the teacher's son had persuaded him.

"Please forget the past Sean-san. Just let them help. Allow them to show you and Hiroko-san respect."

Peters had relented. He trusted the son's judgement

implicitly.

Word spread quickly. Differences were set aside. The villagers would do everything possible to assist.

The day prior to the funeral the locals arrived. The women cleaned the house from top to bottom while the men attended to outside tasks. They swept the path and tinkered with anything they found that needed fixing.

Peters wanted to escape to the mountains, but custom demanded he simply wait. He sat apart, left alone to mourn.

In the end, he decided to pass the time with Hiroko. She had been laid out on the floor in the small tatami room.

She was dressed in a white kimono. A square of silk obscured her face. Peters sat beside her, brushing away any flies or mosquitoes trying to find a footing.

Meanwhile the preparations continued apace. Food and pans were brought in and meals cooked for those coming to pay their respects.

In the afternoon, people started to arrive. The village men looked uncomfortable in their dark suits, their shirts buttoned up tight, pinching their suntanned necks.

Once they had offered up prayers and presented Peters with their condolence envelopes, they were free to relax. They sat around in groups, smoking.

Helpers moved among them handing out refreshments. Sake was poured. Soon the respectful hush gave way to chatter and laughter.

Throughout, the teacher's son oversaw the arrangements. He moved among the guests, thanking them and attending to their needs.

Peters slept that night beside Hiroko. His hand reached out as always, stroking her sleeve, touching her chilled hand.

The following day, the funeral itself took place. The priest arrived to chant the sutras.

Hiroko was now laid out in her coffin, the silk square removed from her face.

The funeral parlour had dyed her hair, concealing her grey streaks for the last time. Her face was made up with unfamiliar blushes. She looked at peace.

Peters stared at her. The villagers searched for a reaction but the Englishman displayed none.

The Buddhist priest did not linger. Peters had chosen the least costly death name for Hiroko to accompany her to the afterlife. Other bereaved families had dug deeper and were more deserving of the priest's intercessions.

During the afternoon, a large car drew up. Akemi Watanabe got out and marched towards the house. Her husband followed in her wake.

As Akemi Watanabe made her entrance, some of the villagers recognised her. Word went round that Hiroko's sister from Tokyo had arrived.

Without acknowledging any of the mourners, the couple passed straight to the coffin. They then turned to Peters to offer formal condolences. Akemi Watanabe's black kimono shimmered like a raven, her face a pale mask.

Afterwards, they sat apart from the others at a small table. One of the ladies offered them refreshments. They refused.

After an interlude, Peters approached. He knew he needed to make amends for his earlier oversight.

Akemi Watanabe could not contain herself.

"You couldn't pick up the phone to tell me my own sister had died!"

Peters recoiled.

"I'm sorry. I wasn't thinking clearly. I apologise."

Akemi Watanabe looked at him. She spoke deliberately as if to a child who had trouble understanding simple sentences.

"Imagine hearing about my sister's death from the police!"

Peters braced himself for further recriminations but Akemi Watanabe changed tack.

"Anyway, what do you plan to do now?"

"Now?"

"With Hiroko gone, what are your plans?"

Peters looked at Akemi Watanabe blankly.

"I haven't really thought about it. Carry on as before, I suppose."

Akemi Watanabe turned away and started to whisper to her husband. Peters, summarily dismissed, returned to the other guests.

Now, at the crematorium, as he picked out Hiroko's bones, he wondered what Hiroko's sister might have meant.

53

Following tradition, Hiroko's ashes would join her forebears in the family grave.

Peters had no choice in the matter. But it did not rest easy with him. He could not accept her lying among those grey granite slabs.

On returning from the crematorium, he transferred a portion of her remains into a small porcelain pot. This was now stored in his backpack.

He was climbing the narrow path into the high mountains. It had rained overnight and the ground was soaked. All around the vegetation steamed as it shed water.

On the steep ascent, he did not stop to catch his breath as others might. He set a relentless pace.

After an hour, he reached the halfway point, a concrete storm barrage spanning a stream. As he picked his way over the narrow walkway, he paused to glance down the mountainside. The village was already just a tiny cluster of roofs far below.

Where the path snaked under trees, mosquitoes lay in wait. Brushing them away with sweeps of his hand, he hastened on into the sunshine.

The path zigzagged up and up until the air was redolent of pine resin. It was the path they always took together. The higher he went, the closer he felt to her.

Eventually the path reached the small clearing with the two rounded boulders side by side. Their special place.

He sat down and removed his backpack. He took out a thermos of tea, an *onigiri* rice ball wrapped in seaweed and a *mikan* orange.

It was the meal they always shared, gazing out over the expanse in front of them. A feast, they always called it.

They rarely felt the need to talk. It was enough to listen to the songs of the mountain. As if on cue, he heard the mournful mewing of a black *tombi* hawk circling high overhead.

Hiroko would have loved that. He pictured her sitting beside him, her hands hugging her knees like a schoolgirl.

Sometimes she would surprise him by turning and smiling. As if she knew exactly what he was thinking.

She often did. Then she would burst out laughing and slap her thigh in delight.

"Spooky!" she would say. It was.

When he had finished, he reached into the backpack. He took out the porcelain pot and a small trowel.

He tested the ground in front of her stone. It was soft. The pine needles formed a rich loam. He started to dig.

He made sure the hole was deep enough. He did not want the pot bearing Hiroko's remains to be disturbed.

After covering the hole again, he stamped down the ground. Finally, he placed a large round rock on top to mark the spot.

He sat down again. Wiping the trowel clean, he put it away in the backpack.

She would always be there now. Whenever he needed her, all

he had to do was climb the path into the mountains.

He filled his cup from the thermos. Before he drank, he poured a little tea over the rock covering her resting place.

He had not intended to say anything. But the words started to bubble up of their own accord.

"I'm sorry, Hiroko. So sorry."

Once the words started, others tumbled out. Words never uttered when she was alive.

Suddenly he felt a pressing need to articulate them. To relieve the crushing weight on his chest.

He talked of their life together. What it had meant to him. How she had saved him from the darkness. How she was his guiding light. How she was within him and always would be.

Finally, the words faded away. The mountain breeze took up the refrain, shuffling the branches overhead.

It was time to go.

He packed his bag and swung it over his shoulders. At the last moment, he leaned forwards and brushed the dark soil with his fingertips.

Then straightening, he retraced his steps down the mountainside. He did not look back.

54

Akira Kato was lying flat on his back, covered in a large white sheet with a piping-hot towel over his face. He almost felt like he was floating.

The hair salon was his refuge when life was not going according to plan. Here he was pampered and primped. Everything was designed to soothe away any unwelcome worries.

Except that day Kato was unable to lay his ghosts to rest. Under the sheet, he shuddered, causing his manicurist to recoil for a second before re-applying herself.

He kept replaying the recent chain of events in his mind.

It had started with a phone call from Akemi Watanabe. She had briskly informed him of her sister's death and requested a meeting.

The news had thrown Kato into a panic. He had left several messages for the city mayor at Yamashiro, only to learn from the town hall staff he would be unreachable for several days.

In desperation, he had rung the private investigator Ito. After making some rapid checks, Ito had rung back to confirm Hiroko Iwasaki had died in an accident.

Apparently, she had fallen from a bridge not far from where she lived. The police had pronounced it suicide.

Afterwards Kato had sat rooted to his chair in his office. His head in his hands.

Members of staff had peered into the office at regular intervals before slipping away. It was obvious their boss should not be disturbed.

Two days later, Akira Kato had crossed the capital to meet with Akemi Watanabe at her office. He struggled to look her in the eye.

"So, Kato-san, I take it your company is still interested in purchasing the property in Yamashiro? Following my sister's death, I am now the new owner."

She had wasted no time. After the funeral, she had immediately contacted the relevant local authorities to press her claim.

Akemi Watanabe knew full well her sister Hiroko and Peters were unmarried. She understood the legal position perfectly. The Englishman had no rights to inherit the property.

Akemi Watanabe had assumed the developer would jump at the opportunity. Instead, she was surprised at his apparent reticence. He seemed to be wrapped up in his own thoughts.

Kato's mind was indeed elsewhere. He was visualising hands pushing Hiroko Iwasaki from the bridge, her plummeting descent to the riverbed below.

He quickly pulled himself together. He had to secure the property. He had no choice.

Akemi Watanabe knew how to drive a hard bargain. The company's initial offer had been more than generous. But she understood the premium she could now command. She had a figure in mind and was hell bent on achieving it.

She never once considered the fact the land had been in her family for generations. She was no custodian of the past. This was business, pure and simple.

But money was not her only motivation. Her mind was set on uprooting the Englishman and sending him packing.

She laid the blame squarely at his door for her sister's misery and subsequent suicide. She was going to make sure he paid.

Under the white barber's sheet, Kato's arms twitched again. This time it was prompted by the disturbing memory of his conversation with the client when he first rang to break the news.

Chen had been sitting in his motor cruiser when he took the call. That morning he had set off from his berth in Yokohama Marina. He had rounded the point of Miura Peninsula into Sagami Bay where he had dropped anchor.

The odd little Chinaman might not cut much of a figure on land, but on the water, Chen was in his element. His antecedents had been pirates, plying the South China Seas, before sailing north to Japan to make landfall in Yokohama.

The sea was in his blood.

Whenever he had the opportunity, he would spend days out on the water alone. He was more than capable of managing the vessel by himself. He had everything he needed on board.

"Yes? What do you want?"

As always, Kato strained to hear the man.

The developer paused. He had tried to rehearse what he was going to say. In the end, he just blurted it out.

"The woman in Yamashiro. The one who wouldn't sell. She's dead."

There was a long silence. In his cabin, Chen stared out through the toughened glass at the misty coastline beyond. The waves were picking up a bit and slapping against the hull.

"Dead, you say? My goodness."

In an instant, Kato knew beyond any doubt. This was not news to his client.

"Yes. According to the police, she committed suicide."

"Suicide? Tell me more."

Kato was forced to reprise the details of how Hiroko Iwasaki had died. Chen did not interrupt.

"And the property?"

"I have been dealing with the sister, the new owner."

"The sister? What about the will you mentioned?"

"It never materialised."

"Just as well. It could have caused unnecessary complications."

Kato tried not to think about the will. He ploughed ahead

"Anyway, my people tell me we shall be in possession of the property in due course. Once all the terms are finalised."

"That's encouraging to hear. Then we can put all this hold-up behind us. Nothing to stop us moving ahead with the project at full speed."

The line was cut abruptly. Mercifully, it stopped Kato asking the overwhelming question consuming him.

His self-recriminations were cut short as the hot towel over his face was peeled back. He stared up at the young woman bending over him.

"Are you ready for your shave, Kato-san?"

He nodded and closed his eyes. He felt the tickle of the badger hair shaving brush as it lathered his face. Then the rasp of the cutthroat razor as it travelled over his cheeks and throat.

55

"This is all perfectly in order."

Sean Peters stared across the desk at the police captain.

"In order? You're joking. How can it be?"

The police captain rarely joked. Neither at the station nor at home. He pushed the letter back across the table towards Peters.

When Peters found it in his mailbox, he had stiffened. Seeing the development company's logo, his first instinct was to throw it in the bin.

Instead, he placed it with all the other post in a cardboard box next to the door. A sizable pile had accumulated since Hiroko's death.

Hiroko always dealt with official correspondence. Even after all these years, the convoluted Japanese was a trial for Peters.

After her death, he did not feel up to deciphering the intricate phrases. He figured, if it was urgent, they would come knocking.

Pulling on his boots, he went out to feed the chickens. Only later, when he came in for lunch, did something prompt him to pick the letter up again.

He sat down at his kitchen table and opened it. He pored over the sentences trying to get the gist. The legal terms were complex. He would have struggled in English.

But the smattering he did understand made him reach for the phone. Half an hour later, he was pulling up outside his teacher's door.

The son met him at the entrance and ushered him into the main room. The old man was sitting reading a book of *haiku* poetry. Peters knelt in front of him.

"I'm so sorry to bother you, Sensei. I received this letter this morning. I wondered if you could look at it."

"Please let me see."

The teacher read slowly. He then passed it to his son. He waited until his son had digested the contents before summarising.

"The letter is from the development company. It says your land now belongs to them. It is a final demand for you to vacate the property. The developers' construction crew will start work there in a week's time."

Exactly as Peters had feared. His teacher, as always, never minced his words.

"I don't understand. We never sold them the land. There must be some mistake."

The old man briefly consulted with his son before turning to Peters.

"You should go to the police. They can check the legality of what has happened."

Peters was reluctant to engage with the police after his earlier encounter. But he realised he had no alternative.

The police captain was nothing if not thorough. He had immediately contacted the developer's office. He asked for Kato, the signatory to the letter Peters had shown him.

As Kato was unavailable, he spoke with his personal assistant. On checking her files, she confirmed the company had purchased the land from one Akemi Watanabe. The sale had gone through without any hold-ups.

When the police captain phoned Akemi Watanabe, she was surprised to hear from the Yamashiro police again. She thought the investigation into her sister's death had reached its conclusion.

She explained that she had inherited the property from her sister. Subsequently, she had sold it to the development company.

"It was of no use to me. Naturally I got a good price for it."

"What about the Englishman?"

"What about him? He didn't even have the decency to marry my sister. He failed to take care of her. And look what happened. My family owes him absolutely nothing."

The police captain was surprised to learn the couple had not, in fact, been married.

He then made a call to the local government office. They confirmed Hiroko Iwasaki's estate had passed to her nearest surviving relative. Unmarried partners, they explained had no inheritance rights under Japanese law.

Once he had ascertained all the facts, the police chief had summoned Peters. As the Englishman sat down opposite, the police chief looked him up and down.

Peters looked dishevelled, even more so than earlier. He had clearly let himself go since his partner's death.

The police chief decided it was time to conclude this sorry business once and for all. To draw a line for the benefit of all concerned.

"After her death, Hiroko Iwasaki's property was inherited by her sister. She, in turn, sold it to the developers, the ones who sent you the letter."

"What? But that can't be!"

"I'm afraid so. I carried out the necessary checks myself with the local authorities. Everything has followed due process."

"But what about the will?"

"Will? What will?"

"Hiroko wrote a will leaving the property to me. The document is at home."

The police captain started shuffling the papers in front of him.

"I know nothing about wills. That is a matter for your legal advisor. If you'll excuse me…"

As Peters drove home, he recalled exactly when Hiroko had shown him the will.

"You never know, Sean. What if I go before you? This document gives you the right to inherit the house and land. All you have to do is take it to the council office and show them."

He had put a finger over her lips to hush her. But Hiroko had grabbed him by the shoulder.

"Sean, listen! This is important. If anything happens, just take this document to the public notary. They will know what to do."

Then they had knelt side by side in front of the family *butsudan.* She had opened the small drawer at the bottom and placed the document there for sake-keeping.

Since that day, the drawer and the subject had remained closed.

Arriving home, Peters hurried into the tatami room and opened the drawer. Staring inside, he felt the ground slipping away beneath his feet.

56

The developers did not waste any time.

Peters heard the low-loader grinding its way up the track. He was sitting in the kitchen.

He was surrounded by the usual clutter. He had made no attempt to pack.

A black Toyota Crown sedan and two large vans preceded the truck. The convoy pulled up at a safe distance from the house.

Three men in dark suits got out. They conferred in whispers before the senior man approached the front door.

Knocking, he leaned forwards to slide it open. He was saved the trouble. Peters suddenly filled the entrance.

As the executive recoiled, his hand rummaged in his briefcase. He produced a copy of the letter Peters had received earlier.

"We are here to take possession of this property. You were notified by post."

The man waved the paper at Peters like a talisman warding off an evil spirit. Peters said nothing.

The man decided to try his luck again.

"This house and the surrounding land are now the property of the New Horizon Development Company. The house is scheduled for demolition today."

On cue, a diesel engine shuddered into life. A heavy-duty hydraulic excavator started to inch its way down from the low-loader.

A group of construction workers now emerged from the two vans and sauntered towards the house. They lined up behind the men in suits.

These men were cut from a different cloth. They were well-experienced at persuading reluctant residents to be on their way.

Peters sized them up.

The men in suits inched forwards, emboldened by the crew at their backs.

"Your personal property will be put on the driveway in front of the house. Please remove it at your earliest convenience. You need to vacate the property now."

"You have no business here. Please leave immediately."

The men in suits hesitated. Peters' simple statement was not open to misinterpretation.

As they withdrew to a safe distance, the construction workers stepped forwards in their place. Their faces were set. They were ready to play their part.

Peters held his hands up. Encouraging them not to escalate the situation. To give them a chance to reconsider.

"I don't intend to let you enter this property. I will defend myself if necessary. Please understand I wish no one any harm."

The construction workers ignored him and started to close in. Peters, in his old *judogi* and comical tee shirt, did not seem to pose much of a threat.

The eight burly construction workers rarely needed to resort to physical force. Most people threw in the towel at the sight of them.

But they could see the foreigner had no intention of giving in. He would need to be taught a lesson.

The leader and largest member of the group stepped forward. It was a well-rehearsed move.

Everyone knew their role. While the leader frogmarched the man off the property, two others would control the access. The remainder would clear the building of possessions. It always worked without a hitch.

The leader circled Peters. He did not anticipate any trouble.

He was somewhat surprised Peters did not react. This is going to be a piece of cake, he thought.

He reached out and grabbed Peters' wrists, pinning them behind him. At this point, people generally tried in vain to wriggle free. The leader prided himself on his iron grip.

But the Englishman did the opposite. Remaining completely relaxed, Peters raised his arms as if unencumbered, swivelled to one side and took a step forward.

The large man found himself spinning through the air towards his colleagues. He landed awkwardly. There was a sickening crunch as his shoulder dislocated on impact.

He struggled into a sitting position, holding his arm. The foreigner meanwhile had resumed his original relaxed stance.

"Get the bastard!"

The men in suits had now retreated to the safety of their car. They had no intention of becoming involved in any unseemly physical violence.

The remaining construction workers now crowded around. The odds were still heavily in their favour.

Assuming they could grab hold of the Englishman.

He always seemed to evade their grasp. At each attack they launched, the man in the *judogi* sidestepped before retaliating with speed and power.

The more frantic they became, the calmer he remained. Like the hub of a spinning wheel.

One of them fell headlong against a water trough. Another sat nursing a severely twisted wrist. A third lay on his back without moving.

The others started to disengage. They knew when they were beaten. This was not what they had signed up for.

"Please leave now."

Peters' voice showed no evidence of his recent exertions.

"If you continue, the consequences are likely to be more serious."

Turning his back on his assailants, he disappeared inside the house, sliding the door behind him.

The construction workers attended to their injured comrades, helping them back to the vans. Meanwhile one of the men sheltering in the black sedan made an urgent phone call.

57

Peters had eaten nothing for 24 hours.

He lay on a small bed in the Yamashiro police station's holding cell, staring at the ceiling.

Following the emergency call from the black sedan, a squad car had been dispatched to the property. When it finally arrived, the indignant businessmen had clustered around to describe what had taken place.

After hearing them out, the senior police officer rang the station. He did not warm to the executives but their complaint seemed cut and dried. The construction workers sitting in their vans nursing their wounds were evidence enough.

He kept his report concise. A foreigner, on being legitimately requested to vacate a property, had reacted violently. Several men had been injured. The man had subsequently shut himself up in the house.

The police officer requested further instructions on how to proceed. The Yamashiro police switchboard transferred him to the police captain.

After some quick-fire questions, the captain rapidly identified the perpetrator as Sean Peters. He ordered the two officers to arrest the Englishman and bring him in.

The senior officer rang off and sat in the squad car staring through the windscreen. He was too old for this type of hurly-burly. But he knew he had no choice in the matter. Duty called.

Urged on by the company executives, the two police officers approached the building. The senior policeman stepped forward and knocked at the door.

"This is the police."

He was met by silence.

"We need to speak with you."

Again, there was no response.

The policeman sighed. He signalled to his younger colleague to stay back.

"Excuse me. I'm coming into the house."

He carefully slid open the door and stepped into the entrance. He was poised to retreat.

He need not have been concerned. From the doorway, he could see the Englishman kneeling at a low table, flicking through a photograph album.

The police captain had summarised the background over the phone. He had described the wife's suicide and the man's subsequent eviction notice.

The officer empathised. One of his nephews had taken his own life. A likeable boy, good at his studies, a popular member of his sports team.

They had found him hanging in some woods. His suicide note apologised for the distress it would cause his family.

He looked at the motionless figure staring at the photos. He thought he understood something of what he was going through.

"Excuse me?"

The foreigner looked up. His eyes were filled with steely resolve.

"May I come in?"

Peters considered for a second and then nodded.

The policeman took off his shoes and padded into the room in his socks. He knelt down and waited.

"What happens now?"

"I'm afraid you'll have to come to the police station with us."

"Why? I only acted in self-defence."

"You'll still have to explain what happened here. Men have been injured going about their lawful business. I'm sure you can appreciate that."

Peters sat for a moment, weighing up the situation. Then he looked around the room, as if making an inventory.

"You realise they're planning to demolish this house?"

"Yes, so I understand. According to my superior, they are within their rights."

Peters stared at the policeman who met his gaze.

"Within their rights ..."

Peters sighed and closed the photograph album. He tucked it under his arm and rose to his feet.

"I'll need to pack a bag."

"Of course. Please take your time."

Peters walked around the house selecting a few personal items. It did not take long. The police officer left him to it, waiting by the entrance.

"OK. That's it."

"Is there someone who can collect the rest of your belongings?"

"Yes. Give me a minute."

Peters walked over to the phone. The teacher's son promised to come over to the house that very afternoon.

The teacher and the son were well aware of the situation. They had been waiting for his call. They had offered to be with him when the developers arrived but Peters had said he preferred to handle it alone.

They knew all about the missing will. The son and Peters had gone to the city hall to meet with two local government officials.

They were sympathetic but adamant. Unless Peters could produce the will, there was nothing they could do.

The two policemen left the house followed by Peters. After seeing the Englishman into the back of the squad car, the older man crossed to the black sedan.

He bent down and fixed each of the company employees in turn with a stern look.

"Make sure all this man's belongings are correctly packed up. They'll be collected this afternoon. I'll hold you all personally responsible for anything missing or broken."

The men in the car nodded.

"And wait until we've gone before you start work."

As the squad car disappeared down the track towards the main road, the heavy diesel engine grunted into life.

58

"I need you to go to Yamashiro City."

Ms Sekikawa raised her eyebrows.

"Sorry? Where?"

Yamaguchi tended to forget Ms Sekikawa had grown up in the United States. There were gaps in her knowledge of Japanese geography.

"Yamashiro. I'll forward you all the details."

Ms Sekikawa waited for Yamaguchi to enlighten her. He rummaged through the paperwork in front of him.

They had not talked a great deal since their fraught earlier exchange. When they did, it was with a new note of formality.

Ligaya Santos was still being held at the Women's Consulting Centre. Ms Sekikawa made a point of travelling across the city to see her whenever she had the chance.

On each occasion, the Filipina pleaded with her to speed up her release. But Ms Sekikawa could only reiterate that her hands were tied.

She did what she could to help Ligaya Santos. On her most recent visit, she had arranged with the Centre to allow the Filipina to make regular phone calls home.

It only seemed to make matters worse. Serving only to underline the distance between her and her family in

Batangas.

Ms Sekikawa continued to press Yamaguchi on the subject. He appeared deaf to her appeals.

She started to see him as an immovable object stuck to an office chair. A barrier to getting things done.

But Yamaguchi had not been sitting on his hands. He had continued to make overtures to the departments concerned.

He understood the woman's predicament and had tried his best to expedite matters. But everywhere he had been met with a brick wall of indifference.

He decided not to mention his attempts to Ms Sekikawa. There was no point in raising her hopes unless he had positive news.

"I had a call from the local police captain up there in Yamashiro. He needs some help with an Englishman he has in custody."

"What's the problem?"

"Apparently there was some kind of assault. The Englishman refused to be evicted from his home. It was due for demolition."

"Isn't that something the local police should be able to handle?"

"Yes, well, they contacted us for assistance. Language difficulties, apparently. I said we'd do what we could to help."

The Yamashiro police captain had been eager to be shot of the problem. He first escalated the case to the prefectural police headquarters. On hearing a foreigner was involved, they had referred him to Yamaguchi's specialist department in Tokyo.

Speaking with Yamaguchi, the police captain had no qualms

about misrepresenting Peters' Japanese ability. Whatever it needed for Yamaguchi's department to take the Englishman off his hands.

The police captain was worried. Since being remanded in custody, Peters had refused to eat. The captain could envisage the situation rapidly spiralling out of control.

When Peters had first arrived at the police station in the squad car, the two officers had brought him to the interview room. The police captain was waiting for them.

"I understand you assaulted some construction workers."

"They assaulted me."

"Not according to eye-witness reports. There were several people present."

"And you believe them?"

"The company employees were perfectly within their rights to take possession of the property."

"I merely asked them to leave."

"You were the one who should have left. Instead, you decided to launch an attack on them."

"You're planning to keep me here?"

"Yes, you'll be held in custody until the case has been investigated."

"Like the half-baked investigation into Hiroko's death?"

The police captain's jaw tightened. He nodded to the senior officer waiting by the door.

"Take him down to the cells."

Peters did not resist. He was locked in one of the holding cells in the basement of the building.

Peters understood the principles of passive resistance. He had witnessed it first-hand in Northern Ireland. He was prepared to tough it out.

When the police captain heard Peters was refusing food, he put him on 24-hour suicide watch. Simultaneously, he escalated the problem up the chain of command.

"So, is this a priority?"

Yamaguchi did not miss the trace of irony in Ms Sekikawa's voice.

"Yes. We must give them whatever support they need."

"Of course."

"Take Hayashi."

"Understood."

As she walked back to her desk, Ms Sekikawa reflected this was not, in fact, such a bad idea. The department did not have much on and she was finding it difficult to keep Hayashi fully occupied.

A trip up north would give him something to get his teeth into.

59

A police car was waiting at the mainline Shinkansen station to meet the two officers who had travelled up from Tokyo.

The prefectural police headquarters was a short drive across the city. They were escorted to the vehicle pool where, as arranged, they were allocated a small squad car.

Hayashi drove while Ms Sekikawa navigated. They headed west through the mountains towards Yamashiro.

They soon found themselves driving through a swathe of peach orchards. Everywhere workers stood on stepladders, clipping and pruning, lavishing care on the ripening fruit.

Ms Sekikawa opened the window.

"Can you smell that?"

Hayashi was concentrating on the road ahead, his forehead almost touching the windscreen.

"Sorry?"

"The peach trees."

"Peach trees?"

Ms Sekikawa frowned at her colleague. City boy, she thought.

She turned and gazed at the trees and the mountain range beyond. Yamaguchi had been right after all. She could do with a breath of fresh air.

She knew she could be difficult. The last weeks had been

quite testing. The change of scene would do her good.

A pity her IT colleague Noriko Muratani was not with her in the car. When not staring at computer screens, she was invariably flicking through gardening magazines. She would have loved these well-tended orchards.

Ms Sekikawa took another deep breath and then shut the window. This was not a holiday. She needed to set an example.

After a few wrong turns in Yamashiro, they eventually pulled up in front of a dull grey building. It was a facsimile of any other provincial police station.

After announcing themselves at reception, Ms Sekikawa and Hayashi were shown into the police captain's office.

He stood to attention to receive them. After the standard formal introductions, he offered them both a seat and came straight to the point.

"The foreigner is being held in the cells. He is currently refusing to eat."

"When was he arrested?"

"Two days ago."

"Has he been charged?"

"No."

Nothing unusual about that, thought Ms Sekikawa. Suspects could be held for over three weeks without charge. And without access to a solicitor.

"I understand there was some kind of affray?"

"The foreigner ..."

"Sorry, does the foreigner have a name, please?"

The police captain bridled at the stocky female police officer interrupting him. He would have much preferred a male officer, rather than a jumped-up woman and her lanky assistant.

"Peters. Sean Peters."

"Thank you."

"He attacked a group of construction workers when they tried to take possession of the property where he was currently residing."

"Residing?"

"He had previously lived there with his Japanese partner. She was the original owner of the property.

"And where is she now?"

"She recently committed suicide."

Ms Sekikawa stared at the police captain. Hayashi momentarily halted his notetaking.

"Suicide?"

"Yes. She threw herself off a bridge."

Hayashi resumed his scribbling.

"Do we know why?"

"Some kind of mental breakdown. She was under pressure to sell the house and land to some developers. Eventually it would seem the pressure became too much for her and she took her own life."

"And the developers now own the land?"

"Yes. The woman's sister in Tokyo inherited the property after her death. She subsequently sold it to the developers."

Ms Sekikawa looked at the police captain. He seemed quite unfazed by the chain of events.

"And you say this man, Sean Peters, attacked and injured several construction workers?"

"Yes. Three required hospital treatment."

"Just one man did this?"

"Apparently he is an extremely violent individual according to those involved."

"Well, thank you for the briefing. Perhaps we could interview the prisoner?"

The police captain picked up the phone and gave instructions for Peters to be brought up to the interview room.

"Second door on the left."

The police captain did not move from his seat. Ms Sekikawa and Hayashi filed out of the office.

60

If Sean Peters' old *judogi*, tee-shirt and *mompe* trousers looked incongruous at the farmhouse, they looked even more out of place in the police station.

He cut an odd figure. Hayashi had trouble concentrating on his note-taking.

His eyes were drawn to the Englishman's grey hair, gathered in a ponytail, and the unruly tufts of beard. He reminded him of some barbarous Viking warrior.

Ms Sekikawa was less distracted. During her time in America, she had seen all sorts of outlandish types.

What surprised her most was Peters' command of Japanese. She wondered why their help had been requested in the first place.

For the purposes of the interview, however, they stuck to English.

"How are you being treated?"

"Fine."

Peters looked tired and ill-kempt. Nevertheless, he sat upright in his chair and showed no obvious sign of distress.

Two local police officers waited outside the room, but Ms Sekikawa felt no physical threat from the prisoner. The opposite, in fact.

"Can you please tell us what happened?"

"What do you want to know?"

"Let's start with the altercation at the house."

"The construction workers tried to make me to leave the property."

"Did they use physical force?"

"One of them grabbed my hands behind my back."

"And you resisted?"

"Yes."

"And the others?"

"They attacked me after I had neutralised the first man."

"How many were there?"

"Seven, I think."

Ms Sekikawa frowned. Seven against one Englishman.

"Can you tell me about the background to the assault?"

Peters sighed and started from the beginning. He described the planned development. Their growing unpopularity among the villagers. The threatening behaviour.

Ms Sekikawa listened without interrupting. Peters came to a sudden halt. He turned his head to look out of the window.

Ms Sekikawa took advantage of the lull.

"We were told about your partner."

Peters leaned forwards in his chair.

"What did they tell you?"

"That she committed suicide."

Peters shook his head.

"No chance. That's just their theory. It's wrong."

"Wrong? Can you prove it?"

Peters shook his head.

"Not in a court of law. But I know without a doubt. Hiroko would never do that. It wasn't in her character. She was a fighter. She never quit."

"So how do you explain what happened?"

"I can't. Except I'm convinced she didn't jump from that bridge."

Ms Sekikawa started to have an uncomfortable feeling.

"I understand you weren't married."

"No."

"So, after her death, her sister inherited the property?"

"It wasn't meant to happen that way. Hiroko wrote a will. She always said she wanted me to have the property if anything happened to her."

"A will?"

"Yes. She showed it to me. All signed and sealed. She kept it safe. But then when the time came, I couldn't find it. It was missing."

Ms Sekikawa sat back, lightly drumming her fingers on the table.

"Thank you, Mr Peters. I think my colleague and I have enough information for the time being. We shall initiate our own investigation."

"Your own investigation?"

"We've been called in from Tokyo to help with your case. Our department specialises in assisting foreigners who have found themselves in difficulty. We'll need to verify all the relevant facts."

"I see."

Ms Sekikawa looked at Peters' haggard face.

"As it is going to take us a few days, may I suggest you start eating again?"

Peters looked at Ms Sekikawa. Personable, smart, efficient. He managed a tired smile.

"OK."

61

"Investigate? For what reason?"

Ms Sekikawa had anticipated this might prove to be a difficult conversation. She had asked Hayashi to wait in the car.

"Following our preliminary interview with Peters, there are some points on which we'd like further clarification."

"I see no need for that. We've already conducted a thorough investigation. You've been given all the relevant facts."

The police captain crossed his arms over his chest. Never a good sign, thought Ms Sekikawa.

"Indeed. Thank you for putting us in the picture. Nevertheless, it would be remiss of us not to do some fieldwork of our own. Familiarise ourselves with the locations highlighted in your report, review some of the witness statements."

"Hardly necessary in my view."

"Perhaps you might find it helpful to speak with Detective Inspector Yamaguchi, my superior in Tokyo? He can explain our working methods more succinctly than me."

"Please wait outside."

Ms Sekikawa got up and left the room. She muttered under her breath as she paced the corridor. The officer at reception gave her periodic glances.

Five minutes later his phone rang. He signalled to Ms

Sekikawa.

"You can go back in now."

The police captain was still sitting at his desk as she had left him. He was looking, if anything, more disgruntled. She stood to attention in front of him, waiting to hear the outcome of his discussion with Tokyo.

"Detective Inspector Yamaguchi and I have agreed you can proceed."

The police captain struggled to articulate the sentence.

Ms Sekikawa's phone call to Yamaguchi the previous evening from the hotel had been timely. She had anticipated resistance from the local police captain.

Yamaguchi had not made any promises but she knew she could depend on him. For a man of few words, he had formidable powers of persuasion when he chose to employ them.

Yamaguchi had left the police captain with little room to manoeuvre. Requesting help from his department, he explained, came with strings attached. Giving his detectives free rein to proceed at their discretion was one of them.

"Could you please assign me a member of your staff to assist? Someone familiar with the locality?"

An hour later they were heading out of Yamashiro. A young female police officer sat in the passenger seat giving directions. Hayashi drove, while Ms Sekikawa craned forwards between the front seats trying to get her bearings.

In no time, they were making their way up into the mountains. They were following the same route Hiroko had taken on the day of her murder.

During the journey, the two women chatted while Hayashi

concentrated on the road ahead. The turns were abrupt, the climb into the mountains precipitous.

The young officer explained she had lived in the city all her life and knew the area well. She had only been on the police force for less than a year.

She had heard her colleagues discuss the Englishman's case, but was not privy to any of the details. Ms Sekikawa filled her in on the relevant background.

When they reached the bridge, they parked on the far side where Hiroko's car had been found. Using the photographs in the incident file, Ms Sekikawa started to figure out the lay of the land.

The three officers proceeded to the centre of the bridge. They studied the high metal protective barrier running the length of the walkway. To climb it would require determination and considerable dexterity.

Ms Sekikawa ruled out the possibility of an accident. The police captain had been right about that.

The three officers peered down at the river far below. They did not speak, each visualising the fatal fall.

They then returned to the car and resumed their journey. When they reached the village, it was noon. They saw no one outside on the streets.

Even the nursery school was silent as they drove past. Ms Sekikawa imagined the children snuggled on their mattresses taking their midday nap. It would be the same in towns and villages all over Japan.

They carried on until they located the track leading up to the farmhouse. The house was no longer there. Just a gash of freshly-bulldozed earth where it had stood.

The excavator's hydraulic grab had made short work of the plaster walls and wooden framework. The remains of the house lay in a neat pile, ready to be loaded onto a dump truck.

The machines had then moved on to the terraced gardens. The rich topsoil, painstakingly nurtured over the years, was scoured with caterpillar tracks.

Hayashi pulled up and the three officers got out. Ms Sekikawa surveyed the scene and then told the others to wait by the car. She picked her way over the rough ground, trying not to get mud on her trousers.

The construction workers were on their midday break. Their feet protruded from the side windows of their parked vans as they napped.

The men in the first van did not appreciate the sharp tap on the window.

"Who's in charge here?"

The three men sat up, glowering at Ms Sekikawa. Their annoyance at being disturbed was tempered, however, when they spotted the police car.

"I am."

The team leader struggled out of the van. The bandaging around his shoulder and chest was visible underneath his shirt.

"We are investigating an assault that took place here. Please come with me."

Shrugging at his co-workers, the man followed Ms Sekikawa to the police car. He sat in the rear seat. Ms Sekikawa climbed into the front.

"Right. Please describe exactly what happened. In detail."

62

The police captain stared at the signed affidavits.

"What's this?"

"Testimony from the construction workers at the site. The ones who claimed Peters assaulted them."

The police captain put on his reading glasses and studied each sheet of paper in turn. Ms Sekikawa found her patience tested.

"You'll see they have retracted their original complaints."

"Kindly do me the courtesy of letting me read through these documents for myself."

Ms Sekikawa sat back and looked around the room. The walls were blank except for a single framed long-service commendation. In Yamashiro, she thought, time ran to a different beat.

Eventually, the police captain fastened the statements together with a paper clip and stared at Ms Sekikawa.

"How exactly did you manage to persuade them to change their statements?"

"No persuasion involved. I interviewed them all individually. It was obvious they had cooked up the story. The details did not fit. Eventually one of them admitted what had actually happened."

Ms Sekikawa had instructed the construction workers in

turn to sit in the back of the small squad car. Her questions were sharp and relentless. Outside, Hayashi and the local police officer exchanged looks as Ms Sekikawa's muffled voice became increasingly strident.

When the men were finally let out, they slunk back to the vans with pinched expressions. They would not forget the experience in a hurry.

The last man to be interviewed slid onto the back seat of the squad car. His eyes were lowered, his hands tugging his cuffs down over his wrists.

By this time, Ms Sekikawa had uncovered enough inconsistencies. She decided not to waste any more time.

"It's clear to me your colleagues aren't telling the truth. You need to tell me exactly what happened. You need to be aware false testimony can have serious consequences. It's time to put a stop to this."

The man shut his eyes. He had had trouble with the police in the past. Small infractions resulting in fines. He knew his record would weigh against him.

He mumbled like a guilty schoolboy.

"OK. The boss tried to grab the foreigner. Like he always does if anyone looks like they are going to give us any trouble. Then he marches them off the site."

"And? What happened?"

"The foreigner just seemed to swivel out of the way. The next thing, the boss was lying there with a dislocated shoulder."

"What did the rest of you do?"

"We all piled in. Big mistake. The foreigner sent us flying too."

"But he never initiated an attack himself?"

"No. He was just defending himself. I've never seen anything like it."

"Thank you."

The man returned to the van to join the others with Ms Sekikawa hard on his heels.

"Everyone out, please."

By now the construction workers knew better than to dally. They fell into line.

"Time for some essay writing. Each of you will now make a clear written statement of what actually happened when you came to take possession of this property. My fellow officers will assist you."

The men sat in their cars with pens and sheets of paper. It took them some time to come up with an acceptable description of the sequence of events.

Armed with the completed affidavits, the police officers headed back to the station.

Based on the new evidence, the police captain realised he had no grounds for holding the Englishman. It was now in front of him in black and white: Peters had acted in self-defence throughout.

He could have done without Ms Sekikawa spelling it out.

"Given these statements, it is apparent the construction workers, not the Englishman, were the ones guilty of assault."

The muscles in the police captain's cheeks tightened. Ms Sekikawa carried on regardless.

"When Peters is released, please arrange for him to be brought to the interview room. I'll be waiting there."

Half an hour later, Peters appeared at the interview room door, flanked by the two officers who had earlier arrested him.

"You're free to go."

"Free?"

"The complaints made against you have been dropped. The men who assaulted you have revised their statements."

Peters raised his eyebrows in surprise.

"Thank you."

He had no idea how this resourceful policewoman from Tokyo had managed to secure his release.

"And the house?"

"I'm afraid it's already been demolished. You can't stay there. Is there somewhere else you can go?"

Peters closed his *judogi* over his chest.

"Yes. I have friends I can stay with."

"Good. Your car has been brought down. It's outside ready for you. Here's my card. Please let me have your contact details later so I can keep you updated with the progress of our investigation."

Peters took the card.

"I appreciate your help. Thank you."

Ms Sekikawa brushed his thanks aside. As they left the interview room, the desk officer helped Peters to complete the necessary formalities for his release.

Ms Sekikawa waited outside. She watched as Peters climbed into his car and drove off.

That's the first part sorted, she thought. Now for the tricky bit.

63

Ms Sekikawa took her usual place in the back seat of the car.

As before, they turned off the highway out of the city and started to climb into the mountains. The landmarks were becoming familiar.

The local officer accompanying them no longer needed to help Hayashi with directions. He was a quick learner.

When they came to the bridge, Ms Sekikawa yet again found herself glancing down into the abyss below as they crossed. Wondering why anyone would choose to die that way.

Ever since their initial recce of the bridge, Ms Sekikawa had nagging doubts about the official version of events. After her interview with Peters, she was even more convinced something did not add up.

He struck her as a no-nonsense type. When he said Hiroko would never throw herself off the bridge, her instincts told her to believe him.

The previous evening after supper at the hotel, Ms Sekikawa and Hayashi had studied the police reports of Hiroko's death. Hayashi had laid out all the documents on his hotel bed. The two police officers sifted through the details, jotting down anything of significance.

Ms Sekikawa could not fault the handling of the investigation. The police captain was quite meticulous. He had devoted most of his limited resources to the case.

Everything was done by the book.

The pathologist's report made sombre reading. Nothing unexpected, all the findings consistent with a fatal fall.

The forensic team's comprehensive review of the scene again suggested nothing untoward. The car only revealed traces of the victim and Sean Peters.

Following standard procedure, the police had conducted house-to-house interviews with the couple's neighbours. Several statements highlighted the friction between them and the other villagers. Some referred to the unpleasant scene at the cherry blossom viewing.

One particular report stood out. A local hunter claimed to have passed Hiroko's parked car next to the bridge on the day she was killed. He reported seeing a woman sitting in the driver's seat.

As he was the only eye-witness, Ms Sekikawa and Hayashi decided it warranted a visit. They had made an early start, collecting the young officer from the police station.

It took them a while to locate the house. It was tucked up a track on the outskirts of the village, quite a distance from the nearest neighbour.

The house looked dilapidated and uncared for. Outside the carcass of a car stood on concrete blocks. A fridge with its door missing lay on its side by the entrance.

Beside the gravel driveway was a large square enclosure. As the officers parked and approached the house, a pack of hunting dogs rushed out from under a large kennel where they had been sheltering from the sun.

They launched themselves at the wire netting, barking in a frenzy. Unable to reach the police officers, the larger dogs turned on the runt of the pack. Flipping it on its back, they sunk their teeth into its flank. The runt screamed in pain and tried to burrow under a sheet of metal lying on the ground.

The police officers knocked on the front door. They had to wait until a man finally appeared.

Ichiro Maeda was as unedifying as his dogs. He was unshaven, with random wisps of beard sticking out from his chin. His hair was streaked with grey and his eyes dull. But he was tough and muscled, typical of forest men.

When he started to speak, he released a blast of stale breath.

"Yes?"

"We are police officers. We would like to ask you some questions."

Maeda looked at them blearily. He seemed reluctant to open the door. But his attitude softened when he spotted the young female officer, half-hidden behind Ms Sekikawa.

He stood aside to let them through.

Once inside the living room, the police officers remained standing. There was clutter all over the floor. A half-empty two-litre plastic bottle of *shochu* stood on the table. Heads of animals stared down at them from the walls.

A stench came from the kitchen. The young police officer could not help wrinkling her nose at the smell. Maeda smirked.

"Oh that? I trapped a boar yesterday. Big one. I'm just butchering it."

With that he pushed past Hayashi and disappeared into the kitchen. He returned with two handfuls of grey offal.

"This will shut those damned dogs up."

He shuffled into a pair of clogs and went outside. Seconds

later the dogs quietened down. He came back in wiping his hands on the back of his trousers.

"Right. What's this about?"

"You reported seeing a woman in a car parked next to Komai Bridge the day Hiroko Iwasaki died."

"Oh that. What about it?"

"We wanted to ask you some more questions."

"Why? I told your colleague everything I saw."

"Would you mind telling us?"

Maeda looked at the three officers and then at the bottle of *shochu*.

"OK, but I hope this isn't going to take long."

"What time was it when you saw the car?"

"Midday. I'd been out to the forest trapping. I was on my way back for lunch."

"Can you be more precise about the time?"

Maeda screwed up his face and scratched his ear.

"Must have been just after one o'clock. The local news was on."

"Can you describe what you saw?"

"A car parked at the end of the bridge."

"What made you notice that car in particular?"

"Well, it's a funny place to stop. Middle of nowhere. A woman sitting in the driver's seat, on her own."

Maeda glanced at young officer, leering.

"Pretty, mind. Easy to remember the cute ones."

Ms Sekikawa decided to let that pass.

"Did you recognise her?"

"Nope. Never seen her before."

Maeda walked into the kitchen and came back with a can of drink. He drank thirstily and afterwards wiped his hand across his face. Ms Sekikawa checked her notebook.

"Did you know Hiroko Iwasaki?"

"No, never met her. Heard her name mentioned from time to time, mind. People complaining about her. Didn't take any notice. I keep myself to myself."

Ms Sekikawa could understand why.

"You didn't stop to speak to the woman in the car?"

"Speak to her? No. Why should I? I mind my own business."

"Can you describe the vehicle parked at the end of the bridge?"

"Small."

"Anything else?"

"Like I told your colleague earlier, a Honda Fit."

"A Honda Fit? What makes you so sure?"

"My brother has one just like it. Same colour, even."

"What colour?"

"Blue."

Ms Sekikawa frowned.

"Blue?"

"Yes. Blue."

Ms Sekikawa flicked through the file.

"Not this car?"

Maeda looked at the photo of Hiroko's red Nissan and shook his head.

"Nope."

"You're sure?"

"I told you. It was the same as my brother's."

Maeda threw his empty drinks can into the corner of the room. It landed on the overflowing rubbish bin before toppling off onto the floor. He was clearly running out of patience.

"And the woman. Is this her?"

The picture was taken of Hiroko Iwasaki the previous year, sitting by a lake. A close-up.

Exhaling loudly, Maeda retrieved some reading glasses from the table and squinted at the photograph.

"Not sure. Might have been. I didn't stop so I can't be sure."

64

The CCTV footage rolled.

Ms Sekikawa and Hayashi sat side by side at the regional National Highways Office staring at a large screen. Once the technician had shown them how to operate the system, he had left them to it.

Their eyes tracked each car as it flashed past. Hayashi's attention never flagged for an instant.

After speaking with Maeda, they had gone through the original eye-witness report. There was no mention of the make or colour of the car Maeda claimed to have seen.

When questioned, the officer who had originally interviewed Maeda admitted the oversight. He was relatively new to the police force and mortified to have made such a basic error.

He had simply assumed it was the same car. It was parked in the same place as Hiroko Iwasaki's red Nissan had been found and Maeda had identified the driver as a woman.

Ms Sekikawa and Hayashi now had a new line of enquiry. Their priority was to locate the blue Honda Fit and its female driver.

The National Highways Office confirmed there were no cameras on the mountain road leading up to the village. The nearest was on a gantry monitoring traffic heading north along the Yamashiro highway. It was positioned just prior to the junction where Hiroko would have turned off.

Not perfect, but better than nothing. Hayashi and Ms Sekikawa planned their strategy over supper the previous evening.

Ms Sekikawa had a healthy appetite but even she was surprised at the way Hayashi tucked away his food. Just when she thought he had had his fill, he pulled the rice container towards him and spooned himself another bowlful.

It was clear she was not going to get much sense out of him until he had finished. She sat back and sipped her tea.

The more she worked with him, the more she approved. He was focused and conscientious.

But she still had not cracked his impenetrable reserve. She could not resist having another shot.

"So, is your mother all right with you being away all this time?"

It was a reasonable opening gambit. She knew he looked after his mother, or the other way round. Either way his mother was bound to miss him on their lengthy trip to the back of beyond.

Hayashi was about to cram in another mouthful but stopped halfway.

"My mother?"

"Yes. We've been up here a while. I just thought your mother might be missing you?"

"No, she is fine, thank you. Well able to manage on her own."

Hayashi finished his mouthful and put down his chopsticks. He then looked straight at Ms Sekikawa, his face devoid of expression.

Ms Sekikawa got the message. Hayashi did not welcome incursions into his private life.

"Good. Well, anyway, let's think about how we are going to approach this CCTV analysis tomorrow."

They had decided to start with what they knew. Hiroko Iwasaki's Nissan must have been caught by the CCTV as it travelled the short distance along the highway. The first task was to pinpoint her car.

It proved harder than they had anticipated. They stared at the continuous stream of traffic for over an hour, pausing the display every time they spotted a vehicle resembling Hiroko's.

Towards the end, Ms Sekikawa's concentration wavered. She kept blinking, trying to maintain her focus.

"That could be her."

Hayashi's sharp eyes had picked out a red Nissan trundling along in the slow lane. Even from the CCTV they could sense the driver was ill at ease. Every time someone raced by, the small car veered towards the hard shoulder.

"Well spotted. Let's have a closer look."

They summoned the technician who showed them how to enhance the image. Hiroko's face gradually came into focus, peering over the steering wheel.

Ms Sekikawa sat studying her features. Shortly after this image had been captured, this same young woman would be lying dead at the bottom of a ravine.

Pulling herself together, she noted the timestamp.

"12:43. Let's say it would take her 30 minutes to get to Komai Bridge. Longer possibly given the speed she was driving. We know Maeda crossed the bridge shortly after one o'clock. When he passed, he only saw the Honda Fit. So, that means Hiroko Iwasaki had yet to arrive at the bridge."

Hayashi took up the reins.

"OK. Assuming the Honda Fit took the same route up the mountain as Hiroko Iwasaki, it would have turned off the main road sometime before her.

"Right. Let's start working back to try to find the Honda."

They did not need to rewind the recording far.

At 12:40 they identified a small blue Honda Fit making swift progress along the inside lane. On enlarging the image, however, they could only make out a man behind the wheel and another in the passenger seat. No sign of a young woman.

Ms Sekikawa jotted down the vehicle's registration.

"I guess we'd better keep going."

They painstakingly rewound two hours of tape. In all that time, they only found two more cars fitting the Honda's description. Both were travelling at speed in the outside lane, too fast to exit onto the slip-road to the mountains. In both cases, the sole occupant was male.

Eventually, the two detectives had to admit defeat. Exhausted, they left the traffic monitoring centre and headed back to the hotel.

As there was no swimming pool, Ms Sekikawa opted for the next best thing: the hotel's *onsen* bath. Relaxing in the steaming water, she slowly released all the tension accumulated during the day.

She found herself mesmerised by the water inlet, constantly replenishing the hot bath with bubbling, sulphurous water.

She imagined its long journey from the bowels of the earth far below.

Invariably when wallowing in her private thoughts, Yamaguchi's face tended to pop up. She pictured him stern-faced, trapped in his glass cube, immersed in weighty reading matter.

She settled back in the bath with a broad smile on her face.

65

The police captain was not given to changing his mind readily.

"This Maeda hardly sounds like a reliable witness."

"I agree. But we checked with his brother. He confirmed he's the owner of a blue Honda Fit. The chances are Maeda would remember seeing an identical model. It's the sort of thing that sticks in your mind."

"But even if there was another car at the bridge around the same time, it doesn't follow it had anything to do with the woman's suicide. It could just be a coincidence."

Ms Sekikawa bit her tongue. She had spent the previous half an hour arguing the new evidence she and Hayashi had produced at least merited further consideration.

She decided she was wasting her time. The police captain was evidently unwilling to entertain any other possible explanations for what had happened at the bridge.

She strode back to the small office they had been allocated. It was little more than a large cupboard. Hayashi looked up as the door slammed.

"I think I may have something."

Ms Sekikawa tried to put the unsatisfactory meeting with the police captain behind her.

"What?"

Hayashi spread out a series of photographs in front of her. They were all of Hiroko Iwasaki's parked car, taken near the bridge on the day of the incident. Each image showed the vehicle from a different angle.

Hayashi looked at Ms Sekikawa, waiting for a reaction. Still bristling from her previous meeting, she was not in the mood for guessing games.

"Sorry? What are you showing me exactly?"

"The position of the vehicle…"

Ms Sekikawa screwed up her face.

"What about it?"

"Well, it's incorrectly parked."

"Sorry? I'm not with you. How is that relevant?"

Ms Sekikawa glared at Hayashi as if he had lost the plot. A woman was dead and Hayashi was concerned about some parking infringement.

"I'm not explaining myself very well. As you see, the right-hand rear side of the vehicle is jutting out onto the carriageway."

"Yes?"

"There's plenty of room in front."

"OK? So what?"

"Why would Hiroko Iwasaki choose to park like that when she could have pulled further forwards, off the road?"

"Maybe she was distraught. In a hurry. Anxious to end her life."

"Possibly. But it occurred to me there might be another

explanation."

"Spit it out!"

Hayashi held out one of the photographs like an olive branch.

"There might have been another car occupying the space in front when she arrived."

Ms Sekikawa grabbed the photograph and studied it. Any thoughts of the police captain had vaporised. The penny had finally dropped.

"You're saying when Hiroko Iwasaki pulled in, another car might have already been parked there?"

"Exactly."

A picture was starting to form.

Ms Sekikawa stood up and started to wave the photograph as if she was conducting an orchestra. Sitting in front of her, Hayashi was content to play second fiddle.

"So, Hiroko Iwasaki pulls in behind another car. Its sole occupant is a woman driver. In the middle of nowhere."

"The Honda Fit."

"Hiroko Iwasaki parks quite carelessly. As if in a hurry. Why?"

Hayashi nodded encouragement.

Ms Sekikawa flourished the photograph again. She was reaching a crescendo.

"She pulls in because the woman in the car in front needs some kind of assistance. Perhaps something is wrong with her car. She's on a lonely road. Hiroko Iwasaki pulls in to help her. It's some kind of emergency. Hence her erratic parking."

Hayashi sat back smiling at Ms Sekikawa. She held up her finger.

"But if there was something wrong with the car, the women would have rung for assistance. There would be a record. We need to check the breakdown services, JAF and all the others …"

"I've already rung them. None of them received a call."

"What about Hiroko Iwasaki's mobile?"

"No outgoing calls from her mobile around that time."

Ms Sekikawa stopped conducting. The orchestra, she realised, was several bars ahead of her.

"But the Honda drives off. Leaving Hiroko Iwasaki lying at the bottom of the gorge."

Ms Sekikawa plumped down in her chair. Now the thoughts start to pile up.

"Well done, Hayashi. Remarkable detective work."

66

"Yes, all the footage."

The technician at the National Highways Office promised to send the digital file over immediately.

Ms Sekikawa could not care less how much food Hayashi ate that evening. He deserved every mouthful.

They had brainstormed ideas throughout the morning. Potential scenarios came thick and fast. They had trouble squeezing them all onto the small office whiteboard.

Ms Sekikawa stood back and stared at the confusion. A jumble of arrows and squiggles worthy of Detective Yamaguchi himself.

A major breakthrough came in the late afternoon. They received a message from a colleague in Tokyo. As Ms Sekikawa had requested, headquarters had run the registration number of the blue Honda Fit from the CCTV footage.

The owner turned out to be an elderly gentleman from Kawasaki Prefecture. He had contacted the police sometime prior to Hiroko Iwasaki's death to report his vehicle missing.

The coincidences were mounting up. They now knew a stolen blue Honda Fit was on the same stretch of road, at the same time, as Hiroko Iwasaki.

Ms Sekikawa decided they needed a closer look at the vehicle and its two male occupants.

Before heading back to the hotel, Ms Sekikawa rang Noriko Muratani. Although it was nine o'clock in the evening, Ms Sekikawa predicted her friend would still be at her desk. The computer specialist picked up after the first ring.

"Yes?"

Ms Sekikawa smiled at the trace of irritation in her friend's voice.

"It's Sekikawa. Am I interrupting?"

"Sekikawa-san? Where are you?"

"Yamashiro."

"What are you doing up there?"

Ms Sekikawa quickly put her friend in the picture.

"How can I help?"

"I'm sending you a video clip. Can you check it out?"

"OK. What are you looking for?"

"Anything you can tell me at all. Any details."

"OK. When do you need it?"

Before Ms Sekikawa could reply, Ms Muratani grunted.

"OK. Top of the pile. Call you later."

The next morning, the two officers left their hotel early. They were at their desks at 7:30.

A message was already waiting for Ms Sekikawa.

"Call me."

It had been left at 5:30 am. Ms Sekikawa's friend had a habit of spending all night at her desk.

Ms Sekikawa rang immediately and started to apologise. Noriko Muratani cut her off mid-sentence.

"Don't worry about that. Anyway, I've managed to find out something interesting from the video clip."

"What?"

Ms Sekikawa listened as her friend gave a lengthy description of the various technical techniques she had used. It was the price she had to pay for asking Ms Muratani a favour.

Eventually she came to the point.

"I've managed to get a reasonable picture of the two men in the front. But there's more. I'm pretty sure someone else is in the back. I can't be certain of course. Chasing shadows, really."

Ms Sekikawa started to think.

"A man or a woman?"

"No way of telling."

"OK, please send me what you have. And thank you."

Ms Sekikawa squeezed through the desks to the whiteboard.

"According to Muratani-san, it looks like there may have been a third person in the back of the stolen Honda Fit."

Hayashi broke off from what he was doing.

"A woman?"

"We don't know for sure."

Hayashi sat with his head on one side.

"But if there was a woman in the back, what happened to the two men? Maeda only saw the woman sitting in the car at the bridge?"

Ms Sekikawa stopped writing on the whiteboard, and nibbled the end of the marker pen.

"Good point."

67

Sean Peters stood up to stretch. The teacher's son followed suit.

Then they bent over and resumed thrusting rice plants into the murky water of the paddy field. The sun danced on the neat rows of green shoots in front of them.

Peters' teacher had insisted he stay with them.

When Peters drove up to the house after leaving the police station, the family were already waiting outside to greet him. The teacher's wife had taken one look at his drawn features and retired to the kitchen to make some food.

"I'm sorry for putting you to this trouble."

The teacher turned and pointed to the small annexe linked to the main house.

"My son has prepared a room for you there. It's yours for as long as you need it."

Every morning they trained. No allowance was made for Peters' condition.

Every afternoon, the son and Peters worked shoulder to shoulder in the fields. Occasionally the father would come to watch.

He would sit on a small rock, his hands resting on his knees. He invariably gave them a piece of well-considered advice before disappearing into the house again.

The family did not discuss what had happened. The past was the past. The priority was to restore Peters' strength, to help him to face the future.

Physically Peters was starting to feel more like his old self. The relentless routine reminded him of his time training with the Royal Marines. The nourishing diet restored him. He felt fighting fit.

But his heart grieved. The nights were the worst. He would lie awake listening to the sounds outside.

Then his fingers would inch across the rough tatami mats in search of Hiroko. He would hold his breath, listening for her own breathing in the darkness. Eventually sleep would envelop him.

He lived one day at a time. After the evening meal, he retired to the annexe. He did not want to impose on the family's kindness more than necessary.

"Sean-san!"

The teacher's wife was calling him from the house. After excusing himself, he squelched his way through the mud to the edge of the paddy field. The teacher's wife beckoned him in the typical Japanese way, as if she was scratching a cat's back.

"The police officers have arrived."

Ms Sekikawa had rung the previous day. She wanted to speak with him before she returned to Tokyo.

Peters saw her standing beside the car with her tall sidekick. As Peters drew close to the house, both officers saluted him.

Ms Sekikawa could see life on the farm agreed with Peters. He looked fit and toughened.

"So, this is the dojo where you train?"

Peters looked at Ms Sekikawa. He owed her. Without her, he would probably still be languishing in the cells, or worse.

"Yes. Every morning. With my teacher and his son."

Ms Sekikawa had asked around about the teacher prior to her visit. One of the senior police officers knew of him.

In an area renowned for martial arts exponents, the teacher's reputation was second to none. According to the officer, for Peters to be accorded the status of his personal student was a great distinction.

It explained the fate of the construction workers. They would not have known what hit them.

"If I may say so, you're looking a great deal better than when we last met."

Peters managed a smile.

"I'm being well cared for."

On cue, the teacher's wife arrived with tea. When the elderly lady withdrew, they started to talk in earnest.

"Before we leave for Tokyo, would you mind answering a few more questions related to our investigation?"

Peters nodded.

"OK."

Ms Sekikawa turned to Hayashi. He delved into his briefcase and produced the CCTV stills Noriko Muratani had sent. He handed them to Peters.

"Please look at these photos. On the day Hiroko Iwasaki died, did you happen to see this car?"

Peters stared at the picture of the blue Honda Fit.

"No, not that I recall."

"Perhaps it passed you as you were cycling towards the bridge?"

"I passed no one. I was on the look-out for Hiroko. I would have remembered."

"And the two men shown here?"

Peters stared at the photograph.

Noriko Muratani had pushed the predictive software to the limit. Out of the shadows of the original CCTV clip, two identifiable faces emerged.

The driver was chubby-cheeked with a pencil moustache and a receding hairline. The passenger, slouched back in his seat, had sharp features, round-framed sunglasses and a shock of hair with a distinctive quiff.

"Never seen them before."

Peters handed the photographs back to Hayashi.

"What has this got to do with Hiroko's death?"

Ms Sekikawa knew the question would come. She was prepared.

"A car matching this description was spotted at Komai Bridge at around the time of Iwasaki-san's death. It may have been this one, captured earlier on CCTV."

"And you think these people might have something to do with what happened to Hiroko?"

"We are making enquiries. It may be unconnected."

Peters reached out and took the photograph back from

Hayashi. His eyes soaked up every detail.

"Where was this image taken?"

"On the bypass outside Yamashiro."

Peters checked the timestamp on the photograph. He was arriving at the same conclusion as the two police officers. He did not need a whiteboard.

"Around the same time as Hiroko was there?"

"Shortly before. We were able to locate your car passing just afterwards."

Peters sat unravelling the information. His thumb made a smudgy imprint on the photograph. Ms Sekikawa was starting to become concerned.

"Please understand we are still gathering information. We need to rule out every possibility."

Peters handed the photograph back to Hayashi. They finished their tea in silence.

"You said you're on your way back to Tokyo?"

"Yes. We'll continue our investigations from there."

"You'll update me on anything you discover?"

"Of course."

With that the two police officers took their leave.

As they drove away from the property, Ms Sekikawa glanced in the side mirror. The Englishman had already disappeared from sight.

68

"Can you run through that again?"

Ms Sekikawa looked at Yamaguchi with exasperation. Sitting in his office in Tokyo, she had just summarised all the latest developments in Yamashiro.

She was tired of explaining the intricacies of their recent findings. Before she and Hayashi left for Tokyo, she had given the local police captain a full status report.

It was slow progress. He had raised endless objections, unwilling to budge from his earlier conclusion. As far as he was concerned, it was a case of suicide pure and simple.

Eventually, Ms Sekikawa had decided enough was enough. Striding over to the police chief's whiteboard, she had drawn out a full flowchart of events to try to help him grasp their significance.

She was not to know that no one was allowed to touch his whiteboard. He had sat at his desk, his face frozen, his fists clenched.

Whatever she said made no difference. Ms Sekikawa finally decided to cut her losses.

She and Hayashi left the building, pausing to thank the local officers for their assistance. Some of them followed the two officers outside to see them off. The police captain did not show his face.

She expected Yamaguchi to be quicker on the uptake.

"From the beginning?"

"Just from the part where you identified the Honda Fit on the CCTV."

Ms Sekikawa started again and then stopped.

"Do you mind if I ask Hayashi to come in?"

Yamaguchi raised his eyebrows. Another recent irritating habit, Ms Sekikawa thought.

"Hayashi?"

"Yes, Hayashi. He should be credited with some first-class police work. He figured it all out, and then paid me the courtesy of letting me think I had."

"Smart chap."

"Exactly. Anyway, probably better you hear it from him. And give him a pat on the back."

Yamaguchi raised his eyebrows again.

"OK, I'll just go and get him."

Ms Sekikawa stuck her head around the glass door of Yamaguchi's office and shouted down the office.

"Hayashi. In here."

The tall officer leaped from his chair, knocking his knee against the desk. He limped across the room to the office.

"Please tell Detective Yamaguchi how you figured out the Honda Fit was at the bridge at the same time as Hiroko Iwasaki's Nissan."

Hayashi drew himself bolt upright. His attention seemed to be on the Inland Revenue building opposite. His summary was unembellished and typically self-deprecating.

At the end, Yamaguchi nodded.

"Excellent work."

Hayashi looked down, abashed. Ms Sekikawa beamed.

"Anyway, where does all this leave us Sekikawa-san?"

It was a good point. She and Hayashi had discussed it on the train back to Tokyo.

"We're following up on the stolen car. It was almost certainly ditched at the first opportunity."

"What about two occupants?"

"I've asked Muratani-san to run the images against the database. She might be able to see if they are already known to the police."

"Good. What about the motive?"

"We were discussing that. With Hiroko Iwasaki dead, her sister inherited the property. She in turn immediately sold it to the company involved in developing the village."

"Which developers?"

"New Horizon Development Company. Run by an Akira Kato."

"Speak with Kato and the sister. See what you can find out."

"We'll get onto it straight away."

"In the meantime, I'll ring the police captain in Yamashiro."

"Thank you. We did not leave on the friendliest of terms."

"I appreciate that. OK, that's it for the moment. Keep me up to date."

Dismissed, Ms Sekikawa hurried Hayashi out of the door.

Back at her desk Ms Sekikawa's phone rang. It was her IT friend Noriko Muratani. There were no preliminaries.

"I'm on my way up."

Moments later the large-boned police officer strode into the department. She made a beeline for Ms Sekikawa's desk.

"Look. I've found a match."

She slapped the photograph of the blue Honda Fit passenger on Ms Sekikawa's desk. Beside it, a printout from the criminal database.

"Wang. Chinese. Police record. He was cautioned after a gangland tussle over territory in Kabukicho. Part of the Chinese criminal fraternity who have taken over Shinjuku."

"When was this taken?"

"Ten years ago."

It was a striking face. The eyes looked back at the camera with an arrogant, untroubled gaze. The man's distinctive quiff was the same as in the CCTV shot.

"Hayashi, over here."

He strolled around to Ms Sekikawa's side of the desk. He bent over the photograph.

"What do you think?"

Hayashi stared long and hard, his eyes narrowed.

"Quite similar."

"OK. We'll pull him in. Thank you, Muratani-san"

Ms Muratani held her ground

"There's more."

She now placed a facial imaging printout on the desk.

It took a second for Ms Sekikawa to make the connection.

"I don't know why I thought of it. The distinctive hairstyle, maybe. I can't be certain, of course."

Ms Sekikawa was already on her feet.

"Well, there's one way to find out for sure."

69

Ms Sekikawa and Hayashi squeezed into the apartment block elevator with two plain-clothes officers.

The men were thick-set and trained for this type of assignment. They both carried New Nambu M60 sidearms and were well versed in using them.

They did not know what they were going to find in Flat B on the 14th floor. It was as well to be prepared.

Ms Sekikawa had driven straight to the Tokyo Women's Consulting Centre in Kiba. When she arrived, she was escorted to Ligaya Santos' room. The Filipina was sitting at her small writing table gazing out of the window.

"Ligaya?"

"Detective Sekikawa?"

The petite woman jumped up and ran across the room. Shocked, Ms Sekikawa found herself locked in a tight embrace. After a moment's hesitation, she reciprocated.

"How are you?"

Ligaya sat down on her bed, clutching herself.

"Please! Do you have any news about when I can go home?"

She looked so distressed Ms Sekikawa was taken aback. It was a while since they had met.

"I am doing everything I can, but you have to be patient."

"You keep saying that. My son is suffering. I need to be there with him."

Ligaya Santos was now in regular contact with her family in the Philippines. Ms Sekikawa guessed the boy's condition had not improved.

"Ligaya, I have something to show you. Some photographs. I want you to see if you recognise anyone in them. OK?"

The woman nodded. She looked confused, unsure what this was about.

Ms Sekikawa went over to the desk and lay an assortment of images side by side. Ligaya Santos got up and stood next to her.

She clamped her hand over her mouth. She immediately reached out and pointed to the photograph of Wang.

"It's him!"

Terrified, she reached out to grab Ms Sekikawa's elbow.

"Are you sure?"

"Sure? Yes, I'm sure. He was the one who assaulted me. He's the monster who ran that place."

Ms Sekikawa wasted no time. From the car she rang Hayashi.

"Are we ready to go?"

"Yes. Everything is in place."

Hayashi had researched Wang's current address. Yamaguchi had secured the search warrant in short order. Police back-up would meet them at the property.

"OK. I have a positive ID from Ligaya Santos. I'll be with you directly."

Ms Sekikawa made good time through the heart of the city. Even along the packed streets of Nihonbashi, the traffic parted for the police siren.

Hayashi was waiting outside police headquarters as she pulled up. Ms Sekikawa was already moving off as Hayashi closed the car door. They took the expressway to Shinjuku and continued west into Suginami-ku.

The two plain-clothes officers were waiting for them outside the building in an unmarked car. They had been dispatched from Shinjuku police station. Ms Sekikawa filled them in on the background and they quickly agreed tactics.

The elderly concierge was in his small office near the entrance. Ms Sekikawa approached him and explained they were there to interview one of the residents.

When she mentioned the name, he nodded with a wry smile.

"The Chinese bloke. He's not here. Left yesterday. Took a suitcase with him. Good riddance."

"You're certain he's gone?"

"That's my job. I am responsible for the building."

"Does he live alone?"

"Yes, but he has visitors. Young women mostly."

He gave Ms Sekikawa a knowing look.

"He's bad news. Nasty piece of work."

"How do you mean?"

"The neighbours are always complaining. Noise, late night parties, women shrieking. You name it."

"And you have to deal with it?"

"Yup. The last time he had three girls with him. Foreign tarts, lying on the bed half naked. He answered the door with his yukata wide open, displaying himself. Dirty bastard. He told me it was none of my business and slammed the door."

"Is this him?"

Ms Sekikawa showed the picture.

"That's him."

"Right. We're going up. Please give me the spare key to the apartment."

The man opened the wall safe behind him and took out the key.

"Thank you. I'll need to speak with you later."

The concierge nodded and withdrew into his office. About time that bastard had his come-uppance, he thought, as he sat polishing his glasses on his tie.

When they rang the buzzer for Flat B on the 14th floor, there was no answer. Nevertheless, the two Shinjuku officers had their holster flaps open, their hands resting on their weapons.

They went in first and made sure the rooms were clear. When Ms Sekikawa and Hayashi joined them, they all put on latex gloves and started the search.

If Ms Sekikawa was asked to predict the contents of the apartment, she would have been right on most counts.

Large HD television set. Sprawling music centre. A bed large enough to accommodate a small family. An expensive wardrobe of gaudy clothes. A well-stocked drinks cabinet. No food. Mess everywhere.

The search revealed nothing of interest. No photographs, no

notebooks, no laptop computer. Nothing to give them an idea of the man beyond the little they already knew.

After an hour, they called it a day. Ms Sekikawa returned the key to the concierge and left her card. He was to call if Wang showed up.

Outside, the two Shinjuku officers returned to their vehicle. They were under orders to keep the apartment block under observation.

Ms Sekikawa drove. She tapped her fingernails on the steering wheel in frustration.

"I can't believe we just missed him."

70

Wang was furious at being forced to go to ground.

But he had no choice. He had had to move quickly. He understood the police could be arriving at any moment.

He had thrown some items into a suitcase and removed any incriminating evidence from his apartment. With a rueful backwards glance, he slammed the door behind him.

He did not acknowledge the interfering concierge as he wheeled his large suitcase past the small office on the ground floor. A large SUV was waiting outside.

His boss had been unsparing. Wang was pivotal to his operations. Having him out of the picture impacted the business.

As Wang listened to the voice hissing down the phone, a chill ran through his body. After the debacle with the Filipina, he was now guilty of another serious transgression.

Mistakes were not tolerated. However well placed you were.

Wang had risen through the ranks. First as a punk enforcer, later as an area coordinator.

Chen had been quick to spot his potential. Behind the young man's ruthless streak was a sharp brain. He had demonstrated a natural gift for organisation.

Chen needed competent men with flair at the forefront of his operation. It allowed him to stay in the background, the hidden hand pulling the strings.

At the outset, he always set his chosen men a simple test. To demonstrate their unswerving loyalty.

Wang's initiation had taken place at Chen's private restaurant in the heart of Yokohama's Chinatown.

From the outside, no passer-by would have even guessed it was a restaurant. Located down a narrow side street, it displayed none of the usual inducements to dine.

If any member of the public did happen to venture across the threshold, the imposing manager would soon set them right. No one was ever foolish enough to linger.

The main body of the restaurant was out of bounds to all but Chen's select inner circle. But even they knew never to enter the exclusive back room without prior invitation.

That was Chen's private domain.

On that particular day, Wang was granted unusual access. The heavy teak doors swung open and two of Chen's trusted minders marched him inside.

Alone, across a sea of empty tables covered with pristine white table cloths, sat Chen. He was engrossed in the array of food laid out in front of him.

As instructed, Wang took an empty seat on the other side of the large circular table. The minders withdrew and stood guard at the door. Wang waited.

Chen continued with his meal as if unaware of his underling's presence. For his part, Wang tried not to stare at the dainty white-gloved hand wielding the ivory chopsticks.

Eventually, Chen broke the silence.

"I have heard positive reports of your activities. It seems you are ready to take on more responsibility in our organisation."

Wang started to breathe more evenly.

"Thank you."

Chen looked directly at Wang for the first time. Wang was captivated by his protruding eyes. He could not help comparing them with the sea bream in the dish Chen had been picking at.

"You will take your orders directly from me from now on. You will carry them out to the letter. Is that understood?"

Wang nodded. He was ambitious. This was the pinnacle of his career.

But he was wary. Life was perilous so close to the flame.

Chen glanced to his left. A signal.

"I need to know I can trust you. A small test."

Wang heard movement behind him. Three men came into his field of vision. Between Chen's two bodyguards was a man with his hands tied behind his back.

As they approached the table, Chen dabbed his mouth with his napkin. He waved a gloved hand towards the bound man.

"I expect you've run across this piece of shit in the course of your daily activities. At one time, he was like you. An ambitious young man intent on forging a long and successful career in our organisation."

Wang stared at the man. He knew him. But he bore little resemblance to the dapper gangster of old, always smartly turned out in flashy suits.

The man's face was a bloodied pulp. The front of his shirt was encrusted with vomit. His hands had been crushed like tenderised steaks.

"Unfortunately, his ideas were above his station. He thought he could ignore the time-honoured precepts of our organisation. He conspired to topple us, to take our share. In short, he betrayed our trust."

Wang sensed a reckoning was imminent. The air-conditioners suddenly seemed to labour.

Chen continued to speak while his eyes roamed over the dishes in front of him.

"So, it's important you can demonstrate your commitment to us here and now. A gesture of good faith, if you like."

Chen tilted his chopsticks in the direction of the doomed man. The two heavies kicked his legs away so he fell to his knees.

One of the men then reached into the waistband of his trousers and produced a loop of hemp rope attached to a steel T-shaped handle. He offered it to Wang.

As Chen picked at a dish of prawns, Wang took the rope. He knew what he was expected to do.

He had no issues with it. He had dispatched people in this way before. He considered himself something of an expert.

The kneeling man squinted through a bloodied eye at Wang. Ignoring him, Wang moved to his rear and fed the noose over the man's head. Then he started to turn the handle.

It did not take long. Throughout Chen paid no attention, continuing his lunch as if oblivious to the man's dispatch.

As the body was removed, Wang resumed his seat at the end of the table.

Chen smiled and pointed to a bowl of diced sea cucumber.

"Try this. It really is something, you know."

71

Ms Sekikawa was peering out of the 43rd floor window. She was wondering if she could pinpoint her home.

Far below her, the Keio Line snaked away from nearby Shinjuku Station like a silver thread running through the cityscape. Somewhere out there was her cramped apartment. With the previous evening's washing-up stacked in the sink.

Akira Kato was behind his stainless-steel desk on the other side of the room. He was giving the detective a fulsome description of his firm's activities. As she had asked him the question, she felt obliged to let him drone on.

He paused for a second as if waiting for a pat on the back. Ms Sekikawa decided to put the boot in instead.

"Kato-san, I'm here to ask about your Yamashiro development project."

Kato's smile did not flicker.

"Yamashiro? Ah yes, of course. A particularly promising venture."

He looked set to launch into another self-congratulatory spiel.

"Your company recently purchased a property from a certain Akemi Watanabe."

In an instant, the wind seemed to drop from Kato's sails.

"That's correct, we did."

Ms Sekikawa had already interviewed Akemi Watanabe. She had not warmed to the woman, noting especially her undisguised contempt for Sean Peters. Nevertheless, she had uncovered nothing suspicious.

"Can you describe the circumstances surrounding that purchase?"

"Of course. I myself made the initial contact with Watanabe-san."

"Was that prior to her sister's death?"

Kato only hesitated for a moment, flicking his long hair back from his eyes.

"It was, yes."

"And the purpose of that meeting?"

"The then owner, now as you say sadly deceased, was reluctant to sell despite the very attractive offer we were making. I thought her sister, Watanabe-san, might be able to put a word in for us."

"Exert pressure?"

"No, certainly not. More to encourage her sister to appreciate the opportunity the development presented."

Ms Sekikawa pressed ahead.

"And then, after her sister's death, Akemi Watanabe comes into the property."

"Indeed."

"And your company was finally able to acquire it from her, allowing your development to proceed?"

"Yes. Watanabe-san was keen to divest herself of the land. We were naturally glad to be of service."

"Were you aware her sister, Hiroko Iwasaki, had received threats prior to her death?"

Kato's eyes travelled across his desk as if he was searching for something he had mislaid.

"Threats? No, I had no idea. I'm shocked to hear that."

"Nothing your company would resort to?"

Kato leaned back in his chair with his palms raised.

"Please, Detective Sekikawa. I can assure you that we are above such tactics."

"You are developing this land on whose behalf?"

"A consortium."

"A Japanese consortium?"

"No, an overseas consortium, in point of fact."

"Based where?"

"The Cayman Islands."

"And who do you receive your instructions from?"

Kato's mouth suddenly became dry. He fidgeted on his chair.

At the outset of the project, the client had been quite explicit. At no point should he be in any way linked with the project.

"From their representatives in the Caymans. But they leave most of the day-to-day operational decisions to us. We are quite experienced in handling these types of projects independently. We only need to involve our clients in high-level decisions."

"Such as what to do when someone has become an obstacle? By refusing to sell, for example?"

Kato smile narrowed to little more than a pout.

"We are naturally obliged to keep our clients abreast of any situation which might have the potential to negatively impact our progress."

"And then, lo and behold, the reluctant owner dies and your problem is solved. Does that not strike you as somewhat fortuitous?"

Kato decided it was time to go on the offensive.

"I don't know what you are implying, Detective Sekikawa. We were all extremely saddened to hear about the owner's death. You surely cannot be suggesting my company was in any way implicated in such a tragedy?"

Ms Sekikawa waited a few seconds before responding. Without cast-iron proof of Hiroko Iwasaki's murder, she had to proceed with caution.

"Kato-san, before I leave this office today, I need all the client details for the Yamashiro project. We'll be contacting them as part of our enquiry."

"Enquiry?"

"Yes. Our continuing investigating into the death of Hiroko Iwasaki."

72

Ligaya Santos had lavished extra care on her appearance that morning. She was sitting on her bed, excited at the prospect of her outing.

Most days she just strolled around the immediate proximity of the centre, breathing in the pine resin from the lumber yards and sitting on the public benches overlooking the waterways.

Sometimes she went further afield but always within easy walking distance. She liked to visit the local parks and watch the school children at play.

Someone from the centre always accompanied her. To make sure she did not get lost. To watch over her.

That day she was all set to go on her weekly shopping expedition. Not far from the centre, a cluster of large discount stores stood near one of the expressway intersections, drawing shoppers from far and wide.

Ligaya Santos loved their energy. The vendors clamouring for attention, the customers driving hard bargains. It reminded her of home.

She had a little money saved up from the weekly allowance the centre gave her for necessities. In addition, the head of the centre had generously given her a loan from her own pocket.

She was in the market for a particular item. A wristwatch for

Cesar.

There was a knock at the door.

"Ms Santos? Are you ready?"

She recognised the voice. Of all the members of staff at the centre, he was the one she felt least at ease with.

Her escort was a portly man in his early forties. Over-polite and distant. He never let her out of his sight as if she was on a leash.

"Yes, ready."

She opened the door. The man was standing outside. He peered over her shoulder before stepping aside to let her pass.

"*Doozo.*"

As they walked down the street, Ligaya Santos kept several paces ahead. She frequently had to wait for him to catch up.

He bustled along behind her struggling to make much headway. Out of breath, he kept pausing to take off his glasses and dab his face with his handkerchief.

He never tried to engage her in conversation. She was glad when they reached the discount store and she could focus on her shopping.

They took the escalator to the ninth floor. Ligaya Santos headed straight for the watch section.

All the expensive items were neatly laid out in display cases. Sales staff were on hand to show them to customers. The watches Ligaya Santos was interested in were kept in large cardboard boxes on a shelf at the back.

Ligaya Santos started examining them one by one. She took her time, trying each watch on her wrist. Cesar would have the best her limited funds could stretch to.

Eventually she decided on one. She ran her fingers over the strap for any imperfections and double-checked the watch face for scratches.

It was a popular brand. She hoped Cesar would like it.

She turned round expecting to see her escort. There was no sign of him.

The floor was packed with shoppers. She ran her eye over the crowd trying to find him.

Perhaps he needed to go somewhere? She was surprised he had not bothered to let her know.

She decided to wait. She kept hold of the watch, not wishing to put it back in the cardboard box in case anyone else took a shine to it.

She felt awkward. What if someone asked her what she was doing? Especially without her escort to speak up for her?

More and more shoppers arrived. The Japanese scurried to and fro looking for bargains. It was cut and thrust, with none of the usual courtesies.

Five minutes passed. She knew she had no alternative but stay where she was. She was starting to panic.

Suddenly, through the crowd, she spotted two department store security staff approaching. A man and a woman. They made a bee-line for her.

She instinctively shrank back. She slipped the watch she was holding on top of the glass cabinet behind her. She did not wish to be caught with goods she had not paid for.

The woman stepped forward. She had a pleasant face.

"Excuse me, are you waiting for your companion?"

She breathed a sigh of relief. Everything was all right. What's more, they addressed her in English.

"Yes, that's right. Is anything the matter?"

"I'm afraid he has been taken ill. He asked us to take care of you."

"Ill? Oh, goodness. Thank you for coming to find me."

"Please come with us. We'll take you to him."

The woman led the way. Ligaya Santos followed with the man. They took the escalators down to the ground floor.

"This way please. He's waiting for you outside."

They walked out through the exit and took a sharp right turn past a line of vehicles. A large white van was parked at the end.

As they neared it, Ligaya Santos' survival instinct suddenly kicked in. She had let her defences drop. Questions started to flood her mind.

How had the guards recognised her so easily in such a crowded store? Just from her escort's description? When he was feeling so ill?

As if sensing her hesitate, the man grabbed her elbow and with the other hand propelled her forwards. The woman swivelled back and seized her from the other side.

The side door of the white van yawned open. With a vicious shove, Ligaya Santos found herself sprawling on the floor inside.

73

"She's been taken!"

Startled, Yamaguchi looked up. It was a brusque entry into his office even by Ms Sekikawa's standards.

"Who has?"

"Ligaya Santos."

Ms Sekikawa glared at her boss.

"The Filipina!"

"I know. What happened?"

"The director of the centre just rang. Apparently, Ligaya Santos was out shopping. She was abducted in broad daylight."

"She didn't just wander off?"

"No. The staff member accompanying her raised the alarm. He was threatened by the kidnappers, tied up in a toilet."

Yamaguchi stared at the pile of reports in front of him. Crime statistics, departmental budget projections, human resource procedure manuals.

"OK. Let's go."

Ms Sekikawa raced out of the office as Yamaguchi grabbed his jacket. She ordered Hayashi to stay put and liaise with the police at the discount store.

Driving to the centre, Ms Sekikawa brought Yamaguchi up to date on the investigation. He listened without interrupting. At intervals, he reached for his armrest as Ms Sekikawa's hands separated from the steering wheel.

When they arrived, Ms Sekikawa led the way into the office. The director was waiting there with Ligaya Santos' escort. The man was perched on a small plastic stool.

Yamaguchi led the questioning.

"Please explain what happened. Take your time. Don't miss anything out."

The man nodded. He kept his handkerchief bunched in his hand as he spoke.

"While Santos-san was looking at watches, a man came up behind me and pressed a knife into my back. I could feel the point through my shirt. He whispered in my ear. He said he'd use the knife if I didn't do exactly what he said. I was petrified."

His eyes petitioned the two officers for sympathy.

"Then he walked me through the department store to the toilet. He told me to go into one of the cubicles."

"Did you get a look at him?"

"No, once inside the cubicle, he put a bag over my head. I never saw his face."

"What happened then?"

"He tied me to the toilet by my wrists. He asked me my name. He said if I raised the alarm, he would come back and slit my throat. He cut me here as a warning. Look."

The man showed the slight nick on his throat.

"And then?"

"He left. I didn't dare move. After a while, someone came into the toilet and I plucked up courage. I shouted for help."

"What happened next?"

"After I was released, I rushed back to the watch section. There was no sign of Santos-san. He must have taken her."

Yamaguchi instructed the man to wait outside the room. He now turned to the director.

"How often has Ligaya Santos been to that department store?"

"Once a week, I believe. She specifically requested it."

"Is it standard procedure to establish a pattern like that?"

"The women are always accompanied. We've never had a problem like this before."

"How long has her escort been working here?"

"Two years."

The director saw where this was leading.

"He has always been a reliable member of staff. Not the most sensitive perhaps, but completely trustworthy."

"Somebody must have tipped off the kidnappers. They knew where to find her and were familiar with her routine."

The director shuffled uneasily in her chair. She was responsible for the centre. Any breach of security would be laid at her door.

"Do you need to interview the other members of staff?"

"Yes. And all the women being held here under protective

custody. Without delay."

74

Ms Sekikawa squeezed into a tight parking space near the discount store main entrance. There was barely room for Yamaguchi to squeeze out of the car.

The local police were already combing the building. Their initial staff interviews had yielded nothing. No one remembered seeing the Filipina.

Surveillance cameras monitored each floor. Checking the recordings, the police were able to locate Ligaya Santos leaving the building accompanied by a man and a woman dressed as security officers.

But once outside the store, the police were stymied. The white van had been parked in a camera blind spot. The kidnappers had done their homework.

"Where do we start?"

Yamaguchi and Ms Sekikawa were standing at the entrance to the store. Yamaguchi was staring out at the car park, trying to visualise what had happened.

"We have to assume it was the original traffickers."

Ms Sekikawa nodded.

"They'll want to set an example."

Yamaguchi knew only too well the type they were dealing with. Calculating and utterly ruthless.

"We need to find her quickly. She won't have long."

Ms Sekikawa slapped her thigh in frustration. She pictured Ligaya Santos back in the clutches of the people she had tried so hard to escape from. Then her thoughts turned to Ligaya's young son in hospital in the Philippines.

"We'll need to contact her family. Let them know what's happened."

Yamaguchi paused for a second before answering.

"Best to hold off for a day or two. No point in causing unnecessary distress at this stage."

After further briefings with the police at the store, Ms Sekikawa and Yamaguchi returned to headquarters. They decided they could be of more use there.

When they arrived, Ms Sekikawa beckoned to Hayashi to join them.

"Detective Yamaguchi's office."

The tall police officer picked up a notepad and hurried across the room.

Yamaguchi sat at his desk with his arms crossed over his chest. Then he stared at each of his subordinates in turn before summarising the situation.

"A man and a woman abduct Ligaya Santos dressed as security guards. We have no descriptions. Faces not visible from the cameras. We lose her outside the building. No information on the vehicle used. Presumably she was taken to a safe house. She could be anywhere. Not much to go on."

The two officers sitting opposite looked blankly at him.

"They may kill her, as an example to the other women not to try anything similar. Or she may be trafficked elsewhere. Alive she is still a valuable commodity. Either way, we don't have much time."

Still no reaction. Hayashi flipped through the pages of his notebook as if searching for inspiration.

"So? Where do we start?"

Ms Sekikawa decided to pitch in.

"Well, if it was her original traffickers, then finding Wang becomes even more of a priority."

Yamaguchi nodded.

"Hayashi, liaise with your former colleagues on the specialist Chinese team in Yokohama. See what they can find out."

"Yes, sir."

"Then start preparing a missing person communiqué, standard procedure. That's it. Regular updates. Top priority."

Yamaguchi stood up. Stacking the reports on his desk, he deposited them in a heap on top of a corner cabinet.

Ms Sekikawa smiled and left the office with a new spring in her step. Suddenly it felt like old times again.

Meanwhile, back at the centre, the director was standing in Ligaya Santos' room. She looked around, her hands hanging by her sides.

On the desk was the framed family photograph. On the chest of drawers, a small mirror and a bag of cosmetics. Items the centre had provided Ligaya Santos to tide her over.

She opened the cupboard in the corner. Inside was a plastic bag containing some toys, a tennis ball and a plastic baseball bat.

The director closed the cupboard door and sat on the edge of the bed. She glanced down at the back of her hands. She wondered how they had come to look so old.

Then, gathering herself, she went to fetch a cardboard box. Places at the centre were in great demand. Someone else would need the room soon.

It did not take her long to pack up Ligaya Santos' meagre belongings.

75

Sean Peters took his usual place at the family dinner table. In front of him were dishes of freshly-picked vegetables from the fields.

After offering thanks to the teacher's wife for preparing the meal, they ate in silence. That day was no different from any other.

Peters had little difficulty falling into the household routine. It followed the same strict rhythms as his life with Hiroko. Training, work in the fields, eating, sleeping.

But despite the family's efforts to make him feel at ease, he realised the clock was ticking. He was anxious not to overstay his welcome.

He had to start thinking about the future. To prepare for a new life after Hiroko.

Peters was always secretly relieved when the meal came to an end. After bidding the family good night, he retired to his annexe. Finally, he could relax, left to his own thoughts.

It was a chance to check his emails. He always made a point of logging on to his second-hand laptop every evening, just in case there was a message.

He only had a few email contacts. Some old friends like George Trevillion, his students, a small group of likeminded environmentalists.

He was surprised to see a new message in his in-tray. He did not recognise the sender. He thought twice about opening it.

When he finally did, he sat for a long time without moving.

The anonymous email was brief but to the point. It was accompanied by an image attachment.

Clicking on the link, Peters recognised the face immediately. The same photo Detective Sekikawa had shown him earlier. The man with the distinctive quiff and dark glasses, lounging in the passenger seat of the car.

The writer identified the individual in the picture as one Wang, a senior member of a Yokohama-based Chinese crime organisation. The email claimed the man Wang was responsible for carrying out Hiroko Iwasaki's murder, acting under orders from his underworld boss.

The writer offered to furnish Peters with the killer's current location. But only on condition the Englishman agreed not to involve the Japanese police.

Peters stared at the message. Trying to read between the lines.

Who had sent it? What was the motivation? Could he trust it?

It was a mystery. But if it was bona fide, he was being offered the chance to settle scores with Hiroko's killer.

It was contrary to everything he believed. Everything his teacher had patiently tried to inculcate in him over the years.

Part of him wanted to delete the message. To put it out of his mind. To forget about it.

But part of him felt suddenly galvanised.

Since Hiroko's death he had been stuck in limbo. Helplessly staring into the void.

Now, after reading the email, a fuse was lit within him.

The former Royal Marine was reawakened. An all-too-familiar feeling flooded through his veins.

He was battle ready. The target identified. His mission defined.

He was primed for action.

And this time, it was personal.

If it needed to be done, he would do it. For Hiroko.

He did not need to involve the police. He could move more nimbly on his own. He had all the skills required for the task.

But first, he needed a second opinion. When he called George Trevillion, his friend did not hesitate.

He immediately offered his unconditional support. He had his comrade's back through thick and thin.

"Understood, Sean. Send over the email, I'll have a look and see what I can find out. I'll phone you tomorrow."

Sean Peters turned in but lay awake on his futon until the early hours. He kept re-playing the image of Hiroko's death.

Of the hands bundling her over the guardrail. Watching her flail in the air as she plummeted to her death.

Only now he could put a face to her executioner.

First thing the next morning, Trevillion phoned Peters.

"Hi Sean. You ready for this?"

"What did you find out?"

"It took me a while. Whoever sent the email made a good job of covering their tracks."

George Trevillion had the latest software at his disposal. He had painstakingly followed the online thread. Eventually he had traced it to its source.

"It turns out the email was sent from a server inside the Tokyo police headquarters."

Peters lowered the phone from his ear and looked through the window of the annexe. He could see the spot where he and the two police officers had talked. Where Detective Sekikawa had first shown him the photograph.

"You're sure?"

"No doubt about it.

"Thanks George. I'll call you back."

It took Peters until lunchtime to reach his decision. Then he sent the anonymous emailer a confirmation. He would not involve the police.

Seconds later, a new email arrived. It included Wang's mobile telephone number and a Tokyo address.

It did not take Trevillion long to confirm the number was currently located at that address.

"Thanks George. Right, time to get cracking."

76

"Gin and tonic."

"Yes, sir."

The Japanese barman at the Paradise Club in the Roppongi Midtown Galleria fussed over the cocktail before placing it in front of Charles Fancourt.

Fancourt downed it in two gulps.

"Another one. And spare me the fucking tea ceremony."

Fancourt always kicked off Saturday night at the Paradise Club. What he did next depended on his mood.

The phone call from Yuki Morigami had come out of the blue. He had not expected to hear from her before the next social event.

She had suggested lunch. He was in two minds. He rarely bothered to eat at midday. But something told him to make the effort.

She had reserved a table at a fashionable French restaurant in Aoyama. Exactly the type of place Fancourt avoided.

Yuki Morigami had pulled out all the stops. She had taken pains to look her best. Her hair was freshly styled, she wore a sleek designer dress.

A bottle of Saint-Emilion Grand Cru was open on the table. Fancourt frowned. He avoided alcohol during working hours.

Something was up. He just could not figure out what.

It took until the flambéed crêpes suzette before he found out. Yuki Morigami leaned forwards conspiratorially.

"Charles, a little bird let me in on a secret."

She sat back, giving her words time to sink in. Fancourt poured himself a glass of water, replacing the jug with exaggerated care.

"What might that be?"

"About you. And your special hush-hush group."

Fancourt stared at her. Suddenly he did not see the gloss, the trinkets.

"Sorry Yuki, I've no idea what you're talking about."

Undaunted, Yuki Morigami forged ahead.

"About the very profitable cartel you run."

She raised her eyebrows and flashed a winning smile. It usually worked.

Not in Fancourt's case. He did not blink. His mind was working double-time.

"As I said, I've no idea what you're talking about."

Yuki Morigami looked flustered. This was not going as she had expected.

"OK Charles. Cards on the table. I know about your stock-fixing party. I want in. You can make room for one more, right?"

Fancourt's eyes half-closed. The restaurant disappeared. The sophisticated ambiance, the well-heeled patrons, the simpering waiters.

It was like a fist grabbing his entrails. The sick-making feeling of suddenly being under threat.

Yuki Morigami bent forwards again. Her voice became more urgent as she tried to seize her opportunity.

"I've got the resources to play. I've got the contacts. And I know how to keep my mouth shut."

Fancourt looked at her mouth. Instead of the glossed lips and polished teeth, he only saw a gaping liability.

Yuki Morigami stretched her hand across the table to brush the end of his fingers. He resisted the impulse to snatch them away. Reaching out for the Bordeaux, he refilled both their glasses.

Yuki Morigami smiled and drank deeply. Fancourt twirled the wine in his glass, studying the blood-red hues.

"So, who on earth has been spinning you all these tales?"

Yuki Morigami coloured up.

"Well, I guess I can confide in you. Frank and I have been seeing each other."

"Frank Deluca? You should know better than believe anything Frank Deluca tells you."

Yuki Morigami's hand snaked back to her side of the table. She waved to the waiter.

Then she turned back to Fancourt. Her seductive smile had become a jagged line.

"Charles, either I'm in, or, trust me, a lot more people are going to know about your little game."

The following Saturday in the Paradise Club, Charles Fancourt downed his second gin and tonic and slipped out into the street.

He hailed a taxi, climbed in and gave well-rehearsed instructions to the driver. They headed westwards, away from Roppongi.

The taxi passed one entertainment hub after another. Some catering for the well-heeled, others for youngsters looking for a cheap night out.

Fancourt's destination lay at the bottom of the pile. When the taxi pulled in, Fancourt paid and disappeared down a crowded side street.

He looked out of place among the Japanese men roaming the narrow alleys, their faces enflamed with alcohol. Here there was none of the usual decorum.

Buildings with cramped frontages rose high above. Each jostled for attention with explicit advertisements.

Massage, striptease, sex shows. The higher you went, the more salacious the offers.

Men with cold eyes stood in the centre of the street distributing leaflets to passers-by, encouraging them to come in and try.

Some of the touts swore at Fancourt. Spitting on the ground as he passed.

Fancourt strode away ignoring them. He was no casual punter.

Eventually he reached the building. It had no advertising boards. It could have been an office block.

With a quick glance over his shoulder, the Englishman ducked inside.

77

The teacher's son was the quiet type. Like his father, he kept his thoughts to himself.

At that moment, his focus was on the busy road ahead as he guided his pickup along the highway. He was part of the stream of traffic heading into the city.

Sean Peters sat beside him in the passenger seat. On his lap was a small rucksack.

He was on the move.

Back at the house he had said his goodbyes. The teacher's wife had covered her eyes with her apron.

She had a soft spot for Sean Peters. Ever since Hiroko's death, she had done everything possible to help him through the difficult time.

Providing kind words of encouragement. Making meals she knew he liked. Thinking of occasional treats.

When the moment came for him to leave, she sensed the finality. She feared she might not see him again.

Tokyo was a long way away. People often did not return.

They had sat together for a final meal the evening before. The *shabu-shabu* pot was centre stage, bubbling away on its portable gas ring. Around it were plates of sliced beef, raw vegetables and tofu.

It was a fine spread, one normally accompanied by

enjoyment and laughter. But, as they swirled the ingredients in the cooking pot, there was a pervading undercurrent of concern.

A few days previously, Peters had knelt with the family before the midday meal. He had explained what he intended to do.

He feared they would not understand. He had thought long and hard before reaching his decision.

His teacher had not said anything. Finally, he had nodded to himself and exhaled loudly. That was as close as he came to commenting.

The other family members took their cue from him. They kept their opinions to themselves. They made no effort to dissuade Peters.

The next days passed quickly. Peters asked if he could leave his belongings with them. He would only need a few personal items on the trip.

They said they would store them in the annexe. They would be there when he returned.

The training routine continued as before but there was a new edge to it. It was clear to all that Peters was gearing up for battle.

The moves had a defined purpose. He had a specific target in mind.

At night, Peters lay awake longer than usual. His mind kept returning to the photograph of the man he intended to track down.

He felt his past was starting to resurface. Life and death struggles. Bloody mayhem.

With Hiroko at his side, he had tried to banish those

impulses, to bury them in the recesses of his mind. Now they were back in plain view again.

The pickup made slow progress. The son seemed content to take his time, as if unwilling to hasten Peters' departure.

Eventually they drew up at the station. While Peters bought a single ticket to the capital, the son disappeared into the station shop. He returned with a plastic bag of snacks for the journey.

They waited together on the platform. They did not speak.

As the train drew in, they turned to each other and bowed. Then they clasped hands.

Peters took his place in the carriage. He maintained eye contact with his friend until he disappeared from view. The son, in turn, waited on the platform long after the train had rounded the bend in the track.

For the first part of the journey, Peters' thoughts were behind him. For the final part, he focussed on what lay ahead.

At Tokyo Station, George Trevillion was waiting to meet him at the ticket barrier. He had taken time off from the office and crossed town to meet his old comrade-in-arms.

"OK?"

"Yup, fine."

They did not have far to go. George Trevillion's apartment was in the heart of Azabu, Tokyo's embassy district. When they emerged from the underground station, Peters was confronted with a very different world from the one he had left behind.

He was surrounded by chic boutiques, restaurants and delicatessens. Expensive foreign cars cruised up and down the main thoroughfare. Well-dressed pedestrians sauntered along the pavements.

In the past, Peters' hackles would have risen. Not the place for him. The antithesis of the life he loved.

But now it was different. He needed to adapt. And quickly.

"This is you."

George Trevillion tossed Peters' bag onto the double-bed. It was where he had stayed all those years before.

"I'll leave you to settle in. Anything you want, it's yours."

"Thanks George."

"No problem. Shall we talk later? Plan of action?"

"Yup. Let's do that."

"Don't worry, chum. We'll get the bastard."

78

"I understand you have something you'd like to discuss."

Charles Fancourt was no stranger to Yokohama. He regularly socialised with the expatriate community living up on the Bluff, the prominent landmark dominating the city skyline.

When the first foreign settlers arrived in Yokohama, the Japanese authorities decided to segregate them. They feared their pernicious influence on the local population.

Now, only the most affluent could afford the Bluff's sky-high prices. Looking down their noses at the port below, the foreign elite could almost forget they were in Japan at all.

They had their own sports clubs, international schools and clinics. All ringfenced against the local riff-raff.

But today, Fancourt was slumming it. Yokohama Chinatown was a stone's throw from the Bluff, but in a different league.

He scurried along the packed pavement, trying to keep a low profile. But the perspiring Englishman could not hope to pass unnoticed. He drew curious glances from all sides.

It was humid and his shirt stuck to his back. He was relieved when he arrived at the restaurant and pushed his way through the pedestrians blocking the entrance to the side street.

He was very rarely summoned to Chinatown.

When he crossed the threshold, a silence fell on the room.

The diners stopped eating and stared at the newcomer.

They only relaxed when the restaurant manager beckoned to the Englishman from behind the counter. Without a word, the burly Chinaman led the way down a corridor to the rear.

As always, the two heavies were waiting outside the double doors at the end. After frisking Fancourt, they ushered him into the private dining room.

Chen sat at his usual place on the far side, surrounded by the chequerboard of empty tables. In front of him was a tray of jasmine tea.

He was taking rapid sips from his tea cup. Like a sparrow from a birdbath.

He did not acknowledge Fancourt until he was seated opposite. Then the brown eyes fixed him and did not waver.

Fancourt's flesh started to prickle. This diminutive man could crush him as easily as the cockroach he spotted inching its way up the table leg beside him.

Fancourt had much to fear. Since his precipitous move to Japan, he had answered exclusively to Chen. And he followed the crime boss' instructions to the letter.

They only met face-to-face when something critical and confidential needed discussing.

Something like Yuki Morigami.

Fancourt's veneer of sophistication meant nothing here. His grating public-school voice cut no ice with Chen.

The Englishman gabbled his message. As if anxious to hasten back to the cocoon of his Mercedes.

He described the meeting with Yuki Morigami. Reported exactly what the woman had said. Outlined the potential business risk.

Chen studied Fancourt. He seemed to digest information as much through his eyes as his ears.

Eventually Fancourt's voice petered out. Chen took another sip of tea.

"I see. Most untimely. What do you suggest, Mr Fancourt?"

"She's a liability."

People merely represented items on Fancourt's balance sheet. Disposable assets.

Chen folded his napkin, pressing down the creases.

First, there was the wretched business with the development in the north. Eliminating the woman had thankfully cleared the blockage there.

The work was now moving ahead apace. His associates in Hong Kong had been placated for the time being.

But then there was Wang. After the police had identified him, he had to be kept out of sight. But tucked away in a safe house, he was of limited use to Chen.

Now he was faced with another mess to clear up. One he laid squarely at the Englishman's door.

When they first told him they were sending Fancourt to Japan from Hong Kong, he had grave misgivings. Especially after his associates had described the Englishman's particular predilections.

Chen was broad-minded. He was familiar with the whole gamut of human depravity. But even he shrank from what he was being asked to facilitate.

Chen had tried in vain to resist the move. But Hong Kong had left him no choice in the matter.

They depended on Fancourt's unique skill set. No one was better at creating an impenetrable financial smokescreen. Under his guiding hand, money simply vanished like a conjuring trick.

"I see. A liability, you say."

Fancourt's fingertips travelled over the pristine white tablecloth. In his mind's eye, he pictured Yuki Morigami as she had been in the French restaurant. Her impeccable appearance, her smug smile.

Then he pictured her naked being ridden by the runt Deluca. Instinctively, he lashed out at the cockroach.

Chen affected to take no notice. He turned to the window.

It looked out onto the main street. Through the frosted glass he could make out the shapes of people rushing past.

He liked crowds. They were good camouflage. Individuals could simply disappear into crowds.

"Is everything set for your next event?"

"Yes. I don't anticipate any complications. We should make the usual killing."

"We would expect nothing less."

Fancourt twitched. He was only too aware of the price of failure.

Later, when Fancourt was escorted from the room, Chen remained at the table.

He had much to consider. He ordered another tray of tea.

After a while, he reached for his mobile phone and made a series of brief phone calls.

79

Ligaya Santos could hear the sea breathing. Rising and falling.

The hot sand burned her feet. Nearby Cesar was playing with his friends.

A conch in his hands. Holding it to his ear.

Ligaya's mother was beside her, plaiting reeds. Dressed as always. A simple brown slip embroidered with flowers.

She could smell her mother's odour. Perspiration and spices. Her mother's arms encircling her.

Whispering to her not to worry. That she would always be with her.

The sea exhaled. She was lifted up into the sky. Towards the light.

She hovered there before opening her eyes.

The face above her was expressionless. In his hand, he held the needle.

She held out her arm. She knew the routine. She felt the cocktail of drugs flood her system.

Making what was to follow possible. She had no strength to resist.

She knew she was going to die eventually. It was just a question of time. Nothing mattered any more.

Across the city, it mattered to Ms Sekikawa. She had just spoken with a senior police officer in Manila. He had promised to break the news to Ligaya Santos' family.

It had been a difficult conversation. She had had to admit Ligaya Santos had been taken while under Japanese police protection.

The kidnappers had left no trace. Yamaguchi's team had nothing to go on. Even the Chinese specialists, with their tendrils extending inside the criminal fraternities, had drawn a blank.

Ms Sekikawa noticed how Yamaguchi now spent less time cloistered in his office. Unread reports were piling up in his in-tray. He roamed around the department, often ending up sitting with her and Hayashi.

Without other leads to go on, they focussed all their attention on trying to locate Wang. He was the lynchpin between Ligaya Santos' abduction and the events in Yamashiro.

They followed up on the stolen car. They examined the contents of his flat. They spoke to known associates.

But he had disappeared. He could be anywhere.

In fact, at that moment, he was standing right next to Ligaya Santos.

His subordinates could never guess quite what he had in mind. He was volatile, unpredictable.

Sometimes he would be eerily still, the calm before the storm. Sometimes his incendiary rage would blow over as quickly as it had arisen. But violence was always the unifying factor.

It kept them on their toes. It was a constant guessing game.

They were certain of one thing: the Filipina was in for a rough ride. Wang had been incandescent after her escape. Furious enough to risk arranging her subsequent recapture.

Wang liked a challenge. He had risen through the ranks by being willing to go a step further than his contemporaries. Where they drew the line, he had no qualms.

As time passed, he became more measured. He had others to do his bidding.

But sometimes, for old time's sake, he decided to get involved himself. To keep his hand in.

The woman in Yamashiro had been a case in point. His subordinates were more than capable of handling everything.

But it had appealed to him. A chance to be close to the action. A much-needed adrenalin burst.

He had fancied a break from Tokyo. He could not remember the last time he had been out of the city.

The planning was always part of the attraction. Sitting with his team, chewing over options.

For the murder in Yamashiro, the brief had been explicit. It was paramount the police believed the woman had committed suicide.

Wang had dispatched his people to reconnoitre the situation. His female assistant had trailed the woman and noted her unvarying schedule.

They had focussed on her fortnightly trips to the supermarket. The long drive on the lonely mountain road.

All alone. Vulnerable.

The bridge provided the perfect location. All they needed was a pretext to make the woman stop. The rest would be plain sailing.

It had gone without a hitch. They had made their way back to the capital on minor roads, ditching the car at a prearranged location. They had then split up and proceeded separately on public transport.

But the police had been smart. They had figured it out. And what was worse, they had tied Wang to the murder.

The moment he was alerted, he had wasted no time in leaving his apartment. Now he was in hiding. Out of circulation. Simmering.

The Filipina had identified him. She posed a constant threat.

She had to go. But there was a time and place for everything.

No point in being precipitous. After all, they could still recoup some of their initial outlay. The Filipina could still have her uses.

Ligaya Santos stirred. She was coming round.

Wang clicked his fingers. One of the men jumped up and grabbed her roughly by the elbow, dragging her out of the room.

She needed to get cleaned up. She was expecting visitors.

80

Yuki Morigami worked hard at keeping in shape. Her body was, after all, one of her most valuable assets.

Even after a tough day at the office, she never missed her evening jog. When she eventually arrived home, she would strip off her work clothes and change into her fluorescent top, elasticated leggings and pink running shoes.

She always made a point of stretching out in front of her high-rise luxury apartment block before setting off. She ignored the stares from male residents as she went through her routine.

She had a regular jogging route around the perimeter of Tsukishima, the small man-made island in Tokyo Bay where she lived. She always completed three full circuits.

As she ran, she liked to glimpse across the narrow stretch of water towards the lights of Ginza. She found their proximity comforting. She never wanted to be far from the action.

On that particular evening, her breathing settled into a steady rhythm. She felt positive, revitalised, finally able to switch off.

She had spent the day mulling over her earlier lunch meeting with Charles Fancourt. It had not worked out as she had hoped. Since then, she had heard nothing from the Englishman.

Now she was in a quandary. She was weighing up the risks of

following through on her threat to expose his secret.

Fancourt had influence. It might backfire on her.

She found Fancourt repellent. Underneath his suave veneer she sensed a chilling emptiness.

But he was a necessary evil. A potential lifeline.

She was sinking fast. Up to her neck in debt.

At first her career had soared. She was the talk of the town. Making money had been easy. She had traded on her looks.

But then came the downturn. She always seemed to be on the wrong side. Scrambling to extricate herself from positions turning ever more toxic.

A savvier trader would have found a way out. But she was convinced she was always right. That she could read the markets.

Her arrogance had cost her dear. She was highly leveraged. When she started to lose, the losses were exponential.

The rumours started. Her credit worthiness was in question. Her personal stock started to dive.

Then Frank Deluca had opened his big mouth. They were recovering from a bout of frantic sex.

The American's guard was down. Inadvertently, he had let slip some of the details about Charles Fancourt's scam.

Afterwards, he told her to forget it. She should not get involved.

Little chance of that. Armed with the information, she realised she was able to chart her escape route.

After all, what did she have to lose?

Her jogging route took her in front of Toyomi Sports Park.

Even though it was already nine o'clock in the evening, the tennis courts were full and would be for another couple of hours.

At intervals along the track were semi-circular sections reserved for anglers. Tsukishima was a popular place to fish.

The island was built on earth dredged a century before. The surrounding water was deep, the fish plentiful.

The fishermen took no notice of Yuki Morigami. They had other things on their minds, their eyes never leaving their floats bobbing in the high tide just below the parapet.

That evening, though, two fishermen turned to stare at her. It threw her off her rhythm. She found herself involuntarily speeding up.

The next time she passed, their attention was fixed on the dark water below. She had half-anticipated further scrutiny.

The third time she jogged by, they grabbed her.

She did not even have time to cry out. A large hand covered her mouth.

On the nearby tennis courts, the rallies continued. No one noticed.

Yuki Morigami was whisked to the stone bench near the water's edge. One of the men covered her fluorescent clothing with a dark blanket. She was now effectively invisible to anyone happening to look in their direction.

Her assailant was a big man. As he pressed down on her mouth and nose, she struggled to breathe. Wide-eyed, she flashed an urgent message to him.

Anything, anything but this.

He was no stranger to dispatching people. He had few qualms

about it.

But he was rarely called on to finish such a striking woman. Something unexpected stirred inside him. He could not put his finger on it.

He would try and explain it later but his associates merely stared at him blankly. He found he did not have the words to articulate the unfamiliar emotion.

It only lasted for a moment. Duty called.

With the help of the other man, he heaved her over the parapet, immersing her head-first in the water.

She bucked a couple of times, trying to jack-knife above the surface but she was too deep. Eventually all movement ceased. The two men watched her final breath escape in a burst of bubbles.

They then signalled to a small motor launch standing off. It drew up alongside and in seconds the body was hoisted aboard and covered in a tarpaulin. The motor launch headed out into the deepest part of the bay.

The whole operation had been completed in less than two minutes.

On land, the two fishermen took their rods apart and packed up their tackle. Then, with a final check to make sure everything was as they had found it, they strolled back to their car.

On the journey back, they did not talk.

81

Ms Sekikawa barely recognised Sean Peters.

He was sitting on a café terrace opposite Harajuku Station in the heart of Tokyo's fashion district. He was drinking a cup of coffee, observing the goings-on around him.

The street was packed. Youngsters in eye-catching outfits strolled up and down. An advertising shoot on the pavement opposite drew a cluster of bystanders.

Peters did not look out of place. His hair was trimmed, the beard had gone. He was sporting a leather jacket, chino trousers and brown leather shoes. He could have been any other foreign professional taking a mid-morning break.

He had been in Tokyo for a week. He had spent the time planning with George Trevillion.

They sat together in the evenings drinking tea. Keeping clear heads.

Peters was in charge of the requirements list. Equipment, premises, fall-backs.

Just like the old days. They were back in Northern Ireland.

In those days Peters had a reputation for settling scores. The hard men along the borders gave Peters' squad a wide berth.

They knew there would be reprisals. He was relentless in rooting out their lairs.

Only Peters was different now. He had become an even more

lethal prospect.

Ms Sekikawa had not expected his call. Nor his request for a meeting in Tokyo. She assumed he was still in Yamashiro.

With the frantic search for Ligaya Santos, Peters had slipped her mind. She had apologised and promised him an update.

She sat down opposite him in the café and ordered a coffee. She thought of commenting on his new appearance, but resisted the temptation. It was none of her business after all.

Ms Sekikawa had walked up from Omotesando Station. In her work clothes and sensible footwear, she felt awkward, out of place among the trendy young set.

When the coffee arrived and the waiter had retreated, Peters leaned across the table.

"So, do you have any news for me?"

Ms Sekikawa paused. She felt she owed him something.

"We believe we have identified one of the men from the CCTV images we showed you."

Peters sat back.

"Who?"

"A Chinese criminal known to the police. We've linked him with another investigation."

"What investigation?"

Ms Sekikawa registered a change in Peters. Not just his appearance. Something in his mode of address. She needed to be wary.

"The disappearance of a Filipina."

Peters waited, stirring his coffee.

"The woman was trafficked to Japan as a sex worker. The Chinese criminal in question was in charge of the brothel. She managed to escape but was recently kidnapped again."

"By him?"

"We assume so."

"Do you have any idea of the man's whereabouts?"

"No. No leads at this stage. He's disappeared."

Peters stared at Ms Sekikawa for a few seconds.

"And you think he's linked with Hiroko's death?"

Ms Sekikawa noticed the almost matter-of-fact way he spoke. This was not the same Peters she had met wasting away in a prison cell in Yamashiro.

"We can't be sure. All we have is circumstantial evidence at this stage."

"Circumstantial?"

"We know he was in the same vicinity, driving on the same stretch of road at the same time. Later a witness saw a similar vehicle parked by the bridge. It's suspicious, but not conclusive."

"I see. Not conclusive."

Ms Sekikawa was starting to worry. It was time to lay down the law.

"Please understand you must not become involved in any way in this investigation. This is a matter for the police."

"Of course. I quite understand."

But Peters was evidently not prepared to leave it at that. As the conversation continued, Ms Sekikawa was aware she was being pumped for information.

She was not used to being on the receiving end. Normally she was the one asking the questions.

It did not take her long to realise Peters was no novice at interrogations. He backtracked, re-checking subjects already covered, trying to prise open doors.

In the end, Ms Sekikawa found she had given away more than she had intended. She beckoned to the waiter for the bill.

"So, what are your plans?"

Peters shrugged.

"Difficult to say at the moment. I'm looking for work. Not easy at my time of life.

"No, I imagine it must be difficult."

"Not much call for gardeners in Tokyo."

Peters struck Ms Sekikawa as anything but a gardener.

"Well, I'd better be getting back. I'll be in touch as soon as we hear anything more."

"Thank you. I'd appreciate that."

Ms Sekikawa left the café and strode away down the street. Sean Peters watched her disappear before gathering up his things and marching off in the other direction.

82

Ms Sekikawa glanced at her watch. She frowned.

Her times were down. She pulled herself up onto the side of the pool and lifted her goggles.

The swimming pool was crowded with recreational swimmers, doing their quota of lengths after work. They churned up and down, splashing and gasping for air.

Her lane was reserved for elite swimmers. They skimmed the surface, hardly seeming to make contact with the water.

She noticed her performance had dropped over the years. She trained just as hard, adopted the latest time-saving techniques, but she knew the trend was irreversible.

At 33 years of age, she was already past her peak. She glanced over at the general swimming lanes.

An elderly lady in a floral swimming cap caught her eye. Her head clear of the water, she paddled up and down with a look of fierce determination.

A sign of things to come.

As Ms Sekikawa dried off in the changing room, she reflected on her meeting with Peters.

It had been on her mind. Apart from his appearance, she had noticed a distinct change in his manner.

Focused. Steely. Professional. A side to him she had not witnessed before.

Oh well, probably nothing to be concerned about, she thought. She stuffed her wet swimming things into her backpack and set off on her long trek back to her apartment.

But she had good reason to be worried.

At that moment, Peters and Trevillion were sitting in a cramped, downmarket bar on the fringes of Shinjuku. Not the sort of venue they would have typically chosen.

They had taken a seat near the window. Their attention was on the building diagonally opposite.

The customers were noisy and for the most part drunk. The Englishmen nursed their drinks, avoiding eye-contact. Nevertheless, provocative comments from the locals kept coming.

It was clear they were drawing too much attention. They would need to find somewhere else. Somewhere nearby.

They paid up and left. Just along the pavement, the Hotel Hime's neon light was flashing. It would stay lit all night.

"Here."

The two men stood outside the hotel and checked their bearings. They sized up the hotel's drab exterior and picked out windows providing the line of sight they needed. Satisfied, they pushed through the main door.

The receptionist sat behind a darkened privacy screen. It spared her customers' blushes. From her side of the glass, however, everything was crystal clear.

She did not like what she saw. Foreign men were trouble. In the past, she had had to call the police. They were often drunk and aggressive. Unpredictable.

"We'd like a room, for several nights, facing the street, on the first floor."

Everything was wrong with the request. Normally rooms were hired by the hour, only occasionally for an entire night. Moreover, customers selected rooms according to theme, not outlook — the schoolroom, the hospital ward, the children's nursery. And two foreign men together? Well…

"All our rooms are booked at the moment."

"All booked?"

"All booked."

The woman looked down at her desk. Hoping when she looked up again, the men would be gone.

"We'll pay well. How much do you want?"

The woman glanced up. Her eyes drawn to the wad of 10,000 yen notes the man had produced.

Business was slow. For foreigners, she had to admit they looked respectable. She had bills to pay.

"Let me see. Rooms at the front are more expensive, of course."

"How much?"

She made a rapid calculation. Working out what she could get away with.

"20,000 yen a night."

"OK. We'll give you 75,000 yen for three days in advance. We don't want to be disturbed. We'll come and go as we wish."

The woman eyed the bills again. It was easy money. Her husband lounging in the room behind watching baseball would surely approve.

"Of course. I understand."

She passed over the key and explained where the room was on the floor above. Trevillion and Peters mounted the stairs.

The room had a dungeon motif, handcuffs decorating the walls. Trevillion ignored the décor, crossing straight to the window. Drawing back the heavy drape, he sized up the building opposite.

From his small bag he took out a camera and attached a long telescopic lens. Squinting through it, he adjusted the lens bringing the entrance of the building into focus. Meanwhile Peters dragged over a couple of chairs and the pair settled down to wait.

They understood the demands of a lengthy stakeout. They were patient men with deep reserves of concentration. They were prepared to be there for as long as it took.

83

The meeting had gone as well as Fancourt had hoped.

The three Malay investors had listened to him as he made his standard pitch. His track record, his investment strategy, the generous returns they could expect.

His patter was couched in sophisticated financial jargon. It had a soothing quality. Designed to allay any concerns.

At a pre-arranged moment, his personal assistant wheeled in refreshments. The Malays talked among themselves. Fancourt radiated encouraging smiles.

The Malays represented a significant tranche of funds. But for Fancourt, it was simply window-dressing, camouflage for cashflows from less reputable sources.

Eventually promises were made and the three men trooped out of the office. Fancourt accompanied them to the lift. With all the sincerity he could muster, he shook hands and bade them a safe journey home.

By the time he had reached his desk, he had put them to the back of his mind. Firing up his screens, he saw the value of his portfolio had ticked up in the interim.

The answer lay in the research. Even as a boy he had an uncanny ability to process and store information. That, combined with a prodigious mathematical brain, meant he was a match for anyone in a field crowded with over-achievers.

He lived and breathed the markets. He could spot opportunities where others stared in vain. He was able to connect the dots, straddling a web of disparate information.

His mind never strayed. Like a surgeon, his scalpel probed for signs of trouble. At the first hint, he cut out the infected part long before others had an inkling anything was awry.

It was why the Chinese had picked him above all others. He always delivered.

His next stock market operation was soon. He enjoyed the power he wielded over his group. People chosen to do his bidding.

Like a general, he demanded complete obedience. Everyone was expected to submit to his leadership and maintain absolute secrecy.

Frank Deluca had broken the golden rule. Divulged what he had promised never to tell.

Fancourt had decided to dump him after the upcoming event. It would take time to cultivate a replacement. Someone with the necessary market clout. Someone prepared to play along.

Once in, there was no escape. Not with the Chinese. Frank Deluca would find that out soon enough.

The Chinese played an integral part. Research alone was insufficient. Arms needed twisting. Information extracted.

He needed them in other ways too.

The Chinese understood his special predilections. They had taken him in hand. They managed everything.

For a second, Fancourt's eyes drifted away from the screens. His father's face rose in front of him. Fancourt's fists clenched.

He was as he always remembered him. Tall, dressed in a three-piece suit, a fob watch in his waistcoat pocket. His hair swept back and pomaded in place. His distinctive after-shave.

In one hand, he carried a scuffed leather briefcase. In the other, a furled umbrella.

His small eyes sat close to the bridge of his nose. His chin was square and dimpled. By the time he arrived home in the evening, it was already smudged with stubble.

He always rang the doorbell of their Surrey home, waiting for it to be opened. The longer it took, the more his temper frayed.

Then he would enter the house without a word. He would drop into his chair in the living room and extract the day's newspaper from his briefcase. He would sit there until dinner, flicking through the pages.

Only then would he speak.

Fancourt was an only child. He remembered a succession of au pairs. They never seemed to last long. Just as he became attached to them, they left. He had always assumed it was his fault.

Soon after his mother died, he was sent away to a preparatory boarding school in the north of the country. Too far to return home during term-time.

He was forced to write letters home. He described the rugger matches. The school choir. The cross-country runs. He received no letters in return.

He did not make friends. The other pupils steered clear. They sensed all was not right with him. That something was out of kilter.

At public school, he was left to his own devices. Cocooned in his academic brilliance.

At university, everything changed. His father married again. A much younger woman. Fancourt found himself persona non grata at the family home.

He was on his own. He realised he needed new skills to survive. Social skills. He threw himself into developing a network of acquaintances.

He found he was surprisingly adept at it. His was always the first birthday card to drop through the letter box. He was the one volunteering to arrange social events. He was always prepared to go the extra mile.

He was the smiling face in the background. Watching. Always watching.

After university, he had been snapped up by a prestigious financial firm. They were quick to appreciate his unique abilities. He had been nurtured and generously rewarded.

Then he had taken off on his own. His success was meteoric.

His fortune set him apart. He existed in a universe where everything was in his grasp. Money became no object. He had complete freedom to indulge himself.

As first, it had happened almost by accident. A window of opportunity. Something had clicked.

In time, the forays became more frequent. His obsession impossible to ignore. Soon he was completely in its thrall.

Fancourt was suddenly jolted back to the here and now. His phone was ringing. A client demanding an urgent update.

His eyes swept the screens in front of him, soaking up the

information. In seconds, he had marshalled all the facts.

The mask slipped back into place as he lifted the receiver.

84

Akira Kato sat slumped in his BMW convertible staring at the ocean.

He was parked overlooking Kujūkuri Beach on Chiba's Bōsō Peninsula. The place he always came when something was troubling him.

He had grown up near this endless stretch of sand. As a youngster he had spent carefree days being buffeted by the giant Pacific rollers.

But on that particular day, he was not paddling in the shallows. He was way out of his depth.

His hands were locked onto the steering wheel. His hair flopped forwards into his eyes but he did not bother to sweep it away.

His phone was turned off. He had no desire to speak with anyone.

After the detective had left his office, he had withdrawn into himself. Trying to come to terms with his actions.

As the waves pounded the shoreline, he charted each milestone in his moral decline. Try as he might he could no longer connect the happy child sketching castles in the air with the tainted man he had become.

It had started as minor infractions. Innocent enough. Standard professional manoeuvres to facilitate the progress of his business.

Before long, it had led to more serious offences. Bribing officials, issuing threats, employing strong-arm tactics.

What would have seemed unthinkable when he started out as a high-minded architect had gradually become his modus operandi. He had always managed to draw a veil over it. Pretend it was not happening.

But this could not be ignored. Not something as heinous as murder.

He knew in his heart he was guilty. If he had not divulged what he had discovered to the client, the woman would still be alive.

He might just as well have been the one launching the innocent victim from the bridge.

He got out of his car and walked down onto the beach. He sat down near the water's edge and kicked off his fashionable brogues.

The damp seeped through the seat of his flannel trousers. The wind whipped down the coastline, peppering him with sand and spray.

Some youngsters were surfing further along the beach. He watched them being churned by the waves before paddling their boards back out through the breakers for another run.

Their bronzed heads sat atop their wetsuits like corks in a bottle. He could hear their shouts of encouragement as they floundered in the surf.

One boy was a cut above the others. He rode his board, balancing on the gathering wave. As it neared the breaking point, the surfer slewed to his left and right in a series of tight turns, eventually sinking down in the shallows.

Kato nodded. That was him. Skirting over the surface, just

managing to keep afloat until he finally ran out of steam.

It was only a matter of time before the police came after him again. The detective was no fool.

She would know he had more to tell. That he was holding something back.

Once they checked the information he had been obliged to hand over, they would smell a rat. If they had any reason to think there was foul play, they would not let it drop.

But the client posed a much graver threat to Kato. If he gave him up to the police, he would spend the rest of his life looking over his shoulder.

He now knew exactly what these people were capable of. Nothing would stand in their way.

He should never have become involved. The moment he realised who he was dealing with, he should have backpedalled fast.

But the money was too enticing. A golden opportunity to cut himself free from his financial difficulties.

Now he was paying the price. He needed to find a way out before it was too late.

His eyes were drawn to a movement near him. A small crab, scuttling across the sand.

He followed its lopsided progress. It was difficult going over the uneven surface, but the crab was persistent.

When it was level with him, it paused, its pincers raised. As if considering its next move.

The crab's eyes swivelled on their stalks, scanning the sky above. Searching for gulls. The crab's tiny claws were no defence against the seabird's aerial attack.

After checking the coast was clear, it set to work. With a flurry, it started to scoop out a hole in the damp sand. Kato watched as it hollowed out its burrow, shovelling the sand behind it.

In no time, the tiny crab had vanished from view completely, leaving no trace.

After a few minutes contemplating the spot where the crab had disappeared, Kato put on his brogues. Then he stood up, brushing the sand from the seat of his trousers.

With a final glance across at the surfers, he made his way back up the beach to his car.

85

Charles Fancourt took a deep breath.

He always pictured market volatility as a stampede. It only needed some sudden stimulus to set it off.

One animal would shy, then another. Suddenly the whole herd would take flight, hurtling pell-mell over the plain, dust and confusion in the air.

In his world, panic made no sound. But it had a colour. Red.

He watched the market tumble on his screens. He visualised the panic on the traders' faces as they scrambled to sell at any price.

Fact played little part. It just required a series of well-coordinated nudges to send the market into freefall.

Timing was everything. His confederates had their orders. They simply had to execute them to the letter.

The pattern was indiscernible. The movements emanated not only from Tokyo but around the globe. Hong Kong, Singapore, London, Frankfurt, New York. Each action innocent in itself, but, when combined, resulted in a seismic shift.

It required funds. Significant funds. Funds the group had at its disposal.

The wave would ripple out, start to gather force, swell and finally crash. The group rode the breaker and then picked up the pieces.

They were prepared. The complex trading algorithms were primed. As the stampeding herd searched for an escape route, the predators cashed in again and again, always a step ahead.

And afterwards, no self-satisfied smiles. No boasts of good fortune. Any enquiry would be met with blank looks. The code of silence was paramount.

Fancourt watched throughout the afternoon, his office door locked, as the blood-letting played out. It was a high-stakes game.

It was never a sure bet. If the tables turned, their losses would be as magnified as their gains.

His breathing steadied as he watched the figures tumble. He could start to relax.

The Chinese bankrolled him. They demanded a healthy return on their capital. So far, he had always delivered.

But in their world, one slip would be one too many. He knew that.

The timing of his group's market intervention was astutely judged. Nothing the authorities could pinpoint. An apparently random series of occurrences.

Afterwards he stayed at home. He avoided the places where people might corner him. Traders curious to dissect what on earth had happened.

But as soon as he retreated into the safety of his luxury apartment, the other impulse started to build. The one he could not control.

He no longer fought it. There had been a time he tried to analyse what was happening. He had even considered seeking help.

But it was too late. Much too late. How could he undo everything that had been done?

There was no greater power to appeal to. No divine intercession to reset the clock. No confessional forgiving enough.

What was done was done. And would be done again.

He sat alone in his apartment, staring at the wall. He recognised the warning signs only too well.

Instead of subsiding, the adrenalin from the day continued to pound through his veins. His mouth was parched, his throat contracted, his knees trembled.

In his mind's eye, the door appeared in front of him. As always, he felt compelled to enter.

He knew only too well the sight he would be met with. The tableau etched on his soul forever.

He would watch his four-year-old self falter. Uncertain. Hesitating to witness what lay beyond.

He would watch his child's hand reach out and push open the door. Hesitating at the threshold, he would eventually totter forwards to the centre of the room.

He remembered the breeze on his face from the open window. Somewhere a dog was barking. Outside a man in the street was laughing.

The sunlight came and went, came and went.

In the room, there was a single repeated sound. Like ship's rigging, straining under the spars.

He came closer. Now his sense of smell took over. The scent was so familiar.

Even at that tender age, he knew everything was wrong. And everything would always be wrong.

Still the sunlight came and went. Still the rigging complained under its oscillating load.

He, of all people, should never have turned that heavy handle. Never have pushed at the solid oak bedroom door and entered.

There should have been a sign saying "Private", "Keep Out".

If she could have spoken, she would have held his hand and guided him back to the corridor outside. She would have smiled her soft, sad smile. Tried as always to disguise the torment behind her eyes.

"Now Charles, you must go back to your room. Where's Ingrid? Isn't she looking after you? The silly girl. Run along now. Mummy's busy, don't you see?"

And he would have gripped her hand, unwilling to let go. To keep her from going back into that room with its open window.

86

"*Mizuwari,* please"

The burly retired policeman turned to the shelves behind him and reached up for Yamaguchi's keep bottle. It was dusty, like the bar.

Ms Sekikawa sat beside her boss at the counter. The tiny watering-hole was wedged between a row of similar establishments down a badly-lit alley in Akasaka.

Apart from a showy camellia in the pot outside the door, there was little to lure passing trade. Just as the owner intended. He liked his peace and quiet.

Ms Sekikawa asked for a *shōchū* highball. After placing the glass in front of her with a grunt, the bar owner retreated to his seat in his corner.

He squeezed a pair of glasses over his boxer's nose and bent over the evening paper. That was quite enough for one day.

"Kampai."

They clinked glasses, drank deeply and exhaled in unison.

The ex-policeman's bar was their regular haunt for late-night brain-storming sessions. They invariably had the place to themselves.

Sometimes after a couple of drinks, they could see cases from a different angle. When Yamaguchi had rung and suggested a night-cap, Ms Sekikawa had given him a thumbs-up from the other side of the glass partition.

It had been a while. It felt like old times sitting shoulder to shoulder at the bar.

"We don't seem to be making much progress."

Ms Sekikawa nodded. The search for Wang had all but petered out. He could be anywhere.

"Wang's the key. He's our link between Hiroko Iwasaki's death and Ligaya Santos."

"Has Hayashi made any progress with the Cayman Islands?"

Ms Sekikawa shook her head.

"Nothing so far. These offshore tax havens are beyond our jurisdiction."

Yamaguchi nodded. Shell companies registered offshore lay behind an impenetrable wall of secrecy.

"What about the Japanese developer?"

"Kato? Odd character. I'm sure he knows more than he's letting on."

"Maybe we should work on him some more."

"I'll get onto it."

Since the abduction of Ligaya Santos, the investigation into Hiroko Iwasaki's death had been largely put on the back-burner.

"Any further contact with the Englishman, Peters?"

"No. Not since our last meeting in Harajuku. Better to wait until we have something new to tell him."

The two officers sat for several minutes without talking. Their brain-storming sessions tended to be rather pensive affairs.

Yamaguchi was the first to break the silence.

"Odd, don't you think, how Wang disappeared just as we went to pick him up?"

"Yes, the thought had crossed my mind too."

During the following pause, the only sound was the intermittent rasp of newspaper pages turning in the corner.

"It's been a while since we've had a drink together."

Ms Sekikawa smiled.

"We should do it more often."

"I meant to ask you how you are finding your new responsibilities."

"You mean Hayashi? It's an interesting change having someone else to worry about."

"It seems to me you're managing pretty well."

"Thank you."

Yamaguchi popped a peanut into his mouth from the bowl between them. Ms Sekikawa turned to her boss.

"To be honest, I haven't quite worked him out yet."

"Hayashi? How do you mean?"

"He's very professional. Diligent. Extremely bright. Intuitive."

"So?"

"I can't put my finger on it. He just seems hard to read."

"Maybe he's a bit reserved. Prefers to keep himself to himself."

Ms Sekikawa glanced at Yamaguchi and nodded.

"I know the type."

87

As his superiors chatted in the bar in Akasaka, Hayashi was at home staring at the television.

He had just had his meal. His mother was in the small kitchen area washing up. As she scrubbed the plates and put them on the rack to dry, she stole a quick look across at her son.

She could always tell when he had something on his mind. Not that he gave much away. It was more a sixth sense they had developed over the years.

They had become inseparable ever since her husband died.

It had been a happy marriage. Her husband had always provided for them. He doted on their only son, making sure he had the best of everything.

They ran a small furniture store in Yokohama on the fringes of Chinatown, servicing both the Chinese and Japanese communities.

At one time, it had been quite successful and the family had moved up in the world. They had even managed to afford a modest apartment on the outskirts of the city.

But financial success attracted unwanted interest. It was not long before the Chinese mob came calling.

She remembered the first time they appeared at the shop. The two men were quite presentable, more like sales representatives. They had waited patiently for all the other customers to leave before they approached the counter.

She remembered how her husband had stood with his arms clamped to his sides, his face pale as he listened to their pitch.

He had told her to go upstairs. To leave him to deal with it.

She knew there was no way out. It was either pay up, or be made to pay.

At first, the protection money was manageable. Her husband had rationalised it as security for the family. Wolves to keep other wolves from the door.

But soon the demands grew. The payments proved harder to find.

At the same time, the store started to struggle. Shopping trends had changed. Their regular customers could find lower prices in the superstores springing up all around.

Their financial difficulties cut no ice with the Chinese. They were deaf to her husband's pleas.

He kept the details to himself, to protect her and their son. She could see the strain it put on him.

She would ask him what was happening, how they were managing to cope. He always told her not to worry. He was handling everything.

By the time Hayashi was in his late teens, his father's health suddenly deteriorated. The doctors diagnosed pancreatic cancer. It was only a matter of time.

Hayashi's mother sat with her son at her husband's bedside over the next two months, watching his rapid decline.

Eventually, the doctors said there was nothing more they could do. They waited for the inevitable.

Her husband rallied at the end. One final effort. It was then he uttered his last words to their son.

"My son, you must look after your mother. You are the man of the house now."

It was only after his death she discovered the eye-watering debts. Her husband had shielded them from the scale of their financial predicament.

The Chinese wasted no time in paying them a visit again. When the family was at its most vulnerable.

She had nowhere to turn.

She finished the last of the dishes and wiped the surfaces dry. Then she came into the lounge and took her usual chair next to her son.

Hayashi was in his father's old armchair. The day after the funeral, he had made this battered old piece of furniture his own.

He had assumed responsibility for the family. He would look after his mother whatever the cost.

His mother was not interested in the television programme. As always, her eyes roamed over the framed photographs around the room.

Smiling pictures of their happy life together. Family outings to the seaside near Yokohama. Her son in a junior high school play. One of him in his baseball outfit, standing next to his proud father.

Then some pictures from the years following her husband's death. Her son's youthful smile replaced with a look of grim resignation.

She could read his altered demeanour in his graduation portrait, dressed in gown and mortar board. And again, more recently, standing to attention as a police recruit.

His mother had always found his career choice puzzling. Her brilliant son could have walked into any top-flight company. Instead, he chose to be a law enforcement officer.

She knew the life he led was dangerous. She understood he was in the front line against violent criminals.

She knew the type only too well. She feared for his safety.

He never discussed his work. She knew never to ask.

But as he sat there on that particular day, she felt compelled. She addressed him in Chinese, the language they had reverted to in recent years.

"Are you all right? Is everything all right?"

She spoke in a low voice as if anxious not to intrude.

Hayashi turned and looked at her. He rubbed his eyes and sighed. He reached across and patted her hand.

"Don't worry, Mum. Nothing for you to be concerned about."

88

The hours of watching were starting to take their toll on Peters.

Trevillion had already stumped up for additional nights at the love hotel. When Peters had offered to foot the bill, the Cornishman had held his hands up in protest.

"It's on me, Sean."

The lady at reception had become used to the two bulky foreigners. They were no fuss and were always punctual with their payments.

The one who spoke Japanese rang down for regular orders for food. When it arrived, she brought it up to the room.

He always took the plastic bag from her at the entrance. When she tried to poke her head around him to see what was going on, he politely closed the door.

From the little she could make out, they were clearly not using the room for its intended purpose.

Changes of clothes lay around on the furniture. A dark blue suit on a hanger was dangling from a decorative set of handcuffs pinned to the wall.

The bed was hastily made and covered with various odd items. Mainly technical-looking equipment she was unable to identify.

On the second day, they had asked permission to leave their

car in the private parking area behind the house. She had agreed after negotiating a separate fee.

George Trevillion had effectively moved out of his luxury apartment. He shared the night shift, while Peters got some shut-eye. Every morning he headed off to the office, leaving Peters to watch throughout the day.

The building opposite saw a steady flow of visitors, mostly men. Trevillion and Peters started to identify the regulars.

They had yet to spot their quarry, but they knew he was there. His phone's GPS told them that.

Peters left the technical side to Trevillion. Back in Northern Ireland, Trevillion was the squad's technical expert. Radios, transmitters, tracking devices, whatever they needed, they turned to the Cornishman.

But the equipment Trevillion was manipulating now was light-years ahead. Sophisticated electronic equipment, linked to his powerful laptop. He seemed to have the world at his fingertips.

Much of it was proprietary to the communications firm where he worked. His particular division was dedicated to the latest tools for tracking and surveillance.

Their clients were all around the globe. Mainly government agencies unconcerned with the niceties of privacy laws.

As the business expanded, the products shrank. Trevillion had shown Peters some of the top-of-the-line offerings. Tiny, barely noticeable, extremely powerful.

Peters had spent too long tending his rice fields. It was all way over his head.

"It's beyond me, George. You carry on."

Trevillion had smiled and clapped Peters on the shoulder.

"Don't worry pal. I've got it covered."

But however long they waited, Wang never showed his face.

As Sean Peters spent his days watching the building opposite, he had plenty of time to think. One question was uppermost in his mind: who had sent him the information about Wang's whereabouts?

If the tip-off came from within the police force itself, why weren't they breaking down the door across the road themselves? Why were they leaving it to him?

One thing was clear: he was being used as the attack dog.

So be it. He owed that much to Hiroko.

As he sat with the camera glued to his eye, his thoughts turned to George Trevillion. His former comrade-in-arms.

George was a West Countryman like himself. He had grown up in a lazy village on the north coast near Newquay. Every summer the tourists would choke the narrow roads, heading for the beaches.

The locals complained, but without full caravan sites and guesthouses they would not survive.

Trevillion had decided to pitch in with the sun-seekers. He bought a surfboard. All summer long he perfected his skills. He became something of a local hero.

He had guts. He rode in all weathers, taking on the most perilous stretches of coast. The big Atlantic breakers held no fear for him.

It could not last. One evening, his father had taken him to the local pub. He did not mince his words. As they sipped their beer he came straight to the point.

"Time you did something with your life, George. What about

the Army?"

The following week he popped into the recruitment centre. After browsing the pamphlets, he had an interview with a recruiting sergeant. The officer had looked at the strapping, sun-tanned fellow opposite and handed him the pen.

Out on patrol in Northern Ireland, in the snipers' sights, Trevillion and Peters always had the other's back. There was an unspoken understanding.

Now, despite their paths diverging, when the question was asked, George Trevillion had stepped up. Peters would have done the same. Without a second thought.

Nothing was too much trouble for George. He had willingly given his time, money and support. It was the measure of the man.

Peters raised the camera to his eye and adjusted the telescopic sights.

Finally, something was happening.

In the narrow parking space in front of the building, adjacent to the main entrance, was a white people carrier. It had not moved throughout the time they had been observing the building.

Someone had climbed into the driver's seat. From where Peters was sitting, he was unable to see who.

He waited with the camera poised.

The people carrier reversed out of the confined parking space. Finally, it turned to face Sean Peters head on.

It was the same driver as in the photo he had been shown earlier. The man behind the wheel on the Yamashiro highway the day Hiroko had died.

89

Charles Fancourt was sitting at the end of the bar, his eyes fixed on the optics in front of him.

Behind him, a group of expats were recounting their latest exploits. Their drunken boasts were accompanied by appreciative guffaws.

But Fancourt's most recent coup was on another level. Beyond anything the braggarts could imagine.

Since the operation, he had moved quickly. His gains were already salted away in secret accounts far from public scrutiny.

He never even discussed the outcome of his nefarious activities with his handler Chen. The Chinaman only cared if something went wrong and he was forced to inform his own superiors.

The bar was packed as always. Fancourt craned his head forwards once again to check the entrance.

Eventually the compact figure of Frank Deluca appeared at the doorway. The American's eyes scanned the crowd until he spotted Fancourt.

He eased his way through the drinkers and sat down next to the Englishman. He clicked his fingers at the barman.

"Manhattan."

The barman took his time serving the American. Eventually

he slid the drink across the counter.

"Here's to you, Charles."

The American leaned across to clink glasses. Fancourt reluctantly reciprocated.

For a man who had just earned a small fortune, Deluca should have been on cloud nine. In one fell swoop, the shady market intervention had put him back on track.

In fact, he was anything but.

One major concern was gnawing away at him. He waited a few minutes before broaching the subject.

"Hey Charles, did you hear the news about Yuki Morigami?"

It was the talk of the Tokyo financial community. One of their own going missing. The police were investigating.

"Yes. Odd business. Her disappearing like that."

Fancourt waved his glass at the waiter, muttering obscenities as he waited to be served.

Deluca paused before continuing.

"So, you don't know anything about it?"

Fancourt swivelled in his seat to glare at the American.

"Me? Why should I know?"

"She mentioned the two of you had met for lunch. I thought maybe she might have said something. Given some indication."

Fancourt turned to face the optics again.

"True. We did have a quick bite together. Just the usual business chit-chat."

"So, nothing out of the ordinary?"

"No, nothing at all."

Deluca leaned closer.

"I don't get it. According to the news, she was last seen in her jogging outfit. Apparently, that evening some residents remembered her leaving the building."

"You don't say? Well, that is strange. Mind you, at night, you never know. There are some odd types around."

Deluca bit his tongue. The police had yet to make the connection between him and Yuki. But it would not take them long.

He had only spoken to Yuki once prior to her disappearance. It was straight after her lunch with Fancourt. She had admitted she had asked Fancourt to include her in his secret market operation.

Deluca had panicked. Furious at her indiscretion, he had decided to steer clear of her.

But when she went missing, he started to put two and two together. And it added up to Fancourt.

He was in a perilous position. He assumed Yuki Morigami must have pointed the finger at him as the source of her information when she met Fancourt for lunch. That meant Fancourt must be aware of their covert relationship.

Deluca knew the rules of Fancourt's game. When Fancourt had rung him to suggest a drink that evening, the warning bells had rung loud and clear.

"Anyway, Frank, drink up."

Deluca turned as Fancourt stood up and grabbed his jacket.

"Where are we going?"

"A little place I know. I think you'll find it interesting."

Fancourt hailed a cab outside the bar and waited for Deluca to get in first. As they travelled through the Tokyo night, Deluca's attempts at conversation gradually petered out.

Fancourt stared out of the window in silence. Deluca used the time to try to organise his thoughts.

The taxi eventually pulled off the main drag and wound its way through a maze of narrow streets.

Deluca was lost. It was a part of the city he was completely unfamiliar with.

Fancourt on the other hand seemed quite at home. He paid the taxi driver who appeared anxious to be on his way.

Deluca did not like what he saw. Groups of poorly dressed men roamed around the streets. There was a pervading smell of urine and vomit. The antithesis of the privileged world he was used to.

Fancourt led the way making sure Deluca kept up. Eventually they climbed some steps and entered a building resembling an office block.

Fancourt waited for Deluca to board the lift first. As it rose, Deluca could hear the muffled sound of music.

The American was increasingly on his guard. He sensed he was walking into the lion's den.

90

Fancourt turned left out of the lift and strode along a darkened corridor. The music intensified.

At the end was a large padded door with a small window at head height. Fancourt rang the bell and stood back. A face appeared and sized them up carefully before opening.

The doorman needed a suit a couple of sizes larger. His biceps and thighs strained at the material. His long hair was tied back in a ponytail. His eyes were compressed under heavy lids.

He exchanged a few words with Fancourt before standing back. For a fleeting instant, Deluca considered making a run for it.

The passageway opened out into a lounge filled with men and women. They sprawled on settees.

Bottles of champagne littered the tables. There was a sickly scent. The conversation was in Chinese.

Deluca had a nose for such things. He categorised the clientele immediately.

Certain bars in his Italian neighbourhood in New York were off limits to regular people. But Frank Deluca had hung around on the fringes as a youngster.

Before he moved upmarket. Before he went to college and clothed himself in a veneer of respectability.

Fancourt walked across to a table in the corner. Deluca could tell the Englishman was a regular at the club.

Drinks and hot towels were brought by an attractive woman in a qipao dress. As she leant over Deluca, the lower half fell open revealing a shapely thigh.

Deluca took no notice. His attention was fixed on the man crossing the room towards them. Chinese, Deluca reckoned.

The man was strikingly handsome, dressed in a dinner jacket and bowtie, his hair pomaded straight back against his skull. He dropped onto the sofa opposite Fancourt and Deluca.

Fancourt made no introductions. There were no handshakes.

"Frank, I need you to listen very carefully to what this man is about to say."

Deluca felt his abdomen churn. The Chinaman opposite smiled, his eyes never leaving the American.

When he spoke, it was a cultured rich voice. Impeccable British English with no perceptible Chinese accent.

It had a discursive quality. As if he was strolling around some Oxford quad discussing philosophy.

"I'm so glad we had this chance for a little chin-wag Mr Deluca. Our mutual friend Mr Fancourt tells me you have been somewhat less than discreet?"

Deluca cursed to himself. Why couldn't he have kept his mouth shut?

For an instant he pictured Yuki's elbows resting on his chest. Her glossy hair enveloping his face like a fragrant tent.

He had reached up and swept her tresses behind her ear. Then he had leaned forwards and whispered.

She had giggled, encouraging him, teasing out all the details. Suddenly he had panicked, realising what he had done.

He had sworn her to secrecy. She had agreed, reassuring him.

"Don't worry Frank. You know you can rely on me."

And then the bitch had promptly contacted Fancourt.

The Chinaman continued in the same mellifluous tone.

"Well, of course, that won't do, will it? And just see what your tittle-tattle has led to? A perfectly lovely girl finding herself buried in the slime at the bottom of Tokyo Bay. What a simply shocking turn of events. And you have only yourself to blame."

In desperation, Deluca turned to Fancourt. If he thought he could find any support there he was mistaken. The Englishman was engrossed in his smartphone, apparently not even listening to the conversation.

"Anyway, that's all in the past. Our problem now is what on earth to do with you."

Deluca's hand strayed to the back of his neck. The room temperature suddenly seemed to have crept up a notch or two.

"We've decided the wisest course of action is for you to pack your things and leave Japan. Chop-chop. Leave and never come back."

"What! You can't force me to do that!"

The Chinaman sat back in his seat with an ironic smile.

"Oh, but we most certainly can."

There was still some fight left in Frank Deluca.

"You're forgetting something."

"Really? Do enlighten me."

"I know too much. What if I tell the authorities about Fancourt's little game? And what you did to the woman?"

The Chinaman brushed some specks of dust from his trouser knees and stood up. Edging around the table, he sat down on the sofa, trapping Deluca between himself and Fancourt.

Deluca felt like a child, sandwiched between their shoulders. The Chinaman turned to face him.

"Mr Deluca. Perhaps it would help if I described the reach of our organisation? It's really quite extensive. In point of fact, I'm hard pressed to think of one place in the world where we aren't represented. We Chinese are quite the travellers as I'm sure you're aware."

The man paused and smiled at Deluca. Allowing time for the point he was making to sink in.

"That being the case, you really would be well-advised to avoid mentioning our activities to a living soul. The repercussions would be swift and, well, simply unspeakable."

The Chinaman reached into his pocket and drew out his own smartphone.

"Perhaps I could draw your attention to some pertinent examples? Now, let's see…. Ah yes. Here we are. A case in point."

He leaned across Deluca and held the smartphone so it was in his eyeline. He then proceeded to flick through a sequence of images. As if he was showing a friend some holiday snaps.

Frank Deluca, the tough kid from Manhattan, caved in without a murmur. He could see his position was hopeless.

He immediately gave the Chinaman the assurances he

sought. A week later he had fled the country.

91

All day, Sean Peters' eyes were glued to the building opposite.

When the white people carrier returned after a couple of hours, the driver unloaded some packages and hurried inside. After that there was no sign of him.

But Peters reckoned the sudden break in routine could signal something was about to happen. He was on full alert.

The sun had already set by the time the driver emerged again. He looked around to check the coast was clear before returning to the building.

Peters nudged George Trevillion. The Cornishman was back from work, ready for his shift. He was sitting beside Peters, tapping away at the laptop on his knees.

"Here we go, George. Action stations."

The two men readied themselves. This could be the moment Wang finally broke cover.

They had already decided their best option was to take him on the move. They assumed he would be well protected inside the building.

But outside, he would be more vulnerable. They could choose the optimal moment to strike.

Sure enough, a few minutes later the driver appeared accompanied by Wang. Peters recognised him immediately. The same arrogant look, the styled quiff.

Peters felt his back tense as he stared through the camera lens.

"There you are, you bastard."

Wang slid into the front passenger seat of the people carrier. Then the driver turned and beckoned to someone behind him in the house.

A few seconds later a tall woman strode out. She had another woman in tow, dragging her by the wrist.

The driver opened the rear door of the people carrier. He helped to shove the smaller woman inside. Then he got into the driver' seat.

Peters sprang to his feet.

"Right, George. At the double."

They had planned for this eventuality. The laptop and camera went into a shoulder bag. Within seconds, they were flying down the stairs.

The woman at reception looked up startled as they rushed past. They were out of the door before she could remonstrate.

Once on the street, Peters waited in the shadows while Trevillion dashed to the parking area behind the hotel. Moments later, a Mitsubishi Outlander drew up beside Peters.

Peters jumped into the passenger seat beside Trevillion. They waited with the engine ticking over.

From there, they had an unobstructed view of the building. The people carrier was still negotiating the confined parking area.

As it drew up directly opposite, the faces of the driver and Wang were clearly visible. Peters and Trevillion shrank back in their seats.

Without paying any attention to the Mitsubishi Outlander, the driver leaned forwards to check the oncoming traffic before pulling out.

"OK, George. Gently does it."

George Trevillion waited a few seconds, allowing another car to pass in front of them for cover. He had no difficulty tailing the white people carrier in the slow-moving traffic.

However, once they reached the main ring road, the pace quickened. Trevillion had to be on his guard not to lose the target.

South of Shibuya the people carrier swung west. Then, before crossing the Tama River, it broke south again.

"They're making for Yokohama."

The traffic was faster and more congested. Trevillion put his foot down, constantly switching lanes to stay in visual contact with their quarry.

After Yokohama Baseball Stadium, the people carrier suddenly signalled and exited the overhead highway. Trevillion found himself in the fast lane and had to cut across to followed suit.

The pace now slowed again and Trevillion dropped back. The people carrier wound its way through a network of city streets, before filtering left towards the bay,

Night was falling by the time they entered the docklands. All around were huge warehouses and storage units.

Trevillion had to be particularly vigilant now to avoid detection. They were the only two vehicles on the road.

Eventually, the people carrier turned into an unlit street backing onto one of the docks. Halfway along, it came to a halt.

A few parked trucks lined the street affording Trevillion some cover. Spotting a side street, he made a quick turn.

He pulled up in the shadow of a fuel storage tank and doused his headlights.

92

Charles Fancourt had all but forgotten Frank Deluca. Out of sight, out of mind.

Once Deluca had agreed to the Chinaman's demands, he was escorted from the night club and bundled into a taxi. Huddled in the back seat, he cut a forlorn, diminished figure.

After seeing him off, the suave Chinaman had returned to the club and thrown himself on the sofa opposite Fancourt. Pointing a flute of champagne at the Englishman, he was quick to make his feelings plain.

"Careless. Extremely careless, Fancourt. Don't expect us to keep cleaning up your mess after you."

Fancourt avoided looking the man the eye. He dreaded to think what would happen if he ever found himself in Deluca's shoes. He knew he would not get off so lightly.

But a week had passed. His mind was elsewhere.

It was Thursday evening. He was sitting alone in his luxury apartment. Readying himself for what lay ahead.

Traffic noise drifted up to him from the street far below. The constant hum seemed to belong to another world. One he felt completely detached from.

His evening meals were normally delivered from a nearby Michelin-starred restaurant. The very best Tokyo could offer, sluiced down with exclusive vintages.

Not that he took much notice of what he ate. He shovelled it down, eyes glued to his laptop, tracking prices around the world. His mind constantly calculating and recalculating his positions.

But, for once, the laptop was closed. The restaurant had been instructed to cancel his supper order for that evening.

He went into the kitchen and opened one of the cupboards. On the top shelf was a neat row of Heinz baked beans cans, bought from a delicatessen across the road.

He reached down one of the cans. Opening it, he emptied the contents into a saucepan. Meanwhile he put two slices of white bread into the toaster and boiled the kettle for tea.

It was a simple meal. One he was well able to prepare himself.

But he took infinite pains. Every element had to be just so.

When the meal was ready, he sat at his dining table. He paused before picking up his knife and fork, staring at his plate.

Then he started to eat. As he chewed, he kept his eyes clenched shut.

He could not expect it to be the same as it had been all those years ago. But it was a reasonable facsimile.

His mother always referred to it as tea. Sometimes sardines on toast, sometimes a poached egg. But on that particular day it had been baked beans on toast.

It only took one mouthful of the tasteless mush. The intervening years melted away.

Once again, he was sitting at the kitchen table with its Formica top. Just the two of them as always. His mother and him.

She would watch him as he ate. Making sure he cleared his plate.

"Thank you for the lovely meal," he would recite once he had finished. She would reach over and pat his head.

Then he would leave the table and wash up at the Belfast sink. He could hardly reach the taps.

Her eyes would never leave him. Afterwards he would climb the steep, carpeted stairs to bed. He would have an hour to himself before she came up to tuck him in and turn the lights off.

Sitting with his eyes closed, chewing his food, he once again journeyed back into his past. Retracing the sequence of events on that fateful Thursday evening long ago.

Once again, he could hear the grandfather clock ticking in the hall. Counting down the minutes.

He pictured his mother sitting at the table, fiddling with her hair. Pushing up the sides of her perm, as it might suddenly collapse.

On that evening, her plummy Home Counties voice had been little more than a whisper.

What exactly had she said? He wracked his brains trying to recall her precise words.

Something about not hurrying his food. About remembering to clean his teeth. About how much she loved him.

He distinctly remembered her reaching out to touch his hair, brushing it out of his eyes. How her hand dropped to stroke his cheek.

He remembered the beaten look in her eyes as she did so. Bruised. Defeated.

Even at that age, he could read the signs. His childish intuition kept repeating an urgent message.

Don't let her go. Keep her close. There is danger.

He had asked her why she was sad. She had merely smiled and patted his hand.

Now years later, he sat in his luxury apartment on the other side of the world, sipping his sugared tea. Trying to unlock the puzzle.

As on every such evening, he sifted through the memories over and over again. But he was only left with a tangle of threads he could never resolve.

Perhaps this evening it would be different? Perhaps finally everything would drop into place?

He stood up and walked into the kitchen to wash up his plate and cutlery. He usually left his dishes for the maid.

When everything was dried and put away, he looked at his watch. Time to be going.

He went into his bedroom. From under the bed, he pulled out a battered suitcase. It had his initials on the lid.

He laid it on the bed. It was locked. From his pocket, he took out his keyring.

93

Peters and Trevillion were now on foot. Both men were dressed for action. Loose dark clothing, black balaclavas, trainers.

They had left the Mitsubishi and worked their way to a position some 50 yards behind the white people carrier. Close enough to see what was happening. Far enough to be invisible in the shadows.

Trevillion had a pair of lightweight binoculars trained on the car.

"Here we go."

Wang got out first from the passenger side. Checking up and down the street, he crossed to the grey two-story building opposite. Opening the front door, he signalled to the other occupants in the car.

Peters and Trevillion watched as the driver seized the small woman from the back seat and frogmarched her towards the building. She was unsteady on her feet, at one point stumbling.

As she regained her balance, Trevillion was able to get a clear look at her face.

"I'm pretty sure that's the Filipina."

Trevillion passed the binoculars to Peters.

"Yup. That's her."

They had both studied the photographs of Ligaya Santos. Peters had received them as email attachments from his anonymous source.

The sender had included some background information about the Filipina. How she had been trafficked, her subsequent escape and re-capture by Wang. The sender seemed to have a personal interest in the fate of this particular woman.

Trevillion turned to Peters.

"What the hell's going on?"

"Nothing good."

They watched the trio disappear into the building. They heard the front door slammed shut behind them.

George Trevillion turned to Peters.

"Do we go in?"

Peters thought for a second.

"You stay put and watch the street. I'll have a quick recce round the back."

"Right. I'll text you if anything happens."

Peters zipped up his anorak and pulled his balaclava down over his face. Then he set off at a jog along the pavement, hugging the shadows. George Trevillion lost sight of him as he neared the building.

Watching Peters in action, George Trevillion could have been back in South Armagh. His comrade still had the same loping run, deceptively quick. The same natural ability to cling to cover, to blend into the background.

Back then, no one came close. Peters was in a league of his

own.

He always led off. He was always the first in the line of fire.

Left alone to watch the building, George Trevillion found the all-too-familiar thoughts start to crowd in. The self-doubts that always preceded any military engagement.

They were now at the point of no return. Whatever happened next would in all likelihood involve violence, its outcome unpredictable.

It was a long time since George Trevillion had found himself in this position. Faced with a life-threatening situation.

He was a different person now. A corporate executive more used to squinting at spreadsheets than staring down the sights of a rifle.

Sometimes, after a few drinks, his cronies could persuade him to open up about his military exploits. The life and death operations he had been involved in.

But he always gave them the edited version. Something his listeners would find easy to comprehend.

He left out the subtext. The stomach-churning fear. The mounting sense of anxiety no amount of training could eradicate.

It was with him now. At his shoulder. Whispering in his ear, as he crouched in the shadows watching the house.

Up until this moment, the whole adventure had been a trip down memory lane. The chance to stand shoulder-to-shoulder with his old comrade-in-arms.

But he realised he was not the same man who had patrolled those lethal streets of Northern Ireland. He had moved on.

In panic, he wondered if he had made a terrible error of

judgement. That he was not up to it any more.

At that moment his thoughts suddenly turned to the Filipina. He pictured her stumbling across the road in front of them.

He did not know what was in store for her. But he could only assume the worst.

In a flash, his own fears receded into the background. It was no longer about him. The trafficked woman's safety was paramount.

He clenched his jaw and muttered.

"Come on, George. Get a fucking grip."

His window for self-doubt came to an abrupt end. Headlights had appeared behind him at the end of the street.

The old instincts kicked in. Trevillion reached for his phone and stabbed out a rapid text message to Peters.

"Company."

94

Charles Fancourt was in a world of his own.

After his ritualised meal, he had gathered the items he would need and packed them in his leather attaché case. Then he had ridden the lift to the ground floor.

The limousine was waiting on the other side of the road with the engine running. When the driver recognised Fancourt, he jumped out and opened the rear door. The Englishman dived inside without a word.

Without needing to be asked, he slipped on the blindfold. Stretching out his legs, he sank back into the plush interior.

He needed to try and relax. He could already feel the tension building as each minute passed.

The car's interior had its usual distinctive smell. The tang of expensive leather upholstery blended with the driver's cheap deodorant.

Deprived of his sight, Fancourt now fell back on his other senses. He had little trouble recognising the familiar landmarks along the way.

The succession of traffic signals. The ramp leading up onto an expressway. The rhythm of the road surface.

Music was playing through the speakers beside him. 1970's American schmaltz. Saccharin melodies Fancourt normally despised.

But these were not normal circumstances. The crooning voice in his ear formed the indispensable prelude to the evening.

It was her song. Over and over again.

He found himself humming it. As he did, her voice came back to him.

It was popular at the time. The catchy tune forever on her lips.

At the sink, hanging out the washing, preparing meals. He could see her now, mouthing the vapid lyrics.

Eyes, lips, hearts. The anatomy of love.

At the hour his father was expected, the singing stopped. The music died.

At the sound of the doorbell, she bundled her apron into a ball and hurriedly changed out of her slippers. Her face taut with anxiety.

From the moment she opened the front door, there was only discord.

It was a lengthy drive but eventually Fancourt felt the limousine slow as it left the expressway. A series of turns through quiet streets followed as they neared their destination.

But Fancourt's journey was just beginning. Within himself. His repeated quest for closure.

Sitting in the back of the car, he now had the attaché case open. His hand rested on a loose woollen garment. His fingers teased out the individual stitches, exploring the woof and warp of the material.

He remembered the first time he had described his

requirements to the Chinese in Hong Kong. They had stared at him mystified.

The telling tarnished the memory. But he had no choice but try to explain. It was imperative they knew.

It all hinged on every detail being right. Like the precise juxtaposition of elements in a still-life painting.

Eventually they sought out an elderly Chinese woman. Someone with the patience to listen. Someone capable of comprehending.

They had sat opposite each other in a small room. He remembered a large floral decoration in one corner. The rattan furniture creaking as he shifted his weight. The single small window covered with a thick velvet drape.

She sat motionless. After a while he blanked everything around, her eyes drawing him in like fissures in the firmament.

If it was a confession, there was no atonement.

But it served its purpose. She understood exactly what was required. When the moment came, everything was in its correct place.

He remembered the first time in Hong Kong when he had put himself in their hands. The blindfold had surprised him. They insisted he wore it.

First, there was the familiar traffic roar as they crossed the Cross-Harbour Tunnel into Kowloon. Afterwards a barrage of sounds he could not identify.

He had not moved during the journey. Waiting. Teeth clenched.

When eventually the blindfold was removed, he was standing outside a door. He needed time to gather himself for what lay beyond.

Then the door swung opened.

He looked around transfixed.

The bed turned back. The crumpled sheets. The dressing table contents scattered on the carpet. The hand mirror, sticks of lipstick, face cream and hairpins all in disarray. The scant furniture upended. The dressing gown with its ripped pocket.

His hand covered his mouth as he let out a squeal of delight. He was back home again.

With the subsequent move to Japan, he was concerned it would not be the same. That they would mess it up.

He need not have worried. Everything had been taken care of just as before.

As the limousine slid to a halt, his mind slipped back to the present. They had arrived.

He was helped out of the car, his legs lifted over the door sill and placed onto the tarmac. Then, like a blind man, one hand resting on the driver's shoulder, he was escorted to the front door.

It would not be long now. He couldn't wait.

95

Ligaya Santos was waking from a nightmare. Only to find herself somewhere far worse.

For weeks, she had tried to assemble her thoughts, but every time she broke surface, the drugs drew her back under. Like being pinned to the seabed by the weight of a suffocating wave.

She had forgotten everything, even Cesar. She had no idea where she was or how she came to be there.

Mercifully the drugs blanked unwelcome memories too. Of the succession of men entering her cramped room.

But the previous week, there had been a sudden, unexpected change. The customers no longer queued outside her door.

She was taken off the drugs. She begged for them. To buffer herself against the brutal reality.

Wang had sat on the bed, his hand squeezing her upper thigh. He spoke in his low voice, his accented English full of menace.

"No more drugs for you. You have a job to do. You need to be ready."

She had shrunk back against the metal bedhead. But there was nowhere to escape.

"You gave me a lot trouble. Now you'll see what happens to people who do that."

Wang's grip tightened. The pain soared. She screamed.

"Stop. Please stop!"

Wang grinned. Then he released the pressure and issued orders in Chinese to the tall woman standing beside him. She nodded.

Ligaya Santos' conditions improved. She was given better food. She was allowed to spend time attending to her personal hygiene. Her scrambled mind gradually began to untangle.

Then that morning a hairdresser arrived. He avoided looking her in the eye. The tall woman had mounted guard, issuing precise instructions.

After he finished, the hairdresser scuttled out of the room. Ligaya Santos did not recognise herself in the mirror. Her long tresses bunched up in tight curls.

Later new clothes were laid out on the bed. Cumbersome garments from another era.

That evening, they had come for her. They took her outside the building and put her in the back seat of the car.

Whatever was happening, she knew it was going to end badly for her. Of that, she was sure.

But she had no will left to resist. She almost welcomed it. The fight had gone out of her.

She sat on the back seat with her head bowed. A lamb to the slaughter.

Eventually they pulled up in a deserted street. As she was hustled across to a building, she looked up. She thought she saw death stencilled on its grey façade.

Cesar was now constantly in her thoughts. She tried to reach out to him. To embrace him one last time.

There was nothing she could do for him now. He would have to learn to survive without her.

They took her downstairs and bundled her into a small room at the end of the corridor. She was told to sit on the low sofa.

The tall woman waited with her, tapping her foot nervously on the floor. She gave Ligaya Santos quick, anxious glances.

Then there was another noise. At the top of the stairs. The sound of people arriving.

She heard footsteps descend. Then another door shutting.

A few moments later, Wang appeared. He held a plastic bag in his hands.

He barked an instruction at the tall woman. She leaped up and dragged Ligaya Santos after her.

Wang pulled an old woollen cardigan from the bag. The tall woman fed it over Ligaya Santos' arms, straightening it over her shoulders. Then she stood in front of Ligaya Santos and buttoned it up from the bottom.

It felt uncomfortable. The night was humid and there was no air-conditioning in the building. The rough wool prickled against her bare arms. She started to sweat.

"Please. Take it off. I can't bear it."

Wang ignored her and spoke with the tall woman. Ligaya Santos had no idea what they were saying. But whatever was planned was imminent.

There was tension in the air. As a performer, she could read the signs.

She remembered standing in the wings with her band back in the Philippines, ready to go on stage. The anticipation, the nerves, the last-minute bravado to cheer themselves up.

The audience was waiting. After taking that first step into the spotlight there was no return, no backing out. She would have to face the music.

She could see it in her captors' faces. Whatever was about to happen, she realised she was going to be centre stage.

Wang opened the door a crack and peered down the corridor.

He turned and gave a last-minute instruction. Before Ligaya Santos could react, the tall woman covered her mouth with duct tape.

Ligaya Santos struggled but the woman was far too strong for her. The two Chinese bustled her out of the room.

Halfway along the corridor was another door. They opened it and went inside.

As Ligaya Santos took in the scene in front of her, she panicked. Her legs suddenly gave way under her.

Wang and the woman dragged her into the room and closed the door behind them. They hurried to complete the final preparations.

96

The blindfold fell away. Fancourt squinted, adjusting to the light. Directly in front of him was the closed door.

Slowly his hand stretched towards the handle.

He turned it, just as he had all those years before. A hesitant push and the room opened up.

He gazed around. Everything was as he remembered. The items strewn on the floor. The furniture overturned.

Earlier, when he had tried to reproduce the scene himself, it was never in such detail. It was amateurish at best.

But with the Chinese there were no half measures. The old Chinese woman had listened. She was a stickler for detail. A constant stream of questions, delving into the layers of his memory.

He painted the picture for her down to the last brushstroke. Every memory engraved on his soul.

Now, standing inside the room, the past rolls into the present. Time fractures.

Fancourt is once again his four-year-old self.

Without prompting, he lunges forwards. His child's mind cannot grasp what he is witnessing.

His mother is standing on a chair in the centre of the room. The flimsy cane seat from her dressing table, covered in floral material.

She is on tiptoe. In her stockinged feet. She sweeps her arms in circles trying to keep her balance.

She is wearing her serge skirt and her purple woollen cardigan. Around her neck, a daisy chain of his father's striped silk ties leads upwards to a hook in the ceiling.

Her eyes swivel towards the door. She sees him.

He should not be here. Not now. Not to witness this.

In her anxiety, she starts to lose her balance. The cane seat cannot support her weight. It starts to topple.

Her stockinged feet struggle to keep it upright. It collapses onto the floor.

The knotted ties around her neck tighten. The silk stretches with his mother's weight.

Her arms start to windmill. Her eyes plead with him for help.

His father's tie bites into her neck. She kicks out.

He rushes forward. He panics. He does not understand.

He tries to help. He holds onto her legs. But it just makes matters worse.

He does not realise she needs to be lifted. But how could a four-year-old boy possibly support his mother's weight? Lift her from the jaws of death?

Her legs now jerk with a violent spasm. He is thrown to the side.

Her eyes are not on him. They are turned, upwards, inwards.

She has no time left for him. She has no time.

He pulls himself up again. He grabs her hand, holding it tight. He is screaming for her.

And as she dies, he feels her final supreme effort. Her fingers lock with his.

A promise never to part.

And that is how his father finds him, hours later. The boy hears him standing outside the front door ringing the bell, wondering why no one is answering.

But the boy ignores him. Holding onto the cold hand, pressing it to his cheek.

He hears his father's key finally turn in the lock. His shouts from the hall.

The boy does not respond.

His father starts his search, racing through the downstairs rooms.

Still no sound from the boy.

He hears his father climbing the stairs, his anger mounting at every step.

And then the silence as he stands at the bedroom door. As he observes the scene in front of him.

His father tries to prise the boy away from his dead mother. To separate the locked, frozen fingers.

Now a grown man, Fancourt is driven to replay the scene. To reach out to the past. To try to re-connect.

As a young man, he had discovered her purple cardigan in a trunk in the attic. He rescued it before his father erased all traces of his first wife.

He stole a fistful of his father's silk ties from his dressing room. Old now, frayed from use.

Wherever he went in the world, he took these cherished

items. The lifeline to his past. His way back home.

He gazes at the woman tottering on the stool in front of him. He does not register her features. He only sees what he needs to see.

The tight perm, the serge skirt, the stockinged feet on tiptoe. The faded purple cardigan. The knotted silk ties.

He yearns to hold her hand. To feel the fingers curl around his own once again in their deadly bond.

Soon the danse macabre will begin. He moves forwards to take his position at her side.

97

George Trevillion spotted the shadow racing back towards him along the line of the buildings.

"Now George. On the double. Keep low."

Trevillion did not hesitate. He sprang after Peters.

On his recce, Peters had crept round to the back of the building, trying to figure out what was happening. The only light was shining through a window in the basement.

Letting himself down into a narrow gully, he had edged along until he could peer inside.

There was not much Peters had not witnessed in his years in the Marines. He had witnessed death at close quarters.

He knew what men could do to other men for a cause. He had been involved in the aftermath of bombings, tasked with picking up the pieces.

But what he saw through the window was beyond all that.

The Filipina they had watched being taken into the house was balancing on a stool in the centre of the room. Around her neck was what looked like knotted neckties, suspended from a steel girder.

Her mouth was taped. She was wearing an odd assortment of clothes. Her eyes screamed fear.

In front of her were the three Chinese. Wang, the driver and the tall woman were standing back, checking their handiwork.

The room was a mess of items strewn over the floor. But despite the clutter, Peters sensed it had been arranged that way with a purpose. The people in the room stepped around the items as if anxious not to disturb anything.

Peters was climbing out of the gully when the text came from Trevillion. Whatever was planned was imminent. There was no time to lose.

The two former Marines ran towards the building. They had to assume the people inside were armed. Peters and Trevillion only had the advantage of surprise.

Peters tried the main door only to find it locked.

"Round the back."

They circled the building and dropped down into the gulley where Peters had crouched earlier. They leaned forwards to peer through the basement window.

The three Chinese had disappeared. They were replaced by a tall Caucasian. He was alone in the room, standing in front of the woman on the stool.

They watched as the man started fingering the woman's mauve cardigan. He then starting running his hands over the material of her dress.

All the while, the Filipina struggled to maintain her balance. The foreigner seemed oblivious to her predicament. He appeared to be mumbling to himself.

Then, in a flash, he moved beside the woman. He reached out and grasped her hand.

With horror, Peters realised what was about to happen.

The former Marine reacted immediately. Smashing the

window pane, he kicked out the jagged slivers of glass.

In a trice, he had slipped through the opening and dropped down into the room. George Trevillion followed suit.

Fancourt seemed to wake from a trance. He looked at the two intruders in shock and then started howling in fury.

In one swift movement, he kicked away the stool supporting Ligaya Santos. She was left swinging, her feet thrashing in the air.

Fancourt then whirled round to face Peters. A second later, he was lying unconscious on the floor.

Meanwhile George Trevillion rushed to Ligaya Santos. He grabbed her legs and lifted her high off the ground, supporting her body weight. Her face was already contorted, her body starved of oxygen.

Peters was immediately at his side. With a penknife, he severed the silk tie above Ligaya Santos' head.

She collapsed into George Trevillion's arms. He gently laid her on the ground, loosening the noose constricting her throat. She coughed, gulping air.

Behind them, the basement door burst open.

The Chinese had strict orders. Whatever happened they were to leave the Englishman Fancourt alone in the room with the victim.

They were never to interfere. They were simply there to clear up the mess afterwards.

When they had heard the window shatter, they took a moment to react. Unsure if this was some unchoreographed departure from the script.

It was only when they heard the sounds of a scuffle, they

realised something was wrong.

They were not armed. Firearms being strictly prohibited in Japan.

Not that they cared about breaking the law. But being caught with guns had unwelcome consequences. It was bad for business.

In any case, they had not expected any trouble. In the past, the event had always gone off without a hitch.

They now wished they had come better prepared.

The driver was first through the door, followed by Wang and Fancourt's chauffeur. The woman hung back.

Trevillion glanced up. Three against one.

Hardly a fair fight, he thought. He continued attending to Ligaya Santos.

For a big man, Peters moved like a dancer. Precise steps followed by thunderous impacts. The three men dropped like rice sacks.

He had only wanted to incapacitate them. They lay on the ground unconscious.

Seeing what had happened to her confederates, the Chinese woman raced out of the basement and up the stairs. Peters sprinted out of the room in hot pursuit.

He caught her just as she reached the front door. He was less than chivalrous as he bundled her back down the stairs and thrust her into the corner by the window where he could keep an eye on her.

Peters bent over Ligaya Santos.

"How is she doing, George?"

"OK, I think. But we had better get her to a hospital pronto."

Peters nodded.

"OK. We'll take these two as well."

He pointed at Fancourt and Wang.

George Trevillion was well prepared. Producing a handful of cable ties from his pocket, he and Peters secured their five adversaries, hands and feet. They dragged the two drivers and the woman outside the room and immobilised them against the steel bars of the staircase.

Trevillion then carried Ligaya Santos to the car while Peters stood guard over their captives. As the Cornishman laid her on the back seat, she groaned, her hands clasped around her throat.

"Don't try to talk. Wait for us here."

Returning to the house, he helped Peters with Wang and Fancourt. The former Marines hoisted the two men over their shoulders as easily as if they were children. They carried them up the street to the Mitsubishi and tipped them into the boot.

Jumping into the driver's seat, Trevillion wasted no time. Putting his foot down, he raced back towards the centre of Yokohama.

98

Ms Sekikawa was working late when the call came. Normally at that time she would have been ploughing up and down the swimming pool.

Hayashi had already left. Just as Ms Sekikawa was packing up, Yamaguchi had wandered out of his office and sat down in Hayashi's chair opposite her.

She had surreptitiously kicked her shoulder bag back under the desk. Suddenly, hurrying off to the swimming pool became less of a priority.

Her boss stared across the desk as if he had something on his mind. She knew the look. The one when he was building up to a question.

Her phone rang before he had a chance to open his mouth. Answering it, Ms Sekikawa's demeanour changed in an instant.

Grabbing her shoulder bag, she jumped up, beckoning to Yamaguchi. She sprinted across the department with her phone clamped to her ear.

Yamaguchi was not far behind. Dashing back to his office, he swept up his jacket and met her at the lift.

"That was Peters. He's found Ligaya Santos. And there's more. We need a fast car."

She had no time for further explanation as the lift doors opened on the ground floor. They headed for the basement car pool. Yamaguchi flashed his ID and was immediately allocated a high-performance police vehicle.

It was a re-enactment of their dash to Yokohama some years earlier to thwart a terrorist attack. Same police vehicle, same route, same urgency.

In no time, Yamaguchi had joined the expressway and they were powering their way south.

While Yamaguchi weaved through traffic, Ms Sekikawa was on the phone to the Kanagawa Prefecture Police Headquarters in Yokohama. Her orders were clear and brooked no discussion.

They should dispatch a team to a deserted building in the Yokohama docks. The three people they would find there should be taken into custody for questioning. They were part of a criminal organisation and should be considered dangerous.

A separate team should go to the Yokohama City University Medical Centre. A Filipina named Ligaya Santos had been admitted to the A&E department within the last hour.

The woman would need round-the-clock police protection. She and Detective Yamaguchi were on their way and would be at the hospital within 30 minutes to liaise with the officers on the scene.

The duty sergeant took down all the details and promised to execute her orders without delay.

Ms Sekikawa sat back and took a deep breath. Beside her, Yamaguchi sliced through the traffic, lights flashing.

She had forgotten how Yamaguchi could drive when the need arose. He did not talk until the road ahead cleared. Then he glanced across at her.

"So, what do we know?"

"Peters didn't say much on the phone. Just where we could find Ligaya Santos and three of the Chinese responsible for kidnapping her."

Yamaguchi grunted.

"Any idea how he managed to track her down?"

"He didn't say. Just told us where to go. That was it."

Yamaguchi accelerated into the next lane. He had a puzzled look on his face.

"Strange. With all our resources we haven't been able to make any progress. And yet this Peters, on his own, manages to locate and rescue the woman, capturing three crooks into the bargain."

Ms Sekikawa had been thinking along the same lines. The Englishman had only briefly seen the photo of Wang and the driver, and she had only mentioned Ligaya Santos' abduction in passing. Nothing much to go on.

"It's beyond me too. There's something we're missing."

"What do we know about Peters?"

"Not a lot. Martial artist. He can clearly look after himself."

"Yes, I remember you mentioning that."

Ms Sekikawa had described in detail how Peters had dealt with the construction workers in Yamashiro. Yamaguchi had been quietly impressed.

He was well aware of the martial arts expertise residing in those remote mountains in the north. Fighting traditions going back generations. If Peters was considered an expert there, he would be a force to be reckoned with.

"Anything else about his background?"

"No. He doesn't give much away. You know the sort."

They sat in silence, wrapped up in their own thoughts, until they pulled up at the hospital. Ms Sekikawa jumped out and rushed into the A&E reception. She flashed her credentials at the receptionist on duty.

"A Filipina was admitted in the last couple of hours. We need to see her right away."

The receptionist nodded.

"Your colleagues have already arrived. They are expecting you. Just a moment, please."

She picked up the phone to inform the police officers the detectives had arrived.

When the foreigner had burst through the automatic doors with the woman in his arms, the receptionist had reacted with calm professionalism. The emergency team had arrived in seconds.

As the team wheeled the patient through to one of the treatment areas, the foreigner summarised the relevant background for the doctor in charge.

He was less forthcoming when it came to filling in the required paperwork.

"I'm afraid I haven't got time for that. The police will be arriving shortly. Please ensure the woman is properly cared for and protected until they arrive."

Despite her anxious requests for him to wait, the man had dashed out of the hospital. She last saw him jumping into a large car parked on the hospital forecourt.

99

Trevillion dropped down from the expressway at the Ukishima interchange. On the other side of the Tama River planes swarmed around the recently-extended Haneda Airport.

Despite the traffic signs being in Japanese, Trevillion drove with assurance. He knew precisely where he was going.

Their destination was the antithesis of tourist-brochure Tokyo. There was nothing quaint about the fuel depots, pipelines and recycling plants. But then, no tourist would ever have any reason for venturing there.

Trevillion's company owned a research facility and warehouse on this wide tract of reclaimed land. He made frequent treks across the city to meet with his managers.

That evening, he was heading for the industrial recycling lot next door. Behind the wire fencing stood ramshackle corrugated sheds alongside towering heaps of discarded scrap.

Whenever he had a coffee-break during warehouse visits, he would idly contemplate the machines separating the junk into piles, trying to work out the logic behind the sifting. Recently he had taken a much keener interest in what was happening on the other side of the wire.

As he and Peters had formulated their plans back in his flat, they had identified the need for a fallback location. Somewhere accessible but isolated.

The recycling facility fitted the bill. It was lightly staffed, just the excavator drivers and a skeleton team of personnel. Only the corrugated hut near the main gate ever appeared to be in use.

Work stopped at five o'clock on the dot when the gates were closed. There was no after-hours security. After all, who would want to steal a used fridge?

On the pretext of a late-night meeting, Trevillion had left his car in his company compound and wandered next door. Slipping over the gate was no problem. He had then tried the corrugated sheds one by one until he found what he was looking for.

One of the smaller sheds at the rear of the site was unlocked. Inside, it was empty. No reason for anyone to visit that particular building, even during the working day.

Peters and Trevillion were now approaching the recycling lot. Trevillion steered the Mitsubishi along the single-track street running behind it. He parked in the shadows.

The corrugated shed he had earmarked bordered the perimeter. Peters got out of the car and approached the chain-link fence. With a pair of bolt croppers, he snipped an opening wide enough for a man to pass. It would only be visible if closely examined.

Returning to the car he opened the tailgate. Fancourt and Wang lay crammed in the boot. Both were awake and struggling at their restraints. Their mouths were taped.

Trevillion and Peters lifted Fancourt out first. Squeezing through the wire fence, they deposited him in the shed. There was an electric light but they did not switch it on. They then returned for Wang.

Leaving the two men lying on the ground, Peters and

Trevillion went outside. There were some items they needed.

They found an old fridge freezer standing next to the recycling stack nearest them. In another, they dug out a large plastic tub which they filled from an outside tap. From the car, they fetched a large cloth and a 10-litre watering can.

It was an ingeniously simple procedure. Recently it had become much more widely publicised but it had its origins with the Spanish Inquisition.

Peters and Trevillion had experienced the method first-hand as part of their basic training. They had both witnessed it used in earnest in Northern Ireland.

They knew how effective it was. The stoutest soul would crumble. Most gave up within minutes as their lungs filled with water.

Wang was first. Peters pulled him over to the fridge freezer and laid him on top. He roped his arms and feet so he was completely immobilised.

Then he stood staring the prostrate man straight in the face.

Peters was not a vindictive man. Over the years, life with Hiroko had all but cauterized the violence in his soul.

But in the half-light, as he looked at the Chinese man struggling to free himself, he had to restrain himself. If he had wanted to, he could have broken his neck as easily as a rabbit's.

Trevillion glanced at his friend. He recognised the look on his face only too well.

"OK, Sean?"

Peters nodded. Trevillion put the cloth over Wang's face. Holding it in place, he started to pour the water from the watering can onto the cloth.

The effect was immediate. Wang spluttered, his body contorting until the water stopped.

Trevillion could not help feeling some empathy with Wang. He understood what drowning felt like.

Many was the time he had been trapped underwater during his surfing days on the Cornish coast. Disorientated, pounded against the shingle by the raging waves above him.

He remembered the saltwater burning his lungs. His arms desperately flailing to reach the surface.

He had been lucky. His fellow surfers had always been there to pull him up. After coughing his guts out, they had all trotted to the pub near the beach to laugh it off.

Wang was not laughing. Between his splutters, he spat out a torrent of Chinese at the two former soldiers.

"Japanese only, if you please."

Back went the towel, on went the water. Peters watched the man writhe, doing his utmost to wriggle free, gasping.

Then he was allowed to come up for air again.

Peters and Trevillion both knew from experience there was little to be gained by asking questions too early. The subject needed a good dosing first. To understand the implications of non-compliance.

In fact, it was 10 minutes before Peters started interrogating him in Japanese. By then, Wang was ready to tell them anything they wanted to know.

100

As soon as the doctor gave the all-clear, Ms Sekikawa went in to see Ligaya Santos.

She was lying in bed, wearing a neck brace. She looked groggy, in shock.

"Ligaya?"

The Filipina stared at Ms Sekikawa. It had been a while since they had last met. A lot had happened in the interim.

Ms Sekikawa glanced at her bare arms lying on top of the sheets. The veins in her upper forearms peppered with tell-tale needle punctures.

Her eyes travelled up to Ligaya's incongruously permed hair and then to the outmoded clothes on the chair beside the bed. Quite untypical of the woman she knew.

The Filipina struggled to maintain her focus. Almost immediately, her eyelids began to close.

"Ligaya, it's me, Detective Sekikawa. Don't try to talk. The doctor says you shouldn't."

In response, Ligaya Santos stretched out her right arm. Ms Sekikawa stepped forwards to clasp her hand.

"It's all right, Ligaya. You're safe now."

The doctor had explained Ligaya Santos had had a very lucky escape. Her neck had only borne her bodyweight for a few seconds. Apart from superficial bruising, her carotid arteries and jugular veins had not been seriously impacted.

The rope had been measured so she would swing, not drop, when the chair was removed. Following their instructions to the letter, the Chinese had staged a drawn-out strangulation.

Ligaya Santos wanted to confide in Ms Sekikawa. To tell her everything that had happened.

How her stockinged feet had scrambled for a foothold. How the noose cut into her neck the more she struggled.

Then, the sudden relief of being lifted. How the unbearable pressure in her temples dissipated in an instant.

How she had clung onto the man as he carried her to the car. How he had laid her down on the back seat like a wounded bird.

How her persecutor and the other foreigner were shut in the boot of the car, inches from where she was lying. How she heard them struggle and groan.

How she had cowered away from them, fearing they might be able to grab her through the flimsy partition.

How, as they drove away, the driver had kept glancing back over his shoulder to check on her. How she had met his gaze, her eyes trying to express her gratitude.

But all this would have to come later. For the time being, it was enough just to sit holding the police officer's hand.

But for Ms Sekikawa, time was against her. She needed to establish the facts as soon as possible. Lives were at stake.

Ligaya Santos had some of the answers. If she could not speak, perhaps there was another way?

"Ligaya, can you try to answer a few simple questions? Just blink once for 'Yes' and twice for 'No'."

There was a pause before Ligaya Santos responded by blinking once.

Ms Sekikawa quickly prioritised the questions she most needed answering.

All she knew at this stage was the scant information Peters had given her over the phone. Where to find Ligaya Santos and the three perpetrators. Nothing more.

When Ms Sekikawa tried to press him, Peters had disconnected. When she tried to call him back, his phone had been turned off.

Slowly, with Ligaya Santos' cooperation, elements of the picture emerged. Ms Sekikawa's primary objective was to establish the identity of all the people involved.

Earlier Ms Sekikawa had contacted her police colleagues in Yokohama. Wang, she learned, was not among the three Chinese they had picked up at the docklands address.

Ligaya Santos blinked to confirm he had been present at the building. Also, that a total of three Caucasians were involved. Two men who had rescued her, and a third foreigner who had tried to kill her.

Wang and the other foreigner had been taken as captives in the car after they left the house. That was all she knew.

The effort exhausted Ligaya Santos. She turned away, her eyes closing.

Ms Sekikawa sat back and tried to piece it all together. Peters had an accomplice, that was clear. They had left three of the perpetrators at the original building for the police. Meanwhile they had driven off with Wang and some other unidentified foreigner.

She reflected on the police officer's report from the crime

scene. The oddly-arranged room. The knotted ties still dangling from the iron girder.

It looked as if the criminals had intended to hang Ligaya Santos. That the execution had been carefully planned.

Beyond that she was in the dark. She could only guess at the motive. Some bizarre ritual? Some act of sexual deviancy?

Leaving Ligaya Santos to sleep, Ms Sekikawa stepped outside the room. Yamaguchi was sitting waiting for her, bolt upright as usual.

She sat down next to him. Taking a deep breath, she went over everything she had learned. He listened carefully without interrupting.

Then he stood up, stretched and fetched two plastic cups of water from the dispenser at the end of the corridor.

Handing one to Ms Sekikawa, he sat down again and took a long sip.

"I don't rate Wang and the other man's chances."

101

Charles Fancourt had witnessed the treatment meted out to Wang. As he was dragged to the fridge freezer and tied down, he was desperate to avoid being put through the wringer too.

"Fucking stop! Stop!"

He had no idea what Wang had revealed to his interrogator. Fancourt was too far away and, in any case, it was all in Japanese. But he had overheard snatches of conversation between his two assailants.

"I'm British, for God's sake!"

If he thought that would carry any weight, he was mistaken. His captors simply tightened the restraints and laid the cloth over his face. He was still proclaiming his nationality as the water started to block his airways.

Trevillion was in the groove now. With Wang, he had struggled with the timing. With Fancourt, he had it down to a tee.

Peters had waited until Wang begged for mercy before posing his questions. He bided his time until all the bluster had drained out of the indignant Chinese criminal.

For Peters, the events that took place in the building in Yokohama were of secondary importance. His questions homed in on a lonely stretch of road near Yamashiro.

He wanted to know exactly what had happened to Hiroko. He wanted to know who had given the orders. He wanted to know why.

The answers dribbled out. Wang assumed he was already a dead man.

If the tables had been turned, death would have been a foregone conclusion. He just wanted to get it over with.

Just tell them what they wanted to hear, then the coup de grâce. Anything was preferable to this excruciating water torture.

The identity of his interrogator had soon dawned on him. The thrust of the man's questions made it obvious.

At first, Wang had tried to work out how the Englishman had managed to track him down. But he soon put it to the back of his mind. He had more pressing matters confronting him.

As he came up for air the final time, he held nothing back. What did it matter now?

Peters made rapid notes as Wang confessed everything he knew. At one point, he dug out Wang's mobile to double-check a telephone number.

Wang rallied for a last lunge. Before he died, he would have the satisfaction of one final twist of the knife.

"She put up a good fight, your bitch. Tried to hold on to the fence for as long as she could. We had to peel her fingers off one by one."

He studied Peters' face. Searching for a reaction. He found none.

"She screamed as she went down."

George Trevillion was unable to understand what was being said. But he had his eyes locked on Peters, reading the tension in his face.

Suddenly, he saw him stiffen. He knew his friend. He stood poised to intervene.

Peters leaned forwards and gripped Wang around the throat. The pressure was slow but even, Wang even managed a grin as his breath leaked out.

"Sean, stop!"

Trevillion reached over and seized Peters' forearm. Gradually he felt the muscles slacken.

Peters released his hold. Wang gulped air into his lungs again.

It was an unexpected reprieve. Wang was hauled off the fridge freezer and dragged to the corner of the shed.

Then it was Fancourt's turn.

As Fancourt was tied down in his place, Wang rapidly reassessed his prospects.

What if the two foreigners did not kill him? There were fates worse than death.

The people he had betrayed would exact a far heavier toll. Not only him, but anyone remotely connected with him would suffer. As he knew only too well, the methods would be infinitely slow and painstaking.

Fancourt, meanwhile, was far more preoccupied with his current predicament than any future repercussions.

He coughed up his information the moment he was allowed up for air. But that did not stop his interrogators going over all the details again several times. Just to make sure his story was consistent.

Peters then ran a check on Fancourt's phone. He confirmed the contact details matched those Wang had given him earlier.

They belonged to the man at the top of the chain. The one they both answered to. The man who had ordered Hiroko's killing.

Fancourt's confession started with the execution room in Yokohama. But it soon rippled far beyond those four walls.

Peters and Trevillion learned what the Chinese received in return for facilitating Fancourt's perversion. The Englishman's unique skill in money laundering.

The two ex-soldiers had trouble following all the financial twists and turns. But eventually, they made landfall on the sun-kissed shores of the Cayman Islands.

It was enough. Others with the necessary skills could dig deeper later on.

The two ex-soldiers cleaned up in exemplary fashion. The fridge freezer and the plastic tubs were returned to where they had found them. The inside of the corrugated shed swept clean.

They dragged Fancourt and Wang to opposing steel stanchions, well apart from one another. They secured them firmly and gagged them.

Once they were satisfied all was in order, the two Englishmen left the way they had come.

As Trevillion turned the car and made his way back up the side street, Peters stared ahead. Neither man spoke.

They parked up near the expressway slip-road. Peters made his second phone call that night to Detective Sekikawa.

Within half an hour, they heard the sounds of police sirens approaching. Two squad cars raced past in the direction of the recycling lot.

With a nod from Peters, George Trevillion started the car. The traffic was light at that hour of the night. They made good time across the city.

102

Back at Trevillion's apartment, the two men downed a quick meal. They then sat drinking tea, discussing their next move.

There was no sense of elation. Just grim resolve at what lay ahead.

Using Trevillion's laptop, they drafted a detailed report. Everything they had witnessed. All the information they had extracted from Wang and Fancourt.

Only certain items were held back. Those would follow later.

When they were satisfied with the contents, Peters emailed the file to Ms Sekikawa.

"How are you bearing up, Sean?"

Trevillion studied his companion. Peters sat on the sofa, cradling his tea mug in his hand. His head was bent forwards, his eyes fixed on a spot on the carpet.

There was a time when this type of operation was bread and butter to the two former Marines. Not any longer.

They were older. And it was personal.

Trevillion had witnessed his old comrade trying to restrain himself during the interrogation. Typing up the report in English with Peters, he was finally privy to the content of Wang's confession.

He now understood the chain of events leading up to Hiroko's murder. The cold calculations that lay behind it.

It took a second or two for Peters to respond.

"I'm OK, George. You?"

"Sure. OK, Sean."

Trevillion finished his tea and stood up.

"I'm going to turn in. Pretty knackered after today."

Peters nodded.

"I'll hang on for a bit."

"Of course, Sean. Long as you like. Help yourself to anything. See you tomorrow."

Trevillion disappeared into his bedroom. He could see Peters needed some time on his own.

Left alone, Peters got up and walked to the window and stared out. Even in the small hours, there was no let up.

Taxis flashed past on the main road. Road crews were out in force making essential overnight repairs. Bars were still open. The neon still lit up the streets.

It was not for him. He yearned for the calm of the countryside. His thoughts turned to their home in the mountains.

The breathless nights when all life stood still. The silence only fractured by the occasional shadowed flight of an owl in search of its prey.

He pictured Hiroko beside him. Her body curled against his side for warmth. Her feet that never seemed to get warm.

"Sean, rub my feet," she would murmur. He always did. Whatever time it was.

It was a simple, private life. They had cut themselves off from everything, happy in their own company.

Was it him? Had he brought this on them? Some echo from his earlier time in the service? Some debt falling due he did not realise was owed?

His mind ran over the faces from the past. The looks of shock and indignation seconds before his gun barrel spat. Any one of them could have demanded reparation. He would have accepted the reckoning.

But not Hiroko. She was not a party to his past actions. She was not to blame. Yet she had paid the price.

For months, he had speculated about what had happened to her on the bridge. But suspicion was not the same as certainty.

Now he knew. He had heard it first-hand from her killer.

The man who had hoisted Hiroko over the railings. Who had prised off her fingers until she fell. Who had watched her plummet to the riverbed. Who had joked with his accomplices.

Peters knew that picture would stay with him for ever. It would never dull. Whatever the future held, nothing would ever erase it. Nothing could ever make amends.

At least they had been able to save a life. The Filipina. They had prevented another pointless murder. That was something.

He thought about the road ahead. He had no choice but keep driving forwards, wherever it took him. Only then could he sit back and take stock, sift through the ashes. Now was not the time.

Was he right to involve Trevillion? Probably not. But he could not have managed without him.

Even if he had told him to stand down, he knew his friend would have taken no notice. Trevillion would never let his comrade go it alone.

All he could do was try to protect Trevillion. To shield him as best he could.

With a sigh, he placed his mug on the breakfast bar. He suddenly realised how tired he was.

As soon as he hit the sheets, he felt himself tumbling into sleep. His last gesture, as always, was to stretch out his hand to the empty side of the bed.

103

Ms Sekikawa waited until Yamaguchi and Hayashi had finished reading Peters' email. It had been waiting for her when she arrived at the office that morning. She had immediately requested a meeting with her two colleagues.

Yamaguchi laid his glasses on the desk in front of him and looked up at his two officers. Hayashi's eyes remained fixed on the text in his hand.

"I assume Peters and his companion extracted this information from Wang and the Englishman Fancourt under duress."

"Without a doubt. It didn't take them long. I doubt Wang would part with this information willingly."

"Indeed. Peters is clearly no amateur."

Yamaguchi sat back in his chair and rubbed his bristled scalp with the palm of his hand.

"He seems to have been one step ahead of us all along. We need to bring him in quickly before the situation escalates any further."

Ms Sekikawa shook her head.

"It's not going to be easy. Whoever is helping him, the other man, must be sheltering him."

"What about Peters' phone?"

"He must have dumped his original mobile. It's untraceable.

Same as the SIMs he used yesterday."

Yamaguchi waved the printout.

"Then there's this other Englishman. This Charles Fancourt."

Ms Sekikawa frowned.

"Apparently the scene in the basement in Yokohama was arranged for his benefit. If Peters had not shown up, Ligaya Santos would almost certainly have died."

"Right. We need to start working on him. He can provide us with vital information about the Chinese underworld's financial operations, here and abroad."

All the while, Hayashi continued to stare intently at the report. Yamaguchi and Sekikawa gave him occasional questioning glances.

"Anyway, now we have both these men in custody we need to set up preliminary police interviews. You and Hayashi head over to Yokohama to initiate proceedings."

"A pity we can't use the same methods as Peters."

Yamaguchi raised his eyebrows at her.

"Meanwhile I'll brief our colleagues in Yokohama on the contents of this note and let them know you are on your way."

Ms Sekikawa and Hayashi returned to their desks. Ms Sekikawa immediately busied herself getting ready to leave. Hayashi seemed to be preoccupied with other matters.

Something's wrong, Ms Sekikawa thought. She did not believe in letting things fester.

"Hayashi? With me."

She led the way to a small meeting room.

"Right. What's the matter?"

"Sorry?"

"Something's up with you. You don't seem to be with us."

Hayashi sat down with his head in his hands. Ms Sekikawa waited, unsure what was happening.

"I'm sorry, Detective Sekikawa. My mother's suddenly been taken ill."

"Your mother? Goodness, I'm very sorry to hear that…"

Ms Sekikawa waited for Hayashi to elaborate. He seemed to struggle to articulate his thoughts.

"She was rushed to hospital early this morning. An emergency operation."

"Oh dear. That's terrible."

Ms Sekikawa was aware how close Hayashi was to his mother. It was not a good time for him to be absent from work, but she did not think twice.

"You should be at her side. Take some time off. As long as you need."

Hayashi stared at Ms Sekikawa.

"Are you sure? What with everything that's happening?"

"Detective Yamaguchi and I can manage. I'll keep you in the loop. Just go and look after your mother."

Hayashi nodded. Gathering his things, he hurried out of the building.

He did not immediately rush in the direction of the nearby subway station. Instead, he ducked round the headquarters building and crossed the six-lane highway opposite.

He made his way along the perimeter path overlooking the Imperial Palace. When he was out of sight of headquarters, he sat down on one of the benches.

He paid no attention to the joggers racing by or the roar of the traffic at his back. His eyes were fixed on the policemen mounting guard on the high ground on the other side of the moat.

They stood rigidly to attention. Every officer prepared to lay down his life for the emperor and the imperial family within. Ready without hesitation to make the ultimate sacrifice.

His train of thought was interrupted by his phone ringing. It was a number he did not recognise.

"Hello?"

"You're wanted. Now."

A rendezvous point followed. The speaker rang off without giving Hayashi a chance to speak.

It was a summons he could not ignore. He had been expecting it.

He sat for some minutes staring across the divide. Then, exhaling deeply, he stood up.

With a final glance in the direction of his fellow police officers, he turned on his heel and hurried back across the road.

104

Peters and Trevillion were in Yokohama.

They had not had much sleep but enough. They had made their move early while the element of surprise was still in their favour.

They assumed it would not take long for news of the gang's imprisonment to reach Chen. If possible, they wanted to catch him off-guard.

They now had a good idea of the man they were after. Both Fancourt and Wang had provided matching accounts.

And they had his phone number. As Peters drove, Trevillion interrogated his laptop, zooming in on their target's location.

"He's in Chinatown. Probably the restaurant."

Wang and Fancourt had described Chen's base of operations. How, closely guarded, he directed his criminal activities from there.

Peters nodded. They would need to proceed with caution. They would be conspicuous.

As they entered Chinatown, it was already bustling with shoppers. Peters had difficulty manoeuvring the Mitsubishi along the congested thoroughfares.

Trevillion held up his hand.

"Hold up, Sean. Somewhere here."

Peters glanced around. The restaurant could have been any one of a number crammed into the maze of side streets.

"Can't you get a closer fix?"

George Trevillion stared intently at the laptop screen before shaking his head.

"This is the best I can do."

"OK. Let's wait a bit and check it out."

The two men settled back in their seats. As with Wang, there was no sense in wading in. Better to wait for an opening.

It turned out they were in for the long haul.

Chen was currently sitting in his private back room in the restaurant. He was surrounded by all his favourite dishes. But, for once, he did not have much of an appetite.

Earlier that morning, he had had an unscheduled session with his fortune-teller. He needed an updated assessment of his prospects.

Sitting at the small folding table in the street, the soothsayer laboured over his charts as Chen fidgeted opposite. Time was against him.

To his frustration, he had just learned the police were holding Fancourt, Wang and three others in custody.

Chen had few illusions. It was only a question of time before they talked and the police came after him.

Eventually the fortune-teller sat back. He took off his glasses and wiped them with a handkerchief before looking Chen in the eye.

"I'm sorry. The danger is imminent. The signs are clear. You may be able to outrun it but I can't be certain of that. But, be in no doubt, to stay is perilous."

"How long do I have?"

"You should not delay."

The man in the dark suit held his palms up towards Chen in a gesture of resignation. Then he started packing away the tools of his trade.

There was nothing more he could do, he thought. He could only say what he saw.

Chen thanked the fortune-teller, passing an envelope stuffed with cash across the table. It would be his final consultation.

Chen realised he had no choice but to make a rapid exit. His former life had drawn quite abruptly to a close.

The organisation in Hong Kong would never forgive him. Fancourt had been put in his safe-keeping. A treasured asset to be protected at all costs. The Englishman held the key to too many secrets.

Chen knew his chances were slight. But with a fair wind he might outrun the organisation and the police.

He was too savvy an operator not to have foreseen the possibility of this day coming. He had well-laid contingency plans.

As soon as he learned the news that morning, he had not hesitated. A series of phone calls set the wheels in motion.

Now, sitting in the restaurant, he picked at the dishes without enthusiasm. Like the last meal of a condemned man, it failed to satisfy.

He kept reflecting on how this state of affairs had come to pass. How his world had suddenly imploded.

He felt cheated. Undone by the death of an insignificant

woman in a remote mountain province.

He pushed away the dish in front of him in disgust.

105

"Mother?"

Hayashi's mother answered the phone on the first ring. In the background, Hayashi could hear the babble of a daytime TV drama.

"Son? Where are you?"

"I'm working."

"Of course, you are. Helping to keep us all safe. Everyone is so proud of you."

Hayashi frowned. He allowed the compliment time to fade.

"Mother, I have to go on another assignment."

"An assignment?"

"Yes. Up north again. Where I was before."

"Will you be gone long?"

Hayashi gazed out of the window at the line of taxis waiting in front of Yokohama Station. A light rain had started to fall.

Up and down the street, pedestrians were sprouting umbrellas like shiitake mushrooms. Mothers with buggies struggled with transparent plastic protective covers to keep their precious charges dry.

He had been one such. His own mother bending over his buggy, tucking him in. Preferring to be drenched herself than allow a drop to fall on him.

His earliest memories were filled with her loving care. How she lifted him from the bath and wrapped him in a cocoon of hot towels. How she picked out the tastiest morsels for him from the dish. How she remonstrated with him in her accented Japanese whenever he misbehaved.

He never took her threats seriously even then. He knew he could always confound her with a giggle and a winning smile.

When he was older, she would sit beside him on the child's stool in his bedroom. Trying to assist him with his homework although it was already quite beyond her. But that never stopped him asking for her help.

After his father's death, he placed himself between her and a pitiless world. Always ready to fight her corner.

It was a sacred duty he took on willingly. She depended on him, unequal to the harsh reality facing her.

He had had to make tough decisions. He had taken them alone. Never breathing a word to her.

He would do it all over again in a flash. To fulfil the deathbed promise made to his father.

"I don't know how long I'll be gone, Mum. It's always difficult to say. I'll try and come back as soon as I can."

"Are you going with your boss? The lady detective?"

"Not this time. I'm going on my own."

I see. I'll be waiting for you. Hurry back. Don't forget to ring me."

"Of course."

"Make sure you have plenty to eat, do you hear me?"

As a youngster he had always looked undernourished, scrawny. His collarbones protruding, his ribs visible through his thin cotton shirt.

It had always been a great source of concern for his mother. Despite the food she shovelled into him, it never seemed to make any difference.

Even now, tall and wiry, he could eat to his heart's content without putting on a single kilo. As an adult, he never sat down to table without hearing his mother's voice echoing in his ear. Insisting he eat his fill.

Hayashi stared through the window at the sudden squall. It was at its fiercest now, the raindrops exploding against the tarmac road like pistol shots.

As if warning him to stay in the shelter of the station concourse. Not to venture out.

To board another train. To go somewhere else. Anywhere else.

"I'd better go now. They are waiting for me."

"Of course. You mustn't keep them."

"Goodbye, mother. Promise me you'll take good care of yourself."

"Goodbye, son. I promise. I'll be thinking of you."

Hayashi waited a moment, unwilling to ring off before his mother. Reluctant to sever the connection.

Eventually, the line went dead. He thrust the phone back in his jacket pocket.

Pulling up his collar, he headed out onto the station forecourt. The taxi driver at the front of queue saw him approach and obligingly opened the automatic rear door.

Back in her front room, his mother listened to the same rain beating against her window. As if it was trying to tap out an urgent message.

Sitting in her usual upright chair, she felt drained of energy. As if, all of a sudden, her life had emptied of meaning.

She frequently felt like that when work took her son away from home. She always missed him terribly.

It was silly she knew. He would soon return and everything would be back to normal.

As she did countless times every day, her eyes panned the living room wall in front of her. Gazing at the family photographs, charting her son's journey from childhood to the fine man he had become.

The memories flooded back. The photographs were a great comfort to her.

106

George Trevillion was having a quick nap. They were taking it in turns to watch the street.

Peters' frustration was mounting. It was impossible to pinpoint Chen's exact location in the warren of restaurants and narrow pedestrian side streets. He felt the impulse to act but had no option but to bide his time.

The streets were crowded, a continuous stream of people strolled by. As the minutes passed, their features merged into a blur. Peters blinked hard, forcing himself to concentrate.

Suddenly he was on high alert. A black saloon had just pulled up opposite.

Three men got out. After cursory glances up and down the street, they dragged another man from the back seat.

He was unusually tall. A distinctive angular cast to his thin face.

"George!"

Peters elbowed Trevillion. The Cornishman awoke immediately.

"What's up?"

"Over there. See the tall one? I've met him before. He's a police officer."

They watched as Hayashi was escorted down one of the side streets. The quartet disappeared from view into one of the buildings.

Peters stared after them.

"What the hell is he doing here?"

Inside the restaurant Chen had been waiting. Gazing around the room, engraving the scene in his memory.

He would miss it. So much of his own past was linked to that silent back room with its sea of white tablecloths.

He thought of the life and death decisions he had made from that very chair.

Some of the condemned faces drifted into his mind like disembodied phantoms. Expressions of disbelief, stubborn resistance or blind terror etched on their ghostly features.

He tapped his fingertips on the tablecloth to banish them. He preferred not to dwell on the past.

His thoughts turned to the future. There was much to consider.

He started to compose a mental check-list. To make sure nothing had been overlooked.

For the first time in his life, he would have to stand on his own two feet. Unable to call on the assistance of others.

He was not unduly concerned. He was by nature a loner.

He turned to the window and watched the silhouettes flit to and fro on the pavement outside. A world apart from the still life of the restaurant's interior.

The door on the other side of the room opened. Hayashi appeared, sandwiched between two giants in dark suits.

Without a word, they advanced across the room to Chen's table. The young police officer was ordered to sit.

Hayashi stared across at the man in the white gloves. They had never met. Chen's identity had always been kept from him.

Wang had been Hayashi's only contact throughout. Everything went through him.

In his final year at university, Hayashi had been picked up on his way home. He was taken to a windowless basement room.

Across a large metal table sat Wang. They were left alone.

Wang had wasted no time laying out the conditions of the deal. They were uncomplicated.

The soaring debts Hayashi's mother had inherited would be written off. In return, Hayashi would join the police force.

He would become the organisation's secret informer. With his talents, he would rise rapidly through the ranks.

Hayashi's mother would know nothing about the arrangement. She would be relieved to learn of a timely windfall. The proceeds of a life insurance policy her husband had prudently taken out without her knowledge.

Wang took care to spell out the alternative. He left no room for doubt.

Either Hayashi's life was theirs. Or his mother's life would be forfeit.

Hayashi had no option but to comply. His overriding priority was to protect his mother.

On graduating from university, the brilliant student suddenly announced he was going to apply to join the police force. No amount of persuasion from his mother could make him change his mind.

He had done exactly as he was ordered. Over the years, he had furnished Wang with a flow of confidential police information.

His mother had been left in peace. She never had any inkling of her son's sacrifice.

But she was always at risk. If ever the flow of information dried up, Hayashi was quickly reminded of the consequences.

On one occasion, his mother had described a near miss she had had. Without warning, a car had mounted the pavement in front of her when she was walking home from the shops.

Hayashi had wracked his brains in vain to find a way out of the trap he and his mother were in. Then he had crossed paths with Sean Peters.

He thoroughly researched the Englishman's military background. He found out what Peters was capable of, the skills he possessed. He decided to use Peters as a wrecking ball against his Chinese masters.

He had assumed Peters would exact lethal retribution on Wang, and then set his sights on the mysterious man sitting opposite him. With both of them eliminated, with luck, he and his mother could make a fresh start.

But he had miscalculated. Instead of eliminating Wang, Peters had delivered him into custody. That morning as he read Peters' report, Hayashi realised time was running out for him.

The net was closing. It was only a matter of time before Wang traded Hayashi for leniency and the police learned of their colleague's duplicity.

He was trapped. If he made a run for it, the Chinese would

wreak their revenge on his mother.

He had been trying to puzzle a way out of his dilemma as he sat on the bench overlooking the Imperial Palace. When the phone call came, summoning him to Chinatown.

Hayashi now only had one priority – to save his mother. That was all he could hope for.

When the man in the white gloves opposite finally spoke, his voice had a reedy quality. Like a cold wind ruffling a bamboo grove.

107

"Wang and one of our most important assets are now in police custody."

Hayashi felt the presence of the two heavies, looming above him. He tried to avoid looking at Chen.

Chen's appetite appeared to have suddenly been rekindled. His eyes ranged over the dishes on the table in front of him.

"You knew about this?"

Hayashi nodded.

"I only found out this morning. I was going to contact you."

"Too late. One of our more reliable sources was quicker off the mark."

Chen sucked the centre out of a kumquat, tossing the skin on a plate.

"Who exactly is responsible for this unfortunate turn of events?"

"An Englishman. The partner of the woman who died in Yamashiro."

Chen sat back and stared at Hayashi.

"That Englishman?"

Hayashi shifted uneasily in his chair. Chen studied him like a pit-viper sizing up its prey.

"Yes. Apparently, he came down to Tokyo seeking revenge for her death."

Chen took another kumquat from the dish. He inspected it carefully before nibbling at the flesh.

"My source informs me you yourself are the original cause of our difficulties. Your actions led to Wang first being linked with the woman's death."

"It was purely accidental. I had no idea Wang was involved. Otherwise, I would have shielded him."

Chen pressed on relentlessly.

"My source says you received plaudits from your colleagues for your excellent detective work. As a result, our organisation has been implicated in this affair. You have brought the police to our door."

Hayashi felt the ground starting to slip beneath his feet.

"As soon as I realised Wang was implicated, I alerted him. I told him to vacate his apartment. That we, the police, were on our way."

Chen sat back. With his chopsticks, he started prising titbits from the dishes in front of him and popping them into his mouth. As he chewed, he started putting the pieces together.

"So, you warn Wang who subsequently goes to ground in one of our safe houses. Then a dumb foreigner, some farmer from up country, manages to capture him and four others at a secret location on the outskirts of Yokohama."

Hayashi's hand gripped the edge of the tablecloth. Chen did not miss tell-tale signs.

"Kindly explain to me how that could happen?"

When Hayashi spoke, his tongue felt like lead in his mouth.

"I've no idea."

Hayashi found his attention kept returning to Chen's white gloves. He noticed how the fingers were now stained with kumquat juice.

"No idea? Well, to me it's obvious. Someone must have betrayed us. Someone who knew both Wang and the Englishman. Someone who could connect the dots."

The tempo of Chen's chopsticks increased before hovering, poised in mid-air. Chen's eyes bored into Hayashi.

"The only person I can think of who fits the profile is you."

Chen spat the words out. The two giants beside Hayashi shifted their weight, readying themselves.

"What is it you policemen say? Means, motive, opportunity. You had them all. You guided the Englishman to Wang. You were tired of fulfilling your side of our agreement. You thought you could be rid of us."

Hayashi realised he was undone. A lethal hush descended on the dining room.

"Of course, that leaves us with the problem of what to do about your mother."

Hayashi lurched forwards, his hands flat on the table, pleading.

"Please, leave my mother out of this. Do whatever you want to me, but leave her alone. She has no part in any of this."

Chen's appetite now seemed fully restored. He delved into the dishes in front of him.

Then, with his mouth full, he paused. With a blank expression, he pointed at the young police officer with his chopsticks.

"Please don't worry about your mother. We'll take good care of her."

He signalled to the two guards. While one of them immobilised Hayashi in his chair, the other slipped the leather noose over Hayashi's head.

As the wooden handle turned, the strap tightened around his throat. Hayashi started to lose consciousness as the pressure mounted.

The final sight etched on his retina as he died was that of Chen. Sitting unconcerned across the table from him, cramming food into his mouth.

108

Peters and Trevillion had spent the last hour waiting for Hayashi to leave the building. There was no sign of him.

"That police officer must be linked in some way with the Chinese. Otherwise, what's he doing here?"

"Maybe he's the one sending you the information."

"If so, he's playing a dangerous game."

Almost immediately, two men emerged onto the side street. Others followed. They formed a cordon around a figure in their midst.

Chen was almost hidden by his tall henchmen. But one tell-tale feature was instantly recognisable.

"That's our man. Look."

Peters had spotted Chen's white gloves. Both Wang and Fancourt had confirmed the underworld boss was never seen without them.

"OK. Let's double-check to make sure."

They waited until the group had emerged onto the main street opposite them. Chen was then clearly visible from the Mitsubishi.

George Trevillion called the number.

They saw Chen pause and take out a mobile phone. He stared at it for a second before thrusting it back in his pocket and hastening on.

He was not expecting a phone call from Wang. And he was certainly not expecting the bogus caller to be staring straight at him from across the street.

At a barked order, Chen's party quickened their pace. Peters started the engine and pulled out.

"Don't lose sight of them, George."

"On it."

It was not difficult to keep track of the party. As they marched along the pavement, the crowds parted to let them through.

George Trevillion pointed to the end of the street.

"Black BMW."

"Right. Got it."

The car was waiting with its engine ticking over. When Chen's group reached it, one of the men held open the front passenger side door for Chen. Three others squeezed onto the back seat.

Those ordered to stay behind waited beside the car, casting suspicious looks in all directions. The Englishmen pulled over to avoid detection.

Trevillion took a deep breath. He could see exactly what they were up against.

Hard men. Trained fighters.

As the BMW drew away from the kerb, the traffic slowed to let it in. Three vehicles now separated Peters and Trevillion from Chen's car.

Peters' foot hovered over the brake as a succession of unwary shoppers sauntered in front of him. He could not afford any mishaps at this stage.

The driver of the BMW was in no hurry. He was careful and observant. He nosed the car through Chinatown's packed streets towards the great gate straddling its entrance.

Sitting in the front seat, Chen felt quite secure. He was well protected. The three men behind him were hand-picked. His personal bodyguards.

Not that Chen expected trouble. No one would be so foolhardy as to start something, especially on his home turf.

The driver slowed to allow some children to cross the road. As he waited, he glanced in his mirror.

A habit learned over the years. As he turned at the next crossing, he checked again. The Mitsubishi he had spotted behind had mirrored his manoeuvre.

"Mitsubishi. On our tail."

None of the men in the BMW turned round. They were professionals, not prone to elementary errors.

"Make certain."

At Chen's order, the driver made a further turn. That confirmed it.

"They're following."

Chen clicked his tongue in annoyance. Such a simple trick for him to fall for.

He reached into his pocket and took out his phone. After a brief conversation, he gave the driver a new destination. He told him to kill time.

Peters and Trevillion kept their distance. They had agreed their approach. They would wait until they had a clear opening before they made their move.

They had calculated the odds. Three bodyguards and the driver. Four against two. They discounted the diminutive figure of Chen. It could be worse.

Suddenly the BMW made a sudden right turn away from the great gate. After weaving through a succession of narrow streets, the car double-backed towards the centre of Chinatown again.

Over the years, the two ex-Marines had lost some of their edge. Trailing the opposition through the streets of Londonderry, they would have been alert to the change of tack. Alarm bells would have rung.

After a while, however, the BMW seemed to settle on a new route. It started to climb briskly out of Chinatown on Yatozaka, heading up onto the Bluff.

Peters followed. As they rounded a bend, they saw Chen's car had pulled up in front of an imposing granite entrance.

Chen was already on the pavement. Without looking back, he strode through the iron gates, his three minders following. The BMW drew away from the kerb.

Peters slipped the Mitsubishi down a side street. Jumping out, he and Trevillion backtracked after Chen and his men.

Trevillion struggled to keep up. Too many corporate lunches. Too many five-star hotels.

Unlike Peters. With his unrelenting training routine, he was an even more formidable fighter than when Trevillion had first known him.

The Cornishman gritted his teeth and put on a spurt. As he caught up with his friend, he glanced across.

Sean Peters' look was one he remembered well. His battle

face. The cheek muscles taut, the eyes steely.

Trevillion knew it was time to ready himself for combat.

In the basement in the Yokohama docklands, Peters had coped on his own. This time, Trevillion knew he would need to make a telling contribution.

They hurried through the gates of the Yokohama Foreign General Cemetery.

Another time they might have stopped to read the inscription at the entrance. Or paused to contemplate the ancient foreign burial ground tiered below them.

The cemetery did not draw crowds. Visitors rarely ventured past the small museum near the gate.

The dead were long gone. Forgotten in this foreign field.

Peters and Trevillion quickened their pace, anxious not to lose their quarry. The steep path snaked downhill bordered on both sides by trees.

The sounds of the city below barely penetrated the cemetery. The dead rested in a stifling silence.

Their peace was about to be disturbed.

109

As Peters and Trevillion rounded a bend in the path, they spotted the men just up ahead. They appeared in no hurry, grouped around their leader.

The two ex-soldiers had assumed the opposition would be armed. They had discussed their tactics. Guns were less of an advantage at close quarters.

Suddenly Peters turned. His expression tightened. Four other men were following them down the path.

"That's why they were pissing about in Yokohama. They must have clocked us. Called in reinforcements."

Trevillion cursed. The opposition was now eight. The trap was sprung. He and Peters were sandwiched.

"Right, George. At the double."

Trevillion took his lead from Peters who was already sprinting towards the group ahead. Seeing them approach, the Chinese shielding Chen were hurried into a poor decision.

Small gravelled tracks accessing the ancient graves fed off at right-angles from the main path.

It was along one of these narrow cul-de-sacs the Chinese shepherded Chen. Above them rose the steep terraced hillside. Below them a sheer drop to the next tier of graves.

As Chen concealed himself behind a marble statue of an

angel, his guards turned to face the Englishmen. Peters was already halfway along the gravelled track, Trevillion only a few paces behind.

By now the reinforcements were also closing in. They approached from the rear in single file, effectively blocking the Englishmen's line of retreat.

Trevillion turned to confront them while Peters concentrated on the men ahead. The battle lines were drawn.

The two ex-soldiers understood speed was of the essence. As Chen's men reached for their weapons, the former Royal Marines launched their attack.

Peters had his closest adversary airborne in seconds. He landed spreadeagled on one of the stone monuments below. He did not move.

As the second man tried to extract his pistol from his jacket, Peters broke his arm at the elbow. A knee to the face sent him also toppling over the edge.

The last of Chen's bodyguards was the most experienced of the three. Made of stern stuff, he had been schooled in unarmed combat from his early youth.

The two fighters traded thrusts and parries, until Peters spotted an opening. He delivered a decisive blow with the side of his hand, followed by another driving the man's nose bone up into his skull.

Peters now turned to help his friend.

Trevillion's adversaries had already gained the upper hand. The Cornishman's nose was broken. Blood was pouring down the front of his shirt. Then a roundhouse kick connected with the side of his head, flooring him.

As he fell, his head smacked against a grave coping. One of

the Chinese produced a blade, stepping forwards to finish him.

All Peters' martial arts training now melded with the untamed instincts of the youth from the backstreets of Plymouth. He flew to his friend's defence.

The Chinese hovering over Trevillion felt the full brunt of the attack. A savage blow to the throat felled him.

The second Chinese managed to parry the first punch before succumbing to the second, a fist driven into his temple. The third spun through the air and landed on some spiked railings enclosing a grave below.

Peters bent over Trevillion. His friend was showing some signs of coming round. Then Peters sensed a movement behind him and swivelled to meet it.

Chen was standing on the path. He was pointing a Glock 17 at Peters. The pistol looked outsized in Chen's childlike gloved hand.

For a second, Peters wondered if he knew how to use it. A second later, he found out.

The gun spat and Peters was rocketed backwards. It was the first time he had ever been shot.

The bullet found its mark. Lower abdomen.

Chen tiptoed over to the Englishman, now spreadeagled on one of the grave slabs. He studied the rapidly-spreading blood stain seeping through the material of his trousers.

It was enough. The man was as good as dead.

Chen was a pragmatist. His current priority was escape.

Looking around he took in the carnage the Englishmen had reeked. He shook his head in frustration.

Stepping around Peters and Trevillion, he thrust the gun in his pocket and hurried back up the path. Taking out his phone, he ordered his driver to meet him at the main gate.

Back in the killing zone, George Trevillion slowly came to and realised with horror what had happened to Peters. He dragged himself to his feet.

"Sean, can you move?"

Peters tried to focus on his friend. His face was grey. Spittle was foaming around the corners of his mouth. Blood was everywhere.

"OK. We need to get you out of here. Keep pressing the wound."

Peters nodded. He knew the routine.

Trevillion levered his friend to his feet. He could not afford to leave him there if any of the Chinese recovered.

Not that it looked likely. They were either dead or incapacitated.

Together they started back up the path. When they reached the main gate, Trevillion left Peters propped up while he hobbled off to fetch the car.

Some passers-by looked aghast at the foreigner, covered in blood, his back to the granite entrance of the cemetery. They gave him a wide berth and hurried on their way.

Twenty minutes later, Peters and Trevillion were admitted to the Yokohama City University Medical Centre A&E department.

Exactly where earlier they had dropped off Ligaya Santos.

110

A few hours later, Chen was buckling his seatbelt on the early evening JAL flight to Vancouver.

After leaving the cemetery, his driver had dropped the crime boss at his house. Chen had told the driver not to wait.

After showering and changing his clothes, he attended to some last-minute tasks before leaving the building. Choosing quiet back streets, he made his way on foot to the nearest railway station.

He usually shunned public transport. On board the train, he stood by himself near the window. On arriving at Yokohama Station, he changed to the shuttle bus bound for Narita Airport.

He sat at the back. He only had a hold-all with him. He kept it perched on his knees throughout the journey.

He had made the flight with plenty of time to spare. Once on board the plane, he wore the customary linen mask covering his mouth and nose. He was barely recognisable under it.

He stared out of the window at the ground crew preparing the plane for take-off. They were efficient and meticulous. He mentally urged them to hurry.

He disliked long-haul flights. Trapped aboard, trying to keep his distance from the other passengers.

But this journey was particularly displeasing. Leaving Japan. Flying into exile.

His hands reached for the inflight magazine. He flicked through the glossy tourist articles extolling the natural beauties of Canada.

Mountains, lakes, endless plains. A vast wilderness ready to explore.

The pioneering spirit was in his genes. Adaptable, resourceful, he was ready to face whatever lay ahead.

His single item of luggage was stored in the overhead locker. He would find everything he needed at his destination.

He was travelling light. Unencumbered. Untraceable.

The police were the least of his worries.

Just before leaving home, he had sat in front of his laptop in his study. The transaction he was about to complete demanded his full attention.

Bringing up the website, he tapped in the username and password. He was relieved to see the introductory screen of sandy beaches disappear, giving him unfettered access to the accounts.

The process was surprisingly straightforward. No complex questions. No unsurmountable hurdles to negotiate.

Fancourt had explained it all to him at one of their infrequent meetings. Just in case Chen ever needed direct access to the funds.

He initiated the transfer and watched as the money changed hands. As the offshore account emptied, his own personal account, held in a different tax haven, was credited.

It was a watershed moment. From that instant, there was no route back. He was a marked man.

He checked his watch and saw the flight was late taking off.

His mind started to run through the possibilities. Calculating what might have gone wrong.

His gloved hand patted the small leather zipped pouch on his lap. Inside was his new passport, issued under a fictitious name, together with all the other documents he needed for his new life.

As it turned out, there was no need for concern. The delay was down to an overweight Canadian bustling onto the plane at the last minute. He was perspiring freely and out of breath.

The steward checked his boarding card stub and then showed him to his seat. Chen watched with growing irritation as the man approached the empty row where he was sitting.

The man stowed his hand luggage and collapsed into the aisle seat. Taking stock of his surroundings, the late arrival turned to his fellow traveller.

"Close thing."

Chen glanced at him over his white mask without replying.

"Shinjuku Station. Nightmare. Wrong train, wrong platform. Conductor didn't speak English. Had to make the flight. Wife meeting me. Big family do. Hell to pay if I miss it."

His staccato bursts were all his heaving lungs permitted. As he calmed, he wondered if his neighbour had understood.

"You speak English?"

Chen paused before nodding briefly.

The large man was encouraged.

"Holiday? Business?"

Chen calculated it would be less conspicuous if he played along.

"Business."

"First trip?"

"Yes."

"Don't worry. You'll fit right in. Big Asian population in Vancouver. Almost outnumber the Canadians."

Chen nodded again. Then he swivelled in his seat to look out of the window as the plane taxied back.

His neighbour took the hint. He rummaged in his briefcase for some papers. Flapping them at Chen, he smiled apologetically.

They did not talk again during the flight.

His fellow passenger was right. Chen would pass unnoticed in Vancouver. He would need to.

When his former associates discovered the Cayman account was empty, they would lift every stone to find him. Their tendrils extended everywhere.

Chen excelled at keeping a low profile. He knew the value of staying out of sight. Like a flounder, camouflaged on the sea bed, both eyes monitoring the ocean above.

But the situation he faced now was of a different order of magnitude. To avoid detection, he needed to be invisible.

A change of identity. A new lifestyle. Total secrecy. No contact with anyone from his previous life.

He had a plan. One he felt confident would work if he stuck to it.

One day, he would once again be able to poke his head above the parapet. Emerge slowly into the light, unrecognisable as the Yokohama Chen of old.

In the meantime, his fate was in his own hands.

111

Ms Sekikawa had assumed her next visit to the Yokohama City University Medical Centre would be to interview Ligaya Santos.

But that evening Yamaguchi received a call from the Yokohama Police Station. There had been a major incident at the foreigner's cemetery on the Bluff. Several dead, others badly injured.

Two foreigners had been admitted to the Yokohama City University Medical Centre A&E department. One suffering from a critical gunshot wound, the other with concussion and minor injuries.

The police had identified the gunshot victim as Sean Peters. The same man responsible for Ligaya Santos' earlier rescue. Peters was currently undergoing emergency surgery.

Yamaguchi and Sekikawa had dropped everything and driven south again. A senior Yokohama officer met them at the hospital reception.

"You're sure it's the same man? Sean Peters?"

"Quite sure. His companion registered them both when they arrived."

"Who is the other man?"

The officer referred to his notebook.

"A George Trevillion. Tokyo resident."

"Have you interviewed him?"

"Not yet. We're waiting for the doctors to give us the OK. As he's British, we thought perhaps you might like to handle that."

"Of course. What about Peters?"

The officer grimaced.

"Not good. They're operating on him as we speak. It seems he took a bullet to the stomach. Lost a lot of blood. I got the impression they don't hold out much hope for him."

"Well, all we can do is wait."

"I've left two officers posted at the Intensive Care Unit."

The Yokohama officer excused himself. He needed to follow up on the others involved in the incident. They were across town at the Yokohama General Hospital.

Yamaguchi found a couple of chairs in reception. He sat down, shaking his head.

"I should have realised. Fancourt and Wang were just stepping-stones. Peters and this other man, Trevillion, must have managed to track down whoever was behind all of this."

"Yes, and we still don't know who that is. No one's talking."

Ms Sekikawa had spent the day with the Yokohama police conducting preliminary interviews with those in custody. Nothing useful had emerged.

Fancourt clearly had much to tell, but he seemed too traumatised to appreciate his predicament. He just kept repeating his demands to see a lawyer, refusing to accept the different custody regulations in Japan.

Ms Sekikawa and Yamaguchi spent the next hour discussing

the case in short bursts before lapsing into silence. Finally, the receptionist came over.

"The surgeon will see you now."

As instructed, they made their way to the Intensive Care Unit on the fifth floor. The two officers on guard saluted as they pushed through the double doors.

A young doctor approached them. His boyish looks belied his experience. He was one of the hospital's top A&E surgeons.

He bent over and took a sip from the water fountain.

"Excuse me. Thirsty work. Please come this way."

He led them across to a large window. Inside the room, a team of nurses were attending to the patient, fixing drips, hooking up a battery of machines.

"We've done everything we can but I'm afraid the patient's prospects are not good. The bullet perforated his abdomen. It shattered on impact. We were able to remove everything we could find but it has done significant damage."

Ms Sekikawa peered into the room. She remembered the rough-and-ready individual she had first met in Yamashiro. Then the well-groomed man she had drunk coffee with in the café in Harajuku.

The drawn figure on the bed bore little resemblance to either.

"Is he conscious?"

"No. He's still coming round from the anaesthetic."

"What about the man he came in with?"

"His injuries are mainly superficial. Some bruising and lacerations. A broken nose. Concussion."

"We'll need to speak with him as soon as we can."

"Not before tomorrow."

"Thank you, doctor. I understand. We'll be waiting in reception."

The surgeon nodded.

"I'll let you know as soon as it's possible."

Returning to the ground floor, Ms Sekikawa commandeered one of the settees towards the rear of the reception area. They had decided to maintain a vigil on the hospital premises in case the situation altered.

Around midnight, Ms Sekikawa dozed off. Her head promptly landed on Yamaguchi's shoulder. In no time, she started to snore.

It was not her usual rattle, more of a noisy purr, Yamaguchi noted.

It had been a while. He recalled the moment years before on the deck of an American warship. Ms Sekikawa sitting next to him, drenched and shivering, her head on his shoulder.

Then he had thought it appropriate to put his arm around her.

Now he felt a strong impulse to do the same. But these were different circumstances. She had not just risked her life in the ocean.

He dismissed the notion. Instead, he contented himself with listening to her steady rumble.

He had to admit it felt comforting to have her head on his shoulder.

112

It was difficult to distinguish night from day in the A&E department.

But the sun was already up as Ms Sekikawa woke and stretched. She felt surprisingly refreshed after her night on the settee.

Yamaguchi could testify as much. She had barely moved a muscle, her head dovetailed into his shoulder.

He, on the other hand, had hardly slept a wink. He spent the night bolt upright for fear of disturbing her.

In a trice, she was back in her stride. Walking over to reception, she returned with two toothbrushes, face flannels and a disposable razor for Yamaguchi.

"There are some showers on the first floor we can use."

They agreed to meet in the small cafeteria for something to eat. It was open 24-hours, offering basic snacks for people waiting for news of A&E patients.

On the fifth floor, the nurse charged with looking after Sean Peters scurried out of the ICU. She returned a few minutes later with the surgeon.

He had managed to grab a few hours sleep and was drinking a coffee in the staff area. He put his cup down the moment he saw the nurse at the doorway and hurried after her.

Back at the ICU, he checked Sean Peters' vital signs. The

message was unmistakeable. The surrounding instrument displays confirmed it.

He gave a series of rapid instructions and left the room. Outside on the corridor, he paused for a second and then hurried to a neighbouring sick bay.

George Trevillion was sitting up in bed. The left side of his face was severely bruised. His eyes still had difficulty focussing after the blow to the side of his head.

But he was conscious. And he could immediately grasp the significance of what he was being told.

Seconds later, he was out of bed. Struggling into his gown, he followed the surgeon to Sean Peters' room.

The nurse placed a chair at the bedside for Trevillion. As the medical staff withdrew to consult in the corridor, George Trevillion stretched out his hand, placing it on top of his friend's.

At his touch, Trevillion felt his friend's fingers twitch. Just enough to tell him he was there.

Both men knew death up close and personal. Most people only had a passing acquaintance, but for them it had been a constant presence, ever at their shoulder.

The figure concealed in the ditch ready to activate the exploding device. The sniper staring through the sights of the high-powered rifle. The decoy sprinting up a side street, glancing back at his pursuers.

They knew death and they accepted it. It was part and parcel of what they did.

"OK, old mate. I'm here now."

Trevillion was not sure if his words registered, but he felt better for articulating them. It was as much for himself as for

Peters.

Peters' eyes remained closed. His breathing was laboured and sporadic, his chest suddenly heaving as if he needed to suck in all the oxygen in the room. His skin had a pallor Trevillion knew only too well.

Trevillion kept talking. As if that could delay his friend's departure.

He spoke of old times together. Their shared dangers. Their shared laughter.

He spoke of the West Country where they both grew up. The endless trudges across Dartmoor's damp peat mires in the dead of night.

He reminded his friend how the dawn light picked out the flashes of purple heather. The dazzling yellow of the gorse. The silhouettes of long-haired cattle against the horizon. The pools of ochre water reflecting the endless sky.

He spoke of Hiroko. The time Sean and she had been blessed to spend together.

He spoke of his regret at not being closer over the recent years. How he had been too caught up in his life in the city.

He spoke of his pride at serving with his comrade once again.

A group gathered at the window behind him looking in. The surgeon and the nurse waited, ready to intervene if required. Anxious to give Trevillion the time he needed.

Beside them stood Yamaguchi and Ms Sekikawa. Summoned from the cafeteria, their meal abandoned.

Beside them, Ligaya Santos.

Ms Sekikawa had rushed up to her room and explained what was happening. The Filipina had not hesitated, scrambling down the stairs to the floor below.

Through the window, she looked at the tragic tableau in front of her. The two men who had risked their lives to save her. One of them now comforting the other as he fought his final losing battle.

She owed them everything. She would never forget.

The minutes ticked by.

And then, almost without warning, for Sean Peters, time suddenly stopped.

113

Yamaguchi and Ms Sekikawa would have preferred to leave Trevillion to his grief, but time was of the essence.

Trevillion and Ligaya Santos were sitting together outside the ICU. Ligaya Santos was holding fast to Trevillion's arm. They were deep in conversation.

"Excuse me? Mr Trevillion? I'm afraid we need to talk with you for a moment."

The Cornishman looked up. He patted Ligaya Santos' hand and released her hold. Then he rose to his feet.

"Of course."

A spare room had been put at their disposal.

"We are very sorry for your loss. We understand you were a close friend of Sean Peters."

"We served in the British Royal Marines together."

Ms Sekikawa glanced at Yamaguchi.

Of course. It made sense. Part of the puzzle explained. The military-style planning and execution, the efficient prisoner interrogations.

"We'll have many questions to ask you, but there is one pressing issue. We have several Chinese criminals in custody, including the ringleader Wang, and an Englishman, a Charles Fancourt."

Trevillion nodded. His face darkened on hearing their names.

"We received a detailed document from Mr Peters yesterday morning explaining what had happened."

"Yes, we thought it best to put it all down on paper."

"Before you moved to the next stage of the operation …"

"Yes. Just in case."

Trevillion looked back in the direction of the room where Peters was lying. Ms Sekikawa waited until she had his attention again.

"I see. We need to know who you were tracking and why. We'll have time to discuss the other details later."

Trevillion, like Peters before him, instinctively warmed to this business-like female detective.

"His name is Chen. Chinese. Head of a criminal organisation. He's the one who shot Sean."

"Based in Yokohama?"

"Yes. Chinatown. He was behind the whole thing. He gave the order for Hiroko to be killed when they wouldn't sell up to the development company."

"How did you establish that information?"

"From Wang. The Englishman Fancourt corroborated it."

Ms Sekikawa stopped short of asking about the methods they had used.

"And how did you locate this man, Chen?

"From his phone number, linked to his headquarters in Chinatown."

Then it was Yamaguchi's turn.

"You were able to track his cell phone?"

Trevillion nodded.

"I work in communications. My speciality is covert surveillance."

"Is that how you found Wang, too?"

"Yes. From his phone number. Plus, a tip-off concerning his hideout in Tokyo."

"Who provided that?"

Trevillion stared at Yamaguchi. He paused before answering.

"Sean received the information from an anonymous source. One of several messages assisting us in our search."

The two police officers glanced at each other, puzzled.

"Can you let us have Chen's number? The one you tracked?"

"Of course. Mind you, he'll almost certainly have dumped it by now."

"I dare say."

Trevillion rummaged in his pockets for the piece of paper with the number and handed it to Ms Sekikawa.

"And here's the address we staked out. A restaurant in Chinatown Chen uses as his base of operations."

Yamaguchi stood up.

"Thank you, Mr Trevillion. We very much appreciate your speaking with us at this difficult time. We'll be in touch shortly. Please be available for further questioning."

"Of course. I understand. I'm not going anywhere."

Trevillion seemed uncertain whether to bow or shake hands. In the end, he just nodded and left the room.

Yamaguchi and Ms Sekikawa hurried to the lift. Yamaguchi was already on the phone.

Their priority now was locating Chen.

114

It was easier said than done. The Yokohama police struggled to discover any official records of Chen or even his current address.

The underworld boss kept his various identities carefully concealed. No one person or administrative body possessed every piece of the jigsaw.

The breakthrough came when police carried out a lightning raid on Chen's restaurant in Chinatown. Some of Chen's men were picked up.

After their boss' disappearance, they had been left rudderless. They were gathered at the restaurant to discuss next steps when the police burst in.

Amongst those swept up in the raid was Chen's driver. Under interrogation, he admitted to dropping Chen off at his residence after the dramatic events at the cemetery.

Apparently only he, among all his confederates, had been privy to the boss' private address. And Chen had sworn him to secrecy.

Yamaguchi and Ms Sekikawa arrived with back-up. After ringing the doorbell and receiving no reply, they forced entry.

The armed squad entered first to make sure the premises were cleared. They then stepped aside for the Tokyo detectives.

The downstairs rooms were unremarkable. A small office, a

kitchen area with washing-up lying in the sink. A sitting room with an ugly sofa and chairs.

Hardly the lifestyle of a member of the Chinese criminal elite.

But Chen's accommodation was not all it seemed. As the search proceeded, one of the police officers drew back a heavy curtain at the end of a corridor to reveal an elevator.

Two officers with drawn sidearms boarded ahead of Yamaguchi and Ms Sekikawa. One of them pressed the elevator's only button.

It rose without a sound. The mechanism was efficient and well maintained.

When the doors opened, plush carpeting led along a hardwood-panelled passageway to a spacious drawing room.

On entering, the police officers paused for a second to take stock. Opposite them, floor-to-ceiling windows framed panoramic views of Yokohama Bay. Dotted around the extensive open-plan living space were pieces of sleek designer furniture. The walls were adorned with abstract artworks.

Opulence in stark contrast to the ground floor squalor.

The armed officers forged ahead. They hastened through all the rooms to check the apartment was empty.

"All clear."

The dimensions of the apartment were surprising. The ground-floor rooms gave no indication of its extent. The penthouse spanned several neighbouring properties.

Every room was sumptuously appointed. Ignoring the decor, Yamaguchi and Ms Sekikawa donned gloves and embarked on a painstaking search.

The refrigerator was full. The cupboards stocked. The wardrobes and drawers crammed with clothes. In the bathroom, the electric toothbrush was still plugged in to charge.

Everything pointed to the owner having just stepped out. That he could be expected back at any moment.

Yamaguchi radioed for a forensic team. He then requested an APB for Chen.

As the APB hit the police network in Japan, Chen was long gone. Already in hiding, living under an alias in Vancouver.

He had left everything in Yokohama pertaining to his old life. Memorabilia, personal items, all his possessions were now open to police scrutiny.

He had made a complete break. Chen no longer existed.

Ms Sekikawa went into Chen's office and started going through the contents of the large mahogany desk beside the window. The drawers were empty except for unused stationery and writing implements.

Nothing of significance. In contrast to the rest of the apartment, Chen had taken care to remove anything incriminating.

Which made the discovery of the items in the locked bottom drawer all the more surprising.

In a small zipped case were several high-capacity storage devices. They were in date order, covering the most recent years.

Later, the detectives debated whether they had been left by mistake. An oversight by a man on the run.

Each memory device contained a film recording. Charles

Fancourt was centre stage in all of them.

The film sets were identical. The same overturned pieces of furniture. The same odd selection of personal items strewn on the floor. The police had no difficulty identifying the location as the basement in Yokohama's docklands.

Only the female protagonist differed in each version.

Each film followed the same script. In the dénouement, the woman was hanged, dying slowly by strangulation.

The evidence was damning. Like his victims, Charles Fancourt was left without a leg to stand on.

Chen knew exactly what he was doing by leaving the films for the police. He had no qualms about sealing Fancourt's fate.

He considered it payback for having been forced to pander to the Englishman's murderous needs. To provide a regular stream of disposable women no one would ever miss. And then having to clean up afterwards.

Faced with the damning film evidence, Fancourt would be certain to crack. And cough up everything he knew.

Chen could bank on the Englishman's photographic memory. His confession would expose every twist and turn in the financial web he had constructed.

His former criminal associates would scramble to limit the damage. To distance themselves from Fancourt's revelations. To shore up their empire against investigation by the authorities.

With their attention distracted, Chen could buy himself valuable time. Time he would use to burrow further out of sight.

115

As Ms Sekikawa stood on the packed commuter train on her way home, she bent slightly and peered out through the carriage window into the night.

The semi-express hurtled along the track. Its horn blared out a warning to stations it was approaching. Level crossings along the route echoed its urgent call.

Every commuter suburb looked identical. The same supermarket chains, restaurants and shopping streets replicated over and over again. Every parcel of land was accounted for, every square foot coveted.

Distinctive features were few and far between. The ponderous silhouette of a temple. A tree-lined park. A dried-up riverbed.

The darkness beyond the train window held an ocean of lives. Each struggling to keep afloat.

It was easy to sink below the surface. To disappear into the Stygian depths where no light penetrated.

Chen had vanished into thin air. The police had searched high and low, checking airports, rail termini, road networks.

Officials sweated his people in custody but they remained tight-lipped. They professed no knowledge of his current whereabouts.

Ms Sekikawa decided to try Akira Kato once again. She had been sceptical of the developer's account. She reasoned he might be more forthcoming, given the recent turn of events.

When she arrived at Kato's plush offices, she was met by his deputy. He explained Kato was unfortunately unavailable.

It transpired Kato had circulated a memo advising the staff he was taking immediate leave. His second-in-command was delegated to run the company in his absence.

Since then, they had seen no sign of him. The deputy had tried to contact him on a number of urgent issues without success. Kato was effectively incommunicado.

Returning to police headquarters, Ms Sekikawa spent some time trying unsuccessfully to track him down. But, as the developer was not central to the case, she and Yamaguchi turned their attention to more pressing matters.

When Fancourt had been shown the recordings found at Chen's secret apartment, he had capitulated immediately. He had no option but to admit his guilt.

In his confession, he was unable to shed any light on the identity of his victims. He had no hand in their recruitment. He was simply the instrument of their dispatch.

Nevertheless, as Chen had predicted, the Englishman was much more forthcoming on other subjects.

Peters' email had provided an overview of Fancourt's financial chicanery. The prisoner now gave the police chapter and verse.

For Fancourt, it came as a welcome distraction. Anything to avoid further discussion of the contents of the films.

Fancourt's memory was prodigious. He had perfect recall of all the transactions he had undertaken over the years on behalf of his Chinese masters.

He laid bare his intricate system of accounts and transfers.

He explained how, with each movement of funds, he could rinse the Chinese money until it emerged fully laundered.

It was too intricate for amateurs to follow. Yamaguchi and Ms Sekikawa called in financial crime specialists on the police force to assist.

Ms Sekikawa could have done with Hayashi's help. Since last seeing him, she had continued to send him regular updates as promised.

He had not once responded. She was beginning to be concerned.

At first, she wondered if his mother's illness had taken a turn for the worse. But, she reasoned, however grave his family situation, Hayashi still had a duty to stay in contact with his employers.

Eventually, after a session at Yokohama Police Headquarters, Ms Sekikawa decided to pay Hayashi a call. On the off-chance of catching him at home.

His house was in a quiet neighbourhood on the fringes of Yokohama. When she rang the bell, there was a long pause before the door was answered by an elderly woman.

Ms Sekikawa and the woman stared at each other for a few seconds. Ms Sekikawa was first to break the silence.

"Hayashi-san?"

"Yes …?"

"My name is Detective Sekikawa. I work with your son."

"Ah yes. Is anything the matter? Where is he?"

"I hoped you could tell me. He has not been at the office for several days. I thought he was looking after you."

"Me?"

"Yes. We understand you recently had an operation. We gave your son some time off to help you to recuperate."

Hayashi's mother stood with her hand clasped over her mouth. Then, glancing up and down the street, the elderly woman beckoned Ms Sekikawa into the house.

They went into the living room. The old woman sat in her usual chair. She looked confused.

"I don't know what you mean, I'm afraid. I haven't had any operation."

Ms Sekikawa leaned forwards.

"I'm sorry? But your son told us you had been ill."

"Why would he tell you that? There's nothing wrong with me."

Ms Sekikawa sat back, stumped. Alarm bells were starting to ring.

"I see. Do you happen to know where we can find him?"

"I assumed you would know. He rang me a few days ago to say he had important work to do. It was quite sudden. Something linked to the earlier investigation up country."

"Can you remember exactly when he rang?"

"Let me see. Yes, it was last Friday."

Ms Sekikawa counted back. The same day he had left police headquarters.

"And you haven't heard from him since?"

"No. It's most unusual. He always makes a point of contacting me. He worries about me a lot, you see."

Ms Sekikawa tried to shield the rising concern from her face.

"Well, thank you Hayashi-san. I'm so sorry to bother you. It's probably just crossed wires. That happens in the police force from time to time."

Ms Sekikawa took her leave as soon as she could. Fending off the mother's frantic questions.

Now, as Ms Sekikawa heard her home station announced, she started to shuffle through the crowds towards the train doors. On the platform, she joined the press of commuters making for the exit.

She could not help instinctively casting her eye over the mass of faces. Searching in vain for the missing police officer.

116

George Trevillion steered his Mitsubishi between the paddy fields. On either side of the road, the ripening rice stalks glimmered in the heat.

He was nearing his destination. On the passenger seat beside him lay a small raku urn containing Sean Peters' ashes.

The cremation in Tokyo had taken place without delay. It was a simple ceremony. The only mourners were himself and Ligaya Santos.

It was as Peters had requested. The evening before confronting Chen, Peters and Trevillion had set down their final wishes in the event they did not make it.

As professionals, they were ready to face that eventuality. They both left a set of instructions in sealed envelopes to be opened in extremis.

George Trevillion was now carrying out his friend's last wishes.

After being discharged from the hospital Trevillion had contacted Yamaguchi. He was, he explained, ready to tell his story and shoulder the consequences.

The interview took place at police headquarters in Kasumigaseki. Trevillion cooperated fully.

He explained about the stake-out at the love hotel and how they tailed Wang to the industrial complex in Yokohama. He described the scene they had stumbled on in the basement and the last-minute rescue of Ligaya Santos.

This much the police already knew from Peters' earlier report. They were more interested in what happened next.

Trevillion admitted waterboarding Wang and Fancourt. He explained how their confessions had led them to Chen, the man behind Hiroko's death. He described how he and Sean Peters had been cornered in the cemetery and the ensuing life and death struggle.

Yamaguchi waited until Trevillion came to the end of his account.

"How were the four Chinese gang members killed?"

"During the fight. They fell awkwardly."

"Mr Peters was responsible?"

"Sean was only acting in self-defence. They were armed and we had no weapons. But they were still no match for Sean. Afterwards, as he was attending to me, Chen shot him."

After the police interview, Trevillion was released. A few days later, Ms Sekikawa had met him in the Ginza. She explained how, in the interim, Yamaguchi had persuaded the police authorities to take no action against him.

Yamaguchi had had his work cut out. But eventually his superiors agreed Trevillion's actions had prevented loss of innocent life. They further adjudged Trevillion and Peters to have acted in legitimate self-defence in the Yokohama cemetery.

Trevillion nosed the Mitsubishi up the narrow driveway to the house. He checked Peters' hand-drawn map and was relieved to see a man appear at the front door, his hand raised in welcome.

"Mr Trevillion? Please come in."

Trevillion followed the son into the house. The teacher and his wife rose to welcome him. Neither spoke English, so the son translated.

As they sat drinking tea, Trevillion told them what had happened. He did not gloss over any of the details. He felt he owed it to Sean to give them a full account.

At the end, they sat in silence. The sliding door at the rear of the room was open and a breeze swept in from the garden.

Outside the day was bright, everything thrown into sharp relief. The pine trees with their needles stretching in the wind. The ripples dancing across the ornamental pond.

Trevillion glanced around the room. Some pictures of the teacher and his students hung on the walls. The compact elderly man sitting surrounded by his students seemed to grow in stature in his *dojo* attire.

Eventually the teacher and his wife stirred themselves. Trevillion understood it was time to be on his way.

At the door, the elderly couple grasped his hands in both of theirs. Trevillion struggled to maintain his composure as he saw the tears well up in their eyes.

They took the son's pick-up. Trevillion cradled the urn on his lap. As they drove away, he turned to see the teacher and his wife bowing in unison, their figures framed by the mountain peaks behind.

The two men did not speak as they made their way along the deserted back roads to the village where Sean and Hiroko had lived. When they came up the track to the property, Trevillion sighed.

They were faced with a wasteland of rutted earth, exposed boulders and dismembered trees. All that was left of the farmhouse and surrounding gardens.

Trevillion placed the urn into his haversack. The son shouldered a small spade. They set off, taking the path up through the trees, the son acting as guide.

He knew the way. He had climbed the mountain path many times with Peters. He shared his love of that natural wilderness.

In the afternoon heat, it was hard going. Trevillion found himself struggling to keep up with the teacher's son. They stopped at intervals to let Trevillion catch his breath.

Eventually they arrived at the clearing. It was as described in Peters' letter.

The two smooth boulders side by side as if placed there by design. The round stone in front marking Hiroko's final resting place.

The son tested the soil while Trevillion sat on one of the boulders and sipped from his water bottle.

"Here?"

The son pointed to the spot beside Hiroko's stone.

"Yes. Perfect."

The son sank his spade into the dark loam. He worked steadily until he had fashioned a sizable hole.

When he had finished, he stood back. Trevillion took the small urn from his haversack and placed it at the bottom.

As the son replaced the soil, Trevillion looked around for a matching stone for Peters' grave. He found one nearby in the thick undergrowth.

Afterwards, the two men rested on the boulders, taking their time before setting off back down the mountain. They contemplated the scene in silence.

Suddenly, the son reached over and touched Trevillion's arm. He pointed into the tall pines in front of them. A flash of green was darting through the canopy.

The woodpecker landed on a fir tree nearby. It stared down at the clearing where they were sitting.

Satisfied the strangers posed no threat, the bird set to work. Beating out its drum roll against the tree trunk.

117

The Marine Trader attracted little attention. Especially when berthed alongside sleeker, more ostentatious craft.

But the 54-foot cruiser produced sufficient power from its twin caterpillar engines to cut through the water at 17 knots if need be. And below decks, the accommodation was luxurious, suited to long spells at sea.

It was custom-built for lengthy solo voyages.

The Marine Trader was fully stocked and waiting for Chen when he arrived at the private marina tucked away on Vancouver Island. He had paid for a year's moorage in advance.

Although some of the marina owners liked to congregate of an evening, others preferred their own company. The small Chinese-looking gentleman was one such. His neighbours respectfully gave him a wide berth.

He had everything he needed on board. He was more than capable of looking after all his needs. No one else stepped foot on the cruiser.

He was regularly out at sea, sometimes for days at a stretch. Familiarising himself with the waters and the complex currents.

Down the Haro Strait, into the Strait of Juan de Fuca and finally into the Pacific. From there, the whole of the North American western seaboard opened up to him.

When he was back at the marina, he stayed on board. When he did venture ashore for necessities, he made sure he was as inconspicuous as possible.

He kept a sharp lookout at all times. The ship's saloon windows gave him a clear line of sight along the pontoon to the dock buildings.

He had intentionally chosen a secluded mooring at the end of the marina. If he needed to make a rapid exit, he could be underway in minutes. He had practised the procedure until it was second nature.

Only one luxury could lure him out of his self-imposed isolation. Freshly-prepared Japanese sushi.

Ever since first tasting the delicacy as a child, he had been hooked for life. As an adult, he would sit in reverential silence in his regular sushi restaurant in Yokohama watching his meal being prepared.

He resisted as long as he could, but eventually the temptation grew too strong. Breaking his strict rules, he decided to cast caution to the wind.

He would cross the Strait of Georgia to the Vancouver mainland. From there, he headed up the Fraser River as far as the Vancouver Marina where he docked.

It was a sensible precaution to distance himself from his hideout on Vancouver Island. In any case, no nearby sushi restaurants could rival the ones across the water in Richmond. And only the best could satisfy Chen's craving.

The Seto Sushi restaurant on Alexandra Road fitted the bill precisely. It boasted authentic Japanese cuisine and was within easy walking distance of the waterfront.

On his first visit, he had not been disappointed. The sushi

master had undergone the obligatory lengthy training in Japan before emigrating to Canada with his family. The food was top notch.

Chen always insisted on a place at the counter, exactly as he would have back home in Yokohama. Although he was not a regular customer, the owners always remembered him and made him welcome.

They found him a secluded seat at the end of the counter, partially obscured from the main body of the restaurant. From there, he had an uninterrupted view of the entrance and could monitor any newcomers.

On that particular day, he had made the short crossing in good time and tied up at his usual, pre-arranged spot. He had locked the boat and set off for the restaurant clad in an anorak with its collar turned up and a New York Yankees baseball cap.

If he happened to pass other pedestrians, he looked down at the pavement, his face concealed behind his broad visor. No one thought to give a second glance to the insignificant Asian shuffling along.

As he slid back the door to the restaurant, the owner looked up from behind the counter. Recognising Chen, he shouted out the customary welcome and gestured to his usual seat.

The owner's wife approached him to set his place and take his drinks order. She did not engage him in small talk.

The tone had been set the first time Chen stepped into the restaurant. He had made it clear from his clipped responses he was not interested in conversation. He was there to eat.

The owner and his wife understood. Wherever possible they anticipated his needs. They made sure the small man in the white gloves was left undisturbed.

Chen avoided times when the restaurant was likely to be busy. But on that particular day, it turned out he was not alone.

A number of other customers were dotted around the body of the room. As he waited for his meal to be served, Chen ran a critical eye over the assembled diners.

Mostly family groups, plus a few harmless-looking individuals eating alone. No one, he thought, to cause him any concern.

Chen was soon engrossed in his meal. So much so that he failed to spot a man on the other side of the room ease his smartphone out of his pocket. After waiting for the right opportunity, he reeled off a series of surreptitious shots.

It only took a few seconds. But long enough to capture several clear images of the small man at the counter gobbling down his sushi.

In hindsight, Chen should have been more cautious. Vancouver was too close to home.

He should have kept on the move. Laying up in the succession of quiet inlets up and down the coast from Lima to Seattle.

The word had raced through the Chinese diaspora. In every city, people were looking. The reward was beyond generous.

Having eaten his fill, Chen settled up and left the restaurant. He made his way back to his boat, ready for a quick nap before sailing back across the strait.

The man in the restaurant scrolled through the shots he had taken. As he did so, he was considering his next move.

He needed to be extremely cautious. He knew exactly who he was dealing with. It would not do to take a false step, to do anything hasty.

But eventually the photographs found their way to their destination. They were examined and, once the man in the baseball cap had been positively identified, a large payment was made to a bank account in Vancouver.

From that moment, for Chen, the clock was ticking down.

118

Ms Sekikawa struggled to accept Hayashi's betrayal. But, as the evidence started to stack up against him, she was left with little alternative.

Returning from her initial meeting with Hayashi's mother, she had confided in Yamaguchi. Together they had tried to work out what was behind their colleague's deception. Why would he lie both to them and his own mother?

They were at a loss. But whatever the motive, a police officer was missing. They had no choice but to alert their superiors.

After weeks of fruitless searching for Hayashi, Ms Sekikawa paid his mother another visit. She had kept the elderly woman regularly informed about the state of their investigation into her son's disappearance.

The round trip to Yokohama took a large slice of her day. But Ms Sekikawa always preferred to update Hayashi's mother in person.

It was not a meeting she looked forward to. The mother's pain was evident. Her questions pointed.

On her most recent visit, Ms Sekikawa had been surprised by the elderly woman's rapid deterioration. Her hair was unkempt, she was wearing a scruffy old robe, she seemed to have given up hope.

They sat at the small table in the lounge as always. No tea was offered. It was no longer a social occasion.

"Have you found my son?"

Referring to her notebook, Ms Sekikawa started to list the actions the police had taken since their last meeting. Her monotone delivery of the facts echoed around the curtained room.

Looking up, she met the elderly woman's desolate stare. Closing her notebook, she decided the time had come for a franker exchange.

"Hayashi-san. Your son misled both you and us, his colleagues. I have no idea why he would do that. I appeal to you to tell me anything you know that might help us to locate him."

"It is quite beyond me, Detective Sekikawa. He's such a wonderful, reliable son. He would never do anything untoward. I simply can't explain it."

Ms Sekikawa stared around the room. It suddenly felt like a mausoleum.

"Has he had any emotional problems? Broken up with a girlfriend, perhaps?"

Hayashi's mother stared at Ms Sekikawa as if she had lost her senses.

"A girlfriend? No. Never."

"Can you think of anything at all? Any change of behaviour you've noticed? Anything out of the ordinary?"

"Nothing I can think of. I'm sorry."

Ms Sekikawa glanced around the room as if searching for inspiration.

"Your son has no financial problems you are aware of?"

The mother shook her head.

"Financial problems? No, nothing of the sort. We put all that behind us a long time ago. We're comfortably off."

Ms Sekikawa slowly straightened in her chair.

"You mean you had money difficulties at some point in the past?"

Hayashi's mother drew her robe over her chest as if there was a sudden draught.

"After my husband died."

"Would you mind telling me about that?"

The elderly woman paused before answering.

"I inherited some debts from my husband."

"What type of debts?"

Hayashi's mother sighed. She decided she might as well continue.

"Unwise debts. To people who never give up pursuing you."

"What people?"

"Local Chinese. People he borrowed money from. Very large amounts."

"What happened?"

"I received daily pressure and threats. They were terrible people, very frightening. Menacing."

"But you say, this was in the past?"

"Yes. By chance, I received a windfall from an unexpected source. I was able to pay off everything we owed. We finally managed to escape from their clutches."

Ms Sekikawa looked at the photographs on the wall. In front of her was the beaming face of Hayashi as a first-year university student. Then, in the next photo, dressed in his police uniform.

The smile was replaced by the deadpan expression she had come to know so well.

"When did this happen exactly? The windfall you received?"

"Let me see. It was a couple of years after my husband died. Those first years were very difficult for us."

"So, it coincided with the time your son was at university?"

"Yes, he was in his final year. I remember clearly."

The elderly woman sighed.

"Then, just when we had nothing to worry about, he suddenly tells me out of the blue he is going to join the police force."

"Did that come as a surprise?"

"A complete surprise. You see, he was a brilliant student. He could have done anything. Excuse me for saying so, but I thought he could have done a lot better than join the police."

And there it was. Like an immaculate *shoji* screen being folded back to reveal what lay behind.

As soon as she could, Ms Sekikawa excused herself. She said she would return before long.

In the car, she stared at the traffic, trying to come to terms with what she had learned.

Hayashi had traded himself for his mother. To free her from her persecutors.

On returning to the office, Ms Sekikawa asked Noriko

Muratani to see what she could discover. Her gifted IT colleague made short work of it.

Following Hayashi's online trail proved relatively straightforward for the computer expert. A couple of days later she drew Ms Sekikawa aside into an empty meeting room.

"As you suspected, Hayashi was the person communicating with Peters via email. It makes for uncomfortable reading."

She swivelled her laptop so Ms Sekikawa could read the compilation of email exchanges with the Englishman.

But one person could put the matter beyond any doubt.

By then, Wang had been moved to a secure unit. The spell in prison had done him no favours.

After festering in isolation, he welcomed any company. Even that of the police woman currently sitting across the table from him.

Ms Sekikawa did not engage him in any superfluous conversation. She took a plain-clothes photograph of Hayashi out of her bag and laid it on the table in front of him.

"Do you know this man?"

Wang glanced at it for a second before responding.

"What's in it for me?"

It did not take much. A slight improvement in conditions. Access to certain luxuries. But nothing that made any material change to Wang's overall prospects.

When Ms Sekikawa left, she knew as much as she was ever likely to. Wang confirmed the man worked for him as an informant. That he had been pressurised to join the police force.

That was all Ms Sekikawa needed to know. On her way back to headquarters, she realised any further search for Detective Hayashi would, in all likelihood, prove fruitless.

119

George Trevillion propped himself up on one elbow and gazed at Balayan Bay.

It reminded him of the long golden beaches back in Cornwall. The fishing boats plying to and fro, the crashing waves, the excited shouts of children in the surf.

For Trevillion, home was now Batangas. He turned on his side and smiled at Ligaya Santos. Sitting between them, Cesar was playing with a starfish he had found at the water's edge.

The boy was still fragile after his long spell in hospital. When Trevillion had arrived in the Philippines, he had made sure Cesar received the best possible treatment.

Beyond Ligaya, her mother sheltered beneath a sunshade, humming to herself. Beyond her, Ligaya's sisters and their children.

A day at the beach was a family affair.

George Trevillion smiled. It had all come as a surprise.

Army life and overseas company postings were not conducive to traditional family life. Over the years, he had resigned himself to living out his days as a bachelor.

Not that he had not had his chances. He was a good-looking man endowed with a west countryman's dry sense of humour.

All that changed in that basement room in Yokohama. When

they severed the rope to free Ligaya Santos, he sensed in an instant their fates had become intertwined.

When Sean died, the two naturally gravitated towards each other. They had spent hours sitting together, talking over what had happened.

Trevillion was a good listener. Ligaya was able to open up about her past. How she found herself in that precarious situation.

He understood. He was not the type to be easily shocked.

Until she told him she would shortly be flying back to the Philippines.

Yamaguchi had received clearance for her to return home. Nothing was to be gained by holding her in Japan. The Japanese authorities recognised their liability for the lapse almost resulting in her death.

Trevillion was fully aware of her son's health issues. He understood how the boy needed his mother in the Philippines.

What he had not appreciated was how much he, Trevillion, needed Ligaya Santos too.

He had taken her to Narita Airport to catch her flight. She kept up a constant chatter in the car. Enough for both of them.

She was excited at the prospect of going home at last. To see her son and family. A chance to put the terrible time she had suffered in Japan behind her.

Trevillion, normally quite articulate, found himself temporarily tongue-tied. It took him until they were standing in the check-in queue before he spoke up.

"Ligaya, listen. I need to ask you something."

She turned.

"Yes, George?"

He found himself staring at the departures board. His eyes searching up and down until he found her flight listing. When he looked back at Ligaya, she was waiting patiently.

"Ligaya, I was just wondering something. If I came to see you in the Philippines, how would that be?"

In answer, Ligaya Santos buried her head in the Cornishman's chest. He reached down and stroked her hair.

"I would like that very much, George. Very much."

"OK."

That was all that needed to be said.

It took a month for George Trevillion to make the necessary arrangements. He spoke with his company managers and negotiated his transfer to the Philippines. They had an office in Manila and were delighted for someone with Trevillion's experience to take charge.

He did not have much in the way of possessions. A couple of suitcases covered it. The rest of the items accumulated over the years he distributed amongst his colleagues.

He had few goodbyes to make. He threw a party at an English pub in Yotsuya he dropped into from time to time. A raucous evening with friends and colleagues.

He doubted he would keep in touch. The ex-pat community was a floating world. Everyone moved on eventually.

Before he left, he had made a point of contacting Ms Sekikawa. He waited for her in a café in Akasaka.

He had not seen her for a while. He smiled as he spotted her through the window, striding up the street.

Purposeful. No nonsense as usual.

"So, you're leaving Japan?"

"Yes. I think I've overstayed my welcome."

"You mentioned something about moving to the Philippines?"

"Yes. That's right."

Ms Sekikawa was hopeless when it came to affairs of the heart. Trevillion had to spell it out for her.

"I'm going to live there with Ligaya."

Ms Sekikawa's teaspoon clattered on the table.

"What!"

"I'm moving to the Philippines to be with Ligaya and her son. We're going to live together as a family."

"A family?"

"Yes."

Ms Sekikawa stared at Trevillion. Gradually, she started to slot it all together.

The tender looks she had witnessed at the hospital. Ligaya's hand resting on Trevillion's arm. The private chats they shared.

For a sharp detective, she could have kicked herself. How on earth had she not realised?

"Congratulations! That's wonderful. I'm so pleased for you both!"

George Trevillion chuckled to himself as he stared out at

Balayan Bay. Recollecting the look of bafflement on Ms Sekikawa's face.

Then he turned to gaze at Ligaya once again. She caught his eye and laughed.

George Trevillion lay back on the sand. He could not imagine wanting to be anywhere else.

As so often, his thoughts turned to Sean. He was certain Sean would have approved.

120

The distress calls of the birds echoed through the pine forest.

No one had taken the narrow path up the mountainside recently. Not since George Trevillion had interred Sean Peters' ashes.

Yamaguchi stopped to double-check the detailed map the teacher's son had drawn. The two police officers had insisted they could find their way alone. They did not want to impose on the family.

Especially after what they now knew.

Ms Sekikawa had been the one to propose the journey north. Yamaguchi had immediately agreed to join her.

To establish exactly where Sean Peters and Hiroko Iwasaki lay buried, Ms Sekikawa had contacted George Trevillion in the Philippines. He had referred them to Sean Peters' martial arts teacher.

They chose to travel up at the weekend. As they approached the remote farmhouse high in the mountains, Ms Sekikawa recalled her earlier visit.

She pictured Peters standing there in his working clothes next to the sensei's son. As if he was one of the family.

They were invited into the house. The father, mother and son sat opposite, waiting patiently for the two Tokyo detectives to explain the reason for their visit.

As the senior officer, Yamaguchi shouldered the responsibility. He had to tread a fine line.

The full facts were only known to a few. Yamaguchi had reported Hayashi's suspected involvement with the Chinese underworld to his superiors. After a lengthy consultation, they decided not to make the matter public knowledge.

They concluded the evidence against Hayashi was largely circumstantial. Much of it centred on a gangland murder suspect's testimony. The collusion between Hayashi and Peters made uncomfortable reading but was deemed inconclusive.

Hayashi had disappeared and was presumed dead. Nothing was to be gained by raking over the coals.

After a carefully-managed internal enquiry, an open verdict was returned. The police would keep the missing officer's file pending until such time as new leads might appear.

Ms Sekikawa understood it was a face-saving fudge. In her heart, she had no doubt about the role Hayashi had played.

Irrespective of his understandable determination to protect his mother, his actions had caused irreparable harm. Lives had been endangered. Lives lost.

Both she and Yamaguchi felt responsible. Hayashi had worked for them. The journey north was a step towards making amends.

She avoided catching Yamaguchi's eye as he stumbled through his explanation. He struggled to clarify why two senior detectives had come such a distance to pay their respects to these two victims in particular.

Yamaguchi was hopeless at embroidering the truth. Listening to him, she shared his discomfort.

The elderly teacher could see it too. Ms Sekikawa watched his face, his eyes narrowing as he heard Yamaguchi out.

He could read between the lines. He knew this was not the whole story. But he also appreciated Yamaguchi had no choice but to provide a sanitised version.

In the end, he politely interrupted Yamaguchi to put him out of his misery.

"Thank you for taking the trouble to come so far. It is greatly appreciated."

Ms Sekikawa and Yamaguchi forced their way up the path without talking. It was overgrown and at points difficult to see where it snaked ahead.

Mosquitoes dogged their tracks. They did not complain. They both considered the mountain trek a form of penance.

Sean Peters should never have been involved in Hayashi's plan. Never set on the trail of Wang and Chen. His ashes had no business on this mountainside.

Eventually, they reached the glade indicated on the map. The two large boulders were unmistakeable.

Ms Sekikawa unpacked her rucksack. She laid out the contents.

A large bottle of water. A box of matches. A handful of incense sticks.

Yamaguchi meanwhile busied himself clearing around the grave markers. He removed the weeds with a small *kama* he had brought.

It was only a temporary reprieve. In no time, the graves would once again be submerged by the rampant undergrowth.

When he had finished, Yamaguchi stood next to Ms Sekikawa. She opened the bottle of water and poured a libation over each gravestone in turn.

Then she lit the incense sticks. Once they had caught, she shook them to extinguish the flames and separated them into two bunches.

They planted the smouldering offerings in the soil. The scented smoke filled the air, mingling with the pine resin.

The two officers then stood to attention with their eyes shut.

When they were ready, they collected their things. Making a final bow, Yamaguchi and Ms Sekikawa retraced their steps down the mountain path.

Hayashi was never mentioned again.

121

Chen woke with a sudden start.

He spent more and more time dozing on the boat. Extended afternoon naps. Turning in early. Sleeping on in the mornings.

He had little to occupy himself apart from his trips out to sea. He found being cooped up on board the Marine Trader increasingly claustrophobic.

Initially, the cabin had struck him as quite spacious. Now, as each day passed, the walls started to close in.

His priority was to stay out of sight, not to draw attention. But that meant spending long hours aboard in solitary confinement.

The sumptuous meals he had always relished were off the menu. He was a limited cook at best. He found himself serving up the same dull offerings day after day until they sickened him.

Without the stimulus of his business activities, his mental acuity started to dull. Others might have found refuge in books. Chen had no interest in reading.

Uppermost in his mind was the fortune locked away in his offshore account. Tantalisingly beyond his reach.

But the end was in sight. He had almost completed his period of self-imposed exile on Vancouver Island.

By his calculations, he could soon start to emerge and carefully re-build his life. His vast funds would afford him a luxury lifestyle screened behind a protective wall of secrecy.

But that was for the future. He still needed to be patient.

Most days he took the boat out. It was important to hone his navigational skills. Just in case he needed to call on them in a hurry.

He invariably circled Vancouver Island and dropped anchor on the sparsely-populated west coast. He would wait out the day, until the late tide bore him back to his mooring at the marina.

Occasionally other vessels would pass. If the situation demanded, he would raise a hand in recognition. Enough to signal all was well and to wave them on their way.

He always had a baited line dangling overboard. The fish were plentiful. They formed a welcome dietary supplement.

He had been lucky that day. He had bagged a gleaming salmon.

He had stood on the deck gutting it, avoiding any mess on his clothes. He was fastidious about such matters and squeamish at the sight of blood.

Later, he chucked a bucketful of the fish's entrails into the sea. He sat on deck and waited. The seagulls soon swooped down, appearing out of nowhere, to fight over the bloodied scraps.

With the salmon stored away in the boat's freezer compartment, he retired to his bedroom for his siesta.

He had not expected to be disturbed.

When he heard the knock, he had woken immediately. He

had lain on the bed in the mid-afternoon sun, wondering what the noise could be. It felt like something had hit the side of the ship.

His mind immediately started to sift through the possibilities. His ship slipping its anchor. Some marine life colliding against the hull.

But another sound followed. And another.

He froze. He knew with absolute clarity it was footsteps on the deck above him.

He was trapped. The only escape was via the hatch.

He had no option but to face whatever was above him. With trepidation, he stood up and tiptoed across.

The footsteps had stopped on the other side of the hatch. Whoever was outside was waiting for him to show himself.

Slowly he pulled open the varnished teak doors.

Tied up alongside the Marine Trader was a sleek fishing vessel. The type available to hire from any number of charter firms around Vancouver Island.

But it was not the boat he was looking at. His attention firmly was on the three men standing directly in front of him.

Two of them looked like they would have difficulty squeezing through the narrow hatch. They stared at Chen deadpan. Their pistols levelled at his chest.

But it was the man standing between them that made the sweat prickle on Chen's forehead.

He was no more than 140 centimetres tall. He clutched a battered leather bag in front of him. The type doctors used when visiting patients.

He wore a full-length plastic raincoat and rubber boots. He

appeared unsteady on his feet as if the sea was not his natural medium. He swayed unevenly at the gentle swell.

One of the giants pushed his way down the ladder below decks. Chen recoiled, flattening himself against the wall.

The underworld boss could not utter a word. His horrified gaze never left the leather bag the small man was holding.

An hour later, a group of men on the other side of the Pacific in Kowloon stared at a large TV screen. It had been set up at the end of a solid oak table just for the occasion.

It could have been a typical video conference call. The men in the room mostly just watched the screen, but at points they interrupted to pose questions.

The process they witnessed was lengthy and precise. Once it was completed, the most junior man in the room stood to switch off the screen.

The men trooped out of the room, satisfied they now had all the information needed.

122

The 20-metre catamaran pulled up alongside the cruiser.

The Royal Canadian Mounted Police West Coast Marine Services Division had received the call late that afternoon. A vessel, it seemed, was anchored a mile off Nootka Island in a remote stretch on the western coast of Vancouver Island.

The caller identified himself as a halibut trawlerman making his way back to port. As the boat was some way out to sea, he had wondered if it was in distress.

He had tried to raise the captain without success. He thought he had better call it in to the coastguard just in case.

The Marine Services Division was made up of 20 officers patrolling a 95,000 square kilometre area running from Washington State up to Alaska. They were stretched thin and did not appreciate wild goose chases.

As they neared the vessel, the helmsman of the police boat sighed. He was coming to the end of his shift. He was looking forward to heading home to Nanaimo to collapse in front of an ice hockey game with a beer.

"Probably just some kids."

Two of the other officers clambered aboard. Nobody was in sight. They hallooed but there was no response.

They were familiar with the type of vessel. The Marine Trader was a common sight up and down the coast. A solid, sensible cruiser, in their opinion. Nothing much went wrong with them.

Dropping down into the main cabin, though, they hastily revised their opinion. Something was most definitely awry.

The aft stateroom's king-size bed was occupied. The small figure of a man lay with his arms and legs outstretched.

They assumed it was a man. It was hard to tell.

The two police officers had seen a lot during their time on the force. Bodies half chewed by grizzlies. Murder victims in remote cabins up the coast. Corpses washed up after being in the water for weeks.

But nothing like this. The victim had been skinned, top to toe.

One of the officers rushed outside to throw up. The other man had a stronger constitution. Clamping a handkerchief over his mouth he inspected the body.

The skin had been removed with precision. Nothing rushed. Like a taxidermist.

He wondered if the man had still been alive. They would need a pathologist to establish that. But he fancied he could still see the horror lingering behind the lidless eyes.

There was one anomaly. The skin had been left intact in two places. On both the victim's hands.

He was still wearing a pair of silk gloves. They had been white originally but were now stained a deep red.

Retreating from the stateroom, the police team conducted a rapid visual search of the rest of the boat. They were careful not to contaminate the crime scene.

In the galley, something caught their eye. The pale tablecloth covering the dining table near the window.

It was stretched taut across the teak table-top. On closer inspection, they noticed it was covered with a patchwork of livid blotches, almost like a rash.

They retreated from the crime scene, standing guard until the forensic team arrived.

Beneath the white gloves, the specialists established the fingertips were undamaged, ready for closer inspection. Prints were taken and run against police databases in Canada and overseas.

Eventually a match was made. The Japanese police claimed the victim. Apparently, they had been searching for this individual for some time.

Such a gruesome death inevitably received a great deal of publicity, both at home and abroad. For a time, the TV channels were full of the story.

Precisely as intended. In no time, the message had rippled through Chinese communities around the globe.

It soon became a cautionary tale whispered around dinner tables. An object lesson to all.

No one could ever hide. No one was ever safe.

123

It was freezing in Katsushika Tokyo Detention Centre. Charles Fancourt drew his legs up to his chin.

There was no heating in the cells. Not for the prisoners.

There was no furniture either. Only the concrete floor. Every morning prior to inspection, he had to store away his thin futon leaving his cell bare.

Some prisoners' relatives bought them cushions from the prison shop. It also sold fresh fruit, sweets, newspapers.

Little extras that made a difference. To help to ease the hours of solitude.

Charles Fancourt had no visitors.

At midday, the small hatch at the bottom of the door slid back and a tray of food was pushed through. It was enough to keep him alive.

At first, he had refused to eat. Now he swallowed the congealed rice and cold fish without complaint.

He no longer shouted through the door, making demands. He no longer drew attention to himself.

The judicial system ground on. His lawyers went through the motions.

He could read the odium in their eyes. His crimes were common knowledge. The newspapers had had a field day.

The police had questioned him at length. A young woman conducted the interviews. Her American accent grated as she chiselled away at him.

The films they showed him left him defenceless. He had capitulated.

The questioning was relentless. They drained him of everything he knew.

In desperation, he had appealed to the British Embassy in Tokyo. But they knew the nature of his offences and declined any assistance.

The crimes were committed on Japanese soil. The Japanese would prosecute them.

He looked at his fingers. They had started to turn blue. He tried to flex them, to bring some colour back.

He wanted to stand up, to swing his arms. But exercise was forbidden. He was obliged to sit still throughout the day.

The rules were strict and enforced. The guards punished any infringement with severity.

All the men in the detention centre had given up their rights to be part of society. They were considered outsiders. They were treated as such.

There was no one he could appeal to. His fate was sealed. He was forgotten.

He was wary of the other prisoners. He assumed there was a price on his head. The Chinese would not let his betrayal go unpunished.

When he was taken to the exercise yard, he kept his distance. To avoid a knife in the back. A wire snaking around his throat in some secluded corner.

But it was only postponing the inevitable.

In time, he knew he would be transferred to the floor above. Such meagre privileges he currently had would be withdrawn.

Then he would meet no one. He would live in the perpetual twilight of a feeble electric light. He would have no privacy, even at night.

He would have ceased to exist.

When the time came, he would only be told a few hours in advance. In an office in central Tokyo, a document would be signed by the Minister of Justice.

There would be no protest outside the prison. No media coverage. Even the condemned prisoner's family only found out after the event.

He would be walked to the place of execution past an image of Buddha. The hangman would be waiting next to the trapdoor.

He hoped it was soon. He welcomed it.

He had spent his life living under a suspended sentence. He had never known freedom.

Ever since he pushed open the door all those years before. To witness his mother gasping for air.

For him, hanging would be a fitting end.

124

The monks knelt on their tatami mats for the morning zazen.

It was two hours before sunrise. The chanting of sutras rippled through the temple buildings, dissipating into the surrounding cedar woods.

It had been that way for almost a millennium. An unchanging routine of meditation and work.

The monks would have to wait another four hours for breakfast. Not that they were impatient. They understood the value of discipline and self-control.

For the novices, it took time to adjust. They came from different walks of life. Some made the transition more quickly than others.

More cossetted individuals struggled. One monk at the end of the row still found the long periods kneeling with his legs tucked beneath him a trial.

He fidgeted, trying to find a more comfortable position. His lower back still ached despite the months of practice.

It was a distraction. It drew him back to the world he had left behind. A world he was trying to forget.

Forgetting the rules for a moment, Akira Kato ran his hand over his shaved head. It was as smooth as marble.

All his life, he had been proud of his long hair. It set him apart. Now, he was glad to be rid of it. To blend in.

The crab on the Kujukuri beach had shown him the way. Burying itself in the sand.

Out of sight, out of mind.

He had left his company in the safe hands of his second-in-command. Then he had simply vanished.

He had been careful to cover his tracks. To leave no trace in the sand.

The initiation had been tough. It had almost broken him.

At every mistake, he had been slapped and kicked. But eventually he had been accepted into the fold.

He had had to leave every vestige of the old Kato behind. Within the monastery he was known by his given name, with a new pronunciation. He had forged himself a new identity.

Every action throughout the day was dictated by the monastic rule. From the way he ate, to the way he walked. The ritualised behaviour even extended to the lavatory.

But he submitted to the monastic strictures without demur. He welcomed them.

It was the only way to atone. For his part in the death of the woman in Yamashiro.

He could try to pretend otherwise. But in his heart, he knew he was as culpable as the thugs who pushed her off the bridge.

The sense of guilt had finally broken him. He could not live with himself.

He shuddered briefly and glanced around. He hoped none of the senior monks had noticed his deviant gesture.

The other monks sat like rocks in the pre-dawn. Each sealed in their own private universe.

Settling back and finding a more comfortable position, Kato exhaled. Then he joined them in the sutras.

"All harmful karma ever committed by me, since of old, on account of my beginningless greed, anger and ignorance, born of my body, speech and thought, now I atone for it all."

125

The old man was taking his daily constitutional stroll.

He had lived in the village all his life. Hardly been anywhere else.

As a child, he had hurtled along the paths at breakneck speed with his chums. Chasing kites, fishing for crayfish in the murky channels by the paddy fields, collecting stag beetles.

Now he needed a stick. Progress was painfully slow.

He tottered past the convenience store, stopping briefly to peek in at the village school with its ever-dwindling class of children.

Finally, he proceeded up the narrow track. His daily circuit of the village always included the place where the Iwasaki woman and the foreigner had lived.

Nothing there now. Just chest-high weeds. He could barely make out the stone wall edging the paddy fields.

No one else came that way. They avoided the place.

He tried to keep an eye on it. He thought someone ought to.

He sat down on the stone at the entrance to the drive. He always stopped there to catch his breath.

All the fuss had all been for nothing. All those grand plans.

They had come with their diggers, ripped up the land and left. Not one brick had been laid. Not one.

Some villagers had cashed in. Headed for the city and beyond.

He had heard many of them wanted to come home. Unable to settle, pining to be close to their roots. More fool them.

He poked at the earth with his stick. Dark. Rich. Fertile.

Nobody knew what really happened back then. There were rumours.

They said Iwasaki-san had not committed suicide. They said she had been murdered. Thrown off the bridge. Dreadful business.

Something to do with gangsters. Scum from Tokyo.

The developers had pulled out. He remembered the smarmy type yapping away at the village hall.

The glitzy presentation. The empty promises.

They would not be coming back. No one would be coming.

The whole area was contaminated for generations. Poisoned.

All over the prefecture, vegetables and fruit were left rotting in the fields. Nobody would touch anything produced in their neck of the woods.

First the earthquake, then the tsunami. Then the power plant explosion and the radioactive cloud.

What did it have to do with them? They were miles away to the west. Up in the mountains.

But they had all felt it. Even in Tokyo.

He remembered looking out at the village and surrounding fields as the earthquake struck. Watching everything buckle and sway in front of his eyes. In all his years, he had never seen the like.

He did not see how the radioactivity would affect them up there. But men with instruments came and took their readings.

They shook their heads. Wrote reports.

Young people moved away. They had the most to lose.

The elderly stayed put. They figured something else would finish them off long before the radiation sickness.

He thought about the Englishman. He wondered what had become of him.

He remembered all the fuss when those construction workers had turned up. How the Englishman had sent them all packing.

He was tough, all right. But after the police took him away, he had never returned. Nothing left for him in the village with Iwasaki-san dead and buried.

The old man spat on the ground. His thick spittle took a moment to seep in. He watched the soil dry.

Then, with a sigh, he struggled to his feet.

He set off again towards the village. Shaking his head as he went.

126

The burly ex-policeman flicked over the pages of the evening edition. He was hunched over, sitting at his small table by the window.

Yamaguchi and Ms Sekikawa perched in their customary places at the other end of the bar.

In recent months, they had been popping in more regularly. It had become something of an after-work ritual.

The bar owner was always pleased to see them. Not that anyone would have guessed by the way he wrestled with his newspaper, as if it was a criminal on the run.

As long as it was only these two sensible police officers, he did not mind. Not those damned youngsters ordering goodness knows what and making a confounded racket.

Work in the International Liaison Department had slipped back into its old routine. The dust had long since settled. The Yamashiro case was in the archives.

Detective Hayashi's disappearance was never brought up. His fellow officers in the department understood the subject was off-limits.

Before long, Ms Sekikawa had found a replacement. A bright young woman, part of the new breed of ambitious female recruits to the force. She fitted in quickly and in no time had made the seat opposite Ms Sekikawa's her own.

Ms Sekikawa twiddled the ice in her drink. Yamaguchi sipped

his whisky and water.

"I meant to tell you, I heard from Ligaya Santos the other day."

Ms Sekikawa made an effort to keep in touch with the Filipina. She felt responsible for what had happened to the young woman when she was supposed to be under police protection.

"How is she?"

"Fine. She says her boy and George Trevillion are inseparable."

"Is that so?"

"Yes, Trevillion is teaching her son to surf."

"Surf?"

"Yes, apparently, Trevillion was a champion surfer in the old days. Back in England."

Yamaguchi pictured the paunchy Englishman.

"Well, I would never have guessed that."

"Indeed. People are difficult to fathom. Hard to know what secrets are lurking beneath the surface."

"Quite so."

Yamaguchi took another long sip. Ms Sekikawa gave her ice cubes another vigorous swirl.

"They made an unlikely couple, don't you think?"

Yamaguchi turned to her and frowned.

"In what way?"

Ms Sekikawa took a noisy slurp through her straw.

"Well, you know. Given their age difference."

Yamaguchi looked even more puzzled.

"Sorry?"

"The age gap. I mean, after all, George Trevillion must be old enough to be her father."

"Really?"

"Yes. He must be in his mid-forties and Ligaya, well, she can only be in her late twenties."

"Not that much of a difference really."

Ms Sekikawa stared at Yamaguchi. He rummaged in the peanut bowl in front of them. Grabbing a handful, he fired them into his mouth one by one, chewing thoughtfully.

When he had finished, he brushed his hands together to remove the salt. Like a sumo wrestler prior to a bout.

"By the way, I wanted to ask you something."

Ms Sekikawa always knew when one of those questions was coming down the track.

"What?"

Yamaguchi turned to look at her again.

"I was wondering if you would like to go to the cinema sometime. If you're free, that is."

Ms Sekikawa sat frozen in her seat. Then she dissolved into peals of raucous laughter.

"You're asking me out on a date?"

"I suppose I am."

Flummoxed, Ms Sekikawa turned and gave Yamaguchi a solid

punch on the shoulder.

"OK."

By the window, the ex-policeman gave his newspaper an extra vigorous shake and let out an exasperated snort.

This was the last straw. What on earth did those two think they were doing?

127

A steel door accessed the roof space above the 22nd floor.

As the man in the blue suit emerged, the wind whipped across, threatening to lift him off his feet.

He leaned forwards and stumbled across to the protective barrier. He held his jacket lapels across his shirt front with one hand, his other hand thrust into his trouser pocket.

The wind funnelled up the front of the skyscraper from the city below. Bringing with it a cacophony of sounds.

Below in his soundproofed office, he never heard anything. He was insulated from the streets. Shielded from the population he had sworn to serve.

His earlier predictions had come to pass. The new man, the former vice-president, was now in charge.

He was not like his predecessors. He was hard-line. Hair shirt. He eschewed the usual perks associated with his position.

If any corrupt officials had been asleep for the previous two years, the 18th Party Congress had been a wake-up call. For men of his rank, there was to be no clemency.

He had nowhere to hide. All his plans were in tatters.

The fortune he had smuggled out of the country had disappeared. Vanished. The project in Japan abandoned.

He had remonstrated with his underworld contacts. People

to whom he had entrusted his life's savings. He demanded to know what had happened.

They had shrugged their shoulders. Someone had absconded with the money. They were doing everything possible to recover it.

He had threatened them. But his threats were empty.

The men were only too aware which way the wind was blowing. They knew he was in a precarious position. His power and influence could evaporate overnight.

He could see it was hopeless. The money had gone.

The previous day, a former associate had contacted him. A man he trusted. Someone he had worked with for years.

It was a simple message. Put your effects in order. They are coming for you.

He had already made his decision. A life sentence in a penal colony was not an option for a man like him.

He swung his leg over the barrier and inched across the intervening few metres towards the edge of the roof.

His glasses misted up in the fine rain. He took them off and stored them in their case.

It was better not to see.

He retreated to the protective barrier to give himself a short run-up.

Then he launched himself forwards.

It was a long way down.

ABOUT THE AUTHOR

T. J. Coulton

T. J. Coulton grew up in Devon, England.

After studying at Bristol University, he spent 10 years working in Sweden and Japan. For the next 20 years, he worked for Reuters in London. Since retiring and returning to Devon, he has dedicated himself to writing thrillers.

"The Chrysanthemum Thrillers" draw on his extensive experience of Japan and East Asia.

THE CHRYSANTHEMUM THRILLERS

Centre stage in THE CHRYSANTHEMUM THRILLERS are two Japanese detectives, Kazuo Yamaguchi and Yuki Sekikawa.

Attached to Tokyo Police's International Liaison Team, the pair handle investigations with a distinctive foreign twist: kidnapping, terrorism, murder.

Tough and resourceful, the two officers will always go the extra mile. Even if it lands them in dangerous, uncharted territory.

The Consignment

In Thailand, Swedish holidaymaker Eva Lindström is gravely injured in the Boxing Day tsunami. She wakes in hospital only to find her 10-year-old daughter Mia is missing.

Her frantic search starts. Eva will not accept her daughter is among the dead.

Eva's quest leads her north to Japan. Lost and confused, she finds help from surprising quarters.

Mia's fate hangs in the balance. Will Eva reach her in time?

Sea Of Trees

A young American teacher goes missing in Japan. Everything points to suicide.

Detectives Kazuo Yamaguchi and Yuki Sekikawa suspect otherwise.

Their investigations lead them to a reclusive religious community in the foothills of Mount Fuji. And the terrible secret hidden behind its walls.

The clock is ticking.

Storm From The North

In the mountainous north of Japan, a couple's life is at risk. Innocent victims of a seismic shift in Beijing's political landscape.

In Yokohama's Chinatown, an underworld boss spins a web of murderous intrigue. Before he finds himself in the crosshairs.

Detectives Kazuo Yamaguchi and Yuki Sekikawa have to unravel the strands. Before more people die.

Printed in Great Britain
by Amazon